# The Dew that Go

### The Tenafly Road Ser

### By

### Adrienne Morris

THE DEW THAT GOES EARLY AWAY

**First edition. October 13, 2016.**

Copyright © 2016 Adrienne Morris.

ISBN: 978-1535506793

Written by Adrienne Morris.

**Your love is like a morning cloud, like the dew that goes early away. Hosea 6:4**

# Chapter One

The suicide of Lieutenant Pierce Fahy at Fort Grant three weeks ago haunted a morning-sick Thankful Crenshaw as she arrived back in Englewood, New Jersey—under the cover of darkness with her family. Thankful's brother Fred demanded her exclusion from his wedding plans. Thankful's humiliation must be kept secret. Fred's fiancée Rose Turner came from important and unforgiving society people, and Fred wanted nothing standing in the way of his promising military career after graduating from West Point.

Margaret Crenshaw, their mother, insisted Thankful stay behind closed doors and guarded her closely as summer turned to fall in the growing suburb of New York City. Although Margaret had been in the same predicament with her husband Graham years ago, she prided herself on timing. She never would have let things show as Thankful had. Margaret had picked a decent Protestant man—not a Catholic in the military! The family whispered, the servants whispered. Even Thankful's little sisters, too young to understand, avoided her for fear of catching whatever it was Thankful had.

Meg, Thankful's twin, pretended to be too occupied at her desk writing letters each evening for talks, but they'd never been close. Graham walked into their room one rainy autumn night after a silent supper.

"How are you feeling, sweetheart?" he asked, Thankful being his favorite.

She sat in bed suffocated by the frilly pillows Margaret insisted upon in the girls' rooms. "I've felt better," she said with a weak smile.

Graham picked up a photograph of Thankful and Meg, sighed, and put it back on the white dresser. "You know, Fred and Buck were unplanned."

"Yes, Father, I know."

"I worry you'll become embittered like your mother," he said, sitting beside her on the bed, "caring for a child before accomplishing anything."

Thankful adjusted the pillows and pulled the blankets up under her pointy chin. Her alert, blue eyes met Graham's tired ones. "But Father, what's a girl to accomplish? I have no real talent for things."

"You've got beauty and intelligence and still ... there is a sliver of hope for a good marriage."

"No. I try to imagine it but ... I don't even think I want that anymore."

"Of course not now, after losing the man you loved." Graham patted her hand.

Thankful bit her lower lip, building the courage to confide in her father. As the pretty child and the good girl she had always garnered the meager scraps of affection she and her siblings spent their childhoods fighting over, but to say this father and daughter were on intimate terms would be a lie. Graham's kind veneer too often covered for his wife's harsh treatment of the less well-behaved Crenshaw children, and Thankful like the others walked a tightrope to please her parents, never certain they'd catch her if she fell. "I *didn't* love Lieutenant Fahy."

Graham pulled back with a pained expression, the disclosure another blow to the idealized image he'd created around his little girl. "Then why did you *allow* for this?"

"I thought, I hoped I could love Pierce because he loved me," Thankful explained. "But he didn't love me, did he? The lieutenant shamed me with Miss Peckham! I made one mistake. *Only one* and for the rest of my life I'll be saddled with *this child* who will look the image of the man who cheated me of everything!"

Graham took her face in his soft hands. "My little princess, I wish I could take your pain upon myself. You're such a beautiful young lady and ..."

"And where has this beauty gotten me?" Thankful asked, impatient with the overused sentiment and how this thing called beauty was the only thing worth measuring. "How will I ever leave this house? How will I explain why I'm not going to Fred's wedding? I want to die! I really do! Father help me somehow!"

Margaret walked in now, always so suspicious and jealous of Graham's time with his children. "Is there something wrong?" she asked, avoiding any interaction with Thankful. "Graham, I need you downstairs to discuss Fred's wedding plans."

"Mama, I'm sorry."

Margaret hesitated at the door as if Thankful's voice was repugnant to her. "Your father and I agreed to wait until tomorrow, but I see he's already broached the subject with you."

Graham stood as if to leave with an uneasiness that bled into Thankful.

"We hadn't talked about anything, Mama. What do you mean? Father, stay. Won't you?" Thankful habitually maneuvered her parents to keep from being alone with her mother.

Margaret, in her perfect supper attire, motioned Graham to move a chair beside Thankful's bed. Sitting with a put-upon sigh, she curled her daughter's hair around her finger as she spoke. "Dear child, your father and I hate the idea of you being absent from a family event where people will talk. I'd be mortified—and saddened—not to have you at my side. I love you so." Margaret delivered a Judas kiss. "There's another way. It's right under our noses, and in this situation it's the most humane plan."

"Father, what is Mama talking about?" Thankful asked, her stomach dropping at the expression on Graham's ashen face.

"Your mother suggested ..."

Margaret interrupted. "Your father is a trained doctor, and we *both* think it best the baby is taken at once—before it's too late. Then you can be in Fred's wedding, flirt with the young bachelors, and get on with your life."

Thankful remained mute.

"It's only an idea, sweetheart," Graham said, taking a step back when Margaret glared at him.

"I hadn't even considered for a second ..." Thankful said, her mind swimming in panic and, yes, excitement—was there still a way out? She'd felt the quickening already, the small bumps against her insides, but she did not feel love for this thing.

Margaret continued, "Of all my girls you have the least maternal instinct. How many times have you complained about minding the children?"

"Yes, but ..." Thankful sought her father's opinion. "But Father, you've always opposed it in your practice."

"Yes, I ..."

Margaret interrupted again. "This is a *special* case. You're not like the stupid farm girls. You still may marry well if we handle this with care, and your father says it's an easy procedure. We could do it tonight after finalizing the wedding plans for Fred."

"Margaret, give the girl time," Graham said.

"Father, do you approve?"

"It worries me that you threaten suicide when it runs all through your mother's family," Graham said, though his words caught in his throat, betraying a reservation.

"Could we bring another doctor in?" Thankful asked.

"No," Margaret said. "Your father will put you under—you won't remember a thing, and I'll be here the entire time with you. No one else has to know, and that's the beauty of it."

"Do you wish you never had Fred and Buck, Mama?" Thankful asked, her teeth chattering now at a decision to be made—a moral decision on such a grand scale!

"Of course that was different," Margaret said. A tender expression crossed her face. "I loved your father then, and he loved me."

Thankful's pregnancy was not the outcome of a lovely, tragic romance. She'd given herself to a lying thief. Was it right to bring a child into the world who'd be hated—even by her? And his grandparents?

"Graham, if it was done later tonight after everyone was asleep—that would be best, wouldn't it?" Margaret asked as she ran her hand over Thankful's forehead and kissed her with a kind and sympathetic sigh. "We want what's best for you, Thankful. You understand that don't you?"

Thankful wanted her mother to understand and love her, and she imagined the freedom and relief she'd have if she said yes. She could start over and do everything correctly this time. "Father, tell me what's right."

Graham folded his arms over his chest, armoring himself. "It's your choice."

Thankful had no faith in her choices and thought she detected anger beneath her father's calm demeanor. "Mama, tell me what to do, and I'll do it."

Margaret smiled for a moment happy that for once Thankful sought her approval. She glanced at her husband wrestling with his demons by the door and said to Thankful with gravity, "Please don't take this wrongly, my love, but you'd make a poor mother. If at some point in the future, when you've grown up and met a good man, then maybe—maybe—things could be different. Having a child now means the door to marriage is forever shut, and you must remain a disgraced spinster living out your bleak years talked of on the streets or hidden like a bad secret in this house and yard."

The bleakness of her mother's appraisal coaxed Thankful's self-hatred into a reckless courage. "Father, I want it gotten rid of tonight!" she said as Margaret cradled her in her arms.

Graham left at once. He told Fred there was trouble with Thankful's baby. The marriage details must wait.

"Is there anything I can do?" Fred asked.

"Please take the children for a walk in town—take them skating ..." Graham said, his usual mild tone clipped enough to concern Fred.

"There's no skating yet. The leaves have barely begun to fall and it's dark out, Father," Fred said, worrying at his father's distress when Graham struggled to respond. "Okay, I'll find something for us to do for a few hours."

Graham went to his office, gathered his equipment, and took it into the unfinished servants' quarters behind the kitchen. An antique bed Margaret had purchased furnished the room. Margaret led Thankful, pale and frightened, into the cool place, tucking her under the cold sheets. Graham said nothing of assurance, though he saw in his daughter's eyes she sought it. He covered her face with a rag, and she floated away.

When Thankful woke, the shadowy forms of her parents stood out of reach.

"But, Graham, there must be a way to save him. I didn't expect him to be so perfect—and he moves still! Graham, you must save him!" Margaret cried. She cradled a pink form in her arms.

"He won't live," Graham said, his voice hollow. "This is what you wanted, Margaret. There is our grandchild, and we've murdered him."

"I made a mistake! You should have stopped me!" Margaret whispered and cried. "He looks so like our boys!"

"Stop it! Just get out of my sight!"

"But what will we do with him?" Margaret whimpered as Graham gathered his things.

"I'll bury him. I'll dig a hole ... he should stop moving soon ..." Graham said, his voice breaking. He moved back to Thankful who pretended at sleep. "She'll be waking any minute. Take it away into the gardener's shed. I'll be out soon."

"But it's terribly cold out tonight, Graham!"

"Death is cold. What did you imagine it was, you selfish piece of ..." Graham stopped himself.

Margaret left the room. Graham and Thankful listened as the backdoor opened and shut. They heard the dry leaves crunching under Margaret's feet. Thankful opened her eyes. Her father stood by the window staring at the worn leather bag Thankful had always associated with his healing power.

# Chapter Two

Graham tapped the reins against the horse's rump as it pulled the sled up the drive to his mother Martha's estate in Peetzburg. He said nothing, his breath white in the frozen air. Graham Crenshaw had once grown a ridiculous mustache for his wife. Margaret liked him to wax and curl it. It pleased him to make her happy, though she soon tired of it when it did not bring him a promotion at her father's banking firm.

Margaret, always formidable, took great care of Graham, but when had he begun to resent it? Graham blamed her for his lack of published medical studies and for using her pregnancies as a way of monopolizing his time. He thought again about the tiny life he'd agreed to snuff out for Thankful's sake—no, for his *wife's* sake and his own. Thankful had never asked for such a thing, and the stricken look on her face when Graham didn't go against Margaret's suggestion told him she never would have considered it.

"I hope you won't always hate me, Father."

They slipped along the shoveled but icy path.

"No tears, Thankful. Please," he said, his tone impatient. He glanced over at his daughter for just a second as the wind and snow swirled. "I don't hate you ... but you know this is best."

"Grandmother never liked me, Father," she said as a shadow passed a lit window.

He sighed, pulling something from his pocket. "Here, take this—a gift for Christmas—you might need ..." He handed her a wad of bills.

"Won't I come home for the holidays?" She held the money at arm's length.

"Your mother and I have decided that—just this once, with Buck away and Fred on honeymoon, the young ones need a proper, quiet Christmas. Your mother says we've neglected them, what with all the excitement lately ..."

"I don't consider what we've done exciting!"

"Now stop. It couldn't be helped, could it? It's too late to cry over spilt milk ..." Graham mopped his brow as snow pelted his cheeks. "Just remember—Grandmother must not be told what really happened. She'd never forgive any of us."

"Yes, of course, Father." Thankful turned her face toward the old federal brick house, unlit but for the one window.

Graham had hitched the horse out front, intending to leave at once—just as soon as he carried Thankful's small case and carpet bag into the hallway. So much of herself she'd left behind in the bedroom of her youth—ribbons from riding contests, lacy underthings, and doilies in a trunk set aside for a wedding. What did she need any of it for now?

7

Betty the housemaid opened the door with a sympathetic, though judgmental, shake of the head. "Miss Thankful," she said by way of greeting. She looked past Thankful and brightened at the sight of the doctor, who had always been her favorite of Martha's boys. "There you are. Come in and warm up by the fire. This traveling can't be good for your heart. Come in, come in."

The door to Martha's sparsely furnished study creaked open, and the old lady appeared in the dim, candlelit hallway. The two women were frugal with heat. Thankful kept her cloak on, not sure where to stand.

"This is becoming a habit with your family, son. Spoiling my Christmas," Martha said. She smiled in her icy way. "Betty, will you go bring the coffee to the parlor, please?"

Betty nodded and walked off as Martha led Graham and Thankful into the frigid room. A tiny fire producing no heat and little light was dying to embers. Martha lit one gaslight on the center table covered with books, puzzles, and a stereograph.

"Mother, is there a shortage of wood this side of the Hackensack?" Graham asked, blowing into his hands.

"What do Betty and I need sitting in the parlor for? I suppose with Thankful here we'll go through our wood quicker."

"Grandmother, that's all right. I'll manage."

Thankful's big eyes were eager for approval in the glow of the gaslight.

"Don't be daft, girl. You may be a Crenshaw, but you're a Brown too, and I won't have a sickly girl complaining in my ear for the rest of the winter—the almanac says it will be right cold all the way through April."

"Mother, you don't believe in pagan weather forecasters," Graham said.

Martha narrowed her eyes. "I don't. I heard Josiah Loope at the store talking nonsense, but it does feel like winter plans to stay and that'll put me out extra for the wood this year."

Graham patted his pocket looking for his billfold.

"Oh, no, son. I don't want your money," Martha said, adjusting a photograph of her dead sons after Thankful touched it. "It's my Christian duty to have pity on sinners."

Graham pulled out his watch. "I had better be going."

"Driving home in the dark?" Martha asked. "I've never heard of such a thing, and Betty's gone to the trouble of making your favorite lamb stew."

Graham coughed, his chest always heavy with mucus. "No, I just think it best ..."

Thankful knew Graham lied. She'd overheard Margaret complain about his idea to stay at the inn at New Bridge. Graham turned uncomfortably away and stood to go.

Betty walked in with coffee and cake—a plain one to be sure. Graham waved it off, in a hurry.

"But, doctor, won't you be hungry all night on the road?" Betty asked.

"No, I'll make do."

They stood for a moment in silence. The clock rang the hour, the dismal hour in early winter when darkness first is full.

"Thank you, Mother, for taking Thankful. I mean for giving her a place to recuperate."

Martha nodded, leading him to the door. Graham looked back once at Thankful who stood still and alone in the gloomy parlor. He hesitated, considered one last embrace, but let himself be pushed out the door by his mother.

Betty set the coffee and cake out and ushered Thankful to a seat by the fire. The housemaid threw more wood on and stirred the coals with the poker when Martha rejoined them, looking as though she might say something about wasted heat but instead taking her seat with a sigh. "Sit with us, Betty," she said. "Thankful, take some coffee at once. You look peaked."

Thankful complied, her fingers tingling still from the icy ride.

Martha nibbled a small piece of dry cake and placed the plate on a side table. The wood popped in the hearth.

"I'm sorry for your troubles, young lady," Martha said. She stirred her coffee. "It's for the best, that's certain. A bastard child has more trouble than you know."

"Pardon, ma'am, but wasn't Father a bastard …" Thankful began.

"Will you begin your stay with an impertinent question?" Martha asked. "Is that how you speak to your elders? Because if it is, you had better go run for your father."

"Grandmother, forgive me."

"You have your mother's lack of common sense, that's what." Martha surveyed her granddaughter. "Christ saved the adulterous woman from a stoning, and I will do the same, but remember, girl, that he also said 'sin no more.'"

"Yes, ma'am. I'm grateful to you for letting me stay."

"Did I have a choice? It's my cross to bear—you children get yourselves into trouble, and suddenly I get popular."

"Ma'am, I didn't want to come. I mean, I didn't want to bother you, but Mama is so very angry at me. I understand, but it's terribly hard to bear her disappointment."

Thankful wiped a tear away, refusing to satisfy her hard grandmother's wish to see her suffer.

"Be happy it ended the way it did, Miss Thankful," Betty said. "A few months here and everybody in Englewood will have forgotten."

"Betty, no one knows anything. I was kept under lock and key until ... until the baby died."

"Good then," Betty said and took the uneaten cakes away to the kitchen.

Martha watched Thankful pull at her curls, as she'd done all her life. "Did your father get rid of the baby for you?"

Thankful took a shaky sip of tepid coffee. "No ma'am." She swallowed hard. "He'd never do such a thing to his own daughter. He's against that—and, and so am I."

"Good, because God may forgive an adulterous, stupid girl, but murdering a child ..." Martha stood now.

Thankful almost spoke, almost said that in a secret place behind the anger at Fahy and the fear of humiliation, she'd named the little boy Silas—as Buck had suggested. Buck wrote infrequently from Fort Grant, and too often those letters were filled with a new Christian convert's platitudes. Once he offered to help raise the baby, but Buck was flighty—he hadn't even seen fit to finish at West Point and now wandered in a desert Thankful wished she'd never known.

Buck couldn't have helped her. It wasn't his responsibility. She remembered the time she'd spilled tea on the new settee in the parlor—the light pink fabric gave away her mistake instantly as Margaret walked in. She said nothing though her eyes bulged and her mouth took on a hideous shape. Thankful and Buck looked on as Margaret ran her white glove over the wet cushion. Her fingers were dark with tea now and she turned to Buck. "What is this?"

"Tea, Mama," Buck said as if Mother were stupid.

"Thankful, go get my brush! Fetch it at once!"

"But Mama, I spilled, not Buck."

Margaret grabbed Thankful by the arm. "Do you know how much this cost your father? Do you know how long I begged him for a pretty settee—for *company*? Buck should have stopped you from drinking in here. He's older and should have known better, but Buck can never be trusted! Now go get the brush."

She ran to her mother's room and stood for a moment before the mirror, running her fingers over the stiff bristles before taking the brush to Margaret.

Buck stood emotionless and waiting.

"Wipe that smirk off your face, young man," Margaret ordered.

Buck's expression remained the same—no smirk, no anything that Thankful could decipher. Margaret snatched the brush from her. Their eyes met, and Margaret almost relented, but turned to her son. Buck yawned, and this enraged her. Margaret lunged at him, but he took a step to the side—a small victory. Margaret got him then. One quick and hard thwack to the face. He stood it well, which infuriated Margaret even more.

Thankful cried.

"Thankful, remember this. Because of your selfishness and gluttony your brother must suffer."

Thankful wanted to say, "Hit me instead, Mama!" but she didn't.

Margaret hit Buck again, the bristle of the brush poking his eye, and he cried out. Margaret dropped the brush and took him in her arms. "Oh, Buckie my little pet, forgive me! Let me see!" She pulled his thin boyish arms from his face. The white of his left eye was red with blood. "Thankful, see what you made me do?" Margaret sobbed and ran for Lucretia the housemaid.

Thankful pulled a handkerchief from her sleeve and wiped Buck's eye though he protested. "Promise me you'll never take the blame again, Buck! Promise!"

"Mama was gonna hit me anyway." He smiled. "Did you see I didn't cry? Ha! I bet she was mad about that!"

Thankful missed him now.

She remembered when baby Silas first moved inside of her under her fingers as they rested on her swollen abdomen in the tiny room out west above Mrs. Markham's kitchen. She remembered it wistfully—the fluttering somewhere deep within her. Now she knew everything that followed. The lieutenant's death, William's demise, and her own, but she had been different out there. Undefined if only briefly.

The lack of eastern definition made her free, but had it been freedom or stupidity? Why now did she want the baby back? She always hated her mother's babies. They were loud work when she liked quiet. At Martha's, quiet hung from the rafters. The soft chimes of the clock in the dining room were the only interruptions. Out west at the fort, even with sentries calling to each other and the small military band announcing the times for drill and food, things had been quiet too.

The noisy place in Thankful's life was Englewood, her bustling hometown, but it wasn't the carriages or the trains that grated her nerves. It was family; the strident bickering of her parents and the simpering loneliness of her siblings—so many of them. The constant banging out of piano keys as her mother tried to give lessons to each of them with no good result. No one in her family possessed real musical talent except maybe Buck. He had at least made an attempt.

In nightmares Silas had William's eyes, and Thankful would wake in a sweat to brood over her men. Willy floated like a willowy ghost between the bawdy houses and saloons of Willcox, Arizona, and Fahy lay moldering in a hole.

# Chapter Three

A loud knock came at the door just as winter thawed. Betty let a short man of slight build in, tramping mud off his hunting boots. "The awful deed is done. My dog is killed."

"A good dog is so hard to find," Martha said, her features softening and her voice full of sympathy and concern.

"Tobey was a fine dog. You must be terrible sad, Mr. Henry," Betty said, taking the man by the arm and leading him to the kitchen.

Mr. Henry wore the rumpled clothes of a poor country gentleman well. His pale green eyes were teary, but Henry didn't cry, only shook his head in sadness at the loss of his beloved lab Tobey as he took a stool at the long work table. "I found the coon too—raving mad—unfortunate creature. What a sad way to start the week."

Henry turned around, gave Thankful the once over and stood. "Forgive me, I hadn't noticed you at first. You must be Martha's granddaughter."

Thankful smiled, took a delicate step forward and held out her hand for him to take. He squeezed it, but not with much interest. Thankful blushed at the slight.

"Have you found work then, Mr. Henry?" Betty asked, setting a cup of tea before him.

"Work?" he asked as he sipped. "I was to help at the wharf, but alas, I'm no good to them now, having traipsed round the countryside looking for Tobey all morning. It wasn't meant to be, and after all that's happened in Haymarket this last week maybe it's best to stay away from the grumbling workers by the water."

Martha nodded. "Those poor policemen just doing their jobs."

"What policemen?" Thankful asked.

"Miss, there's been a dreadful case of laboring men against work in Chicago, haven't you heard?"

"My granddaughter keeps herself from newspapers and the more enlightening books of the world—she has no stock in the community of ideas," Martha said. "Her mother—because she is foolish—has always endeavored to keep her girls just the same."

"I know about the world, Grandmother ..."

"Yes, I'm afraid you do."

A cat brushed around Thankful's skirt, and she booted it away.

Henry rubbed his bristled chin. "I did have an inspiration for a dramatic tune present itself to me as I passed by last year's skunk cabbage," he offered. "Are you familiar with Bruckner's Symphony No. 7, Miss Crenshaw? My tune is of that nature."

Thankful hung her head, ashamed of her ignorance.

"Have you lost your voice, girl?" Martha asked.

Betty turned to Thankful as if offering her a key to Paradise. "Mr. Henry is a composer."

"Martha, old girl, do you mind if I sit at your piano forte for a few minutes—I shouldn't like to forget a gift from God."

"By all means, Henry. Play us something."

The two older ladies followed the man as if he owned the place. Henry walked with heavy feet like a brute in Thankful's estimation, but when he sat and put his fingers to the keys of the piano Thankful grudgingly admitted to herself that his skunk cabbage song brightened her outlook. She took a seat alone at the window, allowing the soft early spring sunlight to fall upon her shoulders as she closed her eyes to listen. The ladies asked for more familiar hymns now, and Henry complied with their wishes, spending most of the afternoon at play as Martha and Betty finished weaving lace, bobbins dancing, for intricately patterned collars they sold to the better people of the county.

Thankful sat with her body straight and her hands clasped on her lap. Once someone had remarked to Margaret that her daughter was a statuesque beauty like the goddesses of old. Thankful smiled to herself remembering the compliment. She opened her eyes and watched as the women worked rhythmically while silently mouthing the words to the hymn. Henry peered into a faraway world, looking only occasionally at his fingers as he played. Thankful had a fair-to-middling voice, but who paid attention to her voice when the very movement of her lips transfixed many a gentleman?

*But after admiration what was there?* Did Thankful admire childless spinsters? Had she ever seen a beautiful childless spinster? Spinsters seemed to come of two kinds—the pale, fearful devotee to an ailing relative, afraid of masculine strength, repulsed by beards and all things sensual, and the embittered spinsters who entertained romantic ideals only to have them dashed by domineering parents or a cruel twist of ill-fated love. Thankful swallowed. Must she come to that?

Thankful studied Martha's hard lines, her prim bun and her busy, veined hands. Did Betty the housekeeper and paid friend ever long for an embrace? Thankful had tasted the delights of sensuality and had given herself to the wrong man, yet even in that—the touch of someone's fingertips—she'd felt more alive than she did now in this unfriendly house with its near-empty rooms and spare decor. Finally, Henry pushed himself away from his music.

"I'll be off now to mother's and will send her your regards, Martha," he said with a wink toward Betty.

"You most certainly will not send a false greeting to your horrible mother," Martha said with a trace of humor in her eyes.

The hair at Henry's temple shone grey as he walked past the sunny glass panes beside the front door, and the lids of his eyes sagged, softening an otherwise angular face. He kept a well-trimmed beard with threads of silver asserting themselves, and his teeth, though fine, were tobacco-stained. Henry turned abruptly, setting his eyes upon Thankful who hung back now.

"Miss Crenshaw, I hope I didn't bore you too much with the old hymns. The young enjoy very modern things."

"I don't know what I enjoy, sir," Thankful replied.

"What a sad state of affairs," Henry said. "Martha tells me you need work—I'm looking for a model for my grand painting themed Goddesses of the Bible."

Martha slapped him. "Don't shock the girl—she might take you up on it!"

Thankful blushed again. "I'd never pose for anything but my own portrait! It's shameful."

"Thankful, hush before you make a fool of yourself," Martha said. "Henry likes to tease me about my devotion to our Lord—he fancies himself an iconoclast when he's really just a country bumpkin."

Henry laughed, bowed and departed.

Martha turned to Thankful. "So what did you think of our Henry?"

"It's wrong of Mr. Henry to ask me to sit for a painting," Thankful said disingenuously, for she was glad for the confirmation of her beauty.

"Miss Thankful," Betty laughed, "he was teasing you for wasting the last hour while the rest of us made use of the time."

At home in Englewood a housemaid who so brazenly spoke her mind wouldn't last a fortnight, but Thankful said nothing.

"Are you offended by what Betty just said, girl?" Martha asked.

Thankful glared at Betty. "No, ma'am."

"Liar," Martha said, turning away.

"Oh!" Thankful gasped. "How dare you, Grandmother! You scolded me for going against her only a few hours ago. Now I hold my tongue and you call me an awful name! I don't know what to do."

"I want you to learn respect for your elders. After what you've done you should be humbled, but you're not. I saw the way you expected Henry's admiration. He was right to note it and tease you about it."

"Why should I care about an unemployed musician?"

"His life has been full of tragedy," Martha said. "Yours has been a dreadful comedy of self-deception. There are no doors opening for you any longer. No man will have you after what you've done. Your father is on a mission to give all of his funds to your brother Buck so you can't even bribe a man to have you."

"But no one has to know!" Thankful cried.

"Would you lie to a husband?" Martha asked.

"I don't know what I'd do!" Thankful said, taking a seat on the stairs. "I only made one mistake. Why must I bear it the rest of my life? It's so unfair." She sniffled and looked up at her elegant grandmother. "And no one loves me. What am I to do about that, Grandmother? I thought a pretty girl would be loved quite easily, and that kept me cheerful about life—but now ... I think and think and come up with nothing. I never wanted children—I suppose you'll say that's selfish—but why have so many children just to put them into—impossible situations? I never wanted any of it. But Grandmother, what else is there? You have a nice house and one friend in Betty, but what a dreary life you lead all alone with no one to love you. I'm sorry, Grandmother but I'm having so much trouble being an unloved spinster when last year I was the favorite in the family to do quite well for myself! I was one of the well-behaved children, and Father—he liked me best. But no longer!" She stopped and cried into her hands.

Martha took her by the arm. "This is where a coddled little girl has to grow up and worry about real life, not flights of fancy looking for love all over the continent on your father's diminishing funds.

"You have no right to treat me this way! You're no better, are you? You committed adultery too! Why do you act so superior?" Thankful wrested her arm free.

"Sex is not the worst sin ..."

Thankful stared at her grandmother. "A lady should never talk as you do!"

"A grown lady would *never* land on my doorstep to eat my food and sleep in my rooms without a care for the future but how a man, any man, might flirt with her!"

"Mr. Henry was far too bold to insinuate I might pose for him."

Martha jabbed Thankful's shoulder with her boney finger. "And there is your problem. Margaret has raised you as an ornament not a lady. Only fools marry for beauty—is that what you want? A fool for a husband? Now it may be the only sort who'll have you, but remember this: With each passing day your once youthful beauty diminishes. Yes, you are already less than you were the last time I saw you. I say this not to be cruel but to remind you that curls do not make a life. A man's approval and quick flirtation mean nothing. Henry flirts with *me,* and I'm old."

"Do you say that to make me jealous? Because I'm not jealous. You may have *Mr. Henry.*"

Martha laughed. "Oh, poor girl, what your horrible mother has done to your mind! I'm in no contest with you. Henry is not for sale. The reason I keep so little company with women is just the very attitude your mother has cultivated in you. I speak for your good and your good only."

Thankful stood now, ready to depart up to her room. "I find your words very hard to believe."

"Of course you do, poor thing."

Thankful huffed. "I'm not poor and not a thing!"

"A long time ago I told your father to leave your mother," Martha said. "Did you know that?"

Thankful, so accustomed to her parents' squabbling, wasn't surprised. "So?"

"It wasn't right how she treated your brother, was it?"

"I don't know what you're talking about. And I don't feel right listening to you bad-mouth my mother—especially since you like to pretend to be above feminine backbiting."

"Of course," Martha replied sadly. "You would have done better under my roof, is all."

"Ha! I doubt it. Now may I go to my room?"

"Answer me this: Is there anything you're good at besides flirting?"

Thankful thought, tapping her chin. "No. Not really."

"Nothing at all?"

"Well ... I won some ribbons at riding long ago ..."

Martha rolled her eyes. "That's a start. Now get changed for riding and take my horse out. Fresh air might reignite that once-active mind of yours."

"What makes you think my mind is all that good?"

"You have the Crenshaw eyes, girl. Now go."

Thankful raced to her room, not to hurry and get ready for a ride but to check her face in the tiny mirror her puritanical grandmother hung to prevent vanity—the glass only large enough to get a sense of one's nose and the territory just around it. Thankful strained to see her curls. She fingered her scalp—was her hair thinning? She forced her face into a smile—yes, there were the crow's feet, though faint, only waiting to ruin her looks completely!

"Thankful! Come now, hurry up before the day is gone!" Martha yelled up when after ten minutes she heard no movement.

With puffed and tear-stained cheeks Thankful descended the stairs twenty minutes later. "It's true, Grandmother. I look practically like a hag!"

Martha shook her head, having none of it and held open the door. "Now get. Don't come back until you can think of one more thing you may be able to help me with while you're here other than exercising my fat horse."

Thankful stormed off to the barn, fitfully sobbing between curses. She kicked over a water bucket on the way and felt good about it though it hurt her toe. "What have I done to deserve such a miserable grandmother and such a boring life?" she asked the trees. "I hate the countryside! I hate stupid men! All of them so weak and dumb and useless! Mama is right!"

She threw open the pristine barn, and there stood Martha's dappled gelding with soft, quiet eyes. Thankful's heart melted. The horse whinnied, and she laughed. "Shall we go for a silly ride, Marty? How just like Grandmother to name you after herself—horrible old bitch." Marty watched her from his stall. "Yes, I shouldn't talk of her that way, should I?" She gathered the tack and a curry comb. How long had it been since she last ran her hands over the soft fur of a horse? Margaret insisted the help take care of grooming the animals. It was as if all touch was suspect but the painful sort. Thankful hugged the horse's neck and hummed a song as she scratched between the affectionate horse's ears. She sang then:

*Tommy's gone on a whaling ship*
*Away to Hilo*
*Oh, Tommy's gone on a damn long trip*
*Tom's gone to Hilo*
*He never kissed his girl goodbye*
*He left her and he told her why*
*She'd robbed him blind and left him broke*
*He'd had enough, gave her the poke*
*His half-pay went, it went like chaff*
*She hung around for the other half*
*She drank and boozed his pay away*
*With her weather eye on his next payday*
*Oh Tommy's gone and left her flat*
*Oh Tommy's gone and he won't come back*

Martha came in now. "So you can sing. Too bad you waste it on low songs. Those aren't welcome here, young lady."

"Can't I have a moment's peace?" Thankful complained.

"I think not if the songs that come to mind are salty! Now stop this nonsense and take Marty out at once. I'd better help with the tack—who knows how you might make a mess of it."

Thankful said nothing, and Martha ignored her flared nostrils and heavy silence. "There, now hop on and go."

Thankful did as she was told and dashed away before Martha could warn her about Marty's idiosyncrasies.

"I'll sing as I wish!" Thankful said to the wind, but atop a fine horse on a sunny afternoon it was hard for Thankful to chain her spirits to self-pity and anger. "Oh, Tommy's gone and he won't come back!" she sang and laughed. As the valley spread before her with the ground and forest edges flecked with the lime-green leaves of spring's earliest growth, she took back her judgment on the countryside. Through a clearing she spotted a tall-masted ship lazily rolling down the Hackensack River and a farmer raising a small barn with neighbors just above the floodplain. No fancy dress, no trolleys, no anything. Maybe one day the rosy air and the frilly skunk cabbage on the boggy, country roadside would be enough for her.

Marty trotted with a snort, puffing his belly a few times and stretching his neck.

"Yes, friend, it's good to be free once in a while." But what was freedom to a horse in saddle being led by the nose? Or to an impoverished and used lady living off the grudging charity of an old hag? Thankful kicked the horse and cantered on a straight path by the river. They stopped at the shore to watch boats pass by. "One day, I'll slip away on a raft. I'll pretend to be a boy, won't I, Marty?" But like Buck, she had been taught to fear the water after a few horrifying punishments in the tub. She shook the memory from her mind—was it a memory or an imagining? "Mathematics," she said with satisfaction. "I'm good with numbers."

Out from a copse of pine trees up ahead on the path raced a man in greatcoat on a bicycle. Thankful, still proud and remembering her multiplication and division skills, did not notice until too late that Marty the horse did not like the look of the man's coat as it flapped over his fast pedaling legs. Marty cried out and bolted for the river, but fearing water as well he reared back, and Thankful slipped from his back and crashed into a thorny shrub.

The man on bicycle followed after her. As Thankful got up she yelled, "For heaven's sake get off that contraption!" It was then that she realized it was Mr. Henry.

Henry threw the bike aside and ran up. "Is Martha's horse all right? He doesn't like to be ridden by inexperienced riders. Did you ask her first?"

Thankful watched in astonishment as Henry raced past her to see about the horse who stood with his head low eating fresh greens. She marched over and pulled the reins from Henry's hands. "How dare you! It was your ridiculous bicycle that spooked him. What kind of grown man are you, riding a thing like that? Don't you have any self-respect?"

"A better rider wouldn't be standing here with blood dripping down her face, young lady."

"An old man shouldn't play the circus clown," Thankful said, checking for blood from a thorn's scratch. "Aren't you man enough to ride a real horse?"

"Oh, listen how the city girl speaks! Very ladylike indeed, but I challenge you to try the contraption. I bet you couldn't stand it a minute and end up in another thorn bush."

Thankful nursed a curiosity for bicycles, but would not give Henry the satisfaction. "No sir. You seem bent on teasing me, and I won't have it. Grandmother warned me about you."

Henry laughed. "Oh, did she? What did she say?"

"She said you flirted even with old hags like herself."

Henry looked sideways. "Now, I bet she didn't say it quite like that. And guilty as charged. Is that all?"

Thankful looked at the gliding river hoping to say something witty. "I suppose so."

"Well, my little Miss Charming, Martha warned me about you as well," Henry admitted.

"No! Grandmother is such a hypocrite! She tells me all about backstabbing women and then this! What did she say?"

Henry petted the horse. "I won't tell. I'm no gossip."

"Fine. Then get out of my way."

He moved aside. "I could be convinced to tell you ..."

"Whatever Grandmother has said about me, I can assure you that ..."

He shook his head with a grin. "No, no. I only ask that you try the bicycle for yourself." He waved his hands as if presenting her with a grand prize. "I saw the way you eyed it just now. You want to try, don't you?"

Thankful smiled. "Well, maybe a little."

"I'll tell you all the awful things Martha said about you *after* you take your turn on *the contraption* as you call it."

Thankful looked Henry over. "I don't see what you gain from this."

"I get to share my enjoyment with others. Plus I owe you, seeing that it is partially my fault for spooking an inexperienced rider."

"I'm not inexperienced!" Thankful said, handing Henry the reins, dusting off her hands, and climbing astride the bicycle with a blush.

Henry tied Marty to a tree and led Thankful to a spot out of the horse's view. He grabbed hold of Thankful's voluminous skirts and folded them over her lap. She pretended not to notice. "Now push off with your foot. Yes, there you go. Try again. You'll get it if you've got any balance and skill at all."

Thankful left the first timid pushes behind and thrust herself forward with a quick once-round on the pedals before gaining her balance and was off. Her heart raced, and she laughed. Upon turning back she lost balance but threw her leg out and caught herself before falling. As Henry raced up she started off again and flew by him with a smirk of satisfaction. Henry stood watching now with hands in pockets and hat tipped back. He was old, but handsome—maybe forty, Thankful thought, quickly putting it out of mind. She must get home to tell Grandmother about mathematics.

"Miss Crenshaw, you cut a splendid figure on my contraption," Henry said with a laugh as she pedaled up.

"You are very forward, sir, but thank you for the ride." Thankful giggled despite herself, not quite wanting to hand the bicycle back. "But now it's time to put away childish things, I'm afraid. Grandmother will worry what's become of her horse."

"Isn't answering to your grandmother a little childish?" he asked rakishly.

She pouted. "No. It's good manners," she said, but felt Henry had hit upon something. How often had she foregone life's pleasures or her own will to appease others? "Sir, may I ask you a question?"

"Of course."

"What do you do when you're not riding bicycles or making music?"

"You mean for a living, don't you?" Henry sat astride the bicycle and looked out over the rolling farmland with a wistful sigh. "I love the spring, don't you? What a time for new beginnings. Ah, but your question ... To someone so used to being a bird in a cage you may find my lifestyle shocking."

"I'm not easily shocked, sir," she said, her curiosity bringing new life to her world-weary words.

"I've never been one to follow society's strictures. Life is quite simple if you allow it to be, but you must have a strong nerve and the discipline to keep to your own ways."

Thankful grew impatient. "So what is it you *do*, sir?"

Henry held out his arms expansively. "It isn't a matter of doing, but being." He settled his hands on the handlebar of his bicycle, watching her reaction with amusement. "You think I'm mad, but you see, I don't care."

"I haven't a clue what you're talking about."

Henry laughed as if she were very young. "Miss Crenshaw, I thought to myself watching you daydream at the window the other day, Here is a beautiful girl—in her prime, the bloom still freshly on her cheeks—sitting like a sad little bird, unable to see the gilded cage she lives in. We all feel a little sorry for trapped birds, don't we? I love Martha and respect her individuality, but while she plays at freedom she cares too much about society—such as it is along the Hackensack River."

"I do hope, Mr. Henry, that you're not about to insult my grandmother," Thankful said, pretending at familial loyalty but only really wanting to hear her voice against this man's perceived wisdom.

"Martha is a friend," he replied, "but she is a rather controlling old lady. I don't allow her to do it to me, and I think that's why she admires me. Why must I defend to you my choices? Why do you insist on seeing me through the lens of a profession?"

"I only asked ..." Thankful began, but he shooed her words.

"Here is the secret, young lady: Money and profession—these are the things that ensnare a man. They are the things that keep ladies in cages. Things—nice things—are the death of people!"

Thankful thought a moment. "Yes, but you do seem to own a nice bicycle ..."

Henry looked caught for a moment. "Take it."

Thankful laughed.

"No. I mean it. I see how you covet it—and why should I want that for you? Today I ride a bicycle. Tomorrow I roam the fields, scavenging songs from the trees while gathering chestnuts to fill my belly."

"But, won't the chestnuts be long since eaten in the fall by squirrels?" she asked.

"Ah, but there's plenty if you know the secrets of the squirrels."

"So you squirrel away chestnuts ..."

He wagged his finger at her and smiled. "You are a clever girl, but look at your unbelief in God's bounty for those brave enough to take life into their own hands."

Thankful shook her head, turning to retrieve Martha's horse, but Henry wasn't finished. He propped the bicycle against a tree and gamely followed her.

"What would you give for total freedom?" he asked.

"There's no such thing, and this conversation has descended into lunacy."

"You are unused to conversing with poets and artists, I see."

"There you are wrong," she said with feeling. "I know a drunken artist."

Henry shook his head. "Another enslaved soul. That's sad. I believe in getting drunk on life."

"You really do speak nonsense. Who makes *your* fine clothes? Squirrels?"

"Now you take things too far, Miss Crenshaw! I see you are one of those poor people who only see things in black and white when there's a world of color. Of course we all need clothing and food, but so many are caught up in all consuming materialism. Why enslave oneself to a closet of coats when one will do? Carrying ten coats to Europe only serves to weigh one down, don't you see?"

"Europe?"

"Yes, I've been there many times—with my music. I studied there and met true Bohemians who helped me see that life is about adventures and deep friendship and nothing more. But caged birds must live off the crumbs of the cruel creatures who imprison them."

Henry's words cut too close and a sudden fear of adventure and another of wasted life battled in her heart.

"Mr. Henry, it's all very well and good for a man to traipse from place to place ..."

He interrupted. "Martha tells me you traveled west on your own."

"What else did she tell you?" she asked, her insides churning.

"Martha said you were the only Crenshaw girl with wits and bravery."

"Did she really say that?" she asked, drinking it up with a self-satisfied grin.

Henry noted a skip in her stride and laughed. "So, to answer your original question, I make music and sell it to taverns and small traveling theater groups. No, I don't make much money, but I make friends. I'm back in Peetzburg staying with my mother only for a short while as I concentrate on a grand symphony I am composing—and to please my mother with a visit. The music I played for you is a small taste of the symphony I imagined the moment I saw Edward Church's masterpiece in New York. Do you know it?"

She shook her head.

"Oh, what you've missed," Henry said, pulling the branch of a wild rose aside with his gloved hands so she could pass unscathed. "Of course the real art is in Europe. You should go."

"Oh, yes, I should leap on a star and travel the world with not a penny in my pocket," she said dismissively, annoyed by Henry's talk. "Some of us must live in a real world without our parents' money. I've been banished from home, didn't you know? My father gave me a bundle of cash as an insulting send-off but hardly enough to venture far beyond Peetzburg."

Henry cupped his ear. "What's that? Violins I hear?"

"It may be humorous to you, Mr. Henry."

"I find no humor in your plight. I feel sorry for you. Time away from your father is the best thing, I say. Now's the time to take life by the horns, young lady. You must be good at something."

"Mathematics," she said, finding her disclosure a depressing one, especially seeing the reaction it provoked in Henry.

"Well, someone has to keep books," he said in a lackluster performance of excitement. "It's a gift not given to me, but I have little need." He yawned. "Pardon me, but I must be back to my music—it calls like the sirens."

Thankful didn't like coming second to sirens. "May I borrow your cycle, sir?"

"I told you that you could have it."

"I'd rather just borrow it, but how will I get the horse home?" She waited for him to step in. When he didn't, she said, "I know you haven't the time, but I'd be so grateful if you'd ride Marty home. I feel a little spooked by him now." A lie, of course.

Henry knew she lied and smiled. "I think I can spare the time—on one condition." She waited.

"Please come to supper at Mother's house tomorrow night," he said. "My parents are gentle souls, but just a little dull, and they love company. I know you must *ask permission* of Martha, but ..."

"Of course I'll come. I can answer for myself," Thankful said. "And a break from politics over supper might be nice." She ran back for the bicycle expecting Henry to wait. In that brief time she imagined a slow-riding Henry admiring her skill as a cyclist, but he waved and said farewell. "I'm in a hurry so I'll just race Marty home for you. Enjoy the contraption as long as you like, but be at my house seven sharp tomorrow evening."

She stood a moment in surprise and disappointment, realizing just how lonely she'd become for company other than Martha and her judgmental housemate Betty. She remembered now a desk in the parlor nearly toppled with papers and maybe those papers were in need of organizing. Bookkeeping (if Martha kept books) was an actual skill. Maybe this meeting with Mr. Henry was not just happenstance. Thankful imagined a bustling business keeping ledgers and things, though she hardly knew past that what bookkeeping entailed. It was a start though, and she was happy not to come home empty-handed to her grandmother, but for now the bumpy road and need for concentration pushed all thought from her mind. Here in this sleepy little town the entire evening stretched before her. The air cooled and only the loneliest of birds called deep within the woods that lined the Hackensack. The street lacked lamps, and the moon was not quite ready to light her way, but she felt no fear. She stopped pedaling for a moment, just coasting along. She would not go home. Not yet. Peepers and frogs began to drown out all other sounds. Turning around carefully, she raced up the road and turned again—each time gaining confidence. The little hill down to Martha's capped the night with adventure as she sped down to the barn.

# Chapter Four

An uneasiness plagued Thankful as she dressed for breakfast dreading mention of her encounter with Mr. Henry. She knew Martha was not fond of Henry's parents, and though it was none of Martha's concern, Thankful worried that her grandmother would be doubly displeased with her for accepting a supper invitation from a man nearly her father's age and for riding a bicycle (now parked in the barn).

Betty's habit was to ring a tiny bell at the foot of the narrow staircase at mealtimes. Thankful had missed breakfast on a few occasions because the tinkling failed to wake her, but on this day she sat dressed in a brown work gown Martha had put aside for her to wear for picking early peas. Martha was already at table, having been up for hours with her Scripture and gave Thankful an impatient tut as she entered, though she wasn't late.

Thankful pulled in her chair and poured tea. "Good morning, Grandmother ... and Betty." Lucretia at home would *never* sit at table for meals, she thought.

"I saw Henry in my barn yesterday," Martha said, scratching butter over burnt toast. "I wondered where you were, but I pride myself on giving people their privacy."

"Grandmother! I was nowhere near the barn," Thankful cried, affronted. "I took a bicycle ride, and Mr. Henry kindly offered to bring Marty home after he got spooked."

"Yes, well I should have mentioned how easily Marty gets terrified," Martha said. "Pass the sausage please."

Thankful handed Martha the plate. "Grandmother, I think I want to be a book-keeper."

Martha and Betty exchanged amused glances.

"I'm good at figuring, and maybe I could be *your* bookkeeper, Grandmother," Thankful said, her spirits sinking as the two women remained silent.

Betty spoke first. "Well, if that isn't providential, Martha, I don't know what is."

Martha nodded. "We've been praying for help tending my farm log. I'm starting a few new ventures this year, and if there's one thing I hate it is numbers. You say you have skill then?"

"At figuring, but I can learn ledgers and such—I helped Father a few times too. And you can thank Mr. Henry for the idea, so I hope you don't mind that tonight I've made plans for supper with Mr. Henry's parents."

Martha held her teacup midair, surveying her granddaughter with concern bordering on contempt. "You don't want to get mixed up with Henry's family, girl."

"It's only supper, and I'm starved for interesting company," Thankful said, oblivious to her grandmother's feelings.

Martha shook her head and poured more tea. She handed the empty pot to Betty to refill in the kitchen. "Henry is too old for you and has no money."

"Grandmother, don't insult me!" Thankful said, rolling her eyes. "I have no interest in Mr. Henry. I *just told* you I want to be a bookkeeper."

Martha dismissed her words with a raised brow and snicker. "Henry's mother is a raving Methodist and puts on airs. She actually believes we have some say in our salvation and that it's pretty free and easy with God! The Bible says only some are chosen. Your father would oppose a marriage to a Methodist almost as much as a Catholic. Stick with the Presbyterians."

"I promise not to touch on the subject of religion as I don't know my own mind on it yet."

"And that's a disgrace," Martha said. "We could have a Bible study here if you're so in need of intellectual conversation, but you've never expressed an interest."

"I have no interest whatsoever," Thankful replied. "I go to church and that's enough."

"I knew Graham shouldn't have married your mother. She has a brain like a sieve and understands nothing of Scripture. I always said she was possessed by demons."

Thankful pondered Martha's words. "I'm not here to defend Mama. Now tonight I will have a pleasant supper with Mr. Henry—your friend. I have a curiosity about houses and décor ..."

"Just like your mother."

"I promise to remain a Presbyterian—for you." Thankful laughed.

"You take your salvation very lightly, young lady, but do as you like. I'm just old and foolish." Martha allowed Betty to pour more tea. "This morning pick the peas like I told you, and this afternoon I'll show you my accounts. I do hope I can trust you to keep my finances out of your conversation tonight—if you take after your mother you'll be inclined to gossip."

Thankful excused herself with a sigh.

***

A furniture maker's employees loaded fine New Jersey chairs and tables aboard a flatboat as Thankful strode north along the Hackensack toward Henry's house. The woods opened up, and on the right a sturdy and substantial red brick Georgian home came into view. A piano played. Lovely music, completely unfamiliar and haunting, floated from the downstairs windows, all open in the first real warmth of early spring. Servants milled in the front yard gathering the last of their gardening tools for the evening. One waved to Thankful when she smiled.

"I'm looking for the Henry home," she said at the gate to the friendly servant.

The servant laughed with a sideways look. "You mean the Demarest house?"

"Mr. Henry said to arrive at seven, and I thought this was the place."

"Henry Demarest."

"Oh. Yes, I thought ... I was confused, but yes. I'm Miss Crenshaw."

"I hadn't been warned of visitors but come along," the servant said with a not-quite-friendly smile as she led Thankful to the front door. "It's not my job to answer the door, so please wait here and I'll run round back."

Thankful adjusted the tulips in her basket and took in the graceful weeping willows swaying to Henry's music in the damp yard. The music stopped abruptly.

"Henry, it's my birthday supper, and I wanted just family, dear."

Thankful's ears burned.

"Mommy, I felt sorry for her staying with Martha all by herself. Have pity," Henry said.

Thankful turned to go as the door opened. Henry pushed past the servant who stood aside, annoyed.

"Miss Crenshaw, a lovely evening isn't it? Oh, and flowers, come right in. My mother loves tulips."

Mrs. Demarest met them with a sweet smile though a hint of impatience escaped from beneath her drooping eyelids. She wore her hair in youthful curls which Thankful thought ridiculous. "Yes, I do love tulips especially pink ones, but I know Martha prefers yellow." She handed Thankful's basket of pale yellow blooms to the servant in charge of doors and led Thankful into the parlor. "You interrupted Henry's playing—a song written for my birthday, dear. Henry please finish it while we wait for my special meal."

Henry dutifully complied, showing no sign of concern or embarrassment.

"We see so little of our son," Mrs. Demarest said, her breath smelling of Madeira.

Thankful nodded. "Mrs. Demarest, I certainly wouldn't have accepted an invitation if I knew this was a special night."

"Oh, no, no. The more the merrier, and you're quite pretty—nothing like your grandmother. Oh, but I promised myself to be civil with Henry's friends. I'm a Methodist, you know, and we pride ourselves on sharing the gospel and God's saving grace. All are welcome here—even Presbyterians."

Thankful, though uncomfortable, could not help but admire the high ceilings and glistening gas fixtures that gave the room an elegant glow. The couches were white and the artwork soft and modern to Thankful's eyes. Henry's music entranced her for it was nothing like the old hymns he'd played at Martha's. When Henry glanced her way, she blushed.

Mrs. Demarest watched her disapprovingly, though when Thankful caught the look the old lady with heavily jeweled fat fingers and wrists smiled serenely. An elderly man stood at the door with a drink in his hand and looking contemptuously at his son but left for the dining room before the piece was finished.

A bell rang over Henry's final notes. Mr. Demarest complained from the other room that the soup was getting cold. Henry led his mother in, beckoning Thankful as an afterthought. Mr. Demarest held a chair for his wife and Henry did the same for Thankful. They bowed their heads in silent prayer and partook of asparagus soup. Thankful hated asparagus and the soup was a trial, but no more so than the silence in the room.

"Father, this is Martha's granddaughter Thankful."

Mr. Demarest nodded Thankful's way but said nothing. His humorless expression was accentuated by his long, thin mouth that turned at the edges and hinted at some sour disappointment in life.

"You have a very lovely home," Thankful said. "The paintings in the parlor are so cheerful. My mother adores eighteenth century Italian still-life artists, but I've never been fond of them."

Mrs. Demarest glared at her son as she passed him a broken piece of bread. Henry ate it. Turning to Thankful she said, "I like still-life paintings. Henry was told to bring back as many as he could afford with *our money* on his trip to Europe, but he brought back things better suited to his tastes, right Father?"

Mr. Demarest grumbled.

"The paintings in the parlor cost more than they're worth. We laugh at the farm-house painting by a German artist with a big name for so little talent. What was his name again, Henry?"

"Carl August Heinrich Ferdinand Oesterley," Henry said, sipping his wine.

Thankful fell into an old pattern. She sat straighter. "I quite like the name."

Henry looked her way in surprise, unused to having an ally.

Mrs. Demarest rubbed her chin in thought. She snapped her fingers to have the soup taken. "Well, you are very young aren't you, Miss Crenshaw. Have you been to Europe to see the great paintings?"

"No," Thankful admitted but with rising anger. "Have *you*?"

Mr. Demarest grunted in approval with a trace of good humor on his face.

Mrs. Demarest glared at Henry again. Henry shrugged.

"No, I have not been to Europe, but my son has and should have known better what to bring back. I asked for two paintings, but he decided to turn our lives upside down."

"Now, Mommy, let's not spoil your birthday meal. Would you want to give Martha something more to talk about?"

Thankful shot Henry a look, but he winked at her with a smile.

"Mrs. Demarest, I'd never speak ill of you," Thankful lied. She couldn't wait to tell Martha her thoughts. But then Martha had warned her about Henry's parents so best to keep quiet to preserve her pride, Thankful decided, as a toppling plate of raw clams was served.

Before Thankful could say no, the servant placed two pink and quivering clams on her plate. Thankful's stomach revolted, and she nearly gagged. The sheen and the goo took her back west to Fahy's exploded brain and the way the insides of a person were so messy. Thankful imagined her baby's flesh, the same gooey mess, buried now in her parents' yard—a yard she could never again sit in at ease. Yet the baby—little Silas—had been whole. Thankful would have given him Buck's name as middle. Would it have been better that Buck had been killed years ago? How many beatings did she witness? How many of Buck's cries from the tub, how many sickening gasps for air did Thankful cover her ears to, tucked safely in bed having herself made it through another day? Yes, maybe it was better that Silas avoided Buck's messy, gooey, horrible life! As Thankful poked the tiny tool at the flesh of the clam, trying at manners, she thought of the many times she covered for her mother, how she'd acted accomplice to the crimes against Buck, and when Silas was killed—pulled from her in a quivering mess and not quite dead—her mother repaid the favor. Silas was brought to the yard—the cold yard—a little quivering nothing ...

Thankful slipped from her chair, and the room went dark.

When Thankful awoke it was in the elder Mr. Demarest's arms as he carried her to the white sofa.

Mrs. Demarest whispered to Henry, "Just like you to take in a fragile specimen on my birthday, but never mind, there's always next year—God willing."

Henry attempted to cover Thankful with a throw as she sat up in mortification.

"Oh, forgive me, Mrs. Demarest ..." Thankful said, but a wave of nostalgia, an unaccountable sorrow crushed her recovery. "I want to go home!" she sobbed.

Henry knelt beside her. "Father will ready the carriage, Miss Crenshaw, and I'll take you to Martha's."

"No! You don't understand! I want to go home to my mother and father! I miss them terribly—and Buckie!" Thankful covered her face and sobbed some more.

A servant signaled when the horse came round to the side porch lit with lanterns like the ones on Chestnut Street. Henry helped Thankful up into her seat and sat beside her. The night was dark and cold now, and Thankful stared out vacantly as the carriage creaked along the rough road.

Henry looked over now and again. "How are you, pet?"

Thankful glanced back, her eyes wet with tears. "I've ruined your mother's birthday and made an enormous fool of myself."

Henry patted her hand. "Would you like to talk about what happened?"

"What's there to say? I fainted when I saw the clams."

"Who's Buckie?"

"Buck is my brother," Thankful began, but saying his name out loud released more emotion, "and I failed him!"

"What's become of him?" Henry asked tentatively.

Thankful paused before answering. "Mama scalded Buck's legs in the tub once—did you know that? Yes, and she made him earn food sometimes."

"Earn food. How?"

"Mama made Buck do things for the rest of us—our little chores and such. It sounds silly, but we let him. We were young, and Mama beat Buck again and again ..." She began to cry. "I never told anyone. Never. I was afraid to tell Father and afraid for myself! I let it happen, and now I tell you all these things years later when it doesn't matter, and why should you care?"

Henry pulled Thankful to him and let her cry, saying not a word for a long while. The horse waited patiently. When Thankful seemed cried-out Henry said, "It's not your fault, young miss. It wasn't Buck's fault either, was it?"

Thankful looked into Henry's eyes from a dark place she kept inside herself. "But I should have told Father ... poor Buck!"

"Do you think if you would have told him things would have been different? I wonder that your father didn't notice."

Thankful pulled away. "No, Father is a good man. He just worked awfully much, and when he was home we all pretended that everything was fine—even Buck pretended."

"Where is Buck now?"

"Buck's far, far away from us all out west. I miss him so much! I was to name my baby after him—his middle name." Thankful cried again.

"You have a child?" Henry asked, his tone hardening slightly.

"No. He died," Thankful said, despair enveloping her. "Mr. Henry, I shouldn't be telling you this, but I fell in love with an unfaithful man ... we were to be married, but he killed himself!"

Henry shook his head in shock.

Thankful turned her face away. "Please take me to Grandmother's. I know how you must despise me now. My father does." She cried into her handkerchief.

Henry looked to the stars and back at Thankful. The horse waited still. Henry turned Thankful by the arm. "Dear girl, we all have our skeletons. I don't despise you. I'm honored that you felt safe enough to unpack your heavy burdens before me. I'll take you home now, but promise you will consider me a friend—despite the clams and my mother."

Thankful laughed. "You're very kind."

# Chapter Five

Just as the sun rose, Martha knocked at Thankful's door and let herself in. Thankful groggily sat up, rubbing her eyes.

"Grandmother, has something happened?"

"No, I just thought I'd see how your evening went."

"Couldn't that have waited till breakfast? What time is it?" Thankful lay back down, pulling the blankets over her head.

"I thought about your suggestion to get sheep, so I'm going to a farm in Dunkerhook to buy a few lambs. I'll be gone all day."

Thankful sighed when Martha tapped her shoulder insistently. "Fine, I'll tell you, though I don't know why you care so much. I fainted when they served clams so they brought me home."

"Fainted? It was rather late when you came home."

"Henry drove me home, and we talked for a while."

"Talked? In the dark?"

"Grandmother, please. We just talked."

Martha seemed mildly disappointed. "Well, what did you think of Mrs. Demarest?"

"She's awful."

Martha laughed out loud. "Isn't she though? And what sort of person serves clams to guests? I never would—they're bottom feeders and disgusting!"

"Mrs. Demarest had no idea I was coming."

"Oh, just like Henry to make a mess of things." Martha acted as if there was more to say, but changed direction. "Thankful, here is some advice. Henry is too old for you."

"You already told me that. Do you think I'm that desperate for marriage? No. I see Henry as almost a father or maybe a good uncle."

Martha shook her head vigorously. "No, no, no. That he is not. He's a half-baked musician and a drifter."

"Well, he has a sensitive soul, and I admire that—and that alone."

"Good," Martha said, exiting the room. "See you this evening—and please organize the papers in the parlor."

\*\*\*

Rain dripped from the eaves all morning as Thankful cleaned the parlor. Betty was not much for keeping dust at bay. When Thankful realized the tune she hummed was Mrs.

31

Demarest's birthday composition, she smiled to herself. Having confessed her sins to Henry lightened her mood a little, and organizing Martha's desk gave her purpose. She looked forward to a long quiet afternoon indoors with Betty and Martha away and plenty of tea to be had, the old ladies being miserly with tea leaves. Thankful dusted off the pianoforte and sat on the bench playing and singing a children's song she'd learned from a French teacher years ago:

*Je te plumerai la tête.*
*Et la tête! Et la tête!*
*Alouette! Alouette!*

A knock came at the opened window and a drenched Henry in sagging hat waved, signaling for Thankful to open the door to him. She got up at once and ran to let Henry in. He laughed, stomping his wet boots in the long, dark hallway.

Thankful suddenly felt she'd been invaded and wished her grandmother was home. She did not smile and stood at a distance with arms crossed.

Henry felt the chill as he hung his wet jacket. "Is everything all right? Where's Martha?"

"She's not here."

"Then I'll wait."

Henry pulled his boots off to reveal threadbare stockings.

"You certainly make yourself at home here, don't you?" she remarked with a nervous laugh. What would Martha say about Thankful having let him in?

"Martha takes music lessons with me."

"Well, you may have a long wait—I don't know for sure when she'll be back as she's gone off to Dunkerhook looking for sheep."

"Sheep? So she's finally taking my advice to use her pasture for something," Henry said. "She could have told me so I didn't have to get all wet in the weather. I'd like some tea if you don't mind."

"Betty's not here."

Henry gave her a wry look. "Don't tell me you don't know how to boil water. I see you know French."

"Of course. I'm not a barbarian."

Henry laughed. "France is lovely. You really should go."

"First I'm planning a trip to the moon," she said as she walked to the kitchen.

Henry followed with a chuckle. "What a pessimist. No wonder you get nowhere."

She slammed the kettle on the cool stove, stoking the small fire within. "What a mean thing to say. And after all I've told you!"

"Nothing you told me last night convinces me you can't someday go to Paris," Henry said, pushing her aside to get more flame going.

"That's well and good for you who gets sent off to buy works of art on your father's funds. Just like Buck!"

"How so? I thought he was the friendless victim of the family," Henry said, recoiling when a spark burned his hand. "Damn."

"I don't like how you use my words against me. Buck is more than that, but—" Thankful hesitated, aware of sounding like a jealous child. "But my father sends him an enormous allowance out of his (my father's) inheritance that no one even knew he had!"

"So your father has a guilty conscience after all," Henry said.

"I suppose I hadn't thought of it that way—but Buck throws the money away!"

"On drink and women?" Henry asked, smiling.

"No. Not Buck. He's become pure as the driven snow and gives the money to the poor. It irks me." She reached for Martha's fine china cups and noticed Henry's admiring eyes. "Sir, I hope you don't think ..."

Henry played innocent. "What?"

"Nothing," she replied, setting the cups down beside the brown stoneware teapot. "Sir, you must promise never to tell a soul—not even Martha—about all that went on long ago. Please."

Henry took a pair of spectacles from his pocket and slipped them on the end of his nose. "Young lady, what do you take me for? Now if you don't mind I'll just read the morning papers in the parlor until Martha gets back—it's coming down in rivers still."

After Henry poured water over a generous helping of expensive tea leaves, she followed him into the parlor, fretting at her upset plans for solitude. "Sir, I've work set out in there."

"I don't mind," Henry said. "I'm sure you won't bother me."

Thankful sat at the desk reading a disorganized ledger. Her mind flitted from one thing to the next. She wondered if Martha would approve of Henry quietly watching her work, but stealing a look she saw that the man with greying temples napped in Martha's one masculine wingback chair that once belonged to Thankful's promiscuous and disappeared grandfather. Had she taken after him? God forbid! Oh, but that was impossible as her father was the bastard son of an unknown man Martha had bedded. Thankful settled in and as the skies brightened and the birds chirped again she heard her grandmother's heels against the slate path. She jumped to greet her at the door.

"Grandmother! You're back earlier than expected!"

"Yes, girl, now move out of the way. I'm soaked," Martha said, throwing her coat on the bench for Betty to take care of after putting her buggy and horse away.

Thankful followed Martha into the parlor.

"The lambs were the sweetest things so we ordered five, but they're not quite weaned—" Martha stopped and stared at Henry just waking with a yawn and stretch. "Henry? What's the meaning of this?"

"Have you forgotten something?" Henry replied, folding the paper and tossing it on the now messy side table.

Martha waited impatiently until Henry tapped the piano.

"Oh, dear." Martha's tone changed. "Forgive me. Of course I'll still pay you for lessons."

"No need," Henry replied. "I used up your good tea, and I only take pay for services rendered. Your granddaughter was kind enough to let me nap. What a very good worker she is, Martha. This room looks far better than it's ever looked, but then it could be the beautiful girl in it." He smiled. "Miss Crenshaw has been a fine hostess."

Martha wasn't happy with this talk. "Thankful is a foolish child, Henry. I thought you would have kept her from gossip. What will the neighbors say about her entertaining a man twice her age?"

"I won't tell if you don't, old girl," he said, putting his finger to her lips.

She laughed. "Now go away. I want peace after such a muddy day."

Henry bowed and left as Betty walked by. "Betty, Thankful is looking to drive you out with her cleaning. Shape up!"

Betty pointed to the barn. "There's a bicycle crowding the barn, sir."

"Tell Miss Crenshaw it's a gift to travel the world on," Henry shouted as he ran off in the renewed downpour.

Thankful heard through the window and grinned at the idea of the bicycle. Betty misunderstood.

"I escaped slavery when your great-grandparents set me free," Betty said, her voice deep and fierce with Martha out of the room. "I went down the river and married an Indian who left me high and dry. I told Martha I'd never take a man in again, and she saw I was a sister to her in spirit. We have a nice life together just as we want it, so don't for a second think you'll take my place."

"I wouldn't want to," Thankful said with a sneer. She went to the messy newspapers, crinkled them, and threw them on the floor. "Are you happy for work now?"

"I'm not easily upset," Betty said. "Young things like you still feel life owes you something. Once you settle in and see the truth of your place in the world it gets easier to enjoy things as they are. Henry has always been a fool, and he plays you like an untuned piano."

"I've been told never to settle and I won't," Thankful said, wondering just how old the prune-faced woman was. "Settling is un-American. Henry is just a friend, you stupid old woman!"

Betty laughed. "This may hurt your feelings, but Martha and me feel pretty certain you'll end up just like us, now that you've gone so wayward."

"Never! I'm going to be a bookkeeper since you're not so very good with numbers, and then I'll travel the world—once I save up."

Betty smiled. "I know how your travels ended up last time." Betty picked up the newsprint and threw it in the hearth.

"Why are you saying mean things to me? At least Henry is optimistic and believes in me."

"Henry Demarest gives you a castoff toy, and you think it means something," Betty said. "He has a lot of cast-offs and his parents' money to burn. Everything is cheap to him. You'll see. I'm just warning you. Don't let your vanity and gifts get in the way of your chastity."

"How dare you talk to me this way? How does Martha put up with you? I'd fire you in a flash!"

Martha came from the kitchen. "Thankful Crenshaw! Shut your mouth!"

"She's a rude and heartless servant, and I wouldn't ..." Thankful began, but her grandmother's face stopped her.

"Everyone isn't here to please you!" Martha scolded. "Your father's let you become spoiled and snobbish. He's given every part of himself away to a bunch of ingrates! Thankful, take advice from your elders with a spirit of humility. What a sad mix of your parents you are—frivolous and serious at the same time. Don't let an old dog like Henry distract you from living the life God's purposed for you."

"What makes you think I want my life?" Thankful said, with a hurt glance Betty's way. "You forget all I've been through."

"Don't insult God!" Martha said. "No one knows why children are taken from us. Be happy you never got to know the poor thing. My sons were ripped from me at the height of their manhood—with only Graham left."

Thankful hated to ask, but was compelled to torture her conscience. "Grandmother, you kept father even though he was illegitimate. Weren't you frightened?"

"I wasn't scared—just caught out. I tried to give him away, but no one would keep him. Kept sending him back," Martha said, impatiently pinning her hair. "Graham as a toddler would starve himself until they sent him back to me, and finally all our options were lost. I was the laughing stock of the town. Your grandfather Seward never liked him—how could he? I had Graham with the only man I really cared for, and after years of Seward's scandalous affairs in the city! Seward had some debts with a storekeeper from town and practically sold Graham off as slave labor—to do the man's haying. Your Uncle Luce was so angry at his father. It almost came to blows on Main Street in front of Mr. Wright's store. Mr. Wright was caught in the middle—Seward told him Graham had fully recovered from the scarlet fever. When Wright found out the truth he took Luce aside, and they came upon the idea of making the big job a contest for all the boys in town. Luce was so grateful that he worked till it nearly killed him and won the contest, of course. He was always proud of that. Graham would have certainly died in that field. Seward was very cruel and even worse after Graham didn't save his brothers in the war. Luce was Seward's favorite." Martha sniffled, picking up a framed picture of her dead son. Fred and Buck had his strong jawline and straight nose.

Thankful looked to the photograph of her young father as an army surgeon. Unlike the portraits of his half-brothers, Graham looked sad and wary. "You didn't want Father? It's the saddest thing I've ever heard. No wonder ..."

"What?"

"Of course it's why Father has stayed with Mama."

"He stays with your mother because he's weak-willed and extremely stupid with his emotions. He thinks sinning before God by having other women will bring him peace. Graham should have married Mai when he had the chance. After your Uncle Luce died she would have married Graham just out of convenience and sympathy. Did your father ever tell you about your cousin? You've a cousin I sent to Europe to study—a good boy. Graham's kept up a correspondence with Mai and her son Reginald for years."

"You're lying!"

"I'm not," Martha said, disliking Thankful's label. "Where do you think your father really was all those times he went to medical conventions? I bet he was doing what your grandfather Seward did."

Thankful sat on the piano bench reliving the times her father came back from the conventions. When she and her siblings were young they'd crowd the windows in wait, searching for their father's freshly painted carriage pulled by his sturdy but humble horse. Father didn't like to put on airs before the country folk he treated, yet even in that she now saw the facade he created to keep others out. Impressions meant the world to him, so much so that his very best qualities were reserved for patients he hardly knew.

Father kept his children as far away from his weakened heart as he could, and on those days when Thankful's siblings tumbled down the front stairs to meet Father in the drive, his look was one of pained tolerance. As the siblings grew into young men and women the distance only became greater, giving the children a clearer view of the cold, forced kisses between their parents. Did Father understand what went on in his absence? Was that the reason he could not bear more than five minutes accepting his children's embraces, or was he just missing a lover he'd left behind at the latest convention?

Mama cleverly hid her abuses in separate boxes. Thankful didn't understand her mother's cutting remarks back then. When Thankful was young she didn't understand her father's wary distances, his silence, and his sudden rages. The rages were rare indeed but so like an all-encompassing and terrifying cyclone that Thankful and her siblings wished for his long weekends away when things were a more mundane sort of misery. All the ponies, the frilly bedrooms, and best schools could not make the Crenshaw home a happy one.

"And the soldier out west—the one you nearly married ..." Martha continued.

"Yes, Lieutenant Fahy was unfaithful too!" Thankful cried. "Why do men have to be so wicked? I hate them all!"

"Thankful, we let them be wicked," Martha said, her mouth severe and with no trace of compassion for her granddaughter. "Don't for one second think you're innocent."

# Chapter Six

Buck Crenshaw, former West Point cadet turned private, had sacrificed everything for God, even giving away his perfect cadet coat to an Apache who'd lost his clothing at cards. He lay on his army cot in the desert trying to get back to sleep after dreaming of his twin brother Fred winding the scarf at Buck's neck tighter until he gagged. It started his day off wrong. Even after the nightmare Buck missed his twin as he inched up in the half-light of dawn.

His sister Thankful's illegitimate baby was dead and Fred had gotten married, all while Buck sat roasting in Arizona at Fort Grant. He ran his fingers over his rippled and still-sore temple. The gash at his neck had healed, but the scarlet mark refused to fade. After some initial improvement, his voice had settled into a weak and rough whisper, though it no longer pained him.

As a visiting cadet, the officers at the isolated military fort had accepted Buck as a green pup but one of their own. Buck's manners, his physical stature, and his intelligence declared his natural place in life amongst those with rank. Now as a private, those same acquaintances ignored him. Most saw Buck as a weird and pitiful failure with his overzealous faith as an eccentricity that had destroyed his career.

The privates despised him. Their master had come to roost, and they could not be themselves. Different, well-educated, obnoxiously neat and superior at drill, Buck annoyed their rough sensibilities and referenced God too much. And then there were the rumors about his manhood and the missionary. So they stayed away.

Joining the army as a private seemed liberating at first to the newly Christianized Buck. No West Point, no exams, no Fred. But in his heart he was no private. Buck had devised a bargain with God that day on the train platform when opening the great divide between himself and everything worldly—family, Thankful, West Point. If he saved William Weldon, his childhood rival, then God would reward him.

Lately Buck's words fell flat when praying. As morning light filtered into the barracks, Buck skimmed Scripture, considering that Jesus, God come to Earth, had favorite people—John, Peter, and James. Having never been anyone's favorite, Buck sighed at his childish resentment.

His father sent money and sentimental letters, but Buck could not enjoy or trust the late interest in him. And the riches Graham insisted he have—didn't Jesus say to give possessions away? Buck donated most of it to the Catholic Church for the poor. God took the money and ran. Every night Buck's stomach ached with hunger. His mother's big meals when home and his West Point diet supplemented with cakes and things bought in town had always kept him well-nourished. Now he was empty.

He considered the Apaches. At least his life wasn't as wretched as a drunken Indian's—but what about the sober ones? They had family, leisure, and they did whatever they pleased. Buck used to do things in hopes of satisfaction—yet nothing satisfied. What did please him? God? Buck hated to think that he needed miracles—but God ought to give a small one to assure Buck He cared.

Today he had time off along with a few men in his company. They clambered into the same coach to town, but the others avoided eye contact and kept to themselves. Buck brooded over Fred and Jesus' favorite apostles, and part of him listened for any snide remarks concerning his face or his friendship with Kenyon the missionary. Buck considered going right back to Fort Grant and sleeping the afternoon away, but the heat prevented napping.

Instead he went to see William. With the money Graham had given him, Buck had anonymously paid William's board. And sometimes Buck brought food and left it outside his hovel. Weren't you supposed to do good deeds secretly?

He knocked at the door of the rubble-strewn shanty of adobe. And again and again, each time with more force. The sound of William's shuffling feet on the floor annoyed him. The door opened a crack. Buck shoved it further, the light hitting William's squinting eyes.

"Willy, let me in."

"I thought you all went home—months ago." William scratched his head. His face was burnt from drinking and his bare feet were swollen. "Has something happened?"

"I thought we'd go get shoes today."

"Today? *We?* Why are you here and in those clothes?" William asked with amusement as he looked Buck over, landing his eyes on the kepi that no one in the West bothered wearing.

"By special permission, I've enlisted. Captain Markham has friends in Washington."

William laughed. "You're a private? What sort of joke is this? You had me until you said *special permission*."

"Well, it's true," Buck said, trying to look proud.

William stared at him. "You've given up your place at West Point and a sure officer's commission?"

"Yes."

William groaned. "But why? What for?"

"For you. I wanted to make sure you were taken care of."

*"What?"*

Buck puffed up, "I stayed for ..."

"What the hell is wrong with you? I heard that you and Mr. Kenyon ..." William tried to shove Buck toward the door.

"No, there was nothing between me and Seth, you idiot," Buck replied, standing his ground, smug in his assurance that a Crenshaw could not be bested by a Weldon.

"I knew it was odd you called him Seth so fast."

"No, we were—*we are*—friends. Seth helped me, and now I can—help you."

"You're a private!" William cried. "Even I never wanted that for myself!"

"I'm a private for *your* sake," Buck yelled, as he adjusted his dusty cap.

"What game are you playing at?" William asked. "What do you want from me? How dare you drag me into your problems! Did you get kicked out of West Point?"

"No, it's just, well ... I believe, I sort of think that—maybe it's crazy—but I believe that God wants me to help you."

"Who says I want help?" William asked, his red eyes puffed and his beard thick and matted. "Did I ask you to destroy your chances for me? *I don't want your help!*"

"Well, I've prayed about it."

"I don't care if you spoke to the Lord in person—you have no rights over me," William said, the look on his face moving from anger to amusement.

"Friends, I thought we might be..." Buck said as a rat crawled over stale bread in the dark corner.

"I don't want a religious zealot as a friend. You've gotten roughed up in life, and now you find God. Take responsibility for yourself—for once. When you were bad it was Fred's fault, and now that you're good it's all God. Who the hell are you?"

Buck pulled his cap over his eyes. "I don't know. I haven't any friends—on my own, I ... I miss my brother, but I hate him."

William scratched his head and sighed. "I can't be your brother."

"I've made a terrible mistake joining the army. I'm hated."

"You joined to be loved?" William said with mocking disdain.

"No." Buck laughed gruffly. Their eyes met for a second.

"They'll like you in time." William cleared paper from a stool and sat.

"You haven't grown to like me."

"There's too much history."

Buck dusted dirt from his sleeve. "I had it in my head we'd get you some shoes. Let me do that before I give this money to Father Diaz."

William eyed the neatly organized cash as Buck pulled it from his breast pocket. "Well, okay. It is awful kind of you to lend me money for shoes, but I won't trouble you to come join me. If you just trust me to pay you back then ..." He held out his hand.

Buck wavered, but questioned his own motives. Maybe William should buy his own boots. Was there any point in humiliating him? Buck handed over most of his cash—more than shoes could possibly cost.

"This is too generous. I'll pay you back." William sifted through the money too happily.

"It's all right—" Buck second-guessed his generosity but remembered Jesus' words: *lend, expecting nothing in return, and your reward will be great.* He sighed. "You might think of buying food or art supplies."

William's expression changed; his jaw tightened.

"I'm sorry. Do as you see fit," Buck said.

"Yes. Well, thank you for this loan. Hmm, I think I *will* get paint." William's eyes betrayed him. "I guess you must have other errands."

"Oh, no," Buck brightened. "Well, today I'm free."

"*Really?* Sorry, but I'm set to meet ... someone pretty soon so ..." William led him toward the door.

Buck hated being lied to. Even bribery had not gotten him a friend. "Yes, I'd better go," he said through clenched teeth.

"I promise to pay you back."

William closed the door on him.

Back out on the street, Buck figured by the shadows it was around one o'clock in the afternoon, and what was there to do? Wiping sweat from his clean-shaved upper lip, he saw the party of soldiers from this morning pouring out of the card parlor and heading for the Buckskin in high humor. Buck ducked between the dry goods shop and the druggist store, embarrassed at his loneliness. He could ask for a transfer. But no. He needed to settle somewhere, and God put him *here*.

Once the soldiers staggered out of sight, he headed toward the Mexican restaurant. He passed the church with a guilty heart. The bit of money he had left was enough for a meal and a ride back on the coach. The poor would have to wait.

"Say there, Mr. Buck Crenshaw!" A toothless and weather-beaten man just greying at the temples jogged up. "Mr. Crenshaw, I haven't drunk a drop in four days now since we last spoke. I got questions fer ya 'bout Jesus. You got some time?"

Buck had plenty of time but dreaded spending it with this man. He remembered the money in his pocket. "Mr.—what was your name again?"

"Joe."

"Well, Joe, I was just going to eat. Would you care to join me?"

"That's awful kind of you, sir, but ..." The man hesitated as if he'd prefer a few coins, but changed his mind. "That'd be just bully."

Buck groaned on the inside, knowing he had enough money for either one nice meal or two meager ones. He smiled falsely as they went inside the dark restaurant.

Once at the table with a small portion of beans and tortillas each, the man mentioned that he was a songwriter but because of the drink had lost his work. He hoped that the Lord would keep him sober now, but Buck didn't believe him and only half-listened as he wondered why he had not been invited to his brother's wedding—not that Buck would have gone. Miss Turner had been his girl, not Fred's, before his scars and lost reputation.

"Anyways, I was sufferin' these last days fer wantin' the drink, but God gave me a distraction—writin' songs again. I wrote this one 'bout you." Once the man started crooning in his alcoholic warble, Buck took notice as did a few of the other customers.

"Joe, now please ... stop," Buck whispered.

"Sir, you're my hero, and I don't care who knows it!" He sang in earnest:

*"Oh, Buck Cren—shaw!*
*He tells of Moses law*
*That Jesus broke us free from.*
*When Jesus was hung*
*And the damage was done*
*All our sins we did flee from.*
*Oh, Buck Cren—shaw!*
*He ain't that much if you seen him*
*But he brought me mercy*
*Even though he's ugly*
*That's my Mr. Cren—shaw!"*

Buck held his fork in mid-air, listening to the tune and the snickering of other diners. His heart burned from the spicy food, and he thought he might be sick. He eyed the door but figured Jesus would sit through the song. Why did God care about the moron sitting across from him? What good was this drunk to the world? Sponging off people, spoiling lunch, and humiliating him with cruel, insensitive songs. This was too hard—trying to be like Jesus. "Pardon me," Buck grumbled as he tossed his payment on the table and marched outside with the whole place erupting in laughter.

By the time he made it into the sun his head roared. He spotted William scuttling across the road—still barefoot, but with what appeared to be a full haversack. Buck followed him at a distance to his hovel. William reached into his bag, broke open a new bottle of whiskey, and took an enormous slug.

Buck ran up infuriated. "Damn you, Willy!"

"Buck!" William stood like a schoolboy caught at dice.

"What kind of fool do you take me for?"

William regained his composure. "Do you really want to know?"

"Empty your knapsack now!"

"No. I'm not in the army, and you're not my superior!"

Buck grabbed the bag and rifled through it. "Where's the rest of the money? You can't have spent it all on four bottles of whiskey."

"It's gone. I spent it." William ripped his bag, his father's old bag, from Buck.

"But shoes, William. You look so foolish, and it's dangerous with all sorts of vermin around. Why wouldn't you just buy a damned pair of shoes?"

"Buck, the thing is—I'm happy with my life."

"What? Well, that's impossible," Buck said, ruffled at the idea.

William's eyes were yellow, strange and unhealthy. "I considered not doing this anymore," he said, pointing to the bottle. "But then I realized, what else have I got? What else can I get? I have no smarts—no anything. It's been hard for me to deal with that, you know. I remember knowing things I don't know anymore. You wouldn't understand, but for me drinking is a pleasure."

"Anyone can take a drink."

"Well, there was a time when I couldn't. My arms were weak, and my mother had to feed me ..." He looked far away and sad, like a child. "Anyway, what does it matter what others do?"

"You should set your sights higher than taking a drink."

William laughed. "Why? So I can be like you? All of these big notions, all of this praising and God tripe and you're laughed at and despised even more than me. You tell me to look higher, but you quit West Point."

Buck's spirit sank. "West Point isn't everything."

"To me it was! I wanted to go there more than anything! I studied for ages and still I couldn't figure at math or write for shit. I tried my damnedest to walk right and even worked up the nerve to visit with Senator Vail."

"Yes, he's a bully fellow."

"I guess he is to you—but Fred stole my place."

"William, I'm sorry for you, but Fred—well—he's unstoppable and brilliant."

"I know. I finally see now that some people are meant for lesser things, and I'm fine with that so just leave me be."

"But you'll die if you keep this up."

"And what loss would that be?"

"God has better plans ..."

"What God? The God that laughs at this wretched body even after I prayed for years to be healed? The God who has only taken you from bad to worse since you've come out on His side? God lost me a long time ago and soon you'll be lost too. I see how disillusioned you are, Buck."

"I'm not as disillusioned about God as I am about you. I used to admire your strength—the way you fought to recover."

"That's nice of you to say when it doesn't matter anymore. In Englewood I was nothing, and here it's the same. The difference is now I don't care."

"If my only two choices are to give up like you or to continue to at least try—something—anything to make life worth living, then I'm going to have to try however painful it is." Buck heard the resolve in his own voice.

"You don't know the first thing about pain. I do." William took a drink.

"I wouldn't wear your troubles as a badge of honor, Willy. It's sickening."

"I'll pay you when I can."

Buck nodded, took a few steps and turned back. "What size are your feet?"

"Why?"

Buck unlaced his army brogans and tossed them at William, who couldn't catch them without losing the whiskey in his bag.

"I don't want your shoes! How will it look for you? Come back and take them."

Buck shoved his hands in his pockets, tuning William out in stockinged feet.

Walking the miles back to Fort Grant would at least waste the rest of the day. "There you are, Mr. Crenshaw." It was Joe again. "Was wonderin' where you went off to. You had better be careful flashin' money around the way you did at our meal."

"I didn't flash money," Buck said, his blood rising again.

"So where ya goin' now, sir?" Joe asked, shuffling along.

"Back to my barracks."

"But the coach, it ain't comin' for a good while, sir."

"I'm walking."

"With no shoes? You're an odd fish, if I may say, sir. You lose your shoes gambling?"

"Of course not! I gave them to a friend." The man repulsed Buck. "Joe, I had better get going now."

# Chapter Seven

Buck squinted as the sun set over the pink desert. Even with the sun falling, his feet sizzled through his thick woolen socks, but the further he got from town the more relieved he felt. The desert upon his arrival seemed a wasteland, but now his eyes and mind made peace with its harsh beauty. The nothingness of the place spoke to him. For so long he'd wanted to be someone and still did, but for this brief time he didn't have to be. God created even the short, squat, and plain desert shrubbery. The weird plants possessed an unknown value and that, for a second, consoled Buck, but soon enough the idea of being only as valuable as desert scrub depressed him so he marched on.

Humility remained out of reach. What did it even mean? If Jesus had come as a cactus there wouldn't be books about him and churches built. Christ wasn't quiet and humble. Buck realized again the pride in comparing himself to God. He considered Peter, Paul, and even Seth Kenyon. God had big plans for them. What if there was no real plan for Buck? What if he wasn't useful to God? And now he stood shoeless and friendless as a private in the army.

He longed for a wife. Fred would have children and a great commission. He'd be friends with senators and successful and ... Buck sat beside the dusty road. His feet were sore and hot—and why? So he could be laughed at by *William*! He could desert the army, but then what would he do? His father wouldn't send funds to a criminal.

He took off his jacket and socks. A slight breeze passed as he crawled over to the shade behind an outcropping of smooth desert stone and fell quickly asleep and into a dream. He was home—in Englewood, but it was now. Doctor Banks and his father were examining Buck still in his private's uniform. Buck shouted in his old voice and his scars were gone, and then he was at West Point with Cadet Streeter. Streeter smiled and smiled until Buck pulled the pillowcase over his head and threw the cadet into an abyss. Buck kept kicking the pillowcase, crushing the cadet's head, never stopping though wanting to until the dream ended and he woke with a start.

Dusk slipped up over him. He fingered the gash at his head, sighing in relief—Streeter hadn't been killed just badly injured and scared from his place at the academy. Buck only allowed himself a second to wonder what Streeter was doing now before turning back to himself.

His spirits lifted a little. He had nothing, but even now in his poverty, even when his efforts seemed so in vain—he had an assurance—a small bit of peace beyond his understanding that must be God. Or maybe the nap had restored him. The world might label him a fool, but now it was for his Father. Even with his mistakes, this Father counted him sinless. Buck remembered a phrase Father Diaz taught him: *Miles*

*Christi sum.* "I am a soldier of Christ," Buck said out loud, and his heart swelled. Jesus loved him and the things, the events from before and the challenges still ahead—all things worked for good for those who believed.

Buck dusted himself off, slipped his socks back on and stepped out on his tender feet. He would try again with William some other time. The sun lit everything like a tiger lily from home. He felt anxious now to get to the barracks to write his father.

In the distance he heard the rumble of stage wheels over the dry, rocky path. He laughed to himself. God had sent him the ride home he needed. He waited and watched the cloud of dust veil the orange sky. The coach came at a clip, and the horses' mouths foamed. Two young men in ranch hats pulled low sat at the helm and didn't seem inclined to stop as Buck waved his hand at them—not unusual for this time of evening in this very desolate part of the world. He jumped a few yards before them into the path. The horses startled and reared but settled at the whisper of Buck's voice. The men were both Apache. A terrified girl from Fort Grant signaled for help from the window of the coach. Buck fingered his small sidearm as the men sitting above him recovered themselves enough to focus their guns Buck's way. He held up his hands.

"Peace be with you," Buck said.

They laughed. One jumped down and stood chest to chest with Buck. The musky smell of Indian disgusted Buck although it came to him that he must evangelize. The Indian ran his hands over Buck's worn uniform jacket.

"Do you want it?" Buck asked, unbuttoning the jacket. The Indian backed up and said something funny to the other. Buck handed the jacket over but remembered something in the pocket. "Just let me take this Bible," he said, but his sudden movement unnerved the Apache. The bigger one jumped from the driver's seat and grabbed Buck's arm.

"It's only a Bible, see?" His insides quaked. He heard the muffled scream of a girl in the coach. "I can show you how to be saved! Please let the girls inside go. Take me, and I'll show you about God." He looked to the heavens, and they looked too for a moment.

"You're one of them missionaries. Took my brother away for school, and he never come back."

"I'm not a missionary ... but everyone will hunt you down and kill more of you if you steal these girls. It's a foolish thing to do."

The English speaker laughed. "Who's the foolish one, wandering the desert tonight by himself?"

"I'm not by myself. I have God."

"Your white god kills my people just like the soldiers he sends with the missionaries."

Buck took the man's arm in a fatherly way—like he'd seen Seth Kenyon do with great results. The bigger man threw him to the ground, but he rose up. "Please let the girls go. They'll only cause you trouble in the end. I beg you to let them go." He ran to the coach door and flung it open. "Let them go."

The Indians walked up to Buck as if annoyed at a mischievous child. He turned to the two girls and whispered for them to get out the other side. One would not. The other hesitated before slowly opening the stage door.

Buck took out his gun and pointed at the men. Was it right to murder? The Old Testament and New gave conflicting ideas.

One of the Indians pulled a knife from his belt and hacked Buck's hand. The girl still in the coach screamed, but the other had slipped behind the reins and sent the horses off with a whip and a cry.

# Chapter Eight

William stirred from his stupor, trying to remember what day it was. Glancing at a half-gone bottle of whiskey and holding his head, he remembered a time when that much drink would have made him sick for days—now every day brought sickness. He thought of the loneliness on Buck's face. At least Buck had his sobriety. He could go home or stay in the desert even as a private with his head held high.

And there were those boots in the corner—army brogans, not so different from his father's long ago. Maybe Buck had thrown them at him in mockery. But it had felt like—though William wasn't sure—it had felt like a genuine act of generosity. Maybe, just maybe, he would try in the future to be nicer to Buck.

He hadn't spent all the money Buck had given him. The whore he'd taken up with lately mentioned a watch he pawned that had ended up in her hands. William counted the money and counted again and lost his place, sipped his bottle, shoved the coins into his pocket, and slipped on the soft boots. Pulling his hat over his dirty hair, he felt expansive. He'd steal a few pencils and draw.

Shadows stretched long as the day neared its end. A large crowd gathered near the Catholic Church—another bizarre saint procession. William sauntered off in the other direction toward the whorehouse but heard someone shout Buck's name and turned. He hobbled over and pushed through the crowd.

"He's dead."

"Who? Who's dead?" William asked.

The respectable people in town made a point of disregarding drunks, but a soldier who'd always shunned Buck replied, "Buck Crenshaw."

"No, it's not possible! How did it happen?"

"Those Apache bastards!" another soldier said, in tears. "They butchered him."

"It's not true. I saw him earlier today ... I mean yesterday. He gave me his boots."

The men standing around surveyed the army brogans.

"Ain't that our Buck—to go and give the very shoes off his feet?" the choked-up soldier said. "We should have let him be with us, boys."

"What'll be done? Where is he?" William asked.

"The army will investigate."

"When? How?"

"We hear Buck saved Miss Tillie and Miss Alice out on the road. The army sent word by telegraph to town. A teamster found his jacket and a pile of burnt remains—the coyotes were already feeding at him—just bits and pieces left—and brought them to the sheriff. The barbarians burnt him so bad."

"But first they cut off his hand."

"No. I don't believe it."

"Who cares? The girls saw it. He's dead, and we're gonna make those goddamned savages pay!"

"How do you know it's Buck?" William asked.

A sergeant gave him a vicious look.

"They found his Bible and a picture of Thankful," the upset soldier said.

"The hand wasn't in the fire?" William asked. "Was his hand—that ring he's got ..."

A young woman in the crowd said, "Oh, he was such a handsome fellow too."

A soldier stared at her. "You're mistaken, miss."

"No, I'm not! Who's ever seen such violet eyes?"

The men glanced at each other. "Miss, he's the one with the cuts and sores and things."

"Yes, that's him," the girl replied and wiped her eyes. "He hardly knew I existed."

Father Diaz ran up. "Is it true about Señor Buck?"

"He's gone, Father," someone said.

The priest groaned. "*Miles Christi sum.*"

"Excuse me?"

"The young man liked to say he was a soldier of Christ. He was such a friend ..." the priest cried and prayed to God. Everyone stood transfixed but uncomfortable. Father Diaz prayed in Latin. When he finished, the priest turned to the soldiers. "Where is the body? I want to pray over it and see for myself."

"It's all burnt but the hand and his things. It's too late to bring him to the barracks—no coach will venture a trip now so what's left of him's at the sheriff's, but it's military property. Guess you'd have to ask permission to pray ..."

The priest waved him off and headed through the crowd toward the sheriff's. William followed him. Diaz glanced back. "You sure you want to be seen by the sheriff, Bill? They might lock you up again."

"Buck was a friend from home and ..."

The priest laughed. "You were his friend? I don't think so. That Buck was lonesome for amigos. He had no friend, Bill, but God. I've never in a long time seen someone so bent on living out our Lord's commands—though he got it wrong half times. He gave an incredible amount of money to the missions. What a loss for the church."

"All you priests care about is money."

"That money, every penny, went to the poor," the priest said. "What do you do with what you've got?"

"I don't have anything. You might give me some of that poor money Buck gave you."

"Buck has given you enough," Father Diaz said, glancing at William's brogans, which were beginning to pinch. "Mr. Kenyon always had such hopes for you—I don't know why. But he also said he thought Buck would die evangelizing. I guess he was half right."

"How do we know he was preaching when he died?"

"Why was Buck walking back to the barracks?" Father Diaz asked.

The money in William's pocket was heavy. He scratched his head and pulled his hat lower.

"Son, when's the last time you bathed?"

William had become immune to squalor and filth—he deserved no better—but he was not immune to insult. His insides burned.

Outside the sheriff's office a crowd milled about, but the people let Father Diaz and William pass. The thin and quick ex-military man, Sheriff Harrison, got to his feet and shook the priest's extended hand. "Padre, here about this Buck Crenshaw case? It's a mighty scandal what these Indians will do and after all the kindness that boy showed those scoundrels. I'd like to hang them one and all, but the law's the law. I suppose the military will take this case as their own and kill more than's guilty, but so be it, I say." When Diaz didn't respond, the sheriff changed direction. "Crenshaw wasn't Catholic, was he? Well, I guess a prayer or last rites are in order so do you want to see the remains? Too gruesome for some, I'd say, Padre."

"We want to see everything," William demanded.

"And who asked you?" The sheriff's eyes were cold and hard. "Padre, if you want me to get rid of this loafer I will, for heaven's sake."

"No, no, Harrison. Bill and Buck are from the same town back east. He's the nearest thing to kin since Miss Thankful went home."

"What tragedy that family has! Fahy dies and now this!" the sheriff said, scratching his chin. "Fine, Bill. You can stay, but don't get too close to me or you'll annoy me again."

The remains, wrapped in an army blanket for now, lay on an old door acting as table. Buck's things sat stacked on a rickety shelf. The acrid smell of burnt flesh came to them first. William stood just behind Father Diaz as the sheriff folded back the blanket and revealed a mess of charred flesh, all in pieces. Skulls look nothing like the man they make, William thought. Right next to it lay a hand, Buck's hand for sure. The ring wrapped around a swollen finger was the one Buck and Fred both had from their grandmother. They belonged to their uncles who died in the war.

"Buck is *really* dead," William groaned.

He saw Buck's Bible and shook his head.

Father Diaz whimpered, then howled and cried a lament. "My dear Holy Father, you mend broken hearts and settle our spirits. I am torn inside over this cruel act and pray to you, my dearest Papa, the light of my life, I pray that your exceptional, young disciple, Buck Crenshaw, is safe in your comforting hands, and that our Blessed Mother Mary will take the poor boy into her warm embrace and heal his many wounds. So many of us will miss him, Father, and sometimes it feels so unfair with our limited understanding that such good people are taken from us."

"Aren't you laying it on a bit thick, Father? He wasn't even Catholic, and Buck wasn't always so good," William said.

The priest glared at him. "Buck spent his last day on earth doing the Lord's work."

"A man who gives up worldly power and prestige to live voluntarily impoverished in the desert hardly leaves things to chance, by golly," the sheriff said. "This young fella was always helping someone—everyone in town laughed about it, said he was damned foolish, but not them he helped. Most appreciated it." He covered Buck's body.

Father Diaz blessed it and sighed. "Buck is dead now. It hardly seems the time to debate his goodness in God's eyes—or man's for that matter. Because he believed, we can be assured that he is with God now."

William scoffed. "Humbug."

"Bill, you came into church once—remember? Had you come because of Jesus?"

"No, just to get some shade," William replied, feeling sorry for Thankful when he touched her picture. Buck had always been her favorite. "Buck and his brother nearly killed a cadet, and they bullied every boy in Englewood and even stole from the poor box at church. They told everyone that my father was an opium eater."

Sheriff Harrison asked, "Well, was he? Your father—was he an opium eater?"

"Yes, but ..."

"Listen, Bill, all I know is that Buck Crenshaw was a different man after he was shot in the face because of you. I met him when he first came out, briefly, and he was surly enough, but after Kenyon got to him, well, there was a change. I ain't much for religion, but Buck was different somehow," the sheriff said.

"Did you know that Buck paid for your friend Ginny to study at a convent in California?" Father Diaz asked.

"A convent? My wife?"

The priest looked surprised. "Married?"

"Well, sort of. We played at it, I guess."

"Ginny was a harlot, and you're a drunk—that doesn't make a marriage," the sheriff said, pulling up his heavy trousers.

"Well, I didn't pay her so it was different." William shook his head. "A convent for Ginny."

"Yes. Ginny will be taken care of in a loving community of women—she's never been properly cared for," the priest said.

William winced at the comment. "How do you know this?"

"Ginny often came to me searching for something. She prayed for you even after you hit her."

William squirmed under the sheriff's judgmental eye. "I never meant for it to happen."

The priest waved him off. "That's what men say. It's very sad to see someone avoid responsibility. But no matter now—she's safe and God is with her and her baby."

"Baby?"

"Yes, Bill, soon—oh, I wouldn't think about it—it could be anyone's." Diaz waved his hand dismissively.

William mulled over the priest's words in silence.

The sheriff directed his words to the priest. "Suppose the Crenshaw family will get word by tomorrow."

"They'll want what's left of the body soon enough," Father Diaz said, taking Buck's little Bible in hand and flipping through it. "When will they send it back?"

William grabbed the book and placed it on the shelf. "I'm gonna take him home," he said.

The men laughed at him. "We'll see about that."

Nothing could be done till morning. William slinked out into the dark. The street was empty, but the tavern and whorehouse were full. The soldiers and a few others plotted revenge, but most people gambled, drank, or slept the same as ever. People died and people were born in life. That's all there was to it.

William opened the door to his hovel. The candles and the oil for his lamps had long since run out. Even in pitch dark he knew where his bottles were. William drank. Sometimes it felt good to have a solid excuse. *To a friend's death.* Well, not quite a friend—he hadn't allowed for that.

Hmm. Another sip. If only his father hadn't been a morphine eater. If only his father hadn't deserted him. If only. But it rang hollow. William's father struggled to quit. His father sent them home—back east—to protect them. And then Papa had come home and helped William recover and spent his earnings on doctors and art supplies and trips ... and what had William done? Come west, squandered his parents' savings, disappointed Captain Bourke and his friends in the army, let Thankful get involved with Fahy, lied to Kenyon, sent his father back to morphine, become a drunk, beaten his prostitute girlfriend, and behaved like an ungrateful wretch to Buck, whose boots he now wore.

*No.* None of these things were *his* fault. Unprepared for life and stripped of his ability to do the simplest of things like keeping figures straight, how could he be expected to behave any differently? Life was unfair. But somewhere in the back of this hollow talk was a voice pointing out that he no longer was a child.

William's conscience kept throwing Buck's boots before him. And then Buck's scarred and changed face before he had turned and walked down the shabby street. Buck's face when it was perfect had so much power to humiliate William, to stomp on his small, tremulous spirit, but the face that looked upon him yesterday—Buck's face had been in transition and it unnerved William. No one ever changed—not really. Not his father, not Buck.

William remembered something he hadn't remembered before, and his heart fell deep into his stomach. Eliza, his little sister, lay sick, and Papa was a vacant house. William heard something and tiptoed from the cot on the porch of their old place at Fort Grant to the window. Peering in through the sliver of light between the curtains, he saw his gaunt father stripped to his union suit. It hung at his waist, and he rocked, cradling his misshapen arm. Papa had always been so careful to keep covered up in front of the children, to hide his weaknesses. But now the horrible sore at his side crawled with infection. His father suffered, battling hidden pain. The old lieutenant cried, and William's heart hardened against him, this repulsive mess beneath a uniform. Papa was a man who cried, and William felt ugly inside and hated him.

But something else came to him now—the praying. A miserable, desperate, unmanly praying that at the time had made William angry. Papa rocked like the awful keeners he had seen once at an Irish funeral. The words floated back to him: "If you exist, take me. I'm weak and useless, but save them. Protect Kate and Eliza." His emotions overcame him now. "And please, God, my boy—don't let him turn out like me—please just protect them from me."

The boy. That is how William remembered it. His own father couldn't stand to say his name.

The sheriff shoved him awake. The man's eyes darted from one mess to another. "What a shit-hole you've set up here, Weldon. Remember when you first came into town with the young recruits and got drunk? Sad day that was, I reckon. Well, pull yourself together, son. You're needed in town."

"But, what have I done?"

The sheriff laughed with a sneer. "I don't know, what *have* you done?"

William sat up and brushed a crawling thing off his arm. *Needed in town* ...

"Well, hurry up, then, Bill. Looks like the family wants you to escort Buck's remains. Foolishness if you ask me. Probably lose it half way to St. Louis. The army's none too happy neither, but it's what the father wants."

"You've heard from Doctor Crenshaw already?" William had wanted to be heroic yesterday taking the body home, but today came with fear and self-loathing.

"Already?" the sheriff asked, exasperated. "It's been three days, and the body moldering in my office! I thought they'd never respond. Suppose you don't have nothing really to pack up," the sheriff said, wrinkling his nose at the smell of the room. "And you ain't gonna wear them things are you?"

William buttoned his shirt to the neck and poured tonic into his matted hair in an attempt at neatness and modesty. He pulled on Buck's brogans and steadied himself before grabbing a pencil and a stiff paintbrush smelling of linseed. William shoved them into his haversack—everything he had to show for his time in the West. He scratched his head, eyes on the last bottle.

"Just take the damned whiskey, Bill. You ain't foolin' nobody."

William had half a mind to leave it, to prove the sheriff wrong. But it *was* half a bottle. He grabbed it and slipped it into his bag.

The sheriff muttered something, but William didn't catch it.

He didn't close the door behind him—nothing in William's adobe cave needed protection. His stomach or something burned, and William held himself. It was a sensation only a few weeks old.

"Bill, what's the trouble?"

"Nothing, sir," William replied, but winced as he caught up with the sheriff.

"Doctor Crenshaw is even going to pay your fare. You New Yorkers—I ain't never understood a one."

"We're from New Jersey, sir."

"Same difference."

"No, sir, people from New Jersey are ..."

"Do I seem like I give a damn about New Jersey?"

"No, sir, I guess not." William wanted a smoke and remembered the money in his pocket, suddenly excited at the idea of buying a few cigars and ... and what was *wrong* with him? Buck was dead. Gone for good. He must bring the body and that awful hand and the army jacket he had coveted and the boots. William sat on the roadside.

"Bill, what the hell?"

"No, I can't do this. I won't. I can't disappoint them all."

"You already have, I'd say. They still want you to bring Buck home," the sheriff said. He surveyed William wrestling with his feelings and held out his hand. "Boy, it's time you go."

William refused the man's hand and staggered to his feet. "I have to get something."

"What? You don't have much time."

"It's for Buck. I'll be at the station in a few minutes."

The sheriff shook his head and walked off. Let Bill Weldon make his own bed, as always.

William ran to the brothel and entered with the sheepish grin he always used when low on funds. A fine old clock ticked away. It reminded him of his grandmother's parlor before it had gotten so neglected.

"Bill Weldon, what are you doing here?" asked the prostitute in a sleepy and slightly irritated way. Her dark eyes alwys struck William as exotic and he'd often come to her as if seeking after worldly mysteries.

"Oh, the watch, miss. I was wondering if you might sell it. Buck Crenshaw's timepiece—it meant something to him."

"I heard you stole his boots. What do you want with his watch? Trying to take his place in the world?" she asked with a cynical grin.

"Will you sell it to me?" William asked.

"And I'm to believe you have money?"

William hesitated. He took it out—all of it—and the woman's eyes widened. "This is all I have ..." he mumbled.

The woman couldn't bring herself to look into the stupid and naive eyes of Bill Weldon and still take the money so she looked away. "I suppose, for you, Bill, I'll take the trade, though that fine piece of jewelry is worth more."

William realized at this point she was laying it on thick, but he was no negotiator and just wanted the watch—for Doctor Crenshaw who had always been so kind. The woman signaled for him to follow her to her room. After a few moments she found the watch and turned to William, so out of his element with all the money he had in the world held out to her for a timepiece that didn't even keep the hours.

"Bill, why don't you come over here and sit awhile?" she suggested, hating herself for falling under the spell of his doe eyes. She should know better, but always opened herself up to the wrong sort.

"No, I'd better not," William replied, but took a step forward. He wanted affection or something like it. "I don't have time."

The money William gave her made her richer than she had ever been. She didn't want to admit to herself that she had taken advantage of him. Being of service for a few minutes was the least she could do. She put away the money and pulled him to the bed. William consented. There were people waiting for him at the train, but soon he'd be back in Englewood where opportunities like this were non-existent.

William waited for the usual sensations. Buck's words to Ginny months ago came to him—*God wants better for you.* He tried, but couldn't get it from his mind. Aggravated, he ran his hands over the woman's breasts, but they may as well have been stones for all the sensual pleasure he got from them. Ginny, now at a convent ... a convent! Celibacy! William went limp. How many times had Ginny pointed out his sexual inadequacies? He had always convinced himself that her words were said in anger only. Had he been so horrible that the experience of him had sent Ginny to a nunnery?

The whore he lay with had seen many men have trouble now and again—after drinking or for more mysterious reasons—so she took it in stride, trying one remedy after another on his body—each more humiliating and disgusting than the last. William considered that he had never slept with a woman sober—except now. And this was horrible! He tried to force himself to feel something! The odor of their unclean bodies suffocated him. William closed his eyes. He opened his eyes. He tried thinking of something else and then focusing on her.

"Bill, you alive or what?" she asked. This was taking more time and effort than she had expected. "Any tricks or anything—you tell me what to do."

"What? No. No tricks. No, it isn't going to happen," he heard himself say, bewildered. "I have to go. I'm sorry, but thanks, I guess." He buttoned his fly and pulled his shirt over his pungent body stink and made for the door.

"Reckon that Ginny was right about you."

"*What was that?*" William's insides were killing him.

"Nothing. Don't forget the watch."

Two merchants, solid citizens, spotted William slinking out of the whorehouse as the pair debated closing shop to join the rest of the town sending off Buck.

William didn't make eye contact with either of them, didn't even notice them. This bothered the merchants, who wanted William to see the disapproval on their faces. They closed shop and accosted him. "Hey, Bill, what kind of son-of-a-bitch goes with a whore before going to a funeral?"

"It's not a funeral." William said, quickening his pace.

"Still, you were practically brothers, from what people say—even if you did steal his boots and get him shot that time."

"I didn't steal his boots! He gave them to me—I didn't even want them."

"Then why are you wearing them?" The heavy merchant trotted beside him, trying to keep up with William's determined, uneven gait.

William just wanted to get to the train and escape, but when he turned the corner he changed his mind. The street and the platform seethed with mourners and curiosity seekers as the army band played a mournful rendition of "When Johnnie Comes Marching Home." William wheeled around, but the merchants grabbed him and dragged him up to the platform.

The sheriff spotted them scuffling with the reluctant escort and interfered. "Ah, the man of the hour," he said to William.

The crowd booed. The sheriff pulled him along the platform. "They want to blame someone, and it's gotten around that you stole Buck's shoes—suddenly they're all Buck's best friends. Funny how people are."

William shouted into the crowd, "I didn't take his shoes!"

"Lyin' drunk!" someone responded. "What's on yer feet? Army brogans!"

William lost his temper, "None of you even liked Buck! Shut up—all of you!"

From nowhere came a piece of adobe, and it hit William's bag, smashing his last bottle of whiskey. Everyone laughed at William's luck. The sheriff rolled his eyes and hustled William into the hot station. Captain Markham, his wife, and a few other officers stood there.

William turned away from them, listening to his bag drip. The army folk listened too for a few minutes, but then the captain addressed William. "I don't know what ever made you decide to punish yourself and your family this way—but maybe it's good you go home and find out."

"No, sir. It's only to bring the body," William replied, looking out the window.

"You wouldn't steal a man's shoes—hell, I saw you shoeless most of the times I came to town. If those imbeciles in the road really knew Buck like they pretend they'd understand Buck's generosity," the captain said.

Mrs. Markham cried. "I was horrible to Buck after that Kenyon debacle—but the boy was more decent than me and never held it against me! It's such a terrible shame—I can't stand it! Poor Doctor Crenshaw and his wife even. To lose a child—it breaks my heart!"

# Chapter Nine

The conductor stood over a sleeping William as the train pulled into the Englewood station. "This is your stop, sir. We're unloading your cargo, so if you would just come with me."

As William stood bleary-eyed, the car lurched, and he brushed against the train-man. The conductor cringed. William had tried to clean up on the journey, but the Crenshaw money had kept him in spirits all the way. Sober now, almost, William felt proud of his small effort, until he saw his mother waiting on the platform in a pressed Sunday suit as if prepared to meet a dignitary.

William's gut burned as he descended onto the platform. The moist, thawing earth of Englewood in late winter being warmed by the sun brought a flood of melancholia. His memories ran just out of reach and the loss of them always hung so heavy in the East.

His mother ran up with his father looking heavier and healthier than William had ever seen him, though still reliant on his walking stick and left by his mother to make his own way. Katherine smothered William with kisses, and he squirmed, miserable and dirty.

John Weldon limped up and after a horrified once-over, looked past William, his jaw set.

"I bet you wish it'd been me who died, Papa," William said.

Weldon flashed a stung look.

"Willy, how can you think such a thing about Papa?" Katherine cried, still tugging at him. "We're so relieved to have you home, but you look, oh, you look terrible!" She ran her fingers over his unkempt beard. "I never should have let you go out on your own. This is all my fault. If only I'd prepared you—my mother never prepared me for anything. I vowed to do better, but I didn't, did I? I promised never to leave you alone. I've thought about that over and over again this year. I'll never forgive myself!"

"Mother! Stop it, please," William grumbled, glancing around the busy station.

"No, your father convinced me you needed to go out west on your own. I *never* should have listened! Maybe if things had been different, and you hadn't been deserted before ..."

This was the thing—the thing William didn't miss. His silent father, squirming over the past. His mother, so devoted and yet—was it anger? She never acted angry, but it *was* anger—sometimes felt for his father, but sometimes for him. William couldn't figure why, and Mother never told. His stomach burned. He took out his flask and drank from it. Katherine's eyes flitted between the men in horror. Weldon stepped forward as if to grab the silver container that once was Uncle Simon's.

"How was your trip home, Papa?" William asked, wiping his mouth on his sleeve. "What?"

"Your trip after you made a fool of yourself coming for me in Arizona."

"You're drunk. And with Doctor Crenshaw relying on you," Weldon said, leaning in close with his breathe smelling of mints. "And here they come."

William froze as his father looked past him. Graham and Fred Crenshaw rounded the corner of the station—and then the crying began as an enormous huddled bunch followed—Margaret and her elderly parents, Martha, Betty, Thankful, Henry Demarest, Meg, Nathan, Abby, and Maddie. The house servants followed—crying. Random townsfolk gathered at the tragic racket. Everyone respected Doctor Crenshaw. William glanced at his father standing there pulling the hair behind his ear.

"Where's my brother, Willy?" Fred demanded, his nostrils flaring.

The trainman stood down the track, supervising the men pulling the box containing Buck's remains from the car. William pointed in that direction.

"Good afternoon, Katherine, John, and ... and William." Graham held out his hand in a mechanical way, his face composed but ashen. "For the last few nights I've been dreaming you'd bring home Buckie alive, and that there'd been a big mistake, but here you are alone." Graham glanced at William's feet. "William, seeing you right now is like being stabbed. My son was shot for you, and he cared for you—and you took his boots. The army doctor said his feet must have nearly been burnt off."

"But ... well, sir, he was set on fire."

"It doesn't matter!" Graham shouted. "The sand would have burnt his feet and maybe delayed him on the road! And look at you—you're wasting the second chance Buck gave you! And wearing the boots still!"

"If it's the boots you're upset over, I'll give them to you for memories if you like." William could hear how drunk he sounded.

"Memories? What memories? There were so few between us." Graham's voice broke. He swallowed hard. "The army ... I didn't want the army for Buck ... they never liked him." He wiped his eyes.

"Sir, heaps of people came to send Buck off. You'd have been proud."

"Proud? Proud that a bunch of hypocritical bums from the West came to see my dead son? I know how those people are! They used him and his foolish generosity. They killed Buck for the money I sent him! All I ever wanted was to provide for him—for my children!"

Fred took his father's arm, flashing William a hateful look. "Father, we need to get Buck now."

"You know we have a schedule to keep, young man," the train man shouted as the whistle blew.

Graham hurried up. "Sir, it's my son ..."

"This is *your* son?" the trainman asked, looking at William and then at the elegantly dressed doctor.

"No, the body is my son," Graham said.

"Oh, by golly, I'm sorry, sir."

Fred stepped in now for his father, who couldn't say another word. "We have a wagon just over there—to bring Buck home."

"Yes, of course. I'm sorry for you, sir. Suppose he was your brother, then."

"Yes," Fred replied, with a sob. He wiped the emotion quickly away before helping a few boys from town carry the box to the wagon under the tree by the station. William stepped after them, but John Weldon took him by the shoulder. "Willy, leave them be."

William's skin crawled. "No," he replied and pulled away. "Doctor Crenshaw!"

Graham and Fred turned to him.

"William, what do you need?" the doctor asked.

"No, it's not me. I have something of Buck's for you. I know he'd want you to have it." William dug in his pocket and produced the old watch.

Graham turned it over and ran his thumb across the inscription.

"Doctor, it was found with his other things," William lied.

Graham hurled it down the platform. "My gifts kill people. I never want to see that piece of shit again!" he cried and stalked off to his horses.

Fred and the rest of the clan glared at William.

"Forgive me, Fred. I thought it might help him."

Thankful broke free of the others, tears streaming from her puffed, red eyes. "You thought it might make you look good to give the watch to him! You drunken moron! I hate you!" She pummeled him with her fists until Fred pulled her back.

"Thankful, stop making a show!" he said, shoving her toward Margaret. Fred got close in William's face. "You ass-lick. You could have kept the watch with my brother's other things. You sicken me! Leave our family alone for once!"

"I know how you're feeling," William mumbled, not content to let the family go.

Fred's eyes widened in wild affront. "You don't know shit!" He shoved William, but not with his usual force, his face contorted in pain and bitterness. "I took care of Buck his whole life! That damned fool! You don't know the half of what he went through, and here you stand trying to steal the thunder again with my father! You're a sick weasel. I really, really wish it had been you. I really do. What good are you? Just tell me!"

"I don't know, Fred. I am sorry ..."

"You ass-suck," Fred said and ran off to his waiting father.

The women and servants stood their ground as William squirmed. "I'm sorry."

Katherine and John stepped forward. Katherine went to Margaret at once and embraced her. "Maggie, Buck was such a good young man in the end!"

Margaret held Katherine close for a long while before releasing her, wiping her eyes and blowing her nose. Graham came back up as she spoke through her tears, her fleshy chin bobbing. "Graham and I have just finished up work at the cemetery. Buck's headstone was chipped." Margaret stared at William.

"Only a small bit," Graham said, refusing to look at any of them.

Margaret huffed. "Buck had enough wounds in life—should we have left an imperfection on him for eternity?"

"It's just a piece of stone," Graham said flatly.

"Don't mind my husband," Margaret said. "It's just everyone he loves dies—so he says. So finally he loved Buck, and that's it. I suppose it's a blessing he doesn't love me."

"Margaret, stop," Graham warned, mopping his face.

"We had better go," Weldon suggested.

"Just like you to desert!" Margaret lectured. "Poor Graham has no friends, and you've avoided him like the plague, John Weldon."

"No, Crenshaw, I hope you don't see things that way," Weldon said, grabbing hold of Graham's arm. "It's j-just ...w-when Eliza died, well, I wanted to be left alone."

"Graham's not the type to desert his family!" Margaret said.

"Your husband is a good man," Weldon offered.

"Am I dead too? You both talk of me as if I'm not right here standing next to you!" Graham complained.

"Crenshaw, I'm sorry."

"Graham, must you shame us with this crying?" Margaret said, leaning in to wipe a tear from his eye. He gently, but with exasperation, pushed her off. "Be a man," she continued. "The rest of us need you to be strong."

"No!" Graham shouted. "I've tried so hard to make you happy! I've even hurt my children! To please you!"

"You're a wonderful doctor, sir."

"Do you know," he said, unable to hide his disgust, "I spent more time nursing you, William, than all of my children combined? You've had more affection poured out over you in one day than my son ever had in all his years. I never did a single thing without thinking of how it might look to others. I could have taken care of my very own children, but I sought credit elsewhere. What a wretched man I am!"

"You're too hard on yourself," Weldon said. "The kindness you showed my family over the years couldn't have been faked."

"We all know the real reason my husband spent so much time on Tenafly Road. Graham wanted to impress Katie," Margaret said with a bitter sniffle.

William plunged in. "Doctor Crenshaw liked my mother because she didn't abuse him the way you do with your words!"

Margaret gasped and slapped William's face. "You were always an awful boy! It should have been you killed, not my Buck!" She collapsed into a heap on the sidewalk and sobbed. "My soul is ripped from me!"

The men and a few ladies passing tried to bring Margaret to her feet, but she fought them. "I despise you all! What sort of men have I surrounded myself with? All untrustworthy and weak and ignorant! Men are the lowest, most revolting creatures on earth!"

William knelt before Margaret, and she stared at him. Something in her eyes—they were the same weird violet as Buck's—told William how much she suffered, how much she had always suffered. Margaret was awful because she was miserable. "Mrs. Crenshaw, you're right to feel as you do. Buck was honorable and good—to women especially, and it's because he probably cared so deeply for you—and Thankful. I don't deserve to live if someone like Buck has to die."

Margaret shook her head. What did it matter to her if William lived or died? "Do you believe in Hell, William Weldon?" It was obvious she hoped William would end up there.

He scratched his face, thinking. "A long time ago I had a dream, I guess it was. I was talking with Eliza, and it was someplace nice. Maybe Buck is there, and he'll care for my sister and Eliza for him. She always liked soldiers."

Margaret wiped her eyes. William teetered to his feet, trying to avoid being caught in her old-fashioned hoops. He offered his hand to her, and with as much dignity as she could muster, Margaret got to her feet.

William walked Margaret to the Crenshaw carriage and helped her in, even tucking the light canvas blanket over her skirts. All the while the small yet building crowd cried and murmured over Buck.

"Graham, I want to go home," Margaret said.

Graham took a step, but Weldon grabbed him again. "Crenshaw, maybe I'll come by sometime."

Graham shook his head. "No, Weldon. I don't want to put you to any trouble."

"It's no trouble ... we might go to the field house sometime," Weldon stammered.

"I don't want to see any of them—not a one," Graham said. "Everyone from the clubs and committees reminds me now of the vapid company I've kept instead of spending time with my son. "Come by, Weldon, if you like. I'm home now most days."

Margaret glared at him. "You shouldn't get so comfortable at home, Graham. It's unhealthy for a man."

"What would you know about health?" he asked. "All you've ever done is poison my children against me."

"Oh, so now they're your children!" Margaret huffed. "It was I who bore them and cared for them!"

"Cared for them? Are you serious? Did you ever say a kind thing to any of them about me?"

"What was there to say?"

"Shut up. I can't stand this another minute."

Graham's complexion rose in color and his eyes darted from face to face, noticing for the first time the gathering curiosity seekers. "What are you all gaping at? My son is dead! You couldn't care less, but this excites you? You're sick excuses for humanity!"

"Doctor." Someone put his hand on Graham's shoulder.

Graham smiled. "I saved your sister, didn't I? Did you ever thank me? Did any of you ever thank me? Half of you never even paid me!" he cried, waving his arms.

"Sir, I was going to send a note of thanks, but ..." the man began.

"A note? A *note*?" Graham laughed. "Did I send you a goddamned note when your sister was sick? You bastard! Get out of my sight!"

"Crenshaw, we need to get you home," Weldon said.

"Home? I've never had a home. I don't know what that would feel like."

William looked to his father, who as usual seemed at a loss.

Fred pushed past John Weldon. "Father, stop making a scene in front of the whole town."

Weldon said, "Graham, you're welcome in my home."

"What?" Graham faltered.

"Papa, what a stupid thing to say," William whispered.

Weldon kept his hands in his pockets but kept his eyes on Graham. "Crenshaw, I understand. You know I do. Not just about losing Buck. You're welcome, more than welcome in my home and in my life. I don't have much, but I do care."

"Why?" Graham asked. "It seems impossible that anyone would. I'm such a failure."

"You're a friend of mine. No one's perfect, but you're all right by me," Weldon said. "Now, go home, friend. See what you still have, what can still be done."

Graham took a long time to respond. He mopped his face again, breathing heavily. "Maybe, maybe sometime I'll come by, Weldon—to see how you are—I mean—if that would be all right."

"Yes, of course."

"When?" Graham asked.

"Anytime."

Graham sighed and coughed as the crowd dispersed. "Thank you, Weldon. I suppose I should take Maggie and Buck home." They watched as Graham, in his heavy body, climbed into his carriage.

Margaret rolled her eyes. "No home? I've slaved to make you a comfortable home!"

Graham didn't respond. The Crenshaw siblings, still crying, piled into the other surreys belonging to various members of the family. The Weldon family turned away.

"Graham!" Margaret cried. "Help him someone!"

Graham held his heart, his eyes bulging in panic as he gasped for air.

"Run for Doctor Banks!" Thankful cried out. Fred ran around the corner to the old doctor's office. The Weldon men and the servants pulled Graham to the ground as the crowd rushed back for more spectacle.

Martha pushed through with Betty. Thankful threw herself upon her father, but Margaret man-handled them out of the way. "Give him space! Get off of him at once!" Margaret dropped to her knees, threw off her hat, and put her ear against Graham's chest. "There's no heartbeat!"

A new round of cries and uproar surrounded the scene as more and more townsfolk gathered. Old Doctor Banks hobbled over and knelt beside his colleague, pressing a worn, wooden stethoscope against Graham's broad chest. His milky eyes saddened as he looked at the distraught family surrounding him. "His heart was always weak, I'm afraid. We knew this would happen someday."

Fred in stunned silence helped Doctor Banks to his feet. Only little Abigail whimpered. The shock had taken everyone's emotions. The crowd remained breathless.

Margaret pushed the frail doctor to the side. "Graham Crenshaw, wake up. You promised to live a long life! Stop this nonsense. Stop feeling sorry for yourself!"

Thankful and Martha corralled the small herd of children out of sight, and they bawled like sheep separated from their master.

"Mama, stop shaking him!" Thankful cried upon returning.

"No, he's alive in there." Margaret tore open his shirt. "Someone needs to bring him to his senses."

"Margaret you disgust me," Martha said, pulling her by the shoulders. "Have some respect for the dead!"

"You're all fools!" Margaret cried. She grabbed the wooden stethoscope. "Land sakes, somebody quiet the children!"

No one moved. Margaret listened and listened again.

"What do you hear, Mama?" Fred asked.

"Shush!" Margaret said and felt Graham's wrist in her hands. She slapped his face. "No dead man I've ever seen in all Graham's years of medicine had this much color." She spoke tenderly now. "Graham, you fooled everyone but me. Wake up. I'm not done with you yet! Wake up!"

The children slunk up at the sound of Margaret's domineering voice and watched in silence. Margaret cried and kissed her husband's lips. "Don't do this to me, Graham. You promised not to die on me or else I never would have married you."

Margaret laid her head on Graham's chest. Her thick hair brushed against his face, and Graham's eyes opened.

"Mama!" Thankful cried.

Martha and the children pushed forward.

"Stand back and give my husband room to breathe!" Margaret shouted. "Graham Crenshaw, listen to me. We will not have you die on us. Do you hear me? I know you do—but blink to confirm it. Blink, I said."

Graham blinked and no more.

"Good, good, my silly doctor. You hear me, now hear this. I don't like you very much, and you don't like me, but I can't bear to part with you. Blink if you understand."

He blinked.

# Chapter Ten

The Weldon family walked off toward their carriage after Graham and Margaret placed the final flowers over Buck's mostly empty coffin. William, still hiding behind the rough western beard, avoided Thankful all morning. She threw him dagger looks even as Henry stood beside her. Surrounded by Crenshaw men, Henry Demarest was short and effeminate. He delighted the family the night before with his perfect performances of the family's favorite melodies on the piano and even made Margaret cry, playing Buck's favorite duet with her. Thankful remembered the awful time Buck had learning it for a recital, and it annoyed her that Henry played it so easily and so well.

Today as Thankful watched William fidget, scratch his beard, and steal the occasional glance at her with his amber eyes, she felt oppressed by loneliness. She turned to Henry, and he smiled in the self-assured way he had and whispered a reassuring word to Martha, who exposed a rare, sad smile. Henry was better than William could ever be. A sudden surge of gratitude came over Thankful.

Henry was good-looking, wasn't he? He'd given her a bicycle and taught her real music. Henry had seen more of the world and great art than William ever would. Last night Thankful sang as Henry played the violin with her younger sisters, and it had been the picture of domestic bliss. Her mind wandered back to Buck, and she cried. Henry rubbed her shoulder.

The shower threatening all morning began in earnest, and the small group of final mourners eyed their dry carriages and buggies. Graham hadn't attended. Doctor Banks insisted upon bed rest, and for once Margaret agreed with the old man. She ran her hand over the box one last time before leading the way back to the conveyances.

Henry whispered to Thankful, "I'm going to take Martha back to the hotel for her shawl—will you come with me?"

"No, Henry—I hope you don't mind, but I'd rather walk."

Henry looked up at the storm clouds and then back into her eyes with great compassion. "I understand, but take my umbrella." He made to embrace her, but she backed away.

"Not here, Henry. Not yet." She looked around, kissed her fingers, and touched his lips. "Do you love me?" she whispered.

"You know I do," Henry said. Martha called to him, and Henry led the old lady away.

Thankful walked the long way home past the substantial homes on land that used to house childhood forts and spring wildflowers. Ice and snow still clung to the edges of last year's autumn leaves. How could Buck be dead? Her family joked and made merry last night. How was it so easy to forget people? Why could she never forget William? The wind tugged at Henry's umbrella and Thankful slogged home.

Countless horses hung their heads along the drive of the Crenshaw house. A crowded house of strangers mourning Buck overwhelmed her so she slipped into the carriage house instead.

"William! What are you doing here?"

William showed Thankful the cigarette between his fingers and took a drag. His hair hung long like always, the rain making it darker, accentuating the buttery color of his eyes and tanned skin. His Adam's apple jutted out just beneath his beard as he swallowed hard.

"You'll start a fire," she said. "You should go."

"I hate being here, you know," he said. "I hate seeing what's happened."

"Then leave. Be a man and have the strength to just leave us all alone."

"I lost my strength when I lost you. And I never knew I had you till you were already gone. Why did you have to go and do that to me?"

"I followed you west!" she cried. "I didn't do anything to you."

"But if only I'd known. I would have been different."

"William, you lie to yourself. Stop lying to me. I need you as a friend right now."

"What do you mean?" he asked, flicking his cigarette out a window and reaching for another.

"Let's run away!"

"Where would we go? Things are the same all over."

"Are they, William Weldon? How did you come to be so different than you were supposed to?"

"You wanted a soldier husband, and you almost got one," he ventured with more than a small trace of bitterness. "That's all you cared about till it didn't work out."

"No, I wanted you, you fool. And you destroyed it all with your drinking."

"I'll stop drinking for you, Thankful."

"Would you? Oh, I don't believe you, but I want to think you would. I look at you now and ..."

"You see a wreck."

"No, William, I see you as you were when you used to come by even on the rainiest days to visit with my father. You were beautiful when you rode up. Right now I see all those years ago and ..."

William kissed her.

She looked up in tears. "Why can't things be like before—before everything went so wrong? Why can't we be young again?" she asked, but he had no answer so he kissed her again.

"You've never stopped being the only girl I've ever wanted."

"Then take me right now."

"Where?"

"Right here. This very instant," she demanded.

"You mean? No, we can't do that. You've been ill-used already."

"And you think I'm tainted, don't you?"

"No ..." William said, glancing out the window into the pouring rain.

"Even though you slept with prostitutes!" she cried.

"No, I meant I can't hurt you. I don't want to. I always wished I could just—be something so I could marry you, but I can't, can I? I'm a drunk, and I want to promise you things, but I saw my father promise and promise, and he never could fully stop. I can't do it to you."

"What say do I have? You own me just like we were married. I'm hostage to you—all men. I have to take what they say and do and just live with it no matter how I feel. What if I want to wreck my life with you? That's what I want! Does anyone hear it? Does God care at all? Let me bury myself in your drinking. I want someone to be mine, and I can never have that when all I want is you."

"You've always been a dream, Thankful, but I'm too stupid to know what to do with you in reality."

"That's the dumbest thing I've ever heard!"

They laughed and awkwardly William took Thankful's hands in his. "I love you, Thankful."

"I love you too."

He kissed her hands.

"If only you hadn't believed all the lies you've told yourself."

"If only you could see they're not lies. I see my mother every day worrying about my father ..."

"That's true love."

"No, it's a sickness. I will never allow it for you. Never. You've been like a sister to me. No. That's a lie. I lie all the time. It won't change. You need better."

"All my life I imagined you'd be a Crenshaw, and I'd be a Weldon. Mama feared it so I knew it was real. We were meant to be together. I always thought you'd be an artist, and we'd have parties with interesting friends and ..."

"Stop it. I can't see myself in that life. I'd be a hindrance to it. Maybe *you* should paint."

Thankful laughed. "I'm no painter, but I can make babies." She cried then.

"Oh, Thankful ..."

"Is that all you have to say? I lose everything for you, and that's all you have to say."

"I never once asked you to follow me west!" he said. "Never in my wildest imaginings would I have thought it! I'm sorry you lost the baby."

"I wanted *you*!" she cried. "You stupid fool! I wanted you! You're weak and mean to come here now to hurt me."

"I came to pay my respects and for my mother. I didn't know it would be like this for you. I wasn't thinking of you."

"Get away from me."

She pushed him toward the door.

He turned to go, but slowly, and Thankful seized on the hesitation. "Oh, don't leave me, please! Stay just for a few minutes with me."

"You're quaking."

He kissed her and led her to the back of the barn. They sat on a bale of hay while Thankful cried.

"I love you. I love you so much, Willy. I don't want to live anymore."

He kissed her again—tenderly on the forehead and then on the lips. "You're beautiful—the only beautiful thing in this world."

"I don't care about tomorrow," she said, unbuttoning his shirt. He felt warm and smooth and a little soft around the middle. His heart beat so soothingly she dreamt for a second of sleeping, but he pulled her face up to kiss again.

"I lied again," William said. "I came because I wanted to see you."

"Willy, don't talk." She traced her hands around the edges of his face. This close he looked so young and innocent she almost believed he was.

"We shouldn't ..." William began but fumbled over her bodice, unclasping the front before dragging her to her feet. Her skirt slipped to the floor, and she stepped out of it.

She undid his suspenders, and they laughed while trying to untangle his boots from his trousers. Every touch was warm and wonderful and home.

And then there was Fred. He pulled open the barn door and spotted them under a horse blanket. "For God's sake!" Fred ranted as he ripped the blanket from them. "Buck is only just buried, and you come here to fuck my sister! Thankful, get dressed! You've become a complete whore, and under Father's roof!"

"I don't care what you think, Fred!" Thankful grabbed the blanket back and wrapped herself in it.

William dressed, head down to avoid Fred's incredulous stare.

"I guess my sister is tramp enough for you now, Willy."

William met Fred's stare now, pulling his long hair from his eyes. "Your sister is a goddess."

"What?" Fred asked in contemptuous disbelief. "Get the hell out of here before I pummel you."

"Go ahead. I don't care." William slipped on his shoes.

Fred watched them both dress. "What's wrong with the two of you?"

"I'm dead, Fred. Don't you know that?" Thankful pulled up her skirt. "Will you give a moment's privacy?"

Fred walked out under the eaves.

"I'm sorry I made you do this," Thankful said to William.

"It's the best thing I've ever done," he said, glancing up as he tied his shoes. "But ... Fred will tell your family."

"I don't care, but you should leave—if you want to."

"Thankful, I'll always love you, but ..."

She couldn't speak. Picking up her wet shawl she brushed passed William and walked toward the house.

William fumbled for his cigarettes again. Fred stormed back in red faced and breathless with anger.

"Don't worry, Fred. I won't be coming back."

"What the hell are you talking about?" Fred whispered, awake to the threat of wandering mourners hearing. "You poke my sister like she was a common trollop, and then you think you're doing something noble by leaving?"

"I've made a mess of things with her," William said with little visible emotion.

"Thankful's not worthy of the Crenshaw name so you can have her, Willy. Take her west where she won't disgrace us anymore."

"Is that all you care about?"

"What do you care about?" Fred asked. "Not my sister, you sneaky bastard. We all know Thankful's a fool around men, but if you loved her you would have kept her from making the same mistake she's already made. Don't act so high and mighty with me. That Demarest character following her around like a puppy dog has money and a mind to marry her—it's her last good chance, and now you do this!"

"I *do* love her," William said.

"Will you marry her?" Fred asked. "Do you have a penny to your name? Do you have a good reputation here or out west? How will you care for her when she's disowned? My mother would never stand for you and Thankful, and my father is in no shape to help anyone. What will you give my sister?"

"I have nothing for her, and it's why I can't marry her. It's always been why."

"You don't even have it in you to fight for her, Willy. That's worse than anything else. Thankful is a fool, but she deserves at least to be fought for. I at least take care of my wife."

"You don't love her," Martha said as she appeared in the doorway.

"Love is overrated, Grandmother," Fred said, taking her hand and kissing it.

"A true Crenshaw you are, Fred. God bless you," Martha replied. She didn't know what she'd stumbled upon and found William of little interest.

# Chapter Eleven

Buck woke up to a scorpion stinging. With eyes puffed shut from sunburn, he batted away the vermin with his good hand—Buck remembered with a jolt—a *good* hand and a *bad* hand. He pulled himself up to sitting, but his throbbing right arm forced him down again. Sand clung to the corners of his parched mouth. A bird of prey cawed in the high distance.

Buck wanted to die. He prayed for it. The pain! The pain! Even burnt alive from the sun and cut up, he shivered. The smell of blood and ooze sickened him, but his insides were empty. He worked up the nerve to run his fingers toward the throb but couldn't look. Here was his limb—slipping further and further down his sore, swollen forearm ... he stopped himself, remembering what had happened. Girls—pretty ones—and Indians—hacking his hand. His fingers were still in motion as the life line, long and deep on his palm, dropped away from him. He fell to his knees watching blood sink into the sand. Then too he remembered the bummer—Joe—from town. Joe had stalked him for the last bit of money in his pocket. The bummer surprised the Indians. They scuffled as Buck slid into a dark dream.

He reached again, moving his fingers along the pulsating mass of flesh, praying it was just a different dream. And as his fingers brushed closer to where his right hand should be he prayed, "Just let me die." But God refused him. The sun dug its heels in the blazing sky—the day seeming like weeks. When the shade of late day finally enveloped him he peered through sore eyes. Something glistened just outside the shadows. Water. He dragged himself to it, on his back and pushing with his legs while cradling the pained limb.

In darkness, he drank with all the life left in him. He braced himself finally and touched it— the place where a wrist should be was wrapped inside a soggy, crusty bandage. He couldn't have wrapped it himself. The stars looked on like cold and faraway saints. An owl questioned its existence with a lonesome call to no one. Buck feared the panthers and the snakes. The ache, the piercing throbs, were so intense he considered drowning himself. The fear of panther claws and the equal fear of drowning kept him indecisive. As a child, Fred had locked him in the cedar chest under blankets, nearly suffocating him.

Was this real life? Was he awake in Hell? But no. He had been a believer. He had professed Christ! He'd been saved. *Saved.* Someone had bandaged his arm, but who? And left him here then to die? Was it a miracle? No. A miracle wouldn't be so bleak and pointless. Miracles didn't bring pain.

Buck's jaw hurt now with his shivering, every part of him throbbing and alive. He tried praying but lost his thoughts and slept again.

This time when the heat of day came on there was talk—like the talk of his young siblings—and he opened his sore eyes again. Two smallish silhouettes stood over him. The sun hid their features. Their voices trailed off when he opened his eyes. One shoved the other, and they both knelt closer to him with the pale blue sky as backdrop.

"Mister, would you like a drink?" the boy asked, his voice older than his round face showed.

Buck nodded. The girl patted his head with a cool rag before turning to watch the boy drag his canteen through the water. "We thought you were gonna die."

The boy came over and cradled his head before putting the canteen to his lips. "How'd you come to be here?"

"I don't know." His throat ached.

"What's your name?"

"Buck."

The boy cocked his head. The girl giggled.

Buck lifted his head for a second. "I don't know where I am," he whispered. "Please let me die."

"Oh, don't say it, Buck. I bet there's people who wonder what's become of you," the girl said, wiping Buck's head with familiarity as if she'd been at it for days.

"My name's Peter and she's Cordelia, my sister. We've been fighting over what to do with you for over a week now. Thought we'd probably not have to do anything if you died, but every day we come back, and here you still are. I guess you wouldn't want to stay here forever. We're just passing through ourselves."

Cordelia nodded. "We're going to Mexico. I've read about it in books, and I think I should like the color of things there," said Cordelia.

"I want to be a Texas Ranger," Peter said, shrugging off his sister's dreams. "You look real bad though."

"I want to be put out of my misery."

"You know there's lots of Indians around here," Peter said.

Buck nodded.

"They're the ones who got your hand, I guess?" Peter asked.

"That's why I want to go to Mexico and be with the Spanish," Cordelia said. "I'm scared of Indians."

Peter flashed Cordelia a superior glance and turned back to Buck. "If you think you can manage it, we could help you to our hideout, and I'll walk to Willcox and slip a note to the sheriff if that suits you. Then we'll just be moving on. We've stayed too long."

Peter shoved his hands under Buck's body pulling him to his feet with Cordelia cradling Buck's sore arm in her hands. They led him to a crevice in the side of a shallow valley. It was cooler out of the sun. Buck quaked all over. Cordelia wrapped her light jacket around his shoulders, not doing much good, though Buck smiled in appreciation. Peter left the two alone now.

"Peter won't be back for hours—maybe not till tomorrow—won't allow himself to be seen by day in town," the girl said, sitting with her hands clasped in her lap. She spoke about the birds and animals they'd seen on their travels and how nice it would be to set up home in Mexico after having escaped something called an orphan train.

*** 

The Willcox sheriff steadied Buck as he climbed up into the train to the strains of the army band playing "Just Before The Battle, Mother":

*Oh I long to see you, Mother,*
*And the loving ones at home,*
*But I'll never leave our banner,*
*Till in honor I can come ...*

The army was Buck's no longer, and what a costly stay it had been, even with promise of a hero's badge. The pomp and huzzahs from the same crowd so eager to mock him only weeks ago offered small solace as the train whistle announced departure and the faces of acquaintances blurred together, waving their hands in farewell from the platform. Mrs. Markham made Buck a fine knit vest and a dressed-up covering for his stump (a design she'd first devised for other young soldiers many years earlier during the war). She even prepared him a package of fried chicken and tucked it beneath his seat in case he got hungry. Buck wondered how he might carry it off at his first transfer.

"Are you certain we shouldn't send word about you to your parents?" she asked.

Buck feared his mother's anger at their last parting would keep him from his father. "I'd prefer to explain things myself, Mrs. Markham, but thank you."

Being discovered and back in Willcox had not ended any pain. His arm throbbed under any exertion, and he sweated and shivered through his clean new clothes. He fumbled to unbutton the hot vest with no success.

Buck had refused escort, insisting he travel alone to deliver his news. The idea of having to entertain and share his weakness with a rough private sickened him, and the fear that his parents might refuse him in front of this private galled him. To sleep forever in his childhood bed surrounded by polished oak furnishings while listening to his siblings and parents bicker over trifling things was his only desire. He might never leave bed again.

His mind wandered to Fred. Always Fred. At the moment he didn't care that Fred had married his girl or that he was probably promoted by now. What did it all matter?

Mama would be disappointed that Buck's life should come to this—an ugly invalid where a successful son should be, but hadn't she expected it? Never again would they play the duets on the piano his mother so loved. Though they hadn't played together in years and it had always been a nerve-racking affair, it still struck Buck as a cruel loss.

Father would ask after his money. How would Buck explain that he'd thrown it away on bummers and drunks?

The sheriff had informed Buck that William had taken Buck's false remains and the ring his grandmother had given Buck back east. Buck *had* been responsible for getting Willy and the bummer Joe out of the desert in the end.

He prayed for forbearance once when a traveler jostled him on the platform at his first transfer, but that was all. He tried to eat for strength, but the constant motion and the sound of metal screeching against metal on the tracks conspired against him. The arid desert slipped away and then the prairies. Small settlements and then larger ones streamed by, and with each passing mile the houses grew more solid and close.

A hint of snow flurried outside the train window on his last day of movement. Had it really been over a year since he'd seen his family? His heart quickened when the conductor announced familiar stops in New Jersey—Princeton, Newark, *Englewood*.

He refused the conductor's arm on the steps down to the platform. The familiarity of every little thing filled him with emotion. He sat on a bench for some time, taking in the new faces and bustle of the once-quiet town, before setting out to find a driver to carry him and his few things up the hill to his parents' home. A man stood scratching the face of his horse.

"Are you for hire?" Buck asked.

The man turned, straining to hear Buck's soft voice, his face lighting with recognition. "Buck? But you're supposed to be dead!" The driver was a boy from Buck's old Kursteiner school days—one who had been with him when he and Fred killed the farmer's chicken—fallen on hard times.

"I feel dead, but I'm not. It was a big foolish mistake."

"Well, you should have seen the funeral you got! Mrs. Crenshaw sent you off tremendously well. Everyone turned out for it."

"Oh, that makes things worse then, doesn't it? Mama will be embarrassed now."

The man remembering Margaret's heavy-handed discipline wondered, but said, "Of course not. She'll be overjoyed. I see you're not yourself though, and we should have you climb in right away—free of charge —I'd be honored to take you home."

The old friend, having caught a glimpse of Buck's arm from beneath his overcoat, drove the horse slowly and spoke only briefly to Buck, not expecting answers to his questions about the West and all that had happened. Once at the Crenshaw house on Chestnut Street, he motioned for Buck to stay still and jogged up to the front door. Buck watched, full of trepidation, as his old classmate delivered the news.

Margaret cried out and much talk came from behind the front door, but Buck couldn't decipher the tone or meaning. He waited in grim silence, unable to move until Margaret, with his siblings trailing behind, raced across the yard and dragged him down from his seat. His arm throbbed against his mother's strong embrace. The driver alerted her to the state of it, and she cried out once more.

"How are you here? Oh, thank God! Thank God! It's really you! The cruelty! Thinking you were dead! Why didn't you send word? What were you thinking? Oh, but never mind. We must bring you inside! Can you make the steps? Children, get the boys in the stable at once! They'll help us! My poor Buck! What have they done to you now? How will you ever work without your hand—and you had such fine handwriting! You look terrible weak! I don't know how I'm taking this shock so well! What a time! I thank God! Thank God! My poor boy!" She ran sobbing toward the stable boys, who trotted past her eager to greet Buck. Margaret clapped her hands for attention. "Boys! Boys! Help our Buck this minute into the house. Bring him to his room. I haven't changed a thing, Buckie, I couldn't bear it. It's just as you left it. Not a thing removed."

Buck stood still, thankful, so thankful for this moment. He covered his face.

"Now, dear, none of that. Everything will be better now that you're back with Mama. Boys, take him in."

Despite it all Buck loved his mother. Mama allowed him home even after everything she thought she knew about him.

"Wait until your father sees!" Margaret gushed. "Oh, just wait! It will bring him back to his old self, I'm sure!"

"Where is he, Mama?"

"Your father has been *quite unwell*—since your death. Oh, but let's not worry about it anymore. You'll make him right—just the sight of you. Doctor Banks thought your father was dead!" Margaret talked all the way through the house as the children danced with delight and awe. Buck was home!

"Now let *me* tell Father first," Margaret said. "The shock of seeing you back from the dead without warning won't do his heart good." She looked Buck over now, her eyes welling with tears (though was there a small flicker of judgment in them even as she smiled?) "You need to be cleaned up and fed. Someone go tell Lucretia that our Buck is back and needs to be fed. A feast!" She shooed one of the stable hands to the kitchen.

"Mama, I need sleep and something for the pain." Buck craved her touch, but it did not come.

"Oh, my poor boy, of course—oh, your poor hand. What will you do?"

"You won't disown me again, will you, Mama?"

Margaret stepped back affronted, but regained her composure and momentary gratitude at the return of her son. "Forgive me that, Buck. I was so disappointed in you—but it doesn't matter now because here you are alive! You will be the very thing to fix your father and convince him to stay."

"Mama, I want to see Thankful ..."

Margaret's expression changed. "She's with Martha now, and I hope she stays there." Margaret saw that Buck didn't approve. "You'll visit with her when you're well, of course."

"But you must tell her right away."

"Well, sweetheart, if only you had sent word to us sooner then maybe we could have arranged for Thankful and avoided so much anguish, but of course, dear—we'll tell your sister." Margaret motioned for Nathan to step closer. "We'll run a bath. I'll have Nathan help you."

Nathan stood, having grown five inches, crying happily. Margaret allowed him and Buck's two youngest sisters to come up now and hug his brother. Buck cried too until Margaret made them stop. "Sit here until the bath is ready, and I'll go tell your father the unbelievable news!"

Buck sat for a moment in the big old chair outside the dining room, but he couldn't wait. He dashed after his mother and overtook her against her protests. "I must see Father myself!" Buck threw open the door to his father's bedroom.

Graham turned from staring at the sliver of light filtering between the heavy draperies in his tomb-like room.

"My Lord in heaven ..."

"Father, it's me, and I'm home!"

Margaret pushed right behind him. "Graham, see, Buck is back among the living. It was all a big mistake! Say something!"

"It's a dream! It can't be true!"

Buck showed his stump. "Here! Look, Father. It pains me, and I need your help."

Graham jumped from bed. "You're real! How can such a wonderful thing be happening? How did ... oh, it doesn't matter right now! Come out into the light." Graham led Buck to the old familiar office and sat him in the best chair. Graham sat for a moment in front of him on an ottoman, peering into his eyes. "My son, how did I ever deserve to have you back?" He began to sob.

"Father, please take away the pain."

Graham rushed around gathering supplies. He ordered Margaret to get hot water and made the young ones, who had followed Margaret in, stand back. The veins at Graham's forehead pulsed just beneath the skin as he unwrapped Buck's bandage. "Will you ever stay out of scrapes?" he asked, shaking his head at the mess. "The doctors out west know nothing!"

"I didn't see a doctor, Father. I wanted you."

"You foolish boy," Graham cried. "I love you more than life, but this has nearly killed me. You must never be far from us again!" He shook his head at the wound and the swollen arm. "We might have to take more of it."

The two little girls cried. Buck called them to him. "No, don't cry, now. You'll both help me, won't you?"

They nodded, resting their little hands on his good shoulder. The warmth of this familial contact overwhelmed Buck, and he cried again too. His little sisters wiped his tears and petted him as Graham gave Buck an injection to lessen the pain. As Buck slept, Graham cleansed the stump with antiseptic and cut loose flesh. He wrapped the stitched skin in clean bandage. Then the family carried Buck to his room and tucked him under the flannel covers of his own soft bed.

# Chapter Twelve

Buck slept in deep darkness for days—no dreams and no nightmares—until one day he awoke to the sun shining on his face as he lay beneath his blankets. Cards, plants, and chocolates lay scattered and massed atop his nightstand and dresser. Fred, Thankful, and even Meg dozed in chairs beside him but leapt at the sound of his voice and pushed each other out of the way to be of service to him first. Thankful kissed his forehead, but Fred shoved her aside, messing Buck's hair. "Don't leave us again, you ass."

Meg stood back, unable to get past her more dominant siblings, but Buck reached out to her with his good arm. "I missed you."

She stepped up and kissed his hand.

Buck's siblings adjusted his pillows and brought more food, reading notes from well-wishers all the while.

"These morons didn't give a damn about you at the funeral," Fred grumbled after examining one card and tossing it aside. "Mama went all out on it, Buckie. Cost a workingman's yearly wages, I bet."

"Fred, must you?" Thankful complained.

"Why can't you stay, Thankful?" Buck asked for the third time that day. "I wish I'd have been here to help you after the lost baby."

Thankful adjusted his covers, but for a second their eyes met, and Buck understood at once that she was hiding something. Fred noticed it too but kept quiet.

"I'll get you your tea," Thankful said and left with a poorly executed smile.

Fred leaned forward, lowering his voice. "You mustn't get her to stay. Mama and Thankful had a falling out, and Mama's been through too much with Father and with you. Even my wedding was overshadowed by family affairs. The strain of it—and Thankful seeing herself as a victim! You're a Christian still, right? You can see how Thankful's motives aren't pure. She brought this little man—a Mr. Henry Demarest—to your funeral. Weak handshake, everyone said so. It's appalling. Grandmother says Henry's not much of a man, but he's got money."

"Thankful wouldn't marry for money, would she?" Buck considered a moment. "No."

Fred moaned with impatience at Buck's faith in Thankful. It was no secret that Fred resented their closeness growing up. "Thankful had the nerve to fault Mama and Father for the baby troubles—how ridiculous! Thankful was endowed with more looks than she could handle—that's all—but to blame the very people who took her back is pretty unchristian to me."

Buck tried to speak, but Fred held up his hand.

"You weren't here, *playing Jesus out west*," Fred said, "but the real work was done by me and Meg after Father collapsed and Thankful ran off to Martha's. Mama went nearly completely unhinged, and I have my own responsibilities, what with marriage and my career. The army only has so much patience for me coming and going. I've barely left the state of New Jersey since getting commissioned. I've yet to prove myself, and today a reporter was here for you—we turned him away, of course. Seems one of those girls you saved has an important uncle working at *The Herald*, and with your resurrection from the dead the story becomes more interesting." Fred popped a candy in his mouth and continued. "I told Mama you wouldn't want the fanfare. They'd do pictures of you, but Mama says this may be the only time you'd convince a girl to take you on. Now you're the hero." Fred said the last part as if it irked him to do so. "And girls like playing nurse."

"I don't want to be pitied."

Fred laughed. "I say use what you've got to get laid. There's no harm in it. God made this happen, right?"

"I have no idea what God's doing."

"You haven't lost your faith, have you?" Fred asked with eagerness.

"No. I haven't ... but ... I'm confused."

"As always, Buckie," Fred joked. "Nothing to be confused about. You wanted to be like Christ—you got it. Now pick up the pieces and live a normal life like the rest of us. Be careful what you wish for next time."

"I never wished for anything."

"Come now, Buck. You've always wanted the spotlight. Just admit what everyone else already sees. Being second to me bothers you. It's okay. I understand, but humility is a hard thing to learn. Now, we can never compete—that would be unfair. We're too different. I'll be an officer and married and you'll be—something else—that you enjoy. And you'll visit and be my children's favorite uncle."

"I'm not a footnote to your life, Fred. And I won't be the *weird* uncle."

Fred laughed. "It's good to see color back in your face. I've missed you so much. Don't take my words so hard. I've always had your best interest at heart. I'll take care of you till the end. We'll find you something useful to do."

Thankful came back in now with Buck's coffee and cookies, fresh baked by Margaret and Lucretia. "Buck, you look so well today."

Fred laughed again. "I'll be back later. I've someone to see in the city for dinner."

"Rose?" Buck asked.

"Lord no. Hang me first," Fred replied with a rakish grin and left.

"I'm leaving too," Thankful said. "Martha waits for me, and I can't stand being with Mama and her silent treatment."

"Thankful, I know Mama's hard, but ..."

"No, she's a monster! She rips away any ounce of joy in Father's life," Thankful said, stirring sugar in her brother's coffee. She pressed the overfull drink to his lips, but he shook his head no.

Buck sat up, his mind wandering back to himself for a second. Maybe he'd take a walk. The throbbing at his arm had lessened and his muscles ached for movement.

"Are you listening?" Thankful asked, impatient with him.

"Yes. I was just wondering when Father has ever been happy."

Thankful came closer and was quieter. "When he was with Mai."

Buck took a chocolate cookie, showing no interest in Thankful's disclosure.

"Buck, Father was in love a long time ago with a girl from Peetzburg who's now our aunt. Did you know we had a cousin in Europe? Grandmother told me all about it."

Buck added more sugar to his cup. His left hand shook a little. "Uncle Luce had a wife. Yes, I knew that. Father still loves Mama despite what he says."

"You're the only one who ever thinks that. Mama is impossible, and you're still a romantic." Thankful sat on the bed next to him, pushing his straight hair from his eyes. She changed the subject. "Will you like me no matter what?"

"Of course," Buck said, preoccupied with the crumbs on his clean sheets.

"Can you keep a secret?"

"I've kept every secret you've ever told me," he said with an open expression.

"A man has fallen in love with me," she said with little enthusiasm.

"Okay."

"So much has happened since you've been gone. I wanted to talk with you so many times."

"Well, go ahead then."

"I wouldn't be surprised if one day this man asked me to marry him," she said, playing with the broach at her collar.

"We're not talking about Willy, right?"

"No, but ..." Thankful surveyed her brother with his bandages, ashamed at her trivial dilemmas and hurts.

"But what?"

"You won't hate me?"

Buck shifted his pillows. "Just tell me."

"On the day of your funeral Henry escorted us—Grandmother and me."

"Oh, the man Fred says has a weak handshake?"

Thankful stared at him. "No one said that to me."

"Okay, so you're in love with a man ..." Buck wanted her to be happy, but a little something inside him was jealous, not just of her chances at marriage but for the way she always avoided real trouble using her good looks and innate intelligence. Wrapped in a cocoon of bandages and warm flannel sheets, Buck saw the world open for Thankful as it had always been.

"Let me finish. On the day of the funeral ... I made a huge mistake. Only Fred knows."

"*Only* Fred?" Buck laughed.

"I didn't mean for it to happen," Thankful said, "but I was so upset over you, and there he was in the carriage house."

Buck turned grim and stiff. "What did you and Henry do in the barn?"

"No, it was with Willy."

Buck's cup rattled in its saucer as he placed it on the small table. "No."

"I thought ... I thought maybe something good would come of it—but he just wanted to—"

"You let Willy poke you in the barn?"

Thankful cried. "I was so stupid! And Fred ... he could ruin everything for me."

"You can't blame Fred for this one. Last time I saw him, Willy was a raving alcoholic. What in God's name were you thinking?"

"You were dead! I was all alone, and I hoped Willy would change. Henry's a nice man. He really is, but ..."

"I don't understand what's happened to you," Buck said. "Fred tells me you blame Mama for your troubles."

"How can you ever defend her?" Thankful whispered. "It makes me think less of you!"

"I no longer care what you think," he said, though he *did* care. "I couldn't possibly care. You've made a mess of things."

"Mama and Father—they forced me!" she sobbed. "If you were here—we could have worked something out about the baby."

"Yes, I would have helped you."

"You didn't help me—you gave me a name for him, but then you left me alone—those pious letters about nothing!"

"I was trying to cheer you up!"

"You failed. Mama and Father ... even Father. They didn't want for me to put him up for adoption—I don't know—maybe I would have gone mad waiting. Mama wanted me to get rid of the baby."

"I didn't think you'd do it," he replied in the naively boyish way he had when he was without Fred. "I was sure once you saw the little thing you'd fight for it. A Crenshaw would never put a baby up for adoption ... but then you didn't even get to find out what you'd do."

"No, Buck. I did decide. Mama wanted it rid of before anyone would know—and before Fred's wedding. Don't you understand? I promised to keep it a secret for Father's sake. I was so scared, and Mama convinced me. I saw Father's troubled expression—but I let him do it anyway! It's a secret—you understand—for Father's practice."

"For the practice? You mean an *abortion*?" Buck's voice hardened. "Father always refused to do that sort of thing ... but for when there was real danger ... were you in danger, Thankful?"

"Only danger of humiliation, of what everyone would say if they found out," she explained, her mouth quivering, "and I hated it! The way my body changed ..."

Buck waved his hand. "Oh, don't talk to me that way—it disgusts me. I'm sorry, Thankful, but you're my sister and ..." Just the thought of her naked with child, the thought of his sister having intercourse with that Fahy!

"I'm disgusting! I shouldn't have told you!" Thankful cried.

"Does Fred know about the baby?"

"No."

"Then you need to marry the weak handshake man at once. You need to do right and be away from here."

"But I'm not sure I have real feelings for Henry," said with wide, unbelieving eyes at Buck's cold and calculating demeanor.

"You've waived your right to feelings. You killed an innocent. God help you. And you've obviously been leading the weak-handed man to think ..."

"His name is Henry!"

"Yes, okay, this Henry probably won't marry you if he finds that you've slept with the town drunkard. Damn it, Thankful. You've done everything wrong!"

"I'm so glad you're alive. I am," Thankful cried. "But I can't stand having you judge me when you're so good now! I'm happy you're a hero, but ... I can't stay!" She ran out, slamming the door behind her.

Buck leaned back in bed deflated. He considered chasing her but didn't. An image of Thankful as a young girl came to mind, laughing in church, covering her rosy lips with her white-gloved hands with such sweet innocence. How could someone so lovely have gone astray? Buck burst into tears. Nothing beautiful lasted—not even the perfect friendship of siblings.

The room Buck had longed for on the long train ride home was small and close now. He needed to get out for a while. He went to his armoire and slipped a pair of pressed trousers off a hanger. Jostling his legs into them and fastening the buttons left him in a demoralized sweat. His shirt stuck to his back and the tiny buttonholes were impossible. Graham entered after hearing him, halfway through a raspy-voiced tirade.

Graham picked up the fine shirt tossed on the floor and helped his despondent son into it. Give yourself time, son. We'll get the best hand money can buy as soon as you're healed and the pain goes away."

"Money fixes everything," Buck said.

Graham opened his mouth but said nothing. He pulled the braces of Buck's trousers over his shoulders and fastened them. "I'm glad you're feeling well enough to dress, but it's too soon to be up and about."

"I need air for a little while."

Graham ignored his words, speaking in a grave tone. "My heart is failing, Buck, but don't let on to the others. I'm just glad I'm able to be with you now before it's too late."

"Father, I've worried about your heart forever, and here you still stand while others are snuffed out."

Graham stopped with Buck's vest in his hand. "Are you angry about something already? You've only been awake a few hours."

"No," Buck said.

"Has your mother said something ridiculous?"

Buck swallowed hard. "No. You never take a stand, and in a man that's a terrible flaw. I can't stomach what you did to Thankful! It's the worst thing I've ever heard."

Graham's eyes bulged and his voice trembled in rage. "Your mother *demanded* it!"

"Do you have to give in to a woman's demands every time? You should have stood up to her. You've both caused Thankful to do something evil! And what's worse is that you've counseled others against it! What would have been so bad about another child running around? We could have taken care of it."

"*We?*" Graham asked, his jowls rising in color. "I've been taking care of my children for a very long time. How dare you! How will you take care of anyone? You have been just as selfish as everyone else in this family in following your own *goodness*. Why didn't you wire us immediately after being found? An extra two weeks or so of mourning your death was a good thing? You'll be reliant on my funds and Mama's cooking for the rest of your life and why? I've had enough. I want peace. I'm expected to be all forgiving, all healing, all-serving! I can't please any of you, and I don't even want to anymore!"

"Father, calm down. You're being emotional."

"No! All morning I was planning for a trip into the city to buy the best prosthetic hand for you. I was even happy imagining you'd be excited, but instead Thankful unceremoniously leaves, and you accuse me of bringing evil upon her. The evil is in all of you who have too much and appreciate little. Is it my fault that West Point considered you poor officer material after the foolishness with that colored boy? Did I find you a sodomite missionary to befriend? Did I steal the liquor to give Fahy and William that led to Fahy's death and your sister's plight? Find someone else to blame for once!"

Buck caught his breath.

Graham sought to reverse course. "Buck ... I didn't mean ..."

"Yes, you did." Buck walked past his babbling father and past his star-struck younger siblings playing marbles on the parlor floor and past his mother who forbade him to leave the house in his present condition.

"What will people say, seeing you?" Margaret cried.

"They'll say I'm an abomination," Buck grumbled. "Don't worry yourself."

Buck climbed the hill, slowing his pace as he went and cradling his swollen arm. The air hinted at snow even this late in winter, but he had no interest in nature. How could every good intention turn out so wrong? But wait—his behavior had not been good-intentioned. Kicking Streeter was revenge. Visiting Thankful in the West was cowardly escape, and plying Willy with liquor was bravado and sick amusement at Willy's expense.

William would never have gone west if Fred and Buck hadn't tortured him so. If Buck hadn't been so eaten up with hatred for him, he would have somehow been able to help Thankful. He hadn't stayed west for William, but for himself—he'd been afraid of going back to the academy. Even the money he'd given the poor had been given in the proud quest for sainthood.

The loss of his hand was God's rightful punishment for all he had done. His brooding steps led to the crumbling O'Toole foundation in the woods on the Palisades. The old Irish man had lost his fortune in the recession of '73. Graham had delivered one of the O'Toole children in the Irish neighborhood. The family lived there even today, having never made it up the hill to respectability.

William and a tall girl sat upon a boulder nearby. Buck recoiled at the sight of them and considered turning away, but the idea that such a drunk could still draw a young innocent alone in the woods annoyed him. He came closer when the girl stood and waved, only then recognizing Willy's cousin Lucy. She still wore spectacles.

"Buck Crenshaw? I thought it was you! Come closer and help me with Willy. My aunt sent me to find him, but he's drunk again. I was praying someone might come along, but I didn't expect you." She took every inch of Buck in behind her glasses. "A real-life hero. The whole city is abuzz, but, poor you, holding your arm just like Uncle John. Why is it that soldiers always lose their arms? It's sad, don't you think?"

He let his sore arm fall to his side, ill-at-ease but hoping to appear nonchalant. "Some soldiers get killed, so I guess I've no right to complain. Oh, forgive me. I forgot about your father."

"That's okay. I forget about him too sometimes since I didn't really know him—except from the pictures in his scrapbook." Lucy said this with no outward malice. The golden braids she wore around her head shone for a second as a quick-moving cloud exposed the late afternoon sun.

"I should have stopped Fred from tossing it into the fire, Lucy. I'll always be sorry for that."

Lucy allowed for a demure smile as if she were only half-listening. "I believe you. Now can you help me? Willy will freeze to death out here, and Uncle John and Aunt Katherine might get upset about that though sometimes I don't know why." She let out a resigned laugh. Buck thought she looked like a peasant girl from a fairytale in her bright layers as she tugged at her dozing cousin.

He stood watching her until she looked up with a hint of impatience.

He crouched down with a sigh. "Come on, Willy, wake up. It's not fair to Lucy out in the cold."

William stirred.

"Oh, so here you are again," William slurred. "Here to make me a fool. I'm the one who brought you home, but you're still the hero."

"And you're still the drunk," Buck said but saw Lucy's look of reproach and regretted it. "Come now. Let's get you home."

William wobbled to his feet, almost as tall as Buck, but even more frail and willowy beneath his much-improved wardrobe—someone had been sewing for him. Buck guided William's arm over his shoulder, wincing as Lucy took her cousin around his waist on the other side. Buck could not prevent his vanity even now as he eyed William's fine features: his perfect jaw line and smooth skin (however fading). What a waste!

The trio shuffled down the hill, listening to William hum and cough. Then Lucy spoke. "Doctor Crenshaw came by asking about a new hand for you. I suppose he'd forgotten that my grandfather's company is sold."

Buck winced again. Lucy spoke of his handicap so breezily he wasn't sure how to take her. "Yes, but I also need a new face." He laughed for show.

Lucy glanced at him with a smile. "No, they're character marks you'd want to keep."

Buck smiled back despite himself. Lucy's voice appealed to him. There was nothing shrill or striving or terribly emotional in it. His face rose in color. He turned away in embarrassment.

Lucy continued, "Your father told us all about what a hero you were."

"Really? It was nothing."

"Were you afraid of the Indians?" Lucy asked.

"Yes, well, no. I didn't have time. It happened so quickly."

"I love how the children saved you," Lucy gushed. "It's like out of an adventure novel."

"Yes, they were very smart for orphans." His face burned. "Now, that came out wrong—but I hardly think of you as an orphan, Lucy—just a nice little girl."

A bit of temper traced Lucy's face, but disappeared as quickly as it had arrived. "I wish I could have saved my parents from Indians. But I'd settle for yours."

"You don't know them then. No one is ever happy, I guess," Buck said, parroting something he didn't want to believe.

"I'm happy." Lucy giggled.

Buck stopped, looking her over. She was tall for her age, he thought. How old was she? "And how are *you* happy?"

"My, you sound as though I haven't any reason to be, but I always have a feeling inside that everything will be all right. I like to imagine it's my father talking to me."

"That's cute."

"No, it's not. You're being condescending just like Willy."

Buck bristled at the comparison.

"Aunt Kate says I've matured into an optimist like my father. Did you know him?" Lucy asked as they drew closer to the street with its lamplights just lit.

"I was in awe of him and jealous that he belonged to Willy."

"Poor Willy."

Buck coughed. "Hmm. Don't you ever get tired of taking care of him? Wouldn't you like having a bit of your own life—not in his shadow? I mean, well, you're kind of pretty and sweet—you shouldn't be taken advantage of."

William stumbled along oblivious to the world.

Lucy kept her eyes on the road, her features stiffened and her response clipped. "I feel honored to care for my family."

"But they're not really—I just mean it seems a shame that you have to be seen like this." Buck slowed his pace, wrestling with his feelings. He didn't know why but he wanted to encourage her, though there was nothing in her person that seemed to need it. "You know, I remember how you stood for me at Christmas. You seem a brave girl, and I only hope that if things ever got too bad for you—I mean with the Weldons—that you'd know you were worth something so they couldn't drag you down to feel like nothing." He paused to look over at her. "Remember that you are something."

Lucy having recovered herself smiled at him. "Buck, no one has the power to drag me down."

He suddenly felt exposed and annoyed. Why was he so easily routed if a little girl could be so secure? Still there was something interesting about her. "Forgive me, Luce. This is all my fault—you know—about Willy."

Lucy adjusted her dark spectacles.

Buck cleared his throat. "William was trying to stop drinking before I met him out west."

"William was sad as long as I can remember. Buck, God forgives you."

"What do *you* know about God?"

Lucy laughed. "What do *you* know?" An omnibus pulled around the corner of Palisades Avenue. "Thank you for helping us out of the woods, but here's our ride."

Buck stood speechless in front of the Athenaeum, chewing on the inside of his cheek as was his habit, as Lucy dragged Willy with the help of a sympathetic neighbor up into the car. She glanced back and waved. This surprised Buck and he waved back, too late. The bus moved off.

Buck yanked his collar which stood half-up and half-down, disheveled in a way that annoyed his sensibilities, but to no avail. It flurried now, and the wind held steady, making everything a blur of gloom at candle-lighting hour.

"Buck Crenshaw! It's you out from behind your family stockade," came a voice from the other side of the street.

Buck turned to see an old classmate from school waiting for a carriage to pass before trotting across to greet him.

"Walter Babcock, nice to see you." Buck tipped his hat with his left hand.

Babcock had always been very congenial though they had traveled in different circles—Buck in Fred's where everyone was good at everything and Walter in the group good at very few things.

"How are you liking the cold weather after the sunshine of the desert?" Babcock asked. All people talked about the weather to acquaintances, but Babcock's voice was full of sincere concern. He'd always been that sort—the sort Fred, and he, trusted least.

"I'm happy to see you," Buck said with a sudden rush of nostalgia. "And what are you up to?" he asked just above a whisper.

"Well, I'm back from seminary, but there's no work in it I'd be cut out for." Babcock threw out a sheepish grin. "So I've taken a job as reporter for *The Englewood Standard*. Living hand to mouth I'm afraid, but I like it. I've always enjoyed people."

"Yes, I remember that. I'm sorry about that little incident over pocket change years ago."

"Change?"

"Yes, Fred and I making you hand over your money in the schoolyard," Buck explained as if it had happened yesterday.

Babcock rolled his eyes back, chin in hand and trying to remember. "Okay, I accept your apology, but I don't recall."

Buck wiped his cold nose. "I've thought about it often."

"Funny what we remember," Babcock mused. "I remember you being quiet."

"Yes."

The wind kicked up a notch.

"Are you off to anywhere, Buck?" Babcock rubbed his gloved hands together. "How about walking up to Stagg's for a drink?"

"That sounds fine. Yes, I'd like that very much."

Once inside Babcock ordered a brandy and Buck coffee.

"So, I'm sure Fred told you I've been around to your house a few times, as have other writers. I hoped I'd have sway since we were schoolmates."

"What do you mean?" Buck asked, adding sugar to his coffee.

"I'd love to tell your story to the world. I'm a fan of soldiers and imagine how difficult it must be when people with no experience of the West and Indians judge the military harshly."

"Are people judging me?"

"Fred says you're afraid to talk."

"I hadn't even considered it. It's not much of a story."

"Well, that's very humble." Babcock patted Buck's sore shoulder. "The story's brilliant and with a happy ending to boot. One of the girls you saved is from a good Philadelphia family. Did you know that? A senator's daughter run away on adventure. Both girls say you were very brave. It will all come out because they want it to, but it would be an honor for me to tell it first and, to be honest, I'd be using you a little because I need a few big stories to impress my editor. I'd let you proof it, of course."

"I'd be glad to help you in any way I can."

Buck grinned, surprised by Babcock's admission of self-interest.

The two sat for a while and talked until Buck's throat gave out in the cigar smoke, and he went home. He slipped past the dining room where everyone ate in silence and crept up to bed.

# Chapter Thirteen

Fred shook Buck awake a few days later. "We agreed that your story was best kept quiet!"

"What are you bothering me about?" Buck grumbled, shielding his eyes from the light of day. "Why do you care so much if I tell the world?" He checked his clock, the pain pulsing at his wrist. "Walter Babcock asked me a favor—you remember him from school?"

"I don't give a damn about Babcock," Fred ranted. "You need quiet and rest."

"And I'm getting plenty." Buck swung his legs off the bed.

Fred shoved him back on his pillow with an aggravated moan. "*The New York Sun* wants the story now. There's a reporter in the parlor."

"Really? I'll just get dressed then."

Fred shoved him again. "There's an artist too. Are you sure you want people to see you?"

Buck pushed Fred out of the way with more strength than he thought he had. "Maybe I'm not the monster you make me out to be. Anyway, I'm not afraid."

Fred changed his tone. "But Buckie, you won't mention your faith, will you?"

Buck laughed, pulling a scarf from his dresser. "Is that what you're afraid of? I'll seem fanatical and the whole world will connect it to you!"

Fred helped tie the scarf at Buck's neck. "You ruined your chances for a career and marriage. That's not my fault, and I won't be dragged down with you. Try to be normal for once, and I'll let you downstairs."

Buck grabbed his wrapper and tossed it over his shoulders. "Move out of the way. I'm going down. You have no say."

Fred ripped the robe from him. "Not like that, you won't!"

Margaret barged in now. "Oh, Buckie, *The New York Sun*! Can you imagine? We must dress you up decent. Fred, go tell the reporter to wait a few moments."

Fred shot Buck a ferocious look before stepping out. Margaret shook her head in tepid disapproval. "Pay no mind to him. He's just jealous. No matter how you mess up you still get the attention he wants. I told Fred to leave you alone since this could be your last big huzzah. He has plenty of time for his career to take off. He'll be a congressman before you know it, I bet." She began pulling stockings from a drawer then motioned for Buck to sit on the settee by the window so she could put them on him.

"Politics is for rascals."

"Well, at least Fred will have a career and a wife," Margaret said, handling Buck a little roughly as she helped him into his slippers. "It's what every mother hopes for."

"I'm sorry again to disappoint you, Mama."

"No, don't be like that. Mothers also have a morbid desire to keep their children babies. I'll take care of you and be happy to do it."

Buck's spirits dropped at his mother's appraisal of his potential. He almost understood Fahy's wish to escape life. For a moment he thought of God, but a fear gripped him. *God's will be done.* What the hell did that mean? His mind raced from point to point. Where would he work? Where would he find meaning or even friendship? He could never go back to Fred now. It would be like putting himself in front of a train.

"Now's not the time to stand here in a stupor. You must make us proud," Margaret scolded as she switched the scarf for a garish cravat at his neck. She took a hat from atop Buck's armoire and sat it upon his head. "Oh, that won't do. I thought it might distract from your imperfections. Well, never mind, let's see—maybe this woolen cap. Of course we'll explain that you're still in recovery."

Buck tore it from his head. "Mama, stop it. I'll go as myself."

Margaret looked on in mortification as he left for the parlor. A quick glance in the mirror at the staircase landing showed him he *was* a wreck, but what did it matter?

The reporter met him at the pocket doors with a cordial shake of his left hand. "Thank you, Mr. Crenshaw, for allowing me this time."

Margaret followed them in and sat beside Buck, willing him with her eyes to behave in a certain way. He wondered where his father was—possibly too ashamed of the spectacle. Buck cleared his throat.

"My poor son has been through tremendous hardship at the hands of the military." Margaret patted Buck's knee.

Buck bristled. "Will you get us coffee, please?"

They waited for Margaret to leave after she first wrapped Buck's legs in a plaid throw. Buck pushed it off as she walked out. After a few formalities the interview began in earnest.

"Mr. Crenshaw, what brought you alone into the desert that day?"

Buck shifted his weight. "Maybe God—I'm not sure."

"God? What do you mean?"

"Maybe it was God's judgment against me."

The reporter glanced at the artist sketching Buck's likeness before continuing. "Why would you think such a thing?"

"I went west to escape judgment at West Point. If it wasn't for Fred then ..."

"Your brother is making a name for himself in Murray Hill politics and has friends in high places. What happened at the academy?"

"Nothing."

The reporter leaned in closer. "But you said your brother ..."

"I didn't mean ..." Buck stumbled over ideas. He played with the tassels on the throw beside him. "Well, yes. I got myself into trouble with a colored cadet. It was my doing. Fred tried to warn me and help, but I was naive and befriended Streeter."

The reporter looked up now and paused a moment before saying, "I've spoken to Mr. Streeter. He claims there was a cover up and that Fred was responsible."

"No! Fred was trying to help me ..." Buck faltered. He considered getting up but didn't. "I take full responsibility for what happened to Streeter. God is judging me for that. I should have come clean at the academy, but I was afraid."

The reporter raised a skeptical brow. "No one I've spoken with sees it that way. But never mind. I'm here because you saved a senator's daughter. That's the story I'm here for today, you understand. So you ended up in the desert how?"

Buck's mind raced again. "I was walking back to Fort Grant. I'd given my boots to a friend—well, he wasn't really a friend ... and I sat for a moment to rest my feet. I heard the stage and saw it race up." He took a deep breath. "I feel unwell. Fred did what he did to protect me at West Point. I can assure you of that. *They cut me*—all of my friends refused to know me because of Streeter. Fred didn't want me to throw away my chances. We went too far ... I ..."

"Mr. Crenshaw, I'm not here to try you. You do look quite unwell. I'm sure you paid more than your fair share for whatever it is you did. My sources say you were brave in trying to help the colored boy. Streeter says it himself, and now you protect Fred. I can write my story without any more words from you—the girls have told me all about your bravery. But I want to know who took care of you for the weeks you were thought to be dead."

"Children."

The reporter looked confused.

"Orphans. They'd escaped a train they said they'd traveled out on. I don't know where they really came from."

"Little angels, maybe," the reporter said with a cynical smile, scribbling again.

"Do you think I'm making it up?"

With the world-weariness of a seasoned veteran, the reporter looked over his spectacles. "Well, how old were they?"

"They *existed*. I don't know their ages. They told me, but I can't recall. I only remember asking them to send word, and then I never saw them again."

The reporter tapped his pencil against his notes. "So, children surviving alone in the desert ... maybe God was watching out for you then," he said more conversationally than as if he truly believed. It would make for a good story.

Margaret came in now as the man closed his notebook and the artist gathered his tools.

"Mrs. Crenshaw, thank you for your time. Your son is very brave and too tired for any more fuss. You must be proud of *him*."

Margaret straightened up at the insinuation. "I'm proud of *all* my children."

The reporter glanced back at Buck and left with his artist in tow.

The house rested for two days while Fred was in the city spending time with his wife in the home just off Fifth Avenue that Rose's father had given them. But on the third day Fred returned to find Buck sipping hot chocolate in the parlor with their parents.

"You had to go and do it. Didn't you, Buck?"

"Do what?"

Fred drew the folded paper from inside his overcoat and flung it at Buck. Margaret and Graham stood looking over his shoulder now. Buck wrestled with the paper until Fred tore it from him, pages flying to the floor.

"See here: 'Private Crenshaw disclosed that he and his brother Lieutenant Fred Crenshaw, lately of Murray Hill, were the, until now, anonymous cadets who were involved in brutalizing a colored cadet at West Point in 1884. One can assume that Cadet Fred Crenshaw's bullying tactics and personal charm will continue helping him rise up the ranks of machine politics in his district.'"

"But Fred," Margaret said, "it says you'll continue to rise up."

Graham shot Buck a look of despair. Was he upset at Margaret's stupidity or at Buck's disclosure?

"All I told him was that I was responsible for the misdeeds at the academy."

"So you admitted misdeeds? You fool! That was behind us."

"The reporter already knew about everything. He'd talked to Streeter. I couldn't lie."

"Why not? I did for you! I put my career on the line for you, and this is how I'm repaid! Father, Mama, can't you see what a fool you've raised?"

"I'm sorry," Buck said.

"Sorry? What good does that do?"

Buck couldn't say.

"You sit there with that dumb look on your face trying to elicit pity! The reporter pitied you. Is that what you wanted?"

"No."

"Listen to this: 'Private Crenshaw appeared a shell of a man, ravaged by his career as a soldier. Racked with self-doubt and a less than stable perception of his own place in the world, he leaves one feeling that his obvious bravery in Arizona and at the military academy came at a very high price indeed.'"

Margaret cried, "What does it all mean?"

"It means that Buck came off as a moron!" Fred threw the page into the fire.

Graham spoke up now. "Why must you always put yourself in the line of fire, Buck?"

"I didn't think."

"What's wrong with him, Father? Can't you make a diagnosis for Buck's behavior?" Fred asked, kicking a cat out of his way. "You may have single-handedly destroyed my career!"

"Now stop it at once, Fred. You played your part—it's only catching up with you now," Graham said.

"I expected you to enjoy this, Father," Fred replied.

"I enjoy none of this! I'm going to Peetzburg."

"No, Graham, don't go!" Margaret cried. "I saved you, remember?"

"You saved me for this?" Graham turned away.

Buck spoke now. "Father, please, I need you."

Graham made to ignore his son's plea, but couldn't. "Buck, I'd stay for you, if only I had an idea how to help you and keep you from trouble, but you find it."

"Father, I want a hand and don't want to be a burden on you and Mama forever. I won't speak to the press ever again and won't leave here until I'm fit and able to control my words."

Margaret cried, sinking into a chair opposite Buck and begging with tear-filled eyes, "Graham, we must never let Buck from our sight again! You must stay for him if not for me! Please say you will!"

Graham stood over Buck now, his breathing labored with nostrils flared. "I will stay—for Buck. But you must promise to stay quiet and let all of us recover from this horrible year. I can't take any more commotion. I'm not able for it."

"Father, I'll do everything I can to make you proud."

"Buck, do us a favor—do nothing. Nothing at all," Graham said.

He kissed his son's forehead and walked off to his study, closing the door behind him.

# Chapter Fourteen

Buck had hoped for relief in telling his tale and in admitting his guilt, but people ignored it. Fred's political and military supporters cared little for a colored cadet long since forgotten. It was obvious to them that Buck had suffered a nervous condition at the academy, making his testimony suspect. If any of Buck's West Point instructors had read the story, it would only confirm their stated doubts about Buck's soldierly qualities. His defection to the lowest rung of military society further proved their assessment. Saving the two girls was a nice footnote to an otherwise dismal military career.

The Friends of Indians (an organization his mother staunchly supported) never liked a story, no matter how true, that reinforced the stereotypical savage Indian image they were trying to eradicate in their well-meaning literature and philanthropic endeavors. The reporter from *The Sun* wrote with mixed motives from the start and came away with only sympathy for *Private* Buck Crenshaw and disgust for his awful social-climber brother. Fred had hidden his tracks on the Palisades of West Point too well.

After the initial flush of pride in their son's valor and relief at his return, Graham and Margaret agreed it was best to let Buck slip back behind the curtains of their home's sedate and respectable veneer. Margaret still squirmed at his fanatical attachment to God (though anyone paying attention would have noticed a great decrease in references to the heavenly Father), and though Margaret didn't admit it, she had not forgiven him for ruining his good looks.

Graham understood his son's need for attention no matter how foolishly he went about getting it. He admired and envied his son's foolhardy bravery and devotion to Scripture (even though he also believed Buck was a fanatic). Graham's absence as a parent had led his offspring astray. Buck's face, his neck, his career—ruined by a father's negligence. Graham's chance at redemption— to save his loved ones— to erase his failures during the war—proved a dismal failure too.

Buck's infirmities reminded him of this every day, so Graham avoided his son. If in the morning he heard his son's quiet feet on the stairs, he'd curse in the kitchen and hide in the pantry while Buck poured coffee. At the same time Graham lavished upon Buck gifts—one being the newest, most up-to-date and expensive prosthetic hand manufactured. Graham saw that his son pretended at how little it pained him those first weeks where the amputation was still tender. He saw how hard Buck tried to please him and appear grateful, and it only made Graham more inclined to stay later at his office, writing notes or sitting by the window and staring out.

Buck tried to convince himself that he was just imagining his father's cooling toward him but suspected it was a repulsion and shame at Buck's failure and weakness.

Buck must reclaim his manhood and "get back into the game," as Fred liked to say. He went fishing with Nathan but grew peevish with his tackle. Buck must be satisfied on the days when he was able to button his own shirt. But in the end this throbbing where real and false met filled him with resentment and despair.

Fred had not needed to worry about Buck's words to the reporter. The picture in the paper captured not a young and brave soldier, but the aftermath of battle—the part no one wanted to see. Nothing in the past could be proven anyway, and Fred, though watchful, kept his distance now using marriage and thoughts of building a family as his excuse.

For years Fred bullied and led Buck astray. Buck complied, desiring his brother's direction and confidence. Alone Buck was just a half. How had Fred so easily discarded the companion he swam in the womb with? Why did Buck still crave what brought unrest and difficulties?

And so, Buck stayed at home, traveling only as far as the church on Sundays. Sometimes he'd watch William slide into his family's pew, looking ragged after a big night out. His natural good looks still led the well-dressed girls' eyes to wander his way (though Willy was too oblivious to see). Buck's childish jealousy flooded the hollowness of his soul, and he grudgingly asked for forgiveness from the god who now seemed so far away.

The First Presbyterian Church spent great sums on ornate stained glass, but being surrounded by so much beauty made Buck feel uglier and of less use than ever. He longed for those first days of belief—the ones where Saint John's gospel came alive for him. He wanted to believe every last miracle unquestioningly, and he wanted to know that God could love him someday—once he'd proven himself.

When he fell backwards climbing into the family carriage, and his younger siblings jumped to prop him up in front of the entire congregation, Buck knew that God was still punishing him. He tried in vain to locate Seth Kenyon. He tried to talk to the church pastor who was too busy visiting the sick and dying to devote time to the state of Buck's spiritual health.

As the forsythia bushes bloomed outside the parlor windows, Buck dreaded the only event that would force him out amongst others this spring. Margaret made known to Rose Turner's father that the Crenshaw family had been offended by their lack of involvement in Fred and Rose's wedding preparations the previous year, so Mr. Turner suggested a more informal anniversary party with opportunities for Fred to meet with the big bugs who'd moved to the "country" along the Palisades but still made their money in Manhattan. Fred, displeased at the idea, fretted much over the mixing of the two worlds, but without Mr. Turner's benevolence and influence he'd have been sent to a faraway post instead of given a high-profile one here in the East.

Arrangements were set for the Englewood Hotel—provincial and shabby and nothing like the places Fred had grown accustomed to in the city. Rose, game as always, insisted on fanciful settings and décor, much to the dismay of the staid hotel management. Fred coached everyone from young Nathaniel to Graham and Margaret on how they should behave and what they should speak about. Graham did not mention that these very important people were acquaintances of his at the field club.

For Buck, Fred held private lessons. No religion. No West Point reminiscing. In fact if it were possible Buck could depart early with a headache.

"Why should I come at all then?"

"Rose thinks it's awful of me to keep you out of our affairs," Fred said. "And it's time you mingled ... just a little. Rose has friends, you know."

Buck saw, because Fred let it be known on his expressive face, that Fred did not think Buck had a chance with any of them. "I *should* like to meet them then. Maybe you'll be surprised."

Fred laughed. "Here, do you need help with your trousers?"

Buck pushed him aside and buttoned the braces himself. Fred rolled his eyes at how long it took and played with a brush from a top Buck's dresser.

"I miss the old Buck."

"Sometimes I do too," Buck replied, hoping for a reopening of their old closeness. It did not come. Fred walked out to annoy his other siblings.

Heavy steps came down the hall and in walked Graham. "Oh, I was looking for Fred."

"He's gone off to bother Nathan." Buck turned toward the mirror to fix his collar.

"Son, I ..."

"Yes?"

"Well, how is your new hand doing?"

"Same as yesterday, Father."

"Oh, I've asked that far too often," Graham said, rubbing his forehead. He touched the small trinkets of Buck's boyhood on the grand old desk that had once been his own —a pocket knife, a small rabbit figurine. "I'm sorry ... my mind is on a thousand things with work and ..." He glanced at Buck's reflection in the mirror.

"Yes," Buck turned to him, leaning against his set of drawers, "I've noticed how busy you are."

"Just like old times, I suppose you think, but ..."

"Father, there's no need to explain. In fact I'd rather you didn't."

"Buck, have you given any thought to what you'd like to do?" Graham faltered. It wasn't exactly what he meant.

"I know you think me a miserable failure, and everyone is angry that you still deposit money in my account ..."

"No, don't worry about the money. It means nothing to me."

Buck wasn't sure how to take the remark.

"Do you need help getting ready?" Graham asked backing toward the door.

"No, not at all."

# Chapter Fifteen

Buck brooded over Fred from his seat near the door that night at the party. In a month Fred would be a lieutenant in the army, and he was already married to the prettiest girl Buck had ever seen, Rose Turner—yet still there was a restless "looking for the next great prize" in Fred's eyes. Buck listened in mild annoyance as Fred talked to men of business and politics.

"Seems to me, fellows," Fred said, in a countrified version of himself, "that a man has to have loyalty to his homefolk, no matter how quaint they may be." Fred nodded toward his father. "Father is an accomplished doctor and scholar, well known in the medical periodicals, but has chosen, as a calling really—which I admire—to help those less fortunate. Even giving away his fortune to a poor relative." Fred glanced Buck's way.

The men sipped their drinks with faraway eyes.

"Yes," Fred continued, oblivious to the men's lack of interest, "so my dear, sweet wife and Mr. Turner arranged this little celebration here at the Englewood Hotel—to make my parents comfortable amongst the likes of you. Mama is the kindest of simple folk —what a dear—but I take after my grandfathers on both sides—*enterprising and forward-thinking*. Grandfather Seward came from Plymouth stock."

One by one the men made excuses and drifted over to the bar, but nothing fazed Fred as he scanned the room for someone who might be of value to him. Finding no one at the moment, he turned to Buck.

"And why are you so glum, Buck? I'm the one bored out of my gourd, and it's my party. But what's to be done? If only Mama hadn't been so adamant about Englewood. No one of any import wants to come to New Jersey. Well, at least next week we'll have tea with the Cartwrights of Murray Hill. You've heard of the silver magnate haven't you, Buckie?"

Buck shook his head.

"Oh, don't be so smug and superior with me, Buck, when you have father's fortune! I need to have connections so I can take care of my girl and the buckets of children she wants—not to mention pretty clothes and things. I've my work cut for me—not like you. You can do as you please now."

Fred searched Buck for signs of temper, but none came. "Do you want me to pity you forever? Wipe that lost look off your face. It's unbecoming of a Crenshaw."

Rose strolled up with a flirtatious wag of her fan for Buck. "And here's the hero of the day hidden off by the door."

Once Fred realized Rose was alluding to Buck, Fred's smile vanished. "Any Crenshaw would have stood for those silly girls," he complained.

"Of course, dear," Rose said, with a kiss, "and that's why I've married the hand-somest of all." Rose hadn't meant to offend Buck. Her color deepened for a moment. "Well, Buckie," Rose said, with an air of familiarity that irritated him, "I've someone who will cheer you up. She's terribly spiritual and so clever I don't half understand a word she says about God."

"I'm happy watching the dancing," Buck said with a half-hearted smile.

"Oh, don't tell me dancing is against your morals now. I remember how much you wanted a dance with me back at the West Point hops."

Rose was oblivious to the effect her words had on both Crenshaws as she waved her fan in Fred's direction—conveying a secret message that reduced his temper but not enough to stop him from reminding Buck of defeat.

"My brother doesn't go in for frolic and hops anymore. It's beneath him. This life is just a veil of tears. Right, Buck?"

"How morbid Freddie is," Rose said with a pout. "And here I am on *my* day looking out for *you*, Buck. Won't you have one dance with my friend? She's spotted you over here and isn't scared at the state of you—I mean your sour expression—especially be-cause she knows all about the way you saved those girls. India read it in the papers before I had a chance to put in a good word. India's that type—a different sort who skirts social convention and a real hoot. I wouldn't want to spend every waking mo-ment with her and her notions, but she does entertain me."

Fred kissed Rose hard on the mouth (to shut her up) and said, "I hope you want to spend every waking moment with me, young lady—and the sleepy ones too."

Rose giggled and pushed away Fred's advances. He held her more tightly. "Oh, you're such a brute!" Rose tickled Fred, and he let go.

Buck groaned at the sight of Fred brought down to public tickling.

"So I'll go fetch Miss Van Westervelt. Be nice and don't act too eager for a friend-ship, and she'll like you a lot," Rose said.

Buck stood to exit as soon as Rose turned to go for her friend, but Fred stopped him.

"Oh, no you don't. I'll not have you embarrass Rosie. This friend of hers comes from the Van Westervelt clan. They've got ins with the railroads. Let her talk to you about the West and Indians, and I'm sure she'll leave you soon enough. What else do you have to do?"

Buck's feelings for Fred were such a mix of anger and awe that it made formulating a response to him difficult.

Fred stood beside him now. "I'd like you to have a good life, if you'd let us help you."

Buck's feathers ruffled again, and he was about to say something unchristian when Fred elbowed him.

"Sakes alive, here she comes. Now make an effort for once."

A swan-necked blonde, as tall as any Crenshaw girl but more regal in attire and posture, strolled over to them and held out her hand languidly.

"How very pleased ..." she said, not seeing fit to finish a boring sentence.

Fred kissed her hand as if kissing a queen. Buck looked off, feigning disinterest.

"I'm Miss Van Westervelt, but I don't stand on convention. You may call me India."

"It's very nice to meet you," Buck said with a diffident nod before snapping open his pocket watch. He hated pretentious names.

India looked at him in the same tilt-headed way that some look at paintings they don't understand. "I hear you played the hero in Arizona recently. Might you take off your glove so I can see your prosthetic?"

Rose and Fred exchanged pained glances, but Buck removed his glove.

India took his hand, running her slender fingers over the polished wood fitting. "*We* can do better," she pronounced. "My father, a few years back, swallowed up a small medical firm that designed them right here in Englewood."

"The McCullough business?" Buck asked with interest.

"I believe so. Does that mean anything to you?"

"Our parents are friends with Mr. McCullough's daughter, Katherine."

Fred sighed. "Acquaintances, just acquaintances, Buck."

"I don't know any of them. The little company was nicely run, and they had good ideas but were too small to make a real difference in the world. I believe the old man died, and the son-in-law had no real interest in it."

"That's Mr. Weldon all over," Fred said to Buck.

India waited for Fred to notice he had interrupted her. She turned to Buck. "We could fit you out with a better model sometime."

"I like this one," Buck said. "It was uncomfortable at first, but I've gotten used to it. My father gave it to me."

"Buck is too sentimental for his own good," Fred said. "He was supposed to be an officer with me but made friends with the wrong sorts. I don't think Father cares if you trade in this fake hand for another."

"I'm impressed by family loyalty and by people who don't follow others like sheep. Isn't there any place else you need to be at your little party?" India asked and pointed toward Rose who had wandered off to socialize with a state senator from New York.

Fred charged off happy enough to leave.

Buck pulled his glove over his thumb and fingers, said nothing and took his seat on the bench against the wall, adjusting the cravat at his neck.

India sat next to him, quiet until her closeness became awkward. "I do hate these gatherings. I've come as a favor to my father. My mother is ill."

"That's nice of you," Buck said with a hint of sarcasm.

"I thought you might understand," she said with arched brow. "Our sort places too much on appearances, beauty, and wealth. These horrible gatherings are a sign of how far our society has gone wrong."

"When someone is beautiful, it's easy to say looks don't matter—having never had to experience homeliness," Buck said. "And how are anniversaries supposed to be celebrated?"

"Well," India began, leaning in close, "you'll find this shocking, but I don't believe men and women should have to be married to have a life together."

"I don't find it shocking. I find it stupid. Someone like Fred would have a different girl every day."

"And will marriage change him?" she asked.

He glanced at Fred in the distance with Rosie. "No, he won't change a bit."

"And why should he? This society is so dishonest. If we look at animals, very few are monogamous. What do we gain by it?"

India seemed anxious for debate, but Buck was in no mood.

"Maybe it's not for you to gain anything by it. You said earlier that you didn't want to be a sheep, but I guess I do. I disagree with your ideas, but I don't want to argue. I want peace."

"Yes, I was told that you've found God out west, and that's what interested me. I care deeply about spiritual things too. After much time in study and research I believe in a bigger God than our *Christian* one. Maybe one day you'll be at my level and will find the peace you search for."

"Thank you for the words of encouragement. Maybe one day I *will* be at your level, and we can talk then, but for now I see my sister wanting a dance."

Buck rose to meet Thankful coming his way. He hadn't spoken to his sister since that day in his bedroom.

"India, did you tell Buck about the community you're joining?" Thankful asked, her voice clipped and cold.

"No, he's too narrow-minded for it." India flipped of her fan.

"Oh, Buck, it sounds *just right* for you," Thankful said. "The leader is a Christian who's experimenting with all sorts of communal living like the apostles, and they study the Bible and do good deeds. It would give you direction—a place to use your Christian energy and *sense of charity*."

"I've never said I was wanting for something to do. God will lead me. I have faith," Buck lied. He hated the bitterness in Thankful. She was falling away from God over the lost baby, and the sins she had committed troubled Buck. Who would join him in heaven?

India interrupted Buck's thoughts. She stood only inches from his body and regarded him with an unusual intensity.

"Would you like to come with me next month to visit Middlemay Acres?" India asked. "It's a short train ride away, and we'll listen to a lecture and have lunch. They all work together and serve up the most healthful meals, I've heard. None of my friends will come because they're scared of new ideas, and they don't want to give up their comfortable existences to serve God."

Earlier in the day Buck had read about the young king who turned away from Jesus for love of his possessions. Was God speaking to him through this girl?

"I came to talk with you because I heard of your faith and bravery. I find those qualities interesting," India said. "So few men possess both."

Buck stood taller and puffed up. "It wouldn't hurt to take a day out in the country, for a lark."

Thankful laughed at Buck as the room grew quiet. Everyone turned their attention to the piano in the corner and Henry Demarest preparing to play. The sudden silence in the gaslit and low-ceilinged room amplified the rustling pages of sheet music as Henry sought after something of the right mood. Thankful glanced around as if his presence and the way he dominated the moments until he found what he was looking for embarrassed her.

Buck and Fred wore the same bored and disdainful expression. Graham checked his watch—that infuriating Crenshaw habit! Party attendees from the best houses in the city and military friends murmured. Henry looked up, the mutton-chop sideburns he wore accentuating the rusticity of his appearance.

Clearing his throat, Henry spoke finally in his deep, masculine tone that surprised and interested the guests. "I am happily put on the spot by Mrs. Crenshaw to play one of these fine pieces of popular music, but I'm afraid my sensibilities wouldn't do them justice. I ask that you forgive my excitement and pride when I offer up my own composition." Henry shifted around on the piano bench, taking a deep breath and running his fingers lightly over a few keys as he spoke by way of introduction. "I'm sure that every one of us has experienced our full share of life's unexpected horrors and the little secrets we cradle like heavy children in our tired souls, but tonight we turn away from the dark and into the light of celebrating new love. Love that transcends age, love that starts people down a new path of experience and pleasure. Forgive my rustic notions, my dear friends. I'm a simple composer, but here is my gift to you. I wrote it for a beautiful sable-haired fairy who in my dreams dances amongst the skunk cabbage ..."

Thankful looked neither left nor right and her face burned. Henry ran his fingers nimbly over the keys, and the small crowd stood transfixed at the boldness, the passion, and the complexity of the music produced by the man pretending at simplicity. A few ladies batted their fans emotionally as their jealous partners looked on unable to deny that the music had a masculine power so pure and unguarded it unsettled them. The composer knew exactly how to play the room; knew what bored New Yorkers would like to hear.

Thankful relaxed, now sending Buck a triumphant look. Buck crossed his arms immune to the spell, being the most puritanical in the family, after all. The music ended with a bold stroke and a final simple melody reminiscent of the sublime longing Thankful experienced in the very woods Henry alluded to. As the last note held and faded he gazed frankly at Thankful before standing with a bow and humble smile. The crowd lavished him with enthusiastic applause.

Buck and Fred rolled their eyes. It took a few moments for Henry to make his way to Thankful as members of the political New York elite congratulated him and wondered when he might be free for receptions in their fine brownstones in Manhattan and Brooklyn. Henry chuckled as he strode over to Buck, Thankful, and Fred extending his hand to shake Fred's. Fred complied but wiped his gloved hand on his trouser leg afterward.

"Thankful, I hope I didn't disappoint your mother," Henry said.

"Oh, no, Mama's eating it up. An accomplished musician at *her* party," Thankful replied.

"I've heard so much about you, Buck," Henry said. "Thankful has spoken highly of you."

Buck hung back, annoyed at Henry's slick and untrue talk.

Fred lit a cigar and made no effort to screen Henry from the smoke. "Your music was invigorating. I'll admit it. You wrote it for Thankful, didn't you?"

"Fred!" Thankful cried.

"You've caught me, I'm afraid," Henry said. "Art is a reflection of true beauty. Thankful is a worthy subject."

Fred laughed. "Thankful lures men in like a siren."

Henry grew serious. "No, that's not what I meant, young man. Thankful is much respected by everyone she meets in Peetzburg."

Fred laughed again. Margaret ran over. "Dear Mr. Demarest, my heart was in my mouth, but you've outdone my wildest expectations. Thank you! If only our poor Thankful had met you when you were young."

Thankful made to escape, but Henry took her hand. They all noted it. He spoke to Margaret with a respectful familiarity. "I'm afraid, you wouldn't have liked me fifteen years ago, ma'am. Too much of a roamer. I've had my fair share of troubles."

"Oh, I don't believe it, sir," Margaret said, tapping her fingers against his chest once before losing interest and moving on to annoy Meg acting the wallflower as the music for a waltz started up again.

India whispered to Buck so softly at the ear his hair stood on end. "Why don't you ask me to dance, my card is empty."

He took her hand. Fred sought out Rosie and the room whirled with rich fabric.

Thankful allowed herself to be carried along by Demarest on the dance floor. While she enjoyed riding the shade-dappled lanes along the Hackensack with Henry on the new bicycle he'd given her, she liked a full room of people and feeling the eyes of the familiar young men she'd known most of her life upon her. Here she could delude herself. The boys of her youth knew nothing except that she was young and lovely enough to have sublime pieces of music written about her.

Henry knew of the latest authors and composers and happily discussed religion and politics with Martha—he sided with the silver men and Martha with the gold. Yes, they were new ideas for Thankful, and she still wasn't sure why people cared so much about coinage, but as the waltz floated on she dreamt that Henry might be the way back to happy society.

Henry talked so easily to even the stodgiest of Fred's acquaintances from the city about bloomers and showgirls, New York's famous corruption, women's modesty and the Rock Springs miners in Wyoming who killed twenty-eight Chinamen. Henry, not a bit like prudish Buck, substituted nicely as friend—better than the original for he lacked the judgmental airs of Buck gone religious. Henry disregarded the conventions of his family's puritanical church, and no one seemed to mind.

At the moment of Thankful's highest reverie, the freest she'd felt in months, Henry kissed her. With all the laughter and friendship and all the closeness and fragrance of perspiration and toiletries, and the awkward smiles and the way Thankful's hair curled down her back, he kissed her—quickly and unnoticed by the crowd so wrapped up in merriment.

"I'm sorry, Thankful. I don't know what came over me. It seemed like the right thing to do—like something out of a silly novel," Henry said with a nervous laugh.

Henry couldn't know how Thankful panicked. He couldn't possibly understand that she enjoyed the kiss in a way—like the cycling and the intelligent talk, but ...

"Thankful," Henry began, his eyes bright and optimistic, "I shouldn't say this because I see I've made you afraid, and our friendship means the world to me, but I'm the sort who talks. Things must be said—and I've fallen in love with you."

Thankful felt a sudden giddiness, a rush of approval, an air of satisfaction that this artistic man of the world who never settled on anything had settled on her!

Henry regarded Thankful tenderly. "Your smile is very adorable, miss, but what does it mean?"

"You make me feel better than I am, Henry. I'm complimented." Thankful saw he had hoped for something more and a guilty compulsion caused her to continue. "I feel the same about you."

"I'm not sure what you're saying."

"Love ..." Thankful began as the music stopped. Thankful glanced around the room.

"Wouldn't it be jolly if we married, secretly, like in the great romances?" Henry whispered and laughed, so lightly, so boyishly.

"Oh, Henry, how you make me laugh." Thankful led him to the punch held in gaudy crystal.

"Thankful, are you trying to kill me? Slow down!" He laughed, but something in his voice had changed—an almost disgusting desperation slipped in—and Thankful regretted having responded in the way she had. She met his pensive, exposed eyes. He was not an unattractive man. He was smart and acted as if she were as well. She handed him a cup of punch and sighed. Henry was a good man.

Thankful's mind said this: *You've kissed people before. You've given your body before. If Henry kisses you again this must be the last man you kiss. And you must marry him or you are truly as bad as everyone thinks. Here is your chance to be the person you were meant to be.* She waited. She felt a flutter of excitement and dread as Henry made an excuse to bring her out for air.

Englewood had grown more sophisticated and bright in the years since Thankful's childhood. A man and woman of comfortable fortune strode by in the night after attending the concert at the Athenaeum, nodding a polite greeting to the couple. Thankful imagined they had made all the right decisions in life, had the best furniture and never suffered a less than well-rounded conversation at the supper table. She glanced at Henry so perfectly suited to being the star in such circles and smiled. His eyes glistened merrily—his assurance returned. He leaned over, hesitating long enough to smile before kissing her.

"I haven't felt this way in a very long time," Henry said.

"So you've felt this way before?" Thankful asked, girlishly.

He was taken aback and looked to see if she was serious. "Thankful, what use would it be to confess our past mistakes?"

She hesitated. "You're right. We should start anew and enjoy this life. The past is finished."

"So what do you think?" he asked.

"About what?" Thankful asked wanting time.

"About marrying!" he replied, grabbing her chin and shaking it with a grin. He wanted an answer.

"You once told me there's more to life than marriage," she reminded him.

"Yes, I did." Henry stopped her from playing with her curls. "But I never said I was against marriage, exactly. We can live here or travel, living as vagabonds. We can do whatever we like—together."

She laughed. "But how will we eat?"

"Do you really care? I imagine you in a turban, like the gypsies wear, and we'd hike along with the weather going south for warmth and north again in summer like the robins ... or we could stowaway for Europe, and I'd show you real paintings."

"We can go to New York to see paintings, Henry," she replied, at once annoyed at her own pragmatism. "You're right. I've been pent up my whole life, and when will I ever have the chance to see things again?"

"One never knows," he said. "We must tell your family of our plans immediately."

"Oh, no!" she said. "We should wait."

Henry looked confused and a little hurt. "Why?"

"This is Fred's night, and to be honest, I don't want them to ruin everything with their spiteful ways. They might think it foolish." She blushed. "We've known each other such a short time. They'd be afraid I'd make the same ..."

He covered her mouth. "Don't say it. Remember? We're starting fresh. This time will be different. We've had such a jolly time so far, and who cares what people think! We will live for ourselves alone."

She laughed uneasily. Selfishness was not considered a virtue in her family.

Martha found them as they re-entered the hotel. "Now's the time to leave—your mother is getting maudlin with drink, and your father's grey with worry—I can't take another minute. Henry please escort me up to my room. Thankful, are you coming?"

Thankful hesitated. She missed her brothers and sisters, but a sudden exhaustion came over her, so she followed the two upstairs.

Martha turned to look at them both at her door. "What's happened?"

Thankful paled. "I'd like for this to be a secret, Grandmother ..."

"We have news for you," Henry announced. "I'll be taking Thankful from you. I hope you don't mind."

Martha turned a suspicious eye on her granddaughter. "Have you found new employment?"

"No, Grandmother."

Henry laughed. "I'm marrying the girl and soon. We thought to tell you first so you could share our happiness. You are happy aren't you, Martha, old girl?"

"Henry, don't call her that," Thankful scolded.

"Henry can call me what he likes. He won't be controlled by you, Thankful." Martha met Henry's eyes. "Are you sure you want to do this?"

"Certain," Henry said confidently, which helped Thankful's queasy stomach.

"Well, Henry, you've never been one to wait. Frankly I'm surprised you'd want to try marriage again."

Thankful's heart stopped. He'd been married?

"I was a different person then—too young," he said, shifting uncomfortably under Thankful's surprised stare.

"Well, we've all made our mistakes, I suppose," Martha said matter-of-factly. She almost smiled, but there was something held back when she spoke. "Thankful is a surprisingly hard worker with a mind for numbers. She is welcome to continue working on my farm."

Henry hugged Martha who pretended to be put off by it. "That would be grand—only temporarily, until we head off to see things."

"God is good," Martha pondered aloud. "Maybe this is just the thing. Thankful's a wanderer at heart, and I'd have figured her chances for marriage were nil. Have you told your parents?"

Thankful and Henry spoke over each other. "Father's heart—I think after is best," Thankful started.

And Henry: "My parents will want to pay for a small celebration, and we'll live with them for a while."

Martha pursed her lips but said nothing.

A strange and excruciating silence hung now.

"Henry, I'll see you tomorrow," Thankful said.

"Yes, take care, my love," Henry said, kissing his fingers then touching them to her nose. "Good night, Martha."

Thankful followed Martha into the room they shared. She stood before the mirror taking off her earrings and necklace.

"Thankful, is this really what you want?" Martha asked as Betty helped her out of her heavy gown.

"Yes, Grandmother." Thankful turned away to wipe a tear.

"I like Henry very much," Martha said, "but I can't say I trust him."

Thankful's body went cold. "Then why would you give consent?"

"I have no right to consent to anything, girl! You're old enough."

Thankful whirled around to face Martha, her eyes full of fear. "But why don't you trust Henry?"

"Maybe it's because he's so willing to marry you."

"Why are you cruel to me?" Thankful burst into tears. "What have I ever done, Grandmother?"

"Get a hold of yourself. Take a seat there and stop crying." Martha sat beside her on the cheaply upholstered bench. "My point was not to hurt you. Henry lost his first wife to influenza, but by all accounts he was a terrible husband and father."

"Henry had children?" Thankful asked.

"He *has* children. Six of them. Henry's not a cruel man. I love the fellow deeply, but he's never made a cent in his life. He's a dreamer and a good soul, but irresponsible, of course, and babied by his ridiculous mother. Although he has real talent for music, he's undisciplined. This you know, I'm sure. He'll love you, Thankful, but he won't take care of you."

Thankful knew what she should say to put her Grandmother at ease, but it did not come easily. "I don't want him to take care of me. I've learned from you to take care of myself."

Martha smiled approvingly with just a small trace of doubt in her eyes. "You're due for an improvement in your salary, girl."

"Grandmother, don't spoil me."

Martha laughed. "Take what I can give you now. You'll need it."

Thankful lay awake all night in a haze of apprehension. The memory of kissing Henry grew more monstrous with each replaying of it in her mind. What had led her to so rashly say yes to him? He had children! But so had she, and she'd killed hers.

Thankful must remember they were both taking a fresh start, and anyone would think Henry a handsome older man. There was something dashing about him, and why did looks matter that much anyway? She could be who she wanted and do just as she wanted with him.

Thankful liked Henry *well enough*. They would be good friends and have funny adventures, but somehow none of it seemed all that adventurous now. What if they stayed in Peetzburg forever? She had grown to like Martha's house and even enjoyed

Martha and Betty in a way. She enjoyed having a small bit of money to put by too, but that would change with Henry minding their finances—she assumed.

The morning came on quicker than Thankful liked, and as breakfast in the busy dining room of the hotel ended Henry joined them at table and sat easily, sharing pleasant stories and a few amusing jokes. Thankful felt almost happy again, but every little thing Henry did caused her to scrutinize him more. A gesture, a laugh, a raised eyebrow, the way he wiped his mouth on a napkin ... she tried to stop. She leaned back in her chair and took the measure of him.

As they stood waiting for their carriage to be brought around and for Betty and Martha to return from a shop across the street, Thankful didn't want to bring up what was troubling her. This was her last hope at marriage.

Henry exuded great sensitivity. "Something's on your mind. What is it?"

"Oh, it's nothing." She glanced at him and then back out into the busy road.

"Don't play. What is it?"

"Henry, I shouldn't let it bother me, but it does. How is it you were married and never told me?"

Henry laughed, but it was defensive and cold. "Well, you never asked. We've spent most times talking *about you*."

She went silent. Thinking. Worrying.

"Is that *all*, Thankful?" He waited a moment. His tone changed. "I loved you from the start. That wasn't the case with my wife. She and I were too different. She liked being settled."

"What if I said I'd like that too someday?"

"I'd laugh. You who has traipsed all across the country on your own." He glanced across the road.

"It wasn't quite traipsing," she said, tugging the hat strings under her chin.

"Well, you're a spirited girl who I can have fun with. Isn't that what we both want?"

"Yes, I'd like to do everything together, but I wonder why you never told me about your children."

It was quiet now and for so long Thankful felt her heart might burst. A milk wagon sped by on the cobbled road and splashed their feet.

Henry sighed. "To be honest, I blocked them from my mind. I haven't thought of them at all since I met you. My mind has been on the lovely creature in front of me."

"You've forgotten about your children ... *your six children*?"

"Well, I wouldn't say forgotten exactly. It's that my mind's at ease about them. I did my part. I got them through the loss of their mother, but my wife's parents are better suited to raising them. You'll never have to see them if that's what you're worried about."

Thankful bristled. "Henry, my concern is over the fact that you didn't tell me any of this before."

"Does it change the way you feel about me?" he asked.

"No, not exactly ... I don't know."

"Is there anything you need to tell *me*?" he asked pointedly.

She hesitated. "No, nothing. My life is an open book to you."

He threw his arm around her shoulders. "Let's not ruin the future dwelling on the past. My parents will be thrilled at the idea of you coming to live with us."

"First I'd like to save some money."

"Oh, you can do that sleeping under my roof. Won't it be fun to ride to work each day? It's a pretty drive, and I'll escort you."

She avoided a kiss. "Henry, I was wondering also ..."

"Oh no, what now?"

"When we travel, how will you make money?"

"Now you sound like all the other small-minded girls. I thought you were more mature and progressive in outlook," he said, shaking his head. "Thankful, have faith. I promise to become more disciplined, but musicians are so inept at selling themselves— you could help me. Would you do that? We'd be a team. I'm so sorry I didn't tell you about everything, but I was afraid you'd judge me harshly. I'm not good with children. None of us were happy—didn't you say your father was the same way, and you suffered under his emotional abandonment keenly. It was better for them that I left completely in one quick go."

"I never thought Father should desert us," she replied, "and I shouldn't have said that about him."

"You have every right to be angry with me, and if it would help, I could bring you to meet them and show you there's no hard feelings between any of us. All I want is to make you happy."

# Chapter Sixteen

Buck woke before dawn on Sunday and searched Scripture for any sign hinting that he should *not* go with India Van Westervelt to Middlemay Acres. Once the sun rose he smoothed his hair over the scar on his forehead and tied a royal blue scarf at his neck in the mirror. Realizing his vanity, he pulled off the scarf and slicked his hair back. All the world should know that Buck Crenshaw was not vain and needed only God's approval. After trying to meditate on God's word for an hour as the songs of robins and red-winged blackbirds just back from winter grew noisy outside, he gave up, grabbed the blue scarf, and left for town.

The whistle from the northbound train sounded in the distance just as Buck jogged onto the station platform, slicking his hair back again in the reflection of the station window. A strong hand grabbed his shoulder, startling him.

"Mr. Weldon!" Buck said as he turned to find Katherine and John dressed in their best old clothes, faded but neat.

"Where are you off to so early on a Sunday, if not church?" John teased, with a friendly smile.

"I could ask you both the same question," Buck said, his eyes upon Katherine.

"Mr. Weldon has a meeting with a specialist doctor tomorrow in the city, and I convinced him to take us early. I don't want him rushing himself into sickness. Someone needs to look after him," Katherine said. "We'll stay in a hotel tonight."

Buck saw India step down from the train, her face framed by a bold peacock of a hat with ribbons the very color of his scarf. Her dress draped low at the front, and she carried a small bag at her elbow. She glanced around for Buck, playing with a locket at her neck.

Katherine and John turned to see what distracted him and smiled as the girl walked up, holding her hat atop her head against a slight breeze. Buck said nothing for a moment, pulling his hat forward and reaching for the scarf in his pocket.

India waited to be introduced, though her expression might have led one to believe she wasn't interested in people who wore yesteryear hand-me-downs.

Buck noted with sympathy Katherine's eagerness as she straightened her skirt. John Weldon kissed his wife's hand. Buck loved them though they did not know it.

"Miss Van Westervelt, I'd like you to meet Mr. and Mrs. Weldon."

Katherine recognized the name and glared at India. John recovered more quickly. "Pleased to meet you, miss. How is your father?" he asked.

"*Weldon* ... where do I know the name?" India mused, tapping her gloved hand to her lips. "Oh, yes, the prosthetics! Father has enjoyed tinkering with the old designs. I was telling Buck how much better we make hands now. Your father had some superb ideas, Mrs. Weldon, but we have the funds to make great advances. I'm so glad you were both ready to sell."

"I never wanted—" Katherine started, but John interrupted.

"Mrs. Weldon misses her father," John said. "She's happy his designs have helped people."

Buck coughed. "My father was so pleased to find one of the last distributors of the old designs for me," Buck said to Katherine, erasing her bitterness. "I would never replace it. It reminds me of home."

India rolled her eyes playfully at his sentimentality. "Well, I suppose we should say goodbye now. We'll miss our transfer, I'm afraid. Mr. Crenshaw, are you listening to me?"

"Yes, of course, Miss Van Westervelt."

"Mrs. Weldon, I *am* sorry for your sadness over the company," India said patting Katherine's shoulder as if touching a mangy dog, "but it makes my father happy to improve things. Come along, Buck. Excuse us."

The Weldons watched as she walked off, looking back for Buck to follow, only once.

"I've only just met her," Buck said by way of explanation. "We're going to a ..."

John smiled at him. "Buck, take my advice, don't marry her. That girl won't make you happy."

"I hadn't even considered it, Mr. Weldon," Buck said resenting any interference, but Mrs. Weldon's compassionate smile smoothed his feelings. William's mother was meek and gentle, traits hardly admired or noticed in most, but Buck like his father appreciated the rare ability she had to put others first.

"Buck is a smart young man with a *gentle* heart," Katherine said, "and will pick the right girl when the time comes, Mr. Weldon."

Buck always wanted to be better in front of Katherine. "I'd want a girl like you someday. If only you had a daughter," he began, forgetting Eliza. "Oh dash it, I'm sorry."

Katherine's eyes saddened, but she laughed. "Now run along, and don't let any girl make you feel small."

"I won't, Mrs. Weldon. And thank you."

The whistle blew its shrill song, and Buck trotted off to make his train. Inside he took a moment to adjust his eyes.

"Mr. Crenshaw, here I am," India said with a royal wave.

Buck laughed. Miss Van Westervelt was such a duck out of water in the cramped car. The train jumped just as Buck took his seat beside her. The two sat in cramped silence, one long feather of India's hat tickling his ear. India kept the veil over her eyes and stared out the window until the train left the station. Was she angry that he had stopped to speak with the Weldons?

"I admire your way with those people," she said as if it pained her.

"*Those people* are two of the kindest I've ever met," he said, happy to take a noble stand for them.

"Well, I've heard that the people at Middlemay are the most intellectually advanced of our generation and come from a few very noteworthy families."

Buck laughed.

"Why does that amuse you, sir?" she asked, lifting her veil.

"You're such a snob."

India adjusted her hat and shrugged. "I'm just not comfortable with people I have nothing in common with."

"But I thought Middlemay Acres has communistic values and such," he said as the conductor punched their tickets.

"Oh, yes, so it does. I was complimenting you. If I join Middlemay ..." India whispered, "my parents will die of shame! But I want to learn how to treat people as equals. I try for the life of me to do it, but some people seem so"—she scrunched her nose and giggled—"they seem so stupid. I mean, I want to talk with people who like to improve themselves. I find that most people don't have initiative, and they bore me. I don't like to be bored."

"I'm surprised you sit with the likes of me. I certainly don't come from one of the important families you're impressed with."

Buck didn't care that she was a snob. She was very enjoyable to watch as she fidgeted with her wardrobe and played with her earbobs.

"I must admit that your family is not what I expected when I first met your brother. Fred's very elegant and intelligent though *conceited*. Your father's family must come from good stock. It's just a sense I have." She waited for a response, but when he just smiled she continued. "I want to learn to be like Jesus, who could dine with sinners and not be disgusted. Is it my fault I was born to money and privilege? I need to be humbled, yet I dread it. I *am* a snob." She laughed. "You, I don't know what to make of."

"I can't help you there. You may want to avoid seeking out your humiliation though. It's not as enjoyable as you might think." Buck felt excited and hopeful for the first time since the West. He wasn't thinking this girl could be his, but her company and the freedom of admiring her with no hopes for himself awakened a long-buried optimism. The day might be fun.

The train pushed through quiet farm country dotted with wandering Holsteins and Jerseys. The first strong light of mid-spring glistened on a passing pond. Buck dozed, his scars tingling under the warm glare of the train windows. India took a small Bible from her purse to read and practice verse, silently moving her soft red lips to the words she sought to memorize to impress the Middlemay folk. Fred and Buck always won the Bible verse contests at Sunday school. God had given them both good memories.

The hours passed in quiet reverie.

The train lurched to a stop. Buck and India hurried out, curious and excited by their new surroundings. The diminutive station with Johnny Jump Ups swaying in regular clay pots had early spring tulips and daffodils for purchase next to a newsstand advertising the happenings in and around the Middlemay compound. India clasped her hands and murmured, "How sweet."

Buck hung behind, enjoying the way India's large bustle, trimmed out with a flirtatious bow and ribbons, enhanced her shape. He tried not to stare, but she waved her hips back and forth with such grace. Buck looked down just in time to avoid tripping over a loose platform plank. If it was in God's plan for him to remain alone (due to his disfigurements), was it sinful to just enjoy looking? Was it adultery if there was no hope? He wasn't sure and would save that debate for the train ride back to Englewood—later.

India turned and acknowledged by the confident expression on her face that she was used to men admiring her.

"Dear Buck, where do you think we might find an omnibus?"

"I guess in the direction of those people."

"Oh, sugar," India complained, quickening her pace and pulling Buck along by his sore wrist.

He hardly noticed.

"I'd heard that Middlemay was a popular sight at the weekends, but I didn't imagine this," India said. "Will they have enough strawberries and cream for all of us, I wonder?"

Buck laughed at her lowered veil and her reddened cheeks brought on by the embarrassment and annoyance at being jostled around on the crowded omnibus without a seat.

"What good practice for your snobbery, Miss Van Westervelt."

He loved her last name for its solid Dutch roots and for the way he felt pronouncing it.

She laughed too at her own ridiculousness. "This certainly is a lark," she said after being shoved by someone's umbrella.

Over the din of the horses and the chatter of the crowd came the faint sound of brass instruments. India's tense shoulders loosened as she leaned over to see the Middlemay Acres entrance up ahead. Buck took in every inch of her ample bosom, thanking God for the design of women's modern dresses.

The crowd descended from the bus and thinned out over the open expanse of lawn. A sparkling lake with two swans and bunches of white ducks and their young lay to the right. The imposing brick mansion with red-roofed turrets spoke of the solidity and prosperity of the community. A rustic gazebo shaded scores of people seated for small confections baked by Middlemay members.

Musicians played nearby. Buck, having grown up with a pianist mother, regarded the gloomy and off-tune music with disappointment, but the valley with its just-flowering fruit trees arching over hundreds of daffodils and tiny, fragrant blue hyacinths lifted his spirits.

"What could possibly be wrong with a place like this?" India gushed under the dappled sunlight of mature maple trees. "My parents are just too caught up in modern industry and capitalism to understand the soul-edifying nature of trees."

Buck smiled at her sentiment and her expensive clothes.

India narrowed her eyes confidentially and took him into her private friendship. "This will be the greatest adventure of my life!"

Buck had nothing in Englewood to go back to but an overstuffed room and the fading notoriety of the stage rescue. India's enthusiasm sparked his curiosity. Maybe God was turning him in a new direction.

"Oh, and that must be the Circle of Improvement," India said, pointing to a fire pit with cut logs encircling it. Three Adirondack chairs sat in the shade just off to one side.

"What's it for?"

"Well, it's a marvelous idea. Richard Rhinedale, the founder—are you sure you've read nothing about the perfectionists?"

"I like their name," Buck said, "but no, I haven't."

"Richard is older and knew all the perfectionists of the forties—the *originals*. God meant for us to experience perfect sinlessness in this life, they said. No longer would the morals of the world— used to control sinners—apply."

"That sounds like heresy."

"Of course, you were a military man and used to rules," India said with a hint of superiority.

He folded his arms. "I *like* rules."

"They're comforting, I'm sure, but do you feel happy? Fred says you're not."

"Fred has no right to say anything since his behavior has a lot to do with my unhappiness," Buck said, catching how childish he sounded before going further.

"I heard you were interested in Rose before Fred got to her," India whispered, "but between us, she's no match for you. She's much more suited to Fred."

"Why? Because she's pretty?" Buck asked, annoyed at himself for still holding such a grudge and a crush.

India laughed. "Rosie's not that pretty, and she's not bright, is she? You'd be bored in a second."

"How do you know?"

"Fred has no respect for women, so it doesn't matter that she's a child. When he gets bored he'll go elsewhere."

"That's a terrible thing to say." He couldn't help but smile. "But it's true—at least the part about Fred. I don't know Rose well enough."

"You know her *well enough*. There's nothing more to her," India said, as she found them a table and waited for him to seat her.

"I don't understand how girls can cut each other so easily without the slightest compunction," he said, seating himself and looking over an illustrated Middlemay pamphlet left on the table. Everyone sat speaking in hushed tones of awe as members of the community visited the tables, bringing fragrant scones. Buck's stomach growled.

"Men always say silly things like that," India said, pulling the pamphlet from his hand and glancing through it herself. "You must realize that Rose introduced me to you to keep Fred from me. Our friendship unnerves her."

"Married men shouldn't have friendships with women," Buck said. He always spoke in a whisper, but here his voice seemed loud with everybody hushed. It was funny to him. "What shall we say when they come to our table? The women do look queer with those short hairstyles."

India held his good hand and pulled him close over the table. "They may look strange, but I've heard they believe that everybody in the group is married to everyone else."

"How could that be *Christian*?" he asked but sat up straight as a Middlemayer came over with an air of quiet dignity.

"Happy Sabbath," the woman said.

India and Buck shot each other amused glances.

"Today we have cinnamon scones with the apple preserves recipe that first made Dick famous in these parts," the matron said in a sincere, reverential tone. Her deep-set eyes hid under heavy brows and her square chin did not flatter, but her voice held the promise of peace.

Buck's natural skepticism felt somehow mean-spirited at the moment, and the warm scone looked like something that might bring fame to its baker. The lady put the plate before him.

"My name is Sonja Rhinedale. If you have any questions about Middlemay please feel free to ask."

India perked up, "Oh, you're Richard's wife! How very exciting to have one of the founders serving us a treat!"

"Here at the farm we all pitch in at every level. It prevents one from becoming bored. Women *and* men cook, serve, and farm. I find, as a woman, being freed from the slavery of cooking three meals a day has left me with so much more time to do what is truly ennobling, like study of the Bible and geography." Sonja took Buck's lifeless hand in hers, seeing he struggled just a small bit with the silverware. "Let me care for you, young man. It would be my honor."

When she released Buck's hand he slid it under the tablecloth, resting it back on his knee.

"Is this enough preserves for you?" Sonja asked as if his desire in even this small thing was of monumental importance to her.

Buck nodded, taken aback.

"If you wouldn't mind," India said, "my friend Buck and I do have questions. I want to know how we can join, and is it true that you know the path to sinlessness? I've been trying to rid myself of the love of dress and vanity. I also feel so angry sometimes at being a girl who's not allowed to use my intelligence for anything serious."

Sonja looked severe for a second, Buck noted, but a frail smile of tolerance for India covered it, and Sonja took her by the chin. "Richard will love you. He is wonderfully adept at helping the young with their doubts."

"I have no doubts," India began, but Sonja turned to Buck.

"And what are you searching for, young man?"

Buck pretended great interest in his saucer, imagining the eyes of the world upon him forcing an answer. "I want a home," he blurted and took a quick sip of the bitter herbal tea in front of him.

Sonja poured honey over the cup. "From our very own bees," she said. "I usually don't say these things to strangers, but the Lord is leading me to tell you that *you've found it*, sir."

Buck glanced at India. "Oh, I don't know ... I only came because Miss Van Wester-velt asked me."

Sonja sat with them now. "I suggest that you open yourself to the idea. Just think about it. Are you planning on staying all day?"

Buck turned to India for answers. She looked as though she might cry behind her proud posture. "India, what would you like to do?"

"I suppose we can stay till evening so that you can make *your* decision, Buck."

"India, what's wrong?" he whispered, wishing they were alone for a minute. "Would you like to see more of the place?"

"I need to serve the others," Sonja said, "but you should stay at least until you hear Dick speak at three." She left them with a sweet smile, but Buck sensed something not quite genuine about her.

India pulled her veil over her eyes and drank from her tea. "Please pass the honey, Buck."

"Did I do something to offend you, miss?" he asked.

"No, of course not. I should have expected that *you'd* be chosen—and I've dreamed of this day for months! I can't *stand* another minute of people underestimating my intelligence!"

Buck laughed. India looked crestfallen.

"Buck, you don't know what it's like for me. I've studied theology all by myself. Who can I discuss it with? My father has forbidden me to go to college—I'll lose my inheritance, and without it I'd have no money for school. I'm a prisoner."

Thankful came to Buck's mind. "But India, you *are* here. And *it is* a nice place. You can stay if you want to, so I don't understand why you're upset."

"Because I wasn't chosen! Don't you see that?"

"You're very sensitive," he said, mildly annoyed at her behavior. "Sonja said her husband would be glad to help you."

"But she said it with a tone. Didn't you think so?"

"No, I didn't notice," he lied. "This was supposed to be a lark."

"But she said God is seeking *you* out and not *me*!"

"India, you're being foolish and ruining your time. I won't allow it. Now eat the delicious scone that Dick made, and let's enjoy the awful music."

India laughed, leaning close again. "I had imagined being so impressive to them. I had lines to say and everything."

Buck rolled his eyes, complimented by Sonja's words to him but sympathetic toward India. "You're a passionate girl. Aren't you?"

"I suppose." She smiled ever so slightly before taking a small bite of the pastry. "You know, Buck, you're very comfortable to be with. You treat me as an equal."

He let her think what made her happy. It made him happy too.

The two of them wandered the grounds, admiring the idyllic farmland vistas. The sheep grazed in new spring pastures with their lambs frolicking around them, and every so often a heifer complained in the distance. Men and women of Middlemay lounged in the shade, finishing intimate picnics beneath dense oaks and chestnuts as the chimes of the bell tower called them to meeting.

Buck and India had spent the last hour scrutinizing the odd dress of the women and mocking the serious and polite way in which the men (and a few women) played croquet. All the while Buck knew that this was the best day of his life. A beautiful girl stood beside him and had not once mentioned his scars. Here he hadn't noticed a single odd look in his direction (or was it that India entranced him so that he had noticed nothing else?). She put her arm through his and whispered a wry comment about a woman's bloomers. The words could have been anything. Maybe God was calling Buck to this weird place. They were Christians—of some sort. And they were nice.

Buck and India strolled toward the meeting, just beginning under a billowing tent. The canvas reminded Buck of his summer at West Point, and he hesitated at the entrance. He had become uncomfortable entering new places where people glanced at unfamiliar faces.

"I hope he's as good as I've imagined," India whispered.

Buck rolled his eyes at her adoration.

Sonja spotted the pair and led them to folded chairs near the front by the podium. "Most visitors have little interest in what Dick actually has to say. They leave on the early train so there's plenty of seats up front."

Buck kept his eyes on the podium, looking for the man of the hour, but it stood empty. India craned her neck, full of expectancy. Soon a pianist began a sweet and unusual melody accompanied by the flute. It had such longing to it that Buck figured it must be a love song. The tent moved in the wind and a soft breeze made him comfortable and relaxed. Around him everyone looked serene and content—but for India, a bundle of energy. He closed his eyes and memories of his mother teaching him piano made his heart ache. He had been young, and the world new.

Just as he opened his eyes, Dick Rhinedale moved behind the podium with a welcoming wave of his hand. Buck had imagined him severe and bookish. His tousled hair and impish grin gave him the air of a charming rogue. The community cheered him on with polite yet enthusiastic applause until he stopped them, as if uncomfortable with the adoration. Richard pulled his tie loose and laughed until the clapping and mur-

muring stopped and the room silenced. Now he looked more serious as he surveyed the crowd, settling first on those he recognized then more steadily on those he didn't. India's hat made a loud statement.

"Welcome, young lady—and welcome *you truly are* by all of our friends. And what brings you?"

India put her hand to her throat, momentarily at a loss for words as she stood. "Sir, I've come because I love God and want to find how I can express that best. I'm so confined as a lady. I would like best to find what my purpose is in life and to love others."

Dick smiled like he had known India for years. "Friends, have we all not felt as this young one does in our lives? Capitalism and the love of all things modern have made living in this country unbearable for most souls sensitive to the plight of men," he said with a long pause, "and of women."

Gentle applause.

"Young sister, you have come to the right place if what you want is an extended family where everyone loves each other with all their hearts, minds, and bodies. Capitalism has brought a greater divide between men and women than any other event in history." Richard waited again for the enthusiastic applause to fade. "Here at Middlemay we eschew any modern convenience that interferes with our ability to treat each other as equals. Men and women take turns at the chores. No one complains of boredom when the sand is constantly shifting, and you will see that great contentment comes from communal living with a firm devotion to the Lord. Here, my child, you can put aside the restlessness that afflicts the youth of modernity. Listen, will you? To the sounds of the babbling brook and the mewing cow. These are the sounds of God, more beautiful than any piece of music contrived to fill the longing of man's soul in the deep hours of the night. Do any of you—the newcomers and curiosity seekers—realize the peace one has when the world is turned off for a while? '*Be still and know that I am God!*' it says in the holy book. Be still, for heaven's sake. When two or more come together—what does Jesus, our lord, say? Yes, his presence is here.

"He wants you to know that He has blessed Middlemay with healings of the mind, body, and soul. He has sent me such words of joy and compassion for you all. Here there is no competition, no selfish hiding away of one's own things when we have agreed to share all we have for the good of the community. Did not even the apostles give of themselves completely? Some of you are searching, searching for the love of God. And here it is presented to you—the sun in all of its glory sets alight the very gifts of God. How simple if only we stay still enough to see them. Here we have a group, a family not bound by the ordinary and life-deadening cares and expectations of this fallen and capitalist society. Here we recognize that everyone has something to offer—no lights under a bushel here. There is no best person or worst job when all is done for the common good of Middlemay and God."

India sat back down with a glow of satisfaction and excitement as the leader moved on. "Isn't he wonderful?" she whispered.

"If everyone is equal then why is he the leader?" Buck asked, more curious than cynical.

"God chose you to be a hero. Why can't God choose him to be a leader? Richard's words are inspiring," India said, flicking her small fan.

"I don't mean to spoil your enthusiasm. I suppose I'm not sure what capitalism has to do with anything," Buck ventured. He did not want to lose this new friendship, and he was unsure how far he could push her in debate.

Richard droned on.

India listened for a moment, her expression rigid. She leaned in to Buck. "Capitalism is selfish. Look how the trains have stolen from the poor and the Indians."

"I *like* the trains, and in the West everyone likes them. Even the poor and the Indians. I've sat next to a few."

"People are too foolish to realize what's not good for them," India whispered. "Even your friends, the Weldons. They sold away their company for nothing. My father is making a fortune off the old man's designs and contacts in the South. Someone should have been there to protect the Weldons from themselves."

His ears burned at the idea of Mr. and Mrs. Weldon being taken advantage of. "Well, maybe *you* should have done something about it. Capitalism isn't responsible for your father's lack of integrity or your lack of will to stop him."

She laughed. "And what could I do but watch? In my father's eyes I am only smart enough to marry and have children."

"Having children mustn't be all bad," he said, realizing he'd offended her. "Well, I like them anyway."

"You can like children all you want and still do other things."

Buck sighed. Who would have children with him? But he stopped himself. Today might still be saved from dangerous debate. He was trying to figure out how this might happen when Richard called to India again.

"Young lady, I see that while I speak up here you and your friend are in a heated discussion. Do my words trouble you?"

India turned to Buck, who replied, "Sir, I'm sorry to have distracted you. It was rude."

"Young man, I'm past my prime and have trouble hearing you," Richard replied, cupping his ear.

Buck stood up, glancing around at the crowd. "I'm sorry I was rude. It was my fault. I wasn't sure if capitalism was the problem."

Richard's grey beard and spectacles softened his features, and he smiled with large white teeth. "You remind me of myself at your age," Richard said, "roughed up by the world and questioning all things. I admire you for not being gullible. It takes strength and intelligence to question authority. Let me ask you a few things. Do you believe in God?"

"Yes, of course."

"Do you believe he has a purpose for you?"

Buck glanced at India, who was smiling at him. "I hope so."

"I *know* I have a purpose," Richard said, "and my friends *know* they do too. It is to bring the kingdom of God to Earth. Do you feel loved? What is your name?"

"Buck."

"Buck, do you *feel* loved?"

Buck couldn't say anything in front of the crowded room of strangers.

"I will ask again, do you feel loved?"

"No, I don't." He took his seat. India clasped his hand, but he hardly noted it.

Before he could regain his composure, a strong hand landed on his shoulder. Richard Rhinedale had come down through the crowd and pulled him to his feet now. His wife Sonja rubbed Buck's back maternally, and the crowd hushed.

"Buck, my wife told me about you in a dream she had *last night*. I believe you were sent here to us for healing. In the kingdom of God there is no shame in showing weakness and need. You have been brought to the fountain to regain your rightful place in the kingdom. Humility is the greatest gift of all and you, my son, possess that."

Buck said nothing as Sonja smoothed his hair from his face. "You are a beautiful child of God, Buck," she said and released him to his seat. The two of them went back to the front of the crowd.

More speech-making followed with a few discussions and a final hymn, but Buck heard none of it. He wondered what India thought of him now. Why on earth had he confessed to *feeling* unloved? It sounded so needy and feminine. His mother had always told him not to beg for attention. It was a humiliation and unacceptable as a family trait. Feelings were personal, and this man had exposed him and made him say things he shouldn't.

India nudged him as the crowd milled out. "Is everything all right?"

"Yes," he said, searching her for signs of disappointment in him.

"What will you do, Buck?"

"I guess we'll head for the train?"

"No, I don't mean about that. You know, about what Richard and Sonja said. They think you belong here. Isn't that interesting? Don't you feel something special about this place? It's like they know you." India put her arm through his again.

He pretended having a beautiful girl on his arm was a normal occurrence but tried to read her still for a sign of hidden motive. She smiled, perfectly at home with him. There *was* something special about this place.

"Did you hear Richard's opinions about women's rights? It was so encouraging," India said, taking a deep breath of the lilac-scented little garden they walked through now. "I've made up my mind to ask them if I can stay."

"When?"

"If I go home and tell, I won't be let come back," she replied, brushing her hand against the full lilac blossoms at her side.

"So you mean to stay from now on?" he asked, his spirits sinking. He had been looking forward to the closeness of the train ride home.

"Now don't you see how bad it is for a girl? I must ask permission to live and breathe. You are free, Buck."

"But will you ever come back to visit?"

"No, I have no real friends in the city anyway. They're all so materialistic and wouldn't understand." She stopped herself. "Oh, silly me, you were meaning would I visit *you*." She was quiet then.

"I meant nothing," he said with a false smile. He picked a few blossoms and gave them over to her.

She buried her nose in the perfume. "I really like you, Buck Crenshaw. Wouldn't it be fine if you ran away from home with me? We could be the best of friends here, and it wouldn't be quite so scary if we were together—as friends."

He had not a single friend in the world, and here was someone who made him laugh. Mama would be angry at Middlemay's lack of denominational affiliation, but Thankful had almost married a Catholic. Buck was an adult now anyway. It might be nice to spend a few weeks exploring this place, and he hated the idea of never seeing India again.

India spotted Richard and Sonja mingling with a few visitors, giving each person their undivided attention before moving on to the next. The couple seemed happy and full of health although they must be ancient—sixty or seventy. India wanted to get closer, but Buck resented waiting for an audience and suggested they peruse the large bulletin board outside the winter auditorium. The list of things happening at Middlemay boggled the mind. How did people have so much time?

"Buck, the remarkable thing is that, since they all share the chores, they're done by early afternoon, and then they have leisure."

"If you're looking for leisure, young lady," a deeper voice from behind them said, "then you'll be sadly disappointed."

Buck and India turned toward Richard who greeted them with a good humored twinkle in his eyes. "India, here you will work until bedtime to bring the kingdom of God into reality. It may feel like play, and that is the point. God wants us to bring joy to one another, and from that work there is no holiday."

India blushed. "Yes, of course."

Buck cleared his throat. It pained him at the end of most days. "Sir, I'm not sure what you mean by the kingdom of God. Are we living in the end of days?" he asked with obvious skepticism.

"The kingdom has already begun. It will come like a thief in the night. It is not as your Sunday school teachers have told you. The beauty of God's plan is already unfolding." Richard outstretched his arm to the twilight scenery. "You can see it here."

Buck glanced around at the lush landscape. "But the Bible says the end times will be horrible and ..." He was overcome with a sudden coughing fit.

Richard surveyed him. "Young man, may I?" He laid his hand against the scar at Buck's neck. "Lord Father in heaven heal this man's wound through me your humble servant. You said we would do more miraculous things than You."

For a few awkward moments Richard held his hand to Buck's neck. Buck's face burned at the unexpected and unwanted intimacy of the old man's hand around his neck, but ... his throat—was the soreness fading? He looked at the evening sky with the first few stars blinking awake. And then a star fell. It disconcerted him and he coughed again. Richard pulled his hand away as if disappointed.

"Dear boy, your faith is weak like the pulse of your blood."

"My blood?" Buck tightened his scarf.

"Mr. Rhinedale is a well-known healer, Buck."

Buck had no respect for anyone who claimed to heal besides doctors.

"The pulse at your neck is alarmingly slow. I'm concerned for your physical as well as spiritual health. Does anyone in your family have heart problems?"

"My father has a weak heart."

"It's my duty to tell you that you are extremely unwell. Did you not sense the beginnings of a healing a few moments ago?"

"I'm not sure."

Buck began to sweat, something he rarely did.

India watched him with fascination.

Buck coughed again. "My throat relaxed, but ... well, the stars ... one fell from the sky."

Richard and India smiled at each other.

"Don't you see, Buck? It was a sign," India said. "Am I correct, Mr. Rhinedale?"

"India, you are my equal but for age, and your observations are as valid as my own. Yes, it was a sign. Something miraculous was about to happen, but Buck wasn't ready for it. These things take the right guidance, fasting, and prayer. Young man, in your physical condition you will be dead in a year if you don't stay."

Buck coughed out a laugh, uncomfortable in his sweaty clothing. It came to him then that his father perspired a lot with his weak heart.

"Son, your complexion is ghostly, and all signs point to the fact that you should stay—at least the night," Richard said.

"But I feel fine."

"We can send word to your family if they'll be worried," Richard added.

"No, that's not necessary."

"Good, then. It's settled. I'll see you're made comfortable and send you a tonic of herbal remedies to sooth your system."

"Nothing with peanuts."

Richard laughed. "Of course not! Many people cannot tolerate them since they've been used in vaccines. Mint tea as a light tonic for tonight is best."

"I don't drink tea as a general rule, sir. Good strong coffee ..."

"Oh, dear boy, that's the worst thing for you! No, you must have tea."

India spoke up now with doe eyes glistening. "Now what shall I do? He was my escort home."

"India, lovey, I didn't think I needed to invite you. You had already decided to stay," Richard said, kissing her cheek in a paternal way.

Buck recoiled at the sudden intimacy.

Richard led them to a rustic bench and trotted off to make arrangements.

"How did he read what was in my mind?" India said, awestruck.

"It was clear by the way you hung off every word he said."

"Now that's unfair. Richard's convinced you—a true cynic—to stay."

"Just for tonight."

Again music escaped from someplace. Buck covered a yawn with his hand. Was he suffering under a great illness? Two middle-aged women found them both almost asleep, leaning against each other on the bench. Even if terminally ill, Buck had never been happier. India's soft hair brushed against his chin.

"Our two weary travelers. Come this way, and we'll make you more comfortable," one lady said in the tone of a lullaby.

The women, with their hair short to the shoulders, looked homely as they led the two into the turreted mansion and up through a hallway decorated with artifacts left by visitors and by people who had experienced healings. Crutches, braces and spectacles hung from the walls with photographs of people made whole again. Buck smiled, imagining what his father would say. Some people had made themselves sick as a trick of the mind and so were probably healed by suggestion, but others most likely faked their conditions.

India whispered to Buck as the two ladies walked ahead of them having their own private conversation, "Even in the Bible there were healings."

"How have you read my mind?" Buck teased.

The women beckoned them in different directions now.

"Sweet dreams, Buck Crenshaw!" India called to him halfway down the hallway.

Buck grinned and waved. His voice wouldn't carry that far.

Miss Hetty Babbitt led him into his room papered in a subdued pink, where a single small light flickered beside the fine mahogany bed. Buck waited for Hetty to leave, but she moved to a chair and sat at the edge of it.

"Is there something I can do for you?" Buck asked.

"Richard thought you might have questions about us I could answer to make your decision about staying easier."

"I have none, but thank you," he said, noting in himself a rising anxiety. "I guess I wouldn't mind the tea Mr. Rhinedale mentioned."

"Yes, here it is. Do you need help undressing?" the woman asked as she edged closer. "I noticed your hand, and Dick says you're unwell."

"No, I'm fine, but tired. I can take it from here," he said trying not to sound short. "Thank you for everything."

"There's a chill in here. I'll be back with an extra blanket."

Buck waited for her to leave before slipping from his trousers and blouse. He folded the soft blankets down, hopped into bed, and covered himself up to the chin. The door opened, and Hetty carried in an extra pillow and another quilt. She tucked the pillow beneath his head.

Buck sighed despite himself. "This is so comfortable."

"We make our own pillows from the softest feathers of our flock, and the blankets are donated by a man healed by Richard," Hetty whispered. She tucked the sheets in and smoothed the extra blanket over the bed, humming a melody from the service earlier in the day. Buck tried to keep his eyes open, but the woman's voice, the warmth of the blankets, and the cool air through the window conspired to lull him to slumber.

# Chapter Seventeen

Buck woke to the sound of cocks crowing and India's urgent knocking at his door.

"Buck, wake up!"

Half-asleep, he rolled from bed and searched for his clothes, finally wrapping himself in a patchwork throw and opening the door a crack. "Yes?"

India pushed the door open. "Look what I've done! I don't know what to make of myself, but the scissors were there—and I know I must leave vanity behind." She had cut her hair in the same fashion as the other Middlemay women. "What do you think? Have I made myself ridiculous?" Her eyes filled with tears.

"Are *you* happy with it?"

"I don't know! It's why I'm here to ask *you*." She poked him.

"Well ... here at Middlemay you'll be the prettiest one of them all." Buck, reading her disappointed expression, added the oft-repeated words from home over bangs cut too short on his sisters. "It'll grow back."

"It *won't* grow back if I stay here."

He sensed danger. "You're still pretty."

"*Still?* That must mean it's awful!"

He had limited sympathy for girls who cut their own hair. "India, you said you were giving up vanity."

She crossed her arms and took a step toward the door as if to leave. His eyes fell upon her new short Middlemay skirt and the shape of her calves.

"What are you staring at?" she asked, laughing now. "Do you like my stockings, Buck Crenshaw?"

"Will I get in trouble for being honest?"

She came close. "There's something about you, Buck. I'm surprised at my feelings, but I find you quite handsome now."

"*Now?*"

"Except for your forehead and your lighter hair, you reminded me too much of Fred, and while I *like* him ... he's *so self-important.* Maybe it's your eyes. You just make me happy. I do hope you'll stay. We'd have fun times."

Buck was excited under his blanket. "India, I ..."

She kissed him, first on the forehead and then on the lips. He wrapped his blanket around her to enclose them both, his heart racing.

A quick knock at the door came as Dick and Sonja entered.

"This is what I was afraid of," Sonja said to Dick. "Lovers passed off as friends."

India pulled away from Buck. "We're not lovers. We just met, and Buck was consoling me over my hair. I so wanted to be one of you, but my vanity!" she cried. "I've been reading about Middlemay for months now and the meaningful work you do and the equality you experience, and now I've gone and ruined it! I went to one of your lectures at Cooper Union, and it changed my whole life. Life hadn't felt worth living. I finally got up the courage and ..."

Richard opened his arms to her, and she tucked herself beneath them.

Buck wondered where his clothes were as he stood in the blanket. India's little speech and the way she wrapped herself around the old man annoyed him.

"There, there," Dick purred, rubbing her back while giving Sonja a supercilious smile. "Miss Van Westervelt is a lost little soul like you once were, Sonja. It's on my heart to let her stay. With the proper guidance she will be a true friend of the Lord's."

Sonja's brows furrowed, but Buck, wearing a colorful patchwork quilt over his union suit, caught her attention and a youthful smile changed her dowdy face. "And what have we here? A modern day Joseph? Caught in life's snares?"

"And I'm as innocent of wrongdoing as Joseph was," Buck replied, though it pained him to say it. "There's been a mix-up about my clothes."

"Yes, there most certainly has, I'm afraid," Sonja said. "Poor Nettie is such a wonderful soul, but sometimes in her eagerness for hospitality, she does silly things. Whilst you were sleeping she laundered your clothes. Nettie feels it's her natural calling to keep everyone in clean things, and Dick preaches *tirelessly* about cleanliness being close to Godliness so"—again Sonja spoke in a clipped way—"so, with the damp night your things are still wet. I'll have a laundress bring up something for you to convalesce in."

"I'd rather get going. I'm perfectly well after a good sleep," he said, vexed over his clothes. At home he thought nothing of the hired girl washing his trousers, but to take his things without asking seemed a bit forward and personal.

"May I ask," India began, "is it true that *all* work is shared in the community—even laundry?"

Dick and Sonja laughed. "Dear girl, don't worry about laundry. Some things are done by townsfolk who, while not ready for our modern ways, still need funds to get by in life. We hire them as a service to the town—to create employment for those who wouldn't find work otherwise."

"Why do you say modern?" Buck asked. "Christianity is old."

"My, Buck, for someone so young and unwell, you're sharp as a tack," Dick said. Sonja nodded in assent. "You ask questions and don't take things at face value. Shrewd as a viper and gentle as a dove."

"Do you mean me? Or yourself?"

Dick paused before laughing. "Both of us—it's how Christ works in us. I see it in you, young man—the makings of a true soldier of God. The world needs young people such as yourself to lead it into the new century—*once you are well.*" Richard signaled for Buck to sit in a wing chair by the window. "Buck, be honest with me. Are you doing all that God sent you to do?"

Buck pulled the quilt tighter around himself. "I don't know what God wants."

"I can see in your eyes you've been through a lot. God humbles those he wants to use for great things, if only you'd be open to new experiences. The kingdom of God has come, and you are freed from sin. You and I and everyone here at Middlemay can experience a sinless life of joy and companionship and be beacons in a world gone mad with gadgets and doodads."

Buck's chest tightened and he coughed. A voice in his head said *run*, but he stayed, unsure if his discomfort was from God or from the intense man who hinted at fulfillment of spiritual promise in Buck. Was it cowardly to leave or foolish to stay?

"Buck had a conversion out west," India explained. "His sister-in-law, Rosie, told me. He's the soldier in the papers who saved those girls from the Apaches. His brother says he's suffering under a nervous complaint since his discharge from the army because of his hand. It was cut off by the Indians."

Dick nodded slowly at the disclosure with an annoyed expression. "Conversion experiences are often counterfeit and from the Devil. We can help you discern, Buck. You've been sent here by God to escape the grips of the Evil One. The Indians are a curious lot but do have a few good ideas—not about chopping off body parts, mind you, but still they are living something closer to Eden than we are." He paused and studied Buck's face. "I'll show you the many burial artifacts I unearthed here on this very property."

"I didn't find anything like paradise in the West, sir. The Indians are no better than the rest of us."

Buck noted India's impatience at his negative responses. Was it Christian to disagree with others even if their ideas were soft and stupid? Maybe Buck *was* too cynical.

"Paradise is in your heart and mind," Sonja said, taking a pressed and folded outfit from a country girl who quietly stepped in the room. "Cotton is a beautiful thing, and we've made these ourselves." She pressed the clothing upon Buck, who just wanted his own things back.

"Cotton's grown in the South, isn't it? On the backs of ex-slaves," Buck said.

India sighed with force, shaking her head. "Buck, you're being a bore!"

"No, no, he's being a man," Dick said. "Cotton is indeed brought up by the South, but we make sure to only do business with those farmers who treat their sharecroppers fairly. Without businesses like ours, the freed slaves would have no work at all."

"You could always bring a few freedmen up to work for you," Buck said.

"Now that is a *brilliant* idea," Dick said, "but one that has failed. As a younger man I often spoke with Mr. Frederick Douglass. I worked for abolition, and after the war I went south to educate and organize the black man, but they were too degraded and not at all appreciative of my work. Let's just say that God was calling me elsewhere. Human slavery is a horrible thing but not as crippling as the yoke of *moral* slavery. Someday we will educate all classes of citizenry on God's freeing moral code for those who are advanced enough spiritually to accept it."

"Dear," Sonja interjected, "the young man looks peaked. It's time we let him dress and breakfast."

"When will my clothes be ready?"

"Come now, Buck. You need your strength, and our breakfast meal is just the thing," Sonja said.

India wanted to scold him, that was plain from the looks she gave him, but he didn't care. Must he take everything at face value here? India's naiveté surprised him.

Once the door closed, he went to lock it but found the lock was broken. He fumbled and rushed into the soft checkered shirt and rustic vest. The loose-fitting trousers made him laugh. He refused to wear the workingman's cap, but his own hat looked out-of-place with the new clothes. The smell of bacon and coffee lured him out. He sighed and pulled the cap on despite his aversion to it.

In the hallway he admired his reflection in the large mirror near the stairs. The cap hid his scar better. India accosted him on the stairs.

"Oh, Buck, you're so dashing in those quaint bumpkin clothes." She giggled, covering her mouth with her small hands.

"You shouldn't laugh," he said, smiling.

"No, I'm being serious. You're handsome." She pulled him closer. "Isn't it exciting? Richard is impressed by you. Iron sharpens iron, he says. I overheard him and Sonja just a minute ago, and you've really won him over."

"I didn't know this was an audition."

"Oh, Buck, you are a hard case—worse than Fred told me—but won't you just listen to Richard's ideas before you dismiss them? I'd really like a friend here."

India, still so pretty even with the mannish hair, kissed his hand, and he laughed.

The two entered the dining hall, and every one of the forty people interrupted their meals to stand and greet Buck and India. Even India blushed. "It's as if they've never seen a handsome young pair," she whispered to Buck, which meant more to him than the welcome.

Richard sauntered over, looking twenty years younger when there was a crowd. He slapped Buck on the back. "Here at Middlemay we're all family."

The enormous breakfast reminded Buck of home but without the hysterics and awful manners. The children sat at a quiet table in the back and were served by the same girl from town they had seen earlier. She seemed happy enough with her job. Buck's attention switched to a table of baked breads dripping with honey and muffins sitting beside Richard's famous preserves glistening in a glass bowl. The Middlemay family had good and expensive taste.

"Everything in this room was donated by an anonymous benefactor," a man at their table said as if reading Buck's mind. "It is so nice to see more young faces. How did the two of you come to be here?"

India waited for Buck to speak first, but spoke when she saw him taken up with the buckwheat pancakes and sausage the girl was now serving. "I've always been ... ashamed of the wealth of my parents," she began, "and on many occasions I've witnessed such a disparity between the rich and the poor in Manhattan. It wasn't fair, and I thought if only we loved those poor hobos and dirty little immigrant children like Christ would, the world could be so much better. I thought the government would do a much better job of leading them out of their backwards ways by now. In fact, it's how I came to be friends with Buck's brother. Fred wants to make the country better through politics. He believes in money being shared more equally. Fred's a silver man, as they say. Why should the big bugs have it all?"

Buck laughed. "Fred said that?"

India ignored him. "My family frowns on women being involved, but I'm certain God wants me to be of service to the less fortunate, and Middlemay is so full of equality and generosity," she explained while buttering a muffin. "I was there when Richard and Sonja presented Middlemay's donation to the library in Greenwich Village. It melted my heart to see how the volunteers were teaching foreign children to read in English. Capitalism is anti-Christian."

"Exactly," an older man in spectacles said, nodding. "Liberty and justice for *all*."

"I hear people grumble about capitalism," Buck said as he grabbed the last of the sausages, "but what's better?"

"Communism, like Christ teaches. Share everything," the man said as if Buck were insane for not knowing. "Remember the apostles in Acts?"

Buck said nothing. His brothers and sisters had always found ways around his mother's order that they share their belongings. The saints of the early church shared voluntarily. Wasn't compelling people to share more like tyranny? He wasn't inclined to debate so took more pancakes instead.

India poured herself and Buck tea. "Buck has an interesting conversion story. First he was wrongly accused of hurting a black cadet at West Point ..."

"You were a military man? We don't condone violence here," the spectacled man pointed out.

"I didn't graduate. I enlisted for a short time but had an accident ..."

India took his hand. "Buck is a real hero. After his conversion he rescued two girls from Indians."

"India, please stop telling people. I just happened to be there," Buck mumbled, pouring more syrup on his pancakes.

A quiet woman said, "We really are family here, Buck. It's obvious that you're here to mend. Sharing your conversion story is a great inspiration to others. We still have our doubts sometimes, and it might help you to talk about it."

"About my conversion?"

"Sometimes it helps to talk," the lady said, making it clear in her unwavering gaze that she would wait.

Maybe it was the feeling of being full and satisfied, or the soft shirt or the gentle prodding of the group at the table, or maybe it was India holding his wrist lightly and pressing him on with her large, wonderful eyes ...

"I've never been a good person. I've been full of jealousies and resentments." He sighed. "I lived through my brother and was a great disappointment to both my parents. I've been cruel and mean through weakness and action. I was especially mean to a cadet—and to a boy back home. I terrorized him my whole life because I was jealous of the way his parents and my father loved him. I thought if only I could be the best cadet or the best Christian, but I wasn't very good at any of it on my own. For a short period when, I was shot by an Indian but saved, I imagined that God had singled me out for a purpose, but now I feel worse because I know there's a God—I have no doubt—but he's abandoned me. I disappointed him or got it wrong somehow."

"Tell us about when you first came close to God," someone asked.

"It was when I was out west with my sister. Thankful sent me to visit her fiancé, and I got shot going after William (the boy I was telling you I bullied). We both ended up at the fort's infirmary, and Willy lay near death for days. There was a missionary there, and I watched him pray so hard for William. He even prayed over me when I pretended to sleep. He read the Bible out loud, and for the first time I was calm enough to really listen. Seth was kind to me. I first just wanted to please him, but then I *really* felt

God's presence in the words." He paused. "But Seth left, and I never heard from him again."

"You can't judge God by his followers."

"Yes, I know," he said. "It was just disappointing to lose a friend—but then maybe he was wanting something from me I could never give. That's what my mother says."

Everyone sat pondering. The spectacled man said, "It's good to read the Bible, but you need someone trustworthy to interpret it for you. Many people get lost doing it on their own."

"At first West Point was perfect, and later I thought the Bible offered simple answers."

The older ones around the table smiled.

"Now I want to meet God directly, and I can't reach Him." No one at home understood his yearnings. The reassuring faces of the elders and the way in which they nodded knowingly at his struggles comforted him.

"Young man, you have a heart for God, and He will never disappoint," another man said. "It doesn't surprise me that He led you here. The stability of Middlemay will be a comfort to you, but more importantly you will experience God's love through so many different people who are on the same journey as you. You will never again doubt God's love for you once you experience life at Middlemay. I was a successful banker before I came here with Anna and our children."

Buck nodded to the woman he took to be the man's wife.

"Oh, no, this is Henriette," the man said. "I sold off everything we owned after spending one evening with Richard. My life has never been the same. Miracle upon miracle. I was in a failing marriage and doomed to pay for my mistake forever. But Richard taught us about how love is in God's kingdom, and Anna and I are much happier now that we don't have to see so much of each other. It's what sin-free living can do."

The bells chimed signaling breakfast's end. The people sang a hymn of thanksgiving. Buck smiled at India.

"Have they assigned you work yet?" India asked him.

"No. You *already* have work?"

"I've told them I'm staying permanently. I don't care if my parents take my inheritance."

Buck took her arm first this morning. He'd imagined doing it all night. "Isn't it a bit rash?"

"Buck," India said, gently pulling her arm from his after spotting Sonja observing them from across the room. "If you knew how much I've prepared myself for this, you wouldn't think I was rash. You'd be proud of my independence."

"I am impressed by you, India, and you are intelligent, I'm sure, but what if this place fails? You'll have nothing to fall back on."

India put her hands on her perfect hips. "That is exactly why I must stay and make certain it doesn't fail. Men can find employment no matter what happens. I'm in bondage to my father. Look, over the kitchen door."

Buck hadn't noticed the large sign "Health, Comfort, Economy and Women's Rights."

"That sign is why I'm here. You have sisters, Buck. Would you want them to be forced into lives they hated?"

Buck shook his head.

Sonja crossed the room at a clip. "I must wrest India from you now, young man."

"Yes, of course—but my clothes?"

"You look very nice, Buck," Sonja said. "Richard has set aside time for you after his morning prayers. Please feel free to walk the grounds or relax in the hammock by the pond. Richard will easily see you from his window when he's ready for you."

Buck wandered down to the pond past a swath of white daffodils. Girls his young sisters' age practiced a country dance in the field beyond as a few boys played their fiddles (not very well). Buck found the hammock —it was probably made from the husks of last year's corn or some such economical thing—and stretched his arms behind his head, dangling a foot off the side to keep himself in motion. That was his problem—always keeping himself in motion. Buck pulled his leg up and crossed it over the other. A toad hummed lazily, and a bee buzzed by, flying off before becoming a nuisance. The water lapped the shore and Buck fell asleep.

*** 

The sun arched over the birches that had shaded the pond in early morning. The warmth and light of midday roused Buck. A small flock of gold chickens clucked in the shade of a berry bush. A window creaked open at the main house, and Richard called to him. "Come sit with me a while."

Buck hadn't decided on anything. It *was* warm out, but he worried about Richard's grim diagnosis of the previous night as he wiped sweat from his brow before waving up at him. An uneasiness settled in his stomach. A girl walked by carrying a basket of strawberries. She tossed Buck one.

"Miss, which door leads to Mr. Rhinedale?" he asked, rolling the strawberry in his hand.

"All doors," she said, laughing. "Richard's the most accessible person you'll ever meet. It's a wonder he ever gets things done."

"What exactly *does* he do?"

"Well," she began, picking a bug from the berries, "he's everyone's caretaker. Like a father ... and he writes and edits the newspaper. Richard spends hours, sometimes days listening to God. Without God sending him, none of this would be here."

She offered Buck more berries, but he declined. The girl showed him the door that led to the circular staircase up to Richard's private study. The upper door opened as he climbed the never-ending stairs, wheezing and ill at ease.

Once on the landing, a breeze from the open windows opposite Richard's desk relieved him. Richard studied Buck's cap with a look of concern at its dampness. "Young man, please take a seat and rest. I saw you out there sleeping all morning and put aside everything to pray for you."

"Thank you, but I'm hardly worth that much effort."

"While we find it hard to understand, God says every one of us is special. I've been called by my Father to spend my days in prayer—as the apostles did in Acts." He flicked through a few pages of his opened Bible.

"I've tried to pray for hours, but always find my mind on other trivial things."

"It's not an easy thing, and only those who've grown enough in the faith should do it. Prayer for the *wrong* thing can send you on a crooked path." Richard paused now, adjusting papers on his desk before casually taking a seat on the couch next to Buck, so close that Buck could see the small blood vessels in the man's eyes. "I see the way you admire your friend, Miss Van Westervelt, and I wouldn't be surprised if you've prayed a small prayer that she'll leave with you."

Buck blushed, looking to the window.

Richard erupted in laughter. "Buck, you're too serious. It's natural to admire the beauty of this world. India is *ravishing*," he said. "God created women as art and more. I sense that your prayers are powerful, and I worry that your prayers will overpower hers and may cause her to go against God's will for her."

"But if everyone is equal, then she should be able to decide for herself."

"Everyone is born *potentially* equal. God revealed to me—through our orchard, of all things, that God gives potential. Some trees blossom, some don't. If two people are called and only one decides to come to God's feast, who will better serve God?"

Buck knew the answer. "Sir, I don't mean to sound disrespectful, but how do you know that God wants India here?"

"By her fruits. She brought you to the place you need to be."

Buck laughed. "Miss Van Westervelt hardly knows me."

"Exactly. How would she know it on her own that God employed her to bring you here to heal and to help usher in a new age?"

Buck cleared his throat. "This is ridiculous."

"That's what Jonah said," Richard continued, showing no signs of frustration. "Are there close people around you that suffer?"

"Yes, of course."

"You'll see after a few days here that it no longer has to be that way. We are in the midst of the beginnings of heaven on Earth. Buck, God sent a message through my wife that you are necessary to Middlemay."

"Sir, I don't understand how I could have *anything* to offer."

"That is *why* God has chosen you. Think of David as a youngster or Joseph when his family despised him. God uses the weak. You know that."

He wasn't sure he liked being described by a stranger as weak or as chosen, but a small part of him liked the idea very much—didn't God use the weak to conquer the strong? His family despised him, and he did happen to save those girls. Maybe he was going to save others. Buck's heart thrilled suddenly at the possibility of purpose though he never would have guessed for it to come through this odd man and community—yet didn't the earliest Christians seem odd? At least he'd be odd with India.

"What would you have me do, sir?"

Richard smiled, and his eyes glistened with emotion. "You are to be *my* apprentice. I will treat you as we all treat each other—as family. My own son, against my judgment, went to Yale Divinity School and lost faith. At first I thought I'd failed him, but God put it on my heart that I was to let go of him for the greater good of Middlemay. As Christ said, *'These are my real family.'* And I believe—this might scare you a little—that you are to replace him ... God provides all things in His goodness. It was as if a bolt of lightning struck last night when Sonja told me that you needed a home. In that very moment I was ready to place a gold ring on your finger and order a feast."

Buck stood up, shaking his head. "Sir, this is a mistake. I only came on a lark."

Richard stood and gripped Buck's shoulders in the rough and fatherly way he had. "And isn't that how God should work? A happy Father sending his children on paths of merriment and joy? Isn't that the Father you always wanted? Struggling under sin and doubt is for those who have no faith. Young man, make no mistake. God has placed you in my hands to bring you to wholeness. Christ's yoke is light. It's now time to enjoy what you've been seeking. Faith has its rewards."

"I want to believe you. I'm so tired," Buck said, sitting again. "But it sounds too good to be true."

An older man brought in tea and milk, poured Buck a cup, and left.

"Some people come here and expect paradise—as they should, but what they fail to realize is that even in paradise there are occupations and expectations. God knows, sometimes I'd rather not be the leader of this undertaking, but there is no one more suitable. Buck, you would be expected to attend Bible study, and there would be chores for you in the field and kitchen—once your strength comes back, of course."

"But my hand is ..."

"Here we do not see imperfection. Where one is weak another is strong. We are the body of Christ, and each has his own strength and weakness. We help each other cheerfully. India tells me you have an allowance from your family."

"Yes, but I'm not sure how India knew of it."

"Never mind that for now. I only ask because you are in no hurry to find work elsewhere then. I have an appointment to attend to in town. Don't get up," Richard said. "There's something about this room that is quite enchanting. Stay and see if you feel it. Here's a pillow. Think about all I've said and pray."

As soon as the old man's footfall faded on the stairs, Buck stood up and studied the titles of the books lining two of the walls from floor to ceiling. Wesley's sermons and a treatise against Calvinist teaching caught his eye. Forced to church his whole life, he had retained only the most elementary knowledge of the history of his faith. The idea of studying under a mentor appealed to him. Hadn't his teachers at West Point recommended academics over the military for him? The breeze at the windows filled the room with the scent of fresh cut grass. Ink spills and blotter paper, along with a well-worn leather Bible and a small angel statue gracing Richard's dark wood desk, charmed Buck.

He imagined writing for the newspaper and discussing theology. Hearing laughter in the yard, he went to the window. Four girls and India sat at a table doing needlework. India stood out as the most beautiful, but the others weren't ugly either. A hawk's shadow from above caused India to glance up and spot Buck.

"Are you trapped in the tower, Buck?" she said with a laugh. "Come join us!"

The others turned their eyes up at him, smiling and waving. Buck closed the curtain, thrilled yet bashful. His sisters' friends at home avoided looking at him after his disfigurement. He found his cap. Again, he spent time before a mirror in the office. The bright red scar on his forehead disappeared under the tweedy hat. The bullet mark on his cheek under his eye was much faded, and he could cover his neck with a scarf.

No, he would have to one day free himself of the scarf, and today—since one wasn't available—would be that day.

He raced down the stairs to be with India. The sunlight blinded him for a moment, and he stood in the yard lightheaded. India came and led him to the table.

"These are our new friends—Molly, Esther, Adeline, and Parmelia."

They smiled coquettishly at him. Buck laughed a little.

"Won't you sit with us a while?" Parmelia asked, adjusting her black and wavy hair into a tiny ponytail which accentuated her pointy features. Her alert, dark eyes stayed on Buck as she unfolded an extra chair, as if they'd been expecting him.

He sat, touching his neck.

"India told us how you saved the girls out west from Indians. You must be very brave."

He smiled, lost for words.

"I'm curious. Dick so rarely allows people into his sanctuary," Parmelia began.

"I didn't break in or anything—he invited me."

"Oh, of course," she continued, leaning toward him. "What did he say to you?"

Adeline stopped stitching. "Parm, you're being nosy."

"*Shush*, you," Parmelia replied lightly.

"But at the last Circle of Improvement you were told that you needed to stop minding other people's business," Adeline said.

"Oh, bother, Adeline. *You* were told to stop taking life so *seriously*," Parmelia replied, rolling her eyes with a smile.

"Sister, I don't recall any such thing."

"Well, next meeting I plan on mentioning it."

Buck hated female bickering. "You two are sisters? You look nothing alike."

"We're all sisters here," Adeline said with a smile just like Sonja's. "We've been here since we were tiny tots."

"Oh, I see," Buck said. "Sonja is your mother, then?"

"Possibly," Adeline said, going back to her stitching. "It's not important to any of us. All of the elders have been our parents."

Buck was quiet.

"Does that make you uncomfortable?" Parmelia asked.

"I just can't imagine my mother giving any of us over to other people's care."

"Uncle Dick says in heaven everything is shared, and so it is here."

He cleared his throat. "Don't you miss having one person who cares for you best?"

India looked up from her needlework. "Buck, your family is large. Were *you* loved best?"

Buck opened his mouth but said nothing, stabbed by her words.

Sparrows and robins chattered in the trees.

"I'm sorry," India said. "I don't know what made me ask such a horrible question."

Parmelia caressed Buck's arm. "He's just the sort a girl would love to take care of, don't you think?"

"Oh, I really am quite well." Buck laughed and coughed.

Parmelia yawned, put her needlework away, and pulled Buck to his feet. "I'm bored with this. Buck, you'll come with me. I'll show you the gardens."

India stood now, forgetting the work on her lap. "Buck and I toured the grounds yesterday."

"Parmelia, we were supposed to get these bags done to sell last week, but you always run off!" Adeline complained.

India saw the opportunity to be needed. "I'll take over for Parmelia if I may."

"That settles it then," Parmelia said. "I'll show you the secret places, Buck."

India gave Buck a nervous look as if something he was doing might affect her chances here. It annoyed him so he gladly sauntered off with the willowy girl dressed in a lavender dress that suited her perfectly.

Adeline stared after them, and Molly and Esther found their voices.

"That Parm is such a creature! No one else would get away with all she does!" Molly whined.

Esther nodded. "It's so unfair. Just because she's Uncle Richard's new favorite!"

India huffed. "Don't mind Buck. He's harmless and out of his league with girls."

"That's not a nice thing to say," Esther scolded.

India craned her neck to see Buck off behind a rose arbor. "Never mind. I don't even think he'll stay."

"If Uncle wants Buck, he'll stay. You'll see," Adeline said.

Parmelia took Buck behind the rose arbor to show him the new plantings and the beginnings of an elaborate fountain to catch the reflection of open sky and summer blooms. She talked of the weather, theology, gossip, and feminism, all the while laughing at her own jokes (and the few Buck attempted). Buck just smiled and smiled. Holding his good hand, Parmelia skipped along to a bench in the shade of a chestnut tree and leaned her head on his shoulder.

"The other girls seemed annoyed at you finishing your work early."

She gave him a droll smile. "I've rescued you from tedious girl squabbling, and this is my reward?"

"I'm sorry, miss."

"You *are* far too *serious*," she said, tickling his chin. "It's just like Uncle Dick says—life is meant to be enjoyed to the fullest. That, Buck, is how we best please God."

"I guess the martyrs saw it differently."

"Do you really want to be a martyr? And who says God was pleased with them? I personally think they were vain."

"The martyrs and saints?"

"*Yesss*. They wanted to be better than everyone," Parmelia replied, stopping to adjust his cap.

"Don't Middlemay people want the same thing?" he asked, pulling away just a little.

"No, that's only the people who are just too stupid to understand. Half the people here are dimwitted followers who think my uncle will erase their sins. If they understood that their sins were already erased by the cross they could be free. But they do try. The girls are just jealous of me because I was picked to be one of Dick's protégés."

He laughed. "What does that mean?"

She looked at him hard. "You really are a babe in the woods." She put her hand to her chest. "I come from *good spiritual stock*. It's expected that I am *spiritually superior* to the others, and so I will receive my training from *the master*. It's Dick's idea, or I should say, the revelation he received from God that good breeding is the key to bringing the kingdom to Earth."

"My father would disagree with that. He's a doctor and delivers every baby he can to the poor in our town."

"I'm sure your father has the best of intentions, but he is doing the world a great disservice. Unwanted and neglected children breed the same and degrade into animals. It's Richard's greatest fear for the Negroes that since they aren't being raised up spiritually one day they'll run the streets like mobs of savages and be worse that their ancestors in Africa."

Buck shook his head. "Everyone deserves a chance. I once knew a black cadet at West Point and ..."

"Did he graduate?"

"No, but neither did I."

"India told us you left to work with the poor out west." She grabbed both of his hands.

He wondered what she thought of the wooden one.

She didn't waste a second on it. "India says you're ashamed of your looks."

He had experienced so many emotions in the past twenty-four hours, he had run out of ways to hide them. "I am."

"Let me tell you a secret. My friends and I think you're very handsome. You'd be too pretty if you didn't have those cuts and scars."

She pulled off his cap and kissed his forehead.

"I don't need your sympathy, miss."

"Attraction and pleasure are from God."

"I know how I look and so did everyone else at home. Suddenly here I'm *transformed*?" he asked with a cynical huff.

"People of the world are blind to beauty, I guess," Parmelia said, with an adorable shrug. "How would I know what they like when I've lived here forever? I don't lie. If it were possible I'd have my first experience with a man like you who has seen the world and turned from it. The men here are ... well ... I don't know." She leaned in again and kissed him.

This time he kissed back and pulled her close. She pulled him even closer. His hands raced over any part of her he could get to. She laughed and kissed him behind his ear.

"Won't you get in trouble?" Buck asked breathlessly.

"Oh, pooh, this feels so delicious!"

"Aren't there rules?"

"All meant to be broken," she replied. "Even my uncle sometimes allows himself hypocrisy. Kiss me again."

Buck complied. This was the best day of his life.

Someone grabbed him by the shoulder, and Buck turned around to find India fuming over them. "I knew you'd get into trouble! How could you?"

Buck straightened his vest and reached for his cap, but Parmelia wouldn't give it back. He laughed.

"This is no joke!" India cried. "This isn't how it's done here. What would Richard say?"

"My uncle would have to admit that passion is his great pleasure and not meant to be denied to any of us, India," Parmelia said. She stood up and kissed India's cheek. "You're perfectly safe. Nothing Buck or I do will affect your admittance. Richard knows what he likes." She paused to look India over "A girl so smart and ready to give herself to others."

India glared at Parmelia until Parmelia laughed and turned to Buck. She kissed him hard and put his cap on his head. "I hope you stay, Buck." Then Parmelia, with a winner's smile directed at India, skipped off.

Buck pulled his cap over his eyes and waited. He had offended India but had no idea why.

"What was that all about?" she asked.

"Kissing?"

"You are very naive when it comes to girls."

"I don't care if I'm naive!" he said with an expansive stretch.

"My father always says that men get into trouble over three things—drink, money, and women."

Buck looked toward Parmelia gathering her needlework. "I'm in no trouble with women."

"*Yet*. I need to know if you plan to stay."

"India, I don't know what to make of you. You care so much about what these people think, and you're so much prettier and smarter. First you want me to stay, and now you seem to want me to go."

"I really thought you'd be more like your brother, but you're so nice. I'm glad you came, but I never did tell you about the rules here, and I'm protective. Fred asked that I'd make sure you were all right."

"Did he?"

"Yes. Frankly I think he was jealous of the attention you were getting over the girls you saved."

"The kiss you gave me this morning—was it for him or me?"

"I only kiss people I want to kiss, and this morning, wrapped in that blanket with your hair all a mess—you were adorable."

He smiled, rubbing his chin.

"But it's different here. I wish I had met you earlier. You may think it's silly, but I truly believe Richard is inspired by God. He has written that knowing someone intimately is the highest art and worship there is."

"That sounds fine to me. I've read the Song of Solomon."

"Yes, well, Richard and the elders say in heaven there is no selfish marriage."

"I suppose that's a good thing."

"Everyone is to share themselves with everyone else."

Buck squinted skeptically.

"It's all for the good of the *community*." She clasped her hands to her chest with a faraway look in her eyes. She paused. Her features hardened then. "When people break off into permanent couples they tend to stifle each other."

Buck hesitated, mulling over India's words. "I guess I sort of looked forward to that."

"My parents aren't happy. Are yours?"

"Most definitely not." He laughed, shaking his head.

"I just hope you don't get scared off by Richard's ideas before thinking them through," India said. "I like you a lot, but I know that I'm still spiritually selfish."

"What do you mean?"

"I was jealous of you and Parmelia."

He was in secret ecstasy. "So what's to be done?"

"Will you stay?" she asked.

He looked out over the field of early grain swaying in the distance. Here he was something already without even trying. Imagine if he tried hard! What was there back in Englewood? Fading memories of a chance rescue. Here he'd learn the Bible's deeper meaning! Every night listening to talks and sermons! Just then under the gazebo, an impromptu concert of Mozart began—how his mother loved Mozart! Buck had been kissed by two different, lovely girls who thought him handsome in some odd way. He'd wear these clothes forever if he could have his way with one of the girls. That wasn't a very spiritual thought, and he glossed over it hoping God really did want him to experience joy and delight.

"Yes, India. I want to stay."

"Then we should speak with Richard tonight and submit ourselves to his guidance in our lives."

# Chapter Eighteen

India and Buck wandered the manicured paths and shady groves of apple trees alight with the last gold of the fading day until the sun slipped behind the blue ridge of mountains to the west. A shower sent them indoors eager for the supper bells. They wandered into a large parlor with windows from floor to ceiling. From them one could see sailboats on a lake beyond the oaks. The diminutive Shetland sheep, brought back by Richard from one of his many travels across the pond to study the rudiments of English agricultural practice, grazed in the emerald-green pasture just a few yards from the mansion. Over the rougher hills one could see rain clouds threatening still.

Buck looked around for food and spotted a small table with teapots and treats. Children lounged, playing chess or reading. A few were at table, finishing their tea and telling secrets in each other's ears. India's cool demeanor betrayed a distaste for children, but Buck who liked them very much, sat at the table and smiled. A small boy ran to the tea table and brought back two cups of greenish tea.

"How did you know I was thirsty, little man?" Buck asked.

The boy shrugged. "It's sage elm tea. I don't like it, so if you finish it we won't have to. It tastes like snot."

India took her cup with trepidation, wrinkling her nose. The children laughed.

"I suppose I'm not fully grown yet," she said with a giggle.

Buck admired her even more.

A girl with long braids gave up her chair and asked to play with India's hair.

"Oh, it's short now," India said with a mix of excitement and regret.

"It's long enough to plait it if you'll let me," the girl said.

India blushed at Buck. "Do you think we're supposed to be here?"

Buck ignored India's concern. "What time is supper?"

The children looked at each other.

"When's supper?" Buck asked again.

"This is it for tonight, sir."

Buck looked at the cheese and crackers in alarm. Raw spring vegetables did not a meal make.

"Sir, would you like my crackers?" the boy asked.

Buck took one with what he thought was cheese and gagged.

India pushed the children aside. "What's wrong, Buck? Is it your throat?"

Regaining his composure, Buck made her sit. "What is *this*?"

Just then a small, thin man with a faint, forced smile entered from behind a swinging door.

"Children, quiet time is over. You may go outdoors."

A ruckus ensued with shouting and racing for the door.

"I'm so sorry to have interrupted their time," India said.

The man cleared the table in front of him.

"It's my week to be their companion in the evenings, but it's not one of my spiritual gifts."

"Did we miss supper for grown-ups?" Buck asked. "Or is today a fasting of some sort?"

India gave him an impatient look.

"We don't have a formal supper at Middlemay," the man informed them. "Women here have so many interests there's no time to waste in the kitchen. Breakfast is our main cooked meal, and we take turns making it."

"I wish I would have known that earlier," Buck grumbled as his stomach growled. He came from a family of big people, and one meal just didn't suffice. The slight man and the way he looked so smugly at them for being starved did not impress Buck. "I'm not good at fasting," he complained.

"You are good at showing your displeasure," the thin man said.

India spoke up. "Please forgive him. His family is used to getting their way in all things."

Buck stared at her disloyalty.

"Well," the man said as he brushed the cheesy spread onto one plate, "God has ways of showing us to be grateful. I'm sure you won't take food for granted anytime soon."

"Do I look like I overeat?" Buck asked.

"No, but your anger over missing one small meal is something you might want to pray about," the thin man said with raised brows.

Buck laughed, assuming India saw the lunacy of the man's stance.

"It's one meal, Buck," she said. "Breakfast is only hours away."

With an impatient grunt, the man took pity on them. "Well, I can make you a small plate of vegetables and bread."

"What about a little meat?" Buck asked.

"We don't eat meat except in the mornings sometimes and on special occasions."

"Why not?"

"In Genesis, in the garden, man ate fruits and vegetables and was satisfied."

"The problem was that Adam and Eve *weren't satisfied*," Buck began.

"Well, they were vegetarians anyway." The thin man wiped his spectacles. "Richard allows that the occasional bit of meat is probably necessary for health reasons—though Richard says that too much concern over one's physical well-being is ungodly. It's been my experience that with meat-fasting and a contrite spirit more aggressive men like yourself are quite tamed after about a month."

Buck huffed. A door slammed behind them and Sonja appeared. "Children, here you are in the baby room! We've been looking for you."

"Ma'am, is it true you don't eat meat?" Buck had never been overly concerned with food before. Maybe he *had* taken his nourishment for granted.

Sonja looked as if his question disappointed her in some way, but then she smiled. "Come with me, and I'll find you something nice to eat. This is all very new to you, and you've not had time to learn our ways. Most ills are caused by lack of spiritual strength, but a tall young man like you from the outside still needs a protein meal to build back up from your injuries. A *kind* God would expect us to pamper you until you are mended."

Buck hardly heard what she said except that he would get a meal. The possibility of skirting the rules brought him an old thrill. He mimicked the thin man's smug smile on the way out.

India whispered to him, "Fred didn't tell me you were such a spoiled child!"

"I'm sure there's tons of things Fred didn't tell you."

"And there's plenty you don't know about Fred yourself!"

"What's that supposed to mean?"

Sonja finished her chat with another woman and turned back to them. "Surely I don't hear any bickering, *children.*"

"Ma'am ..." Buck began, but India pinched him hard.

The trio walked on in silence until they stood outside Richard's room, Buck straggling on the stairs.

India looked back in sympathy now and waited on the landing after Sonja opened the door. "I'm sorry, Buck."

"There's nothing to be sorry about."

He wheezed as he joined India outside the door. The two walked in together.

Richard greeted them with warm embraces and signaled them to sit.

"And how are we faring so far?"

India sat on the edge of her seat. "Oh, I love it here," she said, "but I have so much to learn. I believe God brought Buck and me together here to test my patience and resolve."

Richard laughed.

"Buck, you're not as enthusiastic. Am I correct?"

"Sir, I'm just hungry, and there are so many rules I don't understand. I don't mind rules if I understand what they're for."

"Sonja, get this man steak."

"Well, I don't want her to go to any trouble," Buck said, but his eyes lit.

"Young man, you came here completely ignorant of Middlemay. I would not expect you to understand everything at once. Revelations come over time for most. Even I have grown in understanding God's will."

"I understand that animals shouldn't suffer cruelty, but I can't imagine not eating them, sir."

"Buck, I eat meat whenever I like because it does not control my moods. Others here decided that God was unhappy with the way they made an idol of their food. A few women here were spectacular cooks, and their talents inflicted an unhealthy passion over others. They decided with my guidance to abolish fancy cooking and meat not as a penance but as an act of liberation from something that kept them from God."

"I thought we were supposed to live with joy."

"Young man, if it has not been placed on your heart to give up meat, then you should still eat it. Some of us do, but it's good to let the others have their way sometimes."

Sonja brought in a plate of plain potatoes and butter with a large helping of thinly sliced beef. The meat was rare and laced with glistening fat. She placed it before Buck on a small table.

They watched Buck take his first bite.

"I can't do it," he said, laying the fork aside. "I really was very impatient with the man over at the children's room, and I was short with India. I'm sorry. I never realized I was so attached to good food." He eyed the steak longingly as Sonja took it away, placing it on Richard's desk.

Richard sat next to Buck. "Look how God is working in you, here."

"Sir, pardon me for saying this, but even though you may be right, I feel a certain uneasiness about Middlemay."

"Buck, do you believe in Satan?"

"I think so. Yes."

Sonja moved behind the back of the couch, massaging Richard's shoulders until he shrugged her off. "Sonja, coffee, please. Buck, I am a very well-educated man. My parents sent me to school in England until I was ready to enter Yale. My mind is quite strong. I can say this without conceit because God gave me my intelligence and wisdom to help usher in the kingdom. But it has been a burden also to constantly see the contradictions and complexities of life in this modern age.

"When I was a little older than you I fell into a nervous prostration consistent with someone who ruminates too much and in doing so separates himself from the physical world which God has given us to enjoy. It was revealed to me on a cold, dark night at my mother's that I was under a satanic attack. The Devil, with the help of my undisciplined intellect, was using my thoughts to blind me to the simple yet magnificent truths of the Bible and of life.

"You have been given a strong mind, evidenced by your questioning mentality, but be careful that you are not giving yourself over to Satan's wily ways. I have the sense about you that you hold yourself superior to the average man."

Buck tried to disagree, but Richard held his hand up and continued. "I say this not to insult you, but as a father would do to his own son to prevent him from missing the meaning of his existence. Your pride will make it impossible for God to work in you the great things he has planned. Do you remember when you first experienced God, my son?"

"Yes. It was in the West."

"Do you feel that same closeness now?"

"No. I can't get back to it no matter how I try."

"You are a good man, Buck, but you need proper guidance and someone to push you toward pleasure. I was just telling Sonja that this part of the country is far too prim for its own spiritual good."

Sonja brought in coffee and cakes. They all partook, but Buck was careful to only enjoy a small bit (the steak still sat upon the desk).

"Sir ..."

"Please, call me Dick, for we are to be almost equals someday."

"Yes, I'd like to maybe stay on," Buck said, "but I just don't know how you can help me."

Sonja and Richard smiled lovingly, as if they truly cared about his well-being. Richard got up and walked to his books. "I will show you how to study with vigor, but also how to enjoy life with vigor," he said, pounding his fist into his hand for emphasis. "Your mind needs a plan, a destination, or we are mired in confusion. Do you see how Satan uses that against you?"

"Yes. I'm trapped in indecision."

"Then here tonight you are one of us if you choose," Richard said.

India nudged Buck. She was terribly beautiful under the gaslight and with the small bit of color the outdoors had afforded her that day.

"I'll stay, but only if my friend India does."

Richard frowned. Sonja tsk-tsked.

"India, has already made it clear that she is staying, but Buck, you must realize that here intimacy is a guided thing," Richard said. "It is a spiritual path not entered into without proper training from the elders."

Buck half-listened.

"Just as you will study theology with me, Buck, you will learn self-control and the sexual joy that comes with it from Sonja," Richard said.

"I have no interest in India, sir," Buck lied. This frank talk was so unusual to him—unless it came in its most profane way from Fred and the other boys at West Point. Hadn't they all snickered reading *Aristotle's Masterpiece* and *Fanny Hill: Woman of Pleasure* until the well-worn books were discovered by a prim officer and thrown in the rubbish?

"You understand that in the kingdom all men and women will share their love with the whole society," Sonja said, rubbing Buck's shoulder now. "You look surprised, and, to tell you the truth, the notion shocked me when Richard first brought it up *after* we married."

Buck nodded. "Sir, it would have been fairer to tell her *before* you married."

"God's inspiration comes when it comes, friend."

"It took me a while to warm up to the idea, but Dick and I were such good friends, and I believed so strongly that he was inspired by God that I gave him my entire inheritance to buy this property. My family continues in their support to this day."

Buck wondered if Sonja's family would have been grateful to anyone who might marry a lady so resembling a vulture.

"Do you love each other?" India asked.

"Not in the little girl way you imagine. Romantic love as we know it is a construct of a society meant to make young people swallow the poison of lifetime captivity. We are spiritual partners, Sonja and I. We care for each other deeply, but we are not in love."

Sonja stopped patting Buck's shoulders and gathered the coffee mugs.

"What about adultery?" Buck asked.

"Read your Bible, son. Jesus tells the Pharisees that there are no marriages in heaven."

Buck rubbed his forehead. "I'm not sure I'm ready for this."

"That's fine, because we never let the young folk experience communal love until they've been properly trained and are spiritually ready. Don't worry. The elders have much experience in this regard. I can assure you that when the time is right you will understand that intercourse is the highest form of art and praise."

Buck blushed. "I'm not comfortable with this talk in front of India."

"The world has turned intimacy into something to be despised and ashamed of. Women are supposed to hide their natural urges," Richard began.

"I don't want to hear about that."

"Buck, listen to him," India said.

"You are tainted by the world, Buck. To be ashamed of the sexual organs is to be ashamed of the most perfect gifts of love and unity. It will be a pleasant journey to joy and fulfillment with the opposite sex if you take the time and the chance to open yourself up to the real way God intended. As I was saying, women, if treated properly, will respond to your touch like piano keys to a virtuoso."

Buck's face burned, but India looked perfectly at ease. How could she consider such sinful ideas?

Richard stared at him for a long time. "Son, confess to me how many times you've been with a woman."

"Sir, never." Buck sat straighter.

"This is your full confession then?" Richard asked, unconvinced.

Buck could not tell by the mild, almost amused look on Richard's face if the old man was surprised or disappointed.

"I was saving it for marriage. My parents got married to avoid an embarrassment."

"I see. And are you responsible for their unhappiness?"

Buck hesitated. "No."

"Here there are no bastard children. We love them all as our own. Just think if your parents had been a part of Middlemay."

Buck tried to imagine it and laughed.

"Your parents expressed love to each other and were punished for it by the world and then expected to stay with each other *forever*. Just because I love peaches best doesn't mean I might not sometimes want a plum."

"So you think adultery is a fine thing?"

"Here at Middlemay there is no need of such talk because the goal is for all of us to love one another by giving and receiving freely."

Buck laughed again. "So you mean that one day I may have relations with anyone I want?"

"With guidance, you will spread your love to everyone."

"And the children that come of it? Who will take responsibility?" Buck asked, imagining his own lonely childhood, always wanting time with his parents and never getting quite enough.

"You saw the children in the Children's Room. We are parents to them all." Dick lit a cigar. "Some of us are too busy for children, but some want to care for them directly. It is their choice. My own son—the youngest—knows I am his father, but he's struck up a true friendship with a simple farmer. One day he'll grow more vegetables than I'll ever care to eat. The boy has a say in his own life and all sorts of people to hug on. Isn't that love?"

India wrung her hands nervously. "Richard, Parmelia mentioned something about a selection process when it comes to babies."

Sonja's face lit up. She quit her hovering and pushed in to sit beside India. "Oh, let me tell you the exciting plans we have. With the right guidance from God we can produce children endowed with higher spiritual gifts and better health—though the spirit is the most important. It's why we have the mentoring program. A young man like Buck would need much more spiritual training with the elders before we would allow him to breed."

"This sounds very strange. I've always imagined being married."

"You would still be married in a way, but you would have freedom to partake of all the fruits in the field," Richard said. "So many children are born into families who don't really want them—despise them, in fact." He watched Buck squirm under his seeking eyes. "Have I hit a nerve, Buck? For that I'm sorry, but here every child comes from the best adults—physically, mentally, and most importantly spiritually. Imagine a childhood perfectly in tune with God and humanity—no physical or emotional limitations—a heaven on earth. Perfect love manifest."

"And the girls don't mind?"

Sonja smiled. "Why would they? If they choose to be intimate with a man they are assured he will be well-trained in how to please her—as she will be in pleasing him. If she wants a baby, and the community agrees it would be a proper and good match for breeding, then she produces the baby. When it's done she is free to follow other pursuits, confident that her child is being well-cared-for. If she doesn't want a child, then the men are trained in how to prevent it from happening. This is where we more mature women come in. We will teach you."

"How do you teach us? With books?" Buck asked.

Richard sighed. "Enough information for tonight, young people. Buck, I want you to really think hard about the people you know who are married. Are they being rewarded for their suffering? Is that the sort of God you hope exists?"

Sonja took Buck's hand. "I'll show you to your permanent room. Richard has prescribed a massage to help with sleep, and someone waits for you."

"I'd prefer no massage, ma'am."

"Son," Richard said sternly. "When will you let your guard down for God?"

Buck had nothing to say. He looked to see if India seemed concerned. She shrugged and waved as Sonja led him out.

The ancient woman waiting in Buck's room startled him. They stood in silence for a moment assessing each other. A sudden exhaustion hit Buck again. The old lady led him to his bed. Buck hesitated. He liked old people and didn't want to offend her, but dreaded the touch of her hands. She motioned for him to roll on his belly. He did this uneasily, but once her rubbing began, his tense shoulders relaxed. Touch at home was rare and deeply frowned upon since late childhood. Buck wrestled with mixed feelings of enjoyment and repugnancy. The old lady knew none of this and sang a sweet hymn Buck had never heard before. The massage and song quieted his mind, and as the old lady closed the door behind her he lay in peace.

He rolled onto his back with a contented sigh. How strange life was! He closed his eyes, enveloped in comfort and tranquility. Here his past and the hunted feeling he'd lived with since childhood waited but at a distance as he drifted to sleep.

The door opened and India let herself in.

"Dear Buck, tucked in for the night. You truly are adorable."

"Wait! I've not been trained. You had better leave before the headmaster finds out."

India frowned and sat at the edge of Buck's bed. "You may laugh at Richard and his ideas, but he makes strong points. Do you think it's possible to be attracted to more than one person at once?" She ran her finger along Buck's forearm.

"No ... one person is enough," he said, the idea of sharing India ignited a jealousy he hadn't expected. Why must she touch him and visit him deep in the night when his conscience was in a sleepy state? Nothing good ever came after midnight—or so said his mother. Buck and Fred had been birthed at precisely 12:01.

India tilted her head skeptically. "My parents were in love a long time ago, but now the fire has died between them, and they live in perpetual boredom and disdain for each other. I don't want that for myself."

"Maybe they need to find common interests."

"People *always* say that," she complained. "Do you believe it?"

"I want to. My sister and I enjoyed many of the same things—like music and playing in the woods. I'd hoped to find a girl like that."

"I love the sea," India said.

"I *hate* it," he snapped back. "The chance at perfecting oneself here *is* interesting, but I'm unsure about the sparking part."

"You're such a prude for a boy." She cupped his face in her hands. "It's so funny that Fred is your brother."

"Men should be respectful of women," he said. "It's the one thing my mother asked of me that I've been able to do."

"If you understand respect as ignoring a lady's *sexual desires*, using polite language and relating only the simplest of ideas to me as a means to protect or cage me, then that's not respect but condescension." India was militant.

He pulled himself up against his pillows, his blissful rest over. "Are you accusing me of something?" When women woke him in the night at home it never went well. "Fleshly desires should be private. Sharing them with all and sundry cheapens the whole thing. I'm not sure why you're here at this hour. Would you want to hear every crass thing that floats through a man's mind?"

"Fred tells me everything," she said. "He considers me an equal friend."

"Then he's fooling you. Fred considers no one his equal."

"Fred already has a mistress from Trenton."

"Oh, no," he said. "Poor Rose. Fred is such a rascal. I hope one day he gets what he deserves."

"Why do you have sympathy for Rosie?" she pouted. "She's a fool, and she loves Fred for the wrong reasons."

"What are the right reasons?"

"Goodness, for one." She touched the hair at his temple.

He wondered if India had had many lovers, and it bothered him, but he enjoyed the sensation of her hand on his skin (it was better than the massage even).

"You seem so sweet and naive, Buck."

"Well, I'm not," he replied indignantly. "I've traveled and done all sorts of appalling things. It's why I even consider staying here. I've no other place to go for penance and improvement. You think you understand Fred and me, but you don't. You're the naive one. Just because you have new ideas about love and freedom doesn't mean you're better than me, but flirting with every man—even Richard—will land you in trouble. It's time you leave me alone."

She stood up in shock. "What have I done to bring this dark side of you out? Fred warned me, but I wanted to believe the best in you—and I shall. *It's the Christian thing to do.* I don't *flirt* with everyone. You're jealous because Richard sees something *special* in my spirit."

Buck laughed. "It's your *spirit* he admires?"

"How dare you turn something I'm excited about into something trivial!"

"If you didn't worship Richard like an idol ..."

She moaned in exasperation and opened the door with a violent and dramatic swing. "Fred told me how jealous and small you could be. Now I see it. You don't like me being interested in gaining knowledge from Richard."

"It's not *knowledge* he wants to give you."

"For someone so pious, Buck, you have a mean outlook on people."

"I know more about men than you do."

"You *know* more about Crenshaw men. That I give you," India said. "But Richard is different, and maybe you will learn something from him. I don't know why I ever considered you a friend." She lingered at the door.

"We've only known each other a couple of days, India. I don't like girls who try to play with a man's heart."

"Fred already told me. Crenshaw men have no heart," she replied, satisfied with a cutting remark. She slammed the door, but it popped open so she slammed it again.

"Good job!" Buck shouted. He got up and paced. Why was he fighting with her? What did any of this matter? He took a drink of water and rubbed the wound on his forehead. "Damn it to hell."

Someone knocked now and before he could reply to it the door opened and Sonja entered. Buck stood in his union suit at a loss for the intrusion.

"I saw India in the hallway, crying."

He rolled his eyes. "I suppose I was cruel to her, but she thinks she knows everything! I'm not sure this place is for me."

Sonja nodded with a smile. "If it wasn't for the dream I had about you, I would agree. You are far too confrontational for Middlemay."

"I'm not confrontational!" he shouted, his voice breaking like an adolescent's.

Sonja directed him toward the bed. Buck complied, covering himself in the sweet smelling quilt. He'd steal it when he left.

"I see you've had a rough time in life and ..."

"Oh, please stop," he moaned. "Even I'm getting sick of hearing that! I just want a normal, quiet life. I wanted to serve God, but He keeps setting obstacles. I'll leave in the morning if someone can ever find my clothes."

"Where will you go to find this *normal* life?" she asked, her doubt dripping with compassion. "What sort of work will you do?" Her eyes teared up, and she sighed as if he meant the world to her. She took a candy from her pocket and tossed it to him. He wasn't going to take it, but it was caramel—his favorite.

"I don't need to work. My father has given me his inheritance," he said with his mouth still full of candy.

"That's quite a burden, isn't it?" She handed him the rest of her candies.

He glanced up and unwrapped another. "Yes, it is a bit, though many people wouldn't mind such a burden."

"Do you harbor guilt?"

"Hmm, a little. It's more that I don't have the faintest idea how to use the money for good. *I'm* not particularly good."

"The girl I saw with red eyes down the hallway thinks you can be."

"Why should I care what *she* thinks? She has her eyes on a bigger prize than me. I'm sorry, ma'am. I forget that Richard is your husband, I ..."

"I forget it sometimes too," Sonja said with a sigh. "Yet Dick knows best about most things having to do with the divine. He has helped so many people come to God. When I look at all he has accomplished for the kingdom of heaven, my small complaints seem ridiculous." She tucked him in as if she were just folding laundry.

"Ma'am, are you all right?" he asked when the sheets became excessively tight.

Sonja's eyes misted. "See, you are a sensitive soul. I'm just a little melancholy tonight. Feelings pass, young man. I'll be right as rain in the morning. Do you have any questions before I go?"

"Yes, one. Is it wrong to want just *one* person to love?"

"It's natural to have an affinity for some over others, but natural isn't always best. Once we had a man in our midst who believed that defecating in the hallway was natural. But I digress. Where in the Bible does it say to love just one person? When that happens we tend to put that person before God."

"But then why love anyone at all if God wants so much love for himself?"

Sonja stood, resting her hands on her ample hips. "Your version of God sounds awful selfish."

"Do you love Richard best?" he asked, tossing the candy wrappers on the table beside him.

She gathered them up with an amused look. "What if I said in this moment I liked you best?"

"You'd be lying," he said uneasily. "Don't all women want one sweetheart?"

"You are so young it breaks my heart. It's been a while since I've talked to an outsider your age. I'd almost forgotten what they're like."

"Pretty ordinary, I'd say," he replied. Her cow-like eyes brought up in him a sudden deep sympathy for her. "Do you ever wonder if Richard is using you—for your funds—and not loving you?"

Her gentle face went red and her strong eyebrows set lower now. "Don't speak of Richard that way in my presence. God directs all things, and He has directed me to be Richard's helpmate. I am honored to be at the side of someone so close to God."

"I'm very sorry," he said, though he really wasn't. "I didn't mean to insult you. I just wondered why you couldn't find God for yourself."

She choked back something in her throat and tucked his arms more tightly beneath the blankets. He was trapped in the cocoon. She touched his head for fever.

"Ma'am, you're touching the sore on my head, please stop."

Sonja withdrew her hands, looking pensively out the window lit by the moon and stars. "God didn't design men and women to be exclusive. It's a faulty reading of the Bible and a reliance on the Jewish Old Testament that keeps us trapped. Richard says the time is close—even slowly coming to fruition now— that will bring the full revelation of God's love to earth. I'm excited about that. Loving each other fully and with no boundaries is how we find God."

"Is that what you accept as true?"

"Read 1 John. We are told that how we love others defines us as Christians. At first I was resistant as you are. But in time—I saw my love for what it was—selfish and controlling—satanic."

He guffawed. "*Satanic?*"

"I wouldn't laugh at the evil one." Sonja played with the small brooch at her neck. "I was keeping my husband and my child for myself and keeping them from spreading their love in the world. Richard secretly blames me for our only son together deserting Middlemay. Wilbur was too influenced by me in the early years and could never adjust to our extended family and being separated from me."

"I love my mother, dearly," Buck said, averting his eyes to hide the conflict in his wishful words. Could his mother have been saved the misery of her children's disappointing lives if they had all been raised communally? Buck remembered his mother's dismal attempts at finding a useful hobby to fill her time, with Father so frequently away. Nothing the children did satisfied her. Mama played the piano but never allowed herself to fully enjoy it. Buck always loved seeing her face relax as she played when she thought she was alone. If she had had the chance to find love among many men ... but he still didn't want to accept that monogamy was not God's purpose for him, though married people presented a sad commentary on the institution.

"I understand how you love your mother. Now imagine you could love the people God sends you in such a way that you really bring them joy and in doing so reap that joy for yourself," Sonja said rapturously, "and imagine that in doing this you will also feel God."

"When do *you* feel God?"

Her face was full of longing, but it changed with a sudden put-on expression of contentment. "When I laugh. When I don't take it all so seriously." She patted him through the blanket. "There was a lady here once—she died tragically attempting to chop wood with the men. Chopped her leg open and bled to death."

Buck sat up, pulling himself free from the bedding.

"Her name was Anne. I confess I disliked her intensely because she was the first woman Richard shared himself with after the revelation he had. We both agreed that our sharing time was ... messy and unfulfilling. Have you ever read about the saints called to marriage but not intimacy?" she asked, her eyes bright as if their stories gave her hope. "Sharing herself was Anne's great gift to Middlemay. She was revolutionary, breaking all of our boundaries. There wasn't a single man she didn't share herself with, and all the men loved her mightily in return."

Buck's mind whirled with unspiritual thoughts as he tried to hold a sudden urge to laugh.

Sonja didn't notice, so caught up in her memories. "You are too affected by the world's view of women to see how inspirational she was to everyone here. Even the children loved her in their way—she was the school teacher. Not a selfish bone in her body. I decided once to make her a dress out of my best fabric (I'd been hiding it to make something special for myself, hoping to entice Richard). I presented it to her on her birthday, and I'll never forget what she said in front of the entire community. Anne told me I was filled with a conniving spirit, that I had hidden the luxurious fabric which could have been used for Middlemay's greater good in order to pridefully present her with a thing she could never in good conscience wear. She sat me down as I cried and led me to confess to the others that I had selfish intentions while making the dress. Everyone agreed that I tried too hard to receive love instead of giving without expecting things in return. And they were right. I had been blind to a major flaw in myself. I decided that day to let Richard's revelation take a foothold in my heart. I stopped giving gifts until I was able to do so without expectation of friendship and opened myself to the possibilities that might arise."

"It was nice that you gave the woman a gift and poor manners on her part to say anything but thank you."

Sonja shook her head, obviously pained by his words. "I tell you this because God often lets others be his mouthpiece. You have to open yourself to that. When the elders voted that I should have the honor of training the young men in how to share love it was because I had finally proven to God that I was capable of becoming unselfish."

His eyes wandered up to the ceiling, his ears burning at her words.

"It all starts with being able to control your own desires in order to give the other pleasure. Pleasure is from God through us." She rubbed his leg. "Let me bring you pleasure right now."

He pulled away. "Ma'am, I ..."

"Please call me Sonja. There is no age in heaven. Now relax. Open yourself to the riches of God."

"I'm not sure I can so easily get over my old ideas about ..." he began, but Sonja touched him in a way that he had only touched himself before yet this time no tumult of guilt came upon him.

"Close your eyes, Buck. Let me satisfy a need in you."

Buck wanted to resist until he had time to work things through, but his unfocused mind and the touching overpowered him. She opened her blouse to reveal an uncorseted body. It was old, but it was soft and available to him. He grabbed her, and she stopped his awkward hands and led them to where and how she wanted to be touched. He had no thoughts now— just energy and a rush of profound pleasure.

When she was done showing him a side of God he had been ignorant of, she kissed his forehead, turned out the light beside his bed and was gone. He lay sleepily for a few minutes until his conscience called. Technically they hadn't done anything wrong. It wasn't exactly sex, since aside from a little mindless rubbing he did nothing for her. There was no entering—*was he really having these thoughts?* Was he rationalizing a great evil? How old was Sonja? What would things be like in the morning?

But what if she was right about love and God? In the last two days he'd experienced a lot of pleasures and maybe God finally wanted that for him. Maybe God wasn't like the men at West Point or in the big old church on the hill in Englewood with all of its pompous congregants pretending to love while gossiping about each other between hymns. He was *those* people. His father read at services, and they all went to Sunday school. Buck and Fred had tortured William there. At West Point Buck tried to be a gentleman but almost killed a cadet, and why? Because that cadet had needed help, and Buck was unwilling to stand up for him. Wasn't it clear that all of his scars and sores were deserved because he had been selfish and unloving?

He remembered what Richard said. God had sent him here to be healed. Could love be easier and freer?

Buck sighed and put his hands over his chest, alone with the beat of his heart.

# Chapter Nineteen

Buck awoke before the roosters and wrote home:

*Dear Mama,*

*I have arrived safely at Middlemay and plan to visit for a few days, for it is very peaceful and I think good for my health. I have done many things to disappoint you, and I am sorry. I remember when I loved you best in the world. Only yesterday did I recall those awkward times you tried to teach me the piano, when all I wanted to do was listen to you play. I am sorry I had no talent for it. I wish I would have told you how I admired your skill back then, and I hope one day you will play for me again.*

*Love always your son,*

*Buck Crenshaw*

Buck folded the letter and put it in his pocket, humming a tune he'd heard the previous evening when a group of boys serenaded the girls under their windows. He slipped his cap on and glanced in the mirror. What would Fred say?

Today was Tuesday. What did people do here on Tuesdays? The smell of baking bread and the clatter of dishes led him to the kitchen. He poked his head in, and Parmelia, wearing the same basic uniform as the other women but wearing it better with dangling earbobs and a matching lilac ribbon in her hair, spotted him. He luxuriated in her flowery perfume when she rushed up and dragged him in.

"Sonja didn't tell us we'd have an extra hand," she began and rolled her eyes. "That was an unfortunate choice of words, yet perfectly accurate. Do you forgive me?"

"No need to apologize," Buck said, drunk on her dark beauty.

"I didn't apologize," she said, poking his middle. "I just asked if you forgave me—a little Christian test." She pulled him close, whispering in his ear, "What shall I make your hand do for me?"

Buck's family refused to let him do much of anything.

Parmelia grabbed a basket full of silverware and hung it on his arm. "There you go—set the silverware."

Buck laughed again for no real reason and pushed through to the dining room. Huge bouquets of brilliant red tulips sat upon each table. The sun's early rays lent a rosy tone to the room. He sat for a moment enjoying the peace of the quiet room. Above a large stone fireplace hung a group portrait of the community. Smaller likenesses littered the mantel top. He walked over, trying to see in the faces evidence of God's presence in their lives. The man in charge of children came in pushing a cart with clean plates, his face turning grim when spotting Buck at the fireplace.

"Do you mind setting the silver so I can do my job before everyone arrives?" he asked.

"I'm sorry. I love pictures," Buck said. "So you finally got moved to the grown-up tables?"

"How long have you been here? A day?" the thin man replied, seeing no humor in silverware not set. "I do plenty of work here, and I do it on time. Will you please set the silver?"

"Of course." Buck refused to let this one man (who obviously wasn't one of the spiritual giants) get the best of him. If Middlemay was something close to heaven, how had it produced such a sour man?

Buck placed a fork, knife, and spoon on the table. The man adjusted the setting with a grunt.

"Sir, do you enjoy living here?"

"That's none of your concern," he replied, waiting with plate in hand as Buck fumbled with a knife and fork. The man sighed pushing the knife a little to the right. "It's just frustrating to do work so unsuitable to me. I was promised a stay at the paper. I'm a good writer, but my wife Rebecca doesn't want me to work with her."

"*You're* married?" Buck said, sounding too surprised.

"Yes, why wouldn't I be?"

Buck opened his mouth but had nothing to say.

"My wife is extremely satisfied with our sharing, I'll have you know—although we share with others. One day she'll see."

Buck moved ahead intent on setting the silverware quickly and perfectly.

"That girl you were with yesterday," the man began as he caught up to him, "is she staying?"

"India Van Westervelt? Yes, she is."

"Do you hold any claims on her?"

"I don't hold claims on anyone, sir."

"Then you may enjoy your time here. I blame my wife for everything—getting us involved in this place. I'm as Christian as the next man, and I've been wrongly accused. If my wife wasn't such a favorite amongst the elders I could convince her to leave with me."

"But why would you want to leave? Everything seems so easy. Setting tables and minding children isn't that bad, is it?"

"It wouldn't be if they were my own children. Seeing my wife's resemblance in some of them that aren't mine is galling. And the women here are stuck on themselves, however plain they appear. It's Richard who's jealous and turns them on me."

Parmelia came up and tugged Buck away. "I've come to rescue you from old sour-puss."

Buck wanted to hear more of what the man was saying and pulled back. "I'm not done with the silver."

"Richard wants you in his office before breakfast."

"Please tell me I won't miss the meal. I'm starved!" Buck said, but followed her down the hall.

Once on their own, Parmelia came close. "Has your training with Sonja begun?"

"What do you mean?"

"Oh, your eyes betray you, Buck. You know exactly what I mean. What was it like to touch the old crow?"

Buck shoved his hands in his pockets. "It's bad form to talk about people behind their backs."

"Oh, how noble of you," she said, bowing before him, "but everyone knows about it already, and it will be discussed at the Circle of Improvement."

"What on earth are you talking about?" His palms sweated in mortification. "Nothing happened."

"You lie. Richard will be disappointed that you're humiliated by Sonja and deny knowing her."

"I don't *know* her! How dare you insinuate that I had relations with ..."

"Well, something happened, Buck. It always does with the ones they want to groom for leadership. It's nothing to be ashamed of. You knew before deciding to stay what people do here—didn't you?"

He stopped and adjusted his cap.

"You *didn't* know?" She dropped her head to peek at his eyes beneath the cap, grinning. "Oh bully, you *are* in for *fun* then. How surprised were you when the knock came?"

He laughed in relief. "I was flabbergasted."

Parmelia giggled at his choice of words. "Oh, the tales I could tell you."

"*Tell me*," he urged.

"Uncle Dick awaits. Be happy. He likes you. You'll be treated as royalty for a while. And Aunt Sonja was all smiles this morning at the women's Bible study."

"I promise I did nothing to her."

"If Sonja's happy. Richard's happy. They're all crazy!" Parmelia threw her hands up in the air, laughing.

"If they're crazy, then why do you stay?"

"Where ever would I go? This is my family, and the world is even more lost. Everyone falls short of the glory of God." She stood at the bottom of Dick's staircase, giving Buck a flirtatious wave and wink. In Buck's search for Christian perfection he had disciplined his mind to avoid leering at beauty for fear of offending God (and because he was afraid of seeing repulsion in girls' eyes), but today a flood of physical sensations and urges left him breathless and giddy— even a little shocked. He let himself imagine Parmelia beneath her dress and had to stop halfway up the stairs to collect himself.

"Are you all right?" she asked, staring up from below.

"I'm quite all right, thank you," he said with a smile.

"I like you *a lot*, Buck Crenshaw," she said in a loud whisper, throwing him a kiss.

The office door opened, and Parmelia disappeared. Richard led Buck in.

"How are you feeling today, Buck?"

He blushed. "I feel very well."

"Already, son, you have more color. Give me your arm." Richard took out his pocket watch and rested his fingers on the veins at Buck's good wrist. "Hmm. Still room for improvement. A cup of sage tea and a solid siesta each afternoon for you. Were you up late last night?"

Buck squirmed. "Not very, sir."

"How was your massage?"

"I didn't mean for anything to ..."

"That old girl has been giving back massages for years with good results."

Buck had forgotten *that* massage. Was it only last night?

"Oh, it was nice. Sir, what should I be doing for work?" Perspiration ran down his face.

"Son, I don't like the way your skin glistens this moment. It speaks of some nervous complaint."

"I have no nervous complaint, though everyone tries to accuse me of it," Buck said, pulling a handkerchief from his pocket.

"So your condition is well documented among your friends and family?" Richard noted, taking a book and then another from his shelf.

"I misspoke, sir."

"No one misspeaks. It's what your soul longs to confess." Richard turned his cool, appraising eyes upon Buck.

"Sonja ..." Buck began, wiping his clammy hands on his trousers, "she came to visit me last night, and since there's no locks on the doors ..."

"Sonja is starting too soon with you." Richard unblinkingly peered into Buck's eyes until Buck could stand it no longer. "Did you feel that what you were doing was wrong?"

"I didn't do anything, I ..."

"But you didn't stop it."

"No. I'm sorry. I should have, but I couldn't help it." Buck wiped his face.

"Do you see how weak the world has made your will? If you are *truly* saved you will grow in maturity as a Christian and be able to make wise choices. Only unsaved people *can't help it*. Sonja will show you how to use your manhood in a disciplined and useful way." Richard patted Buck on the back. "You may not believe it to look at her, but Sonja has trained our most popular sharers."

"Popular?"

"Men who are spiritually excellent make splendid lovers, and God rewards his people with plenty of honey," he said with a sly wink.

"It all seems so wrong ... I worried you'd be angry."

"Dear son," Richard said with just the slightest pity and condescension, "do you know why I picked you?"

"I haven't the faintest clue."

"Many dreamers pass through our doors with not the least amount of intelligence or suspicion about our ways. They are easily led down any garden path, but God gave us brains for a reason. India is intelligent too, but in a womanly way that can be quite dangerous for her without the right guidance from the elders. She is more a devotee than a convert. You have the makings of a true convert. I'm thinking of Paul on his way to Damascus. Look at you—battered and bruised. I sense our daughters see something in you—you possess a virile masculinity God wants bred into this community. If God thought a lackey could be trained to carry my torch I would have already died from the headaches that sometimes torture me—my thorn—as they say. But God has answered a prayer. He has sent someone worldly enough, yet young enough to finish my work."

"Sir." Buck's head spun. "I've never finished anything I've attempted to do and have many reservations about Middlemay."

"Perfect. God loves to send me challenges—because He knows I can handle them and turn them for his greatness. I see God working in your life."

Buck felt a slight tug of annoyance. "But you hardly know me."

The country girl who worked for Middlemay knocked gently at the door and scuttled behind the desk and into another small closet or room, appearing a few moments later carrying a chamber pot.

"Young lady, please tell someone I need my coffee to steady my concentration in prayer," Richard ordered peevishly, "and send up some sage tea too."

"Yes'm, sir," the girl replied, offering Buck a timid smile.

Buck smiled back. "She seems a nice little thing."

"Poor girl comes from hardscrabble stock. Middlemay took her in as a youngster—but she's not bright and didn't take well to our parenting style—kept running back to her family's hovel down the road. It's for the best really. She *is quite attractive* and it would be difficult for some of the men who haven't the true calling for breeding to keep away from her. She doesn't possess the strength of will to stop them."

"She looks too young to be an object of interest. You make the men to be like animals ... why do you allow them to stay?"

Richard shook his head. "Most of our problems come from the men who were late converts—weak-willed men following stronger wives. Right there that tells you a lot. I firmly believe that women should be given more responsibility in life, and I'm for them voting on most things (as I assured India last night), but men come above women ever so slightly in God's plan. God has confirmed it many, many times. So these men come here led by their wives, and I roll my eyes and push up my sleeves knowing God has sent me yet another challenge. These men will never be whole, I'm afraid, because they give their power away to women. I suppose it benefits the community financially because women tend to be more generous, but we do struggle with a few embittered men—we call them *eunuchs*. If only they were like our misbehaving rams—off with their heads!" He laughed uproariously.

Buck pretended at amusement. "I met a sour man in the children's room yesterday."

"This type of man is extremely threatened by men with true masculinity. Sometimes I secretly wonder if they are filled with the evil one's spirit to undermine us, but then the women are usually so capable and generous. There are mysteries even I haven't fully solved, son."

Buck thought a moment. "But can the men leave if they want?"

"Yes, of course, but where would they go? They love their wives. The problem is that they love them exclusively. This suffocates any love the woman might feel in return. Once the woman sees that in our system she has the right to decide who pleases her best and the right to decide if she chooses to be a child bearer, well, it is hard for them to be confined to the same old lover who obviously has not fulfilled his duties—or quite frankly cannot." Richard waited to make sure that Buck understood precisely what he alluded to. "Some men are not meant to produce offspring. God has shown me this many times. Some couples produce children who are at a great disadvantage mentally. It's heartbreaking. Take a good look at the children born here. Most of them are far more intelligent and possess a greater degree of natural morals than children on the outside." Richard read Buck's face. "You will need time to digest many of these ideas, I'm sure, but you have a strong mind and come from good stock, according to India."

How late did India stay with Richard last night? Buck wondered. "Sir, India's a good girl. I hope ..."

"Don't fret, Buck. I will protect her," Richard said with a hint of aggression.

"I wouldn't want India to jump into anything."

"Young man, let her go. I admire your chivalry. You will be the perfect man for God's work here, but you don't own India. Her soul longs for freedom, and she's told me that her feelings for you are secondary to her love of God and this grand experiment."

Buck's natural temper flared. "Good for her, then."

Richard laughed at him. "Mark my words. You will experience more pleasure than you can handle. Surely the sacrifice of one girl is worth it."

"India isn't mine to sacrifice, sir."

"From now on no one will be *yours*," Richard said, leading him to the window open to the magnificent verdure of Middlemay and outstretching his arm expansively before continuing, "Everything will be *ours*."

Buck's head pounded. His desire was for just one girl, but until two days ago he had no chance with any girl. Maybe with more training he'd understand better. He said a quick, silent prayer, asking for guidance. His moral compass whirled. "Sir, what do you want me to work at? Having siestas and the like will be a torture after a few days."

Richard shook his head in tolerant disapproval as the thin man from breakfast brought in coffee and tea. Buck could smell breakfast off the man's clothes as he placed the tray before them on a table by a window. The man pretended at good humor. "Sure is a good day for study, Richard. Hope it goes well."

Richard nodded but said nothing. The man's smile disappeared as he turned away and trudged off.

"That's the man I met yesterday. He despises me," Buck said.

"Come take a seat," Richard said. "Don't take Arnie's actions personally. He is one of our hard cases. His wife Rebecca is one of the best damn writers of her generation and uses her skills to defend our cause and inspire future converts. Arnie was her childhood sweetheart and everyone expected them to marry (though he's no match for Rebecca). Most old-time farmers are incapable of progressive ideas. The only things he's taken to are meat and cider fasts. He does it to prove his religiosity. His forays into sharing were a disaster. We don't expect a man his age to come under Sonja's intensive training—and that might be something God will lead us to change—but he has no skill at lovemaking. It's sad too, because his pride won't allow him to improve. The women say he is not greatly endowed, but with training he could still get by." Richard waved him on to take up his tea. Buck dutifully complied.

"Frankly I don't think Arnie's truly saved," Richard continued, "but his wife is so important to Middlemay that we allow her pleas to keep him here sway us. It's hard having a Jesus-filled heart sometimes—as you'll see. The men pray for him daily. I take my own time to pray for him. At the moment Arnie is being shunned so you shouldn't allow him to bring you into conversation."

Buck's stomach dropped at the memory of Milford Streeter's shunning and what happened when Buck broke the unspoken agreement amongst the cadets. "I won't say a word, Father."

Richard's face lit up at Buck's words. For Buck it had been an odd slip of the tongue.

"Today, young man, you will catch up on Middlemay's vision by spending time at the printing press with Arnie's wife."

Buck's breath caught in his sore throat, and he coughed.

"Buck, every young man who comes here gets excited at the thought of unbridled passion."

"I wasn't thinking that."

Richard smiled. "In time, son. But for now you will be under Rebecca. She's an elder, and Sonja and I think it best you spend most of your time with the more advanced thinkers. They will be better able to answer questions you may have."

"Sir, I thought everyone was equal here?"

"Yes, but we all have different roles, and some are farther along the same path. Rebecca will show you past issues of the paper. In the afternoon—after your siesta—which I demand of you as your caretaker—you may visit with the workers in the field. It's admirable that you care about the common man as Jesus told us to do."

"Father," Buck began this time to please the man, "may I ask what you do all day?"

"That is a fair question," Richard replied, wiping his glasses. "There was a time when I picked up a pitchfork and harvested potatoes. Those memories when Middlemay was small and poor I remember with great fondness, but with great responsibility comes great sacrifice. It came to me on a particularly hot afternoon of spreading manure that God wanted me indoors to pray for the others. Just as the apostles and Moses were forced to hand over their work to others so they could spend more time in the more important work of prayer."

Buck had always thought the apostles were just trying to avoid work—he thought the same of most priests and ministers. He tried to hide his skepticism by glancing out the window. Two young children sang as they herded a flock of sheep into a nearby field. A few adults lingered with Bibles in hand at the edge of the new peony garden. Buck imagined them discussing an important insight they had come upon in Scripture. They looked so happy and at peace even if their clothes were ridiculous.

"That happy scene could not come about without much prayer," Richard said with an intense, almost angry light in his cool blue eyes.

Buck nodded, but could not return Richard's gaze.

"As important as you think your conversion was, Buck, you still do not believe in the power of prayer, do you?"

Buck wanted to defend himself, to prove he was a remarkable Christian. For a moment he considered lying but replied, "I had hoped more of my prayers would be answered. I pray less now, with less devotion and wonder if God hears me or is fond of me."

Richard slapped him on the shoulder. "Buck, it's sad that your view of God is so dismal. Again I thank Him for sending you and India. Jehovah knows what you need better than you do. Are you feeling blissfully happy and filled with wonder?"

Buck hesitated. "Since coming here I've laughed more, but I don't feel blissful yet."

"I love your frankness," Richard said. He sat back, sighed and then leaned in toward Buck with hands on knees. "This is the trouble. You've been saved intellectually, but you haven't exercised your capacity to be filled with the love of God."

"How do I do that?" Buck asked, with great interest.

"This is the secret. You are free *now*. The laws of Moses no longer apply. The kingdom of heaven is *now*."

"What do you mean by that?"

"Do what you enjoy. Do what *feels* right. Do nothing at all," Richard said with convincing excitement.

"That sounds sinful."

"It can be *if* you're not saved. You say you've been saved," Richard said, his stern intensity resurfacing.

"I think so ..." Buck said, suddenly unsure and nervous.

"Son, I believe you have been. Unsaved people will do things with hidden intent and selfishness. Do you remember how you were before finding God?"

"Yes, I was an awful person with no spine whatever."

"Then now's the time to stretch that spine! Grow into the man God wants you to be. Nothing is chance. You came to us for a reason. For one day do exactly what you want to do. God will fill you with the spirit of love. It happens here all the time, and you won't feel any guilt because you will know that everything is going to God's plan."

"So I can burn this place down if I want?" Buck asked with a laugh.

"Is that what you want to do, Buck? Don't be silly about things. You're teasing God. Now, will you try for one day to see the world as God intends it for the truly saved? I will pray for you. I believe in you, son."

*"Do you?"*

Richard pulled the watch from his vest. It looked to be a fine one. He saw Buck admiring it and snapped it shut. "A gift from my wife. I remember having to pawn it when we first started here, but Sonja bought it back when her parents' money came."

Buck coughed. "That was nice of her, sir."

"Sonja is a nice lady."

Buck nodded.

"Young man, you must be starved, and we've missed breakfast."

Buck stood to go—not sure where the printing press was. "Oh, I'm fine. I'm not that hungry this morning."

"Buck, you avert your eyes every time you lie." Richard laughed. "Remember what I said. I believe in you."

"Yes, sir."

"Would you like for me to get you a plate of maple sausage a man in town makes for me, or maybe some eggs?"

Buck's stomach ached with hunger, but he sensed this might be another spiritual test. "If I could have a little bread, maybe?"

"Bread it is then. A girl will bring it over to the print shop," Richard said, leading him to the door. "Enjoy your day!"

# Chapter Twenty

Buck yawned and stretched. His stomach grumbled and he considered retreating to his room but headed toward the pond instead. A young man about his age strolled by with his head deep in a book, whistling. At the last moment he looked up and extended his hand. "So you're Buck Crenshaw. I'm Edmund."

"Could you point me toward the printing room?" Buck asked, in cold disinterest. Edmund in his spectacles and ill-fitted clothes looked extremely foolish and stupid.

"I'll take you there," Edmund offered.

Buck gritted his teeth with a forced smile. To his surprise Edmund didn't say much, just strolled along amicably.

"So, what are you studying?" Buck asked, growing more edgy with the silence between them.

"Oh, Greek. It's a hobby my chums have taken up so we can communicate in code when the girls come round. It's just for frolic, but the elders are impressed because they think we do it to study the Bible." He laughed, pulling his spectacles off to reveal a much more handsome face than Buck had given him credit for.

"How long have you been here?" Buck asked.

"I was born here."

"Do you like it?"

"Yes, of course. It's perfect here." Edmund pushed his spectacles up the bridge of his nose. "You're a skeptic, aren't you? Father said you were, but he has plans for you."

"How is it that you know?" Buck asked, irritated and curious.

"I see him sometimes early in the morning. I take after him. We both enjoy a morning stroll just at dawn."

"Is he your real father?"

"I suppose he's everyone's father ... but yes, I am a product of his love for my mother."

"Who's your mother?"

"Oh, she died a long time ago in a chopping accident."

"So—you never want to leave?" Buck asked, very interested now.

"I've left and returned. No one holds us here," Edmund said sheepishly. "I grew homesick and didn't enjoy the sideways glances of the lost when I quoted Scripture." He adjusted his glasses in embarrassment and changed course defensively. "And the language everyone uses! I couldn't get through a day without feeling abused by it. Cussing is so common."

Buck stood transfixed. The man standing next to him acted normal, yet so different. Buck hardly noticed cussing. "So what plan does Richard have for you?"

"None that I know of," Edmund replied. "He lets me be. I'm good at most things so I help at everything."

"Why wouldn't he pick you to be ..."

"A leader?" Edmund grinned, throwing his well-formed and handsome head back. "I have my mind in the clouds most days. Dick thinks I'm a spiritual giant like my mother was and that suits me fine. I get to be an example for the Middlemay breeding program. And—I get the girls," he said with a winning smile.

Buck did his best to keep up with the athletically built Edmund, who strode over the manicured hillside in long confident strides.

"Do you like sport?" Edmund asked. "We get up a game of baseball every Wednesday evening. You should join us. It's fun. No need to worry about your hand. None of us are very good, and you can play outfield or something."

"Okay," Buck replied, enjoying just being asked. How long had it been since he was invited to join anything without his brother's assistance or his father's money? He couldn't remember. "Edmund, thank you."

Edmund tipped his cap. "Any time, friend." He grabbed a handful of strawberries from the truck garden as they cut through it, offering a few to Buck who declined them. "Off to learn all about us from Rebecca?"

"From old newspapers, I think."

"You'll learn a sight more from Rebecca," Edmund replied in a whisper. "She was my first, and I still take refresher courses from her quite often."

"I was under the impression she was old," Buck said, swatting away a mosquito.

"She is, but you'll see." Edmund popped the last strawberry in his mouth, wiping the juice on his sleeve.

Buck sat on a rustic bench, wheezing. He habitually held his neck, feeling the scar for fear it might burst with over exertion. "Does it bother you that most other Christians probably think your version of marriage is completely sinful?"

"Is that what *you* think?" Edmund asked, joining him on the bench affably.

"I'm not sure," Buck said with a sideways glance, "but yes, I think it's sinful."

Edmund laughed. "I see why Father likes you. I don't care what outsiders think now that I'm back. I only worry that Middlemay might go away. Don't you think it's lovely?"

"Yes, very." Buck glanced around.

"I worry that if the hypocrites have their way the children here will be split up. I had a great childhood with tons of cousins, uncles, and aunts. I've given two children to this place, and I want them raised the way I was—God willing."

"How old are you?"

"Twenty one," Edmund said. He looked into Buck's eyes with a sudden penetrating seriousness. "Don't you like children?"

"You just seem too young," Buck said. "I mean, I can't imagine having them yet. I want to wait until marriage."

"I've been married to the community since I was sixteen. There was a period of training so I wouldn't bring unwanted children into the world ..." Edmund stopped. "This bothers you, doesn't it?"

"Actually, I was thinking about my sister who's been through a rough time. I wish she had met someone like you."

Edmund said nothing.

"But how do you take care of your children?" Buck asked.

Edmund shrugged. "I don't have to. It's not for me. I enjoy them, but I have my own things to do. The community cares for them. The two girls I shared with wanted to have children with me, and my father and the elders agreed that we'd produce fine little Middlemayers, so that's what was done. One of the little boys is having trouble breaking from his mother—which I thought might be a problem when I shared with her, but it's getting better. Miriam is a great girl, and she'll distance herself from Frankie in the end for his own good and hers."

Buck struggled to keep up with his feelings. Edmund's friendliness appealed to him, but his attitude was so alien. "My sister disgraced herself and ... got rid of the child."

"Excuse me for saying this, Buck, but in the world out there what else can your sister do but be victimized by men who take no responsibility for their actions? What sort of meaningful work has she to do?"

Buck shook his head. "She has nothing to speak of—and I thought she was smart."

"Now imagine all the girls here who have the chance to do more than just make babies. None of us need be shackled with sole responsibility for anyone else. We all love each other unconditionally and share every part of ourselves. It's what Christ teaches, isn't it?"

"I suppose," Buck replied skeptically.

"We have a billiards table in the young men's hall—did you know that?" Edmund asked. "We play for who gets to muck the barn and other chores. Come by tonight." He pointed now to a building with thatched roof and whitewashed exterior which looked more like a fairy cottage than a print shop under an enormous chestnut tree. Waxy green vines clung to beautifully crafted trellises and chipmunks scuttled under foot as Buck walked along the stone path. Forget-me-not flowers poked through cracks in the stone walls and the sound of singing floated out of the multi-paned glass windows. It reminded Buck of the cottage in Englewood his father had always regretted selling to please his mother.

A woman with long auburn hair, loosely braided, came from behind a blue door and waved him in. "We thought you got lost, Mr. Crenshaw. Do come in. I'm Rebecca."

Buck caught his breath. Rebecca was older, but her hair hung around her comely face in the most appealing way.

"Cat got your tongue?" she asked. When she smiled, the crow's feet at her eyes betrayed her age, but her expressive mouth and wide-set green eyes energized her entire being. "Young man, is there something wrong?"

"I'm very well, excuse me," Buck finally said, his mind muddled. "I thought everyone cut their hair short here."

Rebecca put her hands through her hair, and it glistened in the dappled morning sun. "I've never been one to follow a trend. Richard believes women should concern themselves with more practical things than hair, but I always tell him that if God wanted women with short hair He would have found a way to make it stop growing. Any other questions?"

"No," Buck replied in stupid awe and embarrassment.

Rebecca lacked the innocence of the girls Buck had met earlier. She carried her well-proportioned body with an understanding of the power it had over men. A weed on the manicured path caught her eye and she bent to uproot it, exposing more cleavage than he had ever seen in real life. Would she fall completely out? He couldn't look away, but when he finally regained his manners their eyes met, and Rebecca tossed the dandelion aside and held out her hand for him to help her to standing again.

"You can come right in," she said.

He blushed. "I-I'm not sure what you mean ..."

Rebecca turned from him, all business now, speaking over her shoulder as she went. "I take it you have questions about theology and our breeding program."

"It sounds so scientific."

"You *are* a romantic, aren't you?" she said, as if this were something to be gotten over. "Richard warned me you'd be a tough nut to crack." The shelves lining the walls of the low-ceilinged room were stuffed to capacity. The smell of ink mixed with that of mildew and tomcat spray.

"Ma'am," Buck began, following her at a cautious distance. "I've only been here a couple of days and don't understand why I've become so important."

Three older men peered over the half-wall to have a look at him.

Rebecca shooed the printers back to work and directed Buck to a pile of old papers in her office. She pointed to a chair and made Buck sit. Taking an apple from her desktop, she bit into it and then offered him a bite. Buck shook his head no, watching the smallest drip of juice escape the corner of her mouth. She wiped it absently with her finger as he looked on in disgust and excitement. The workers laughed and chatted in the adjacent room, rolling the sticky ink over the letterpress.

"We've closed our doors to most seekers in the last year or two," Rebecca said between lusty bites. "I believe Richard has settled on the idea that Middlemay will not be ushering in a great sea of communism as he had originally envisioned. There was a time when he thought God would not allow him to taste death until the world was changed, but lately his health is failing. He was greatly disappointed in the defection of his son, Wilbur. Everyone here is so used to Dick being their leader, and I believe him when he says that God has not put it on his heart to give over that leadership to a member of the community. You are the first young man to visit with no agenda in a very long time. You are a blank slate."

"Well, I don't know about that."

Buck's heart quickened at the thought that God had sent him here to lead.

"So many have come in the last few years to take advantage of our sexual practices or to avoid work."

"I don't even think I want to have sex ... yet," he replied, wanting to convince this woman of his pure motives. "And I have my own money."

Rebecca pulled her hair over her chest and played with it. "If you stay you have a long way to go. Think hard about what it means to love everyone and to share *everything*. Nothing, including your body, is your own. People of the world accuse us of free love, but nothing about it is free."

"You seem not to like it here."

"No, I love it here," she said, "but it's not for the faint of heart. It's demanding to always put others first. It's the most rewarding and spiritually edifying thing in the world, but you will be challenged under very watchful eyes to strip away all that is not love for God and the community."

He sat up straighter, exhilarated. "I've prayed for God to use me in any way He likes. I didn't expect this, but I want to be challenged and used at *any* cost."

Rebecca gazed at him in that wise old way adults often look at children. "Here is a sticking point. Your money. It's expected to be shared."

"I've never been at peace about it anyway. I only want it used for good."

Rebecca flipped through a very old paper breezily. "And your money is from your father? Will he mind?"

"He's given it to me, and I'm an adult. I don't see how it will trouble him," Buck said irritably.

"Before you came here had you ever heard of us?"

"No," he said, feeling under a very harsh microscope. "Are you well-known?"

She smiled again and handed him a paper from 1855. "We've been here a very long time. I'm surprised you haven't heard of us."

"Ma'am, I don't mean to offend you, but I only came to escort Miss Van Westervelt as a favor. I don't like being regarded with suspicion."

"Maybe I've become too suspicious of outsiders," Rebecca admitted. "Sonja told the elders she had a dream about you before you arrived, and that's highly unusual. Yet I would hate for you to disappoint Richard as his son did."

"I just want to serve God," he said, hiding a sudden fear. Would he disappoint again?

Rebecca appeared to be satisfied for the moment. She came close and kissed him on the cheek. "Richard will bring you to the very feet of God, mark my words."

Left to himself for the rest of the morning, he perused the old articles Richard and others had written over the years. He liked the closeness of this big family and the confidence everyone had in themselves and God. He liked Rebecca, Parmelia, India, and even Sonja, but Richard's appraising eyes and grim expression when the leader thought no one looked discomfited him. Yet Buck felt he could write *at least* as well as the authors of this newspaper and could not help be complimented at the idea that something was impressive enough to convince Richard that Buck was a leader. *What might Fred think of that?* Buck smiled.

Rebecca came in around the time noon dinner would be served in the real world. She threw him a mealy apple from last fall, and Buck gobbled it down—the promised morning bread had never caught up with him.

"Any questions, Buck? You are a focused young man."

"It's all so interesting and different. I do have one question. What about Edmund?"

Rebecca's face lit up. "Oh, isn't he a card? One of the nicest boys we have. A true product of good breeding."

"But why can't he be in charge?"

"Edmund's foolish in a way—in the nicest way. In fact he really illustrates what life can be like with God. He has handled his breeding position with the utmost tact and sensitivity, and the girls adore him ... the boys too. Edmund's the most popular boy here, but he has absolutely no ambition to lead. Even Richard forgives him and believes that he is untouchable. Most of us think he has reached a level of perfection that the rest of us can only dream of. Edmund is what convinced us that selective breeding is so special and God's real purpose for this community."

For a second Buck felt jealous but then remembered his own leadership potential. The front door opened and in walked Richard. Rebecca turned to him with a grin, and the two embraced and kissed. Buck watched from behind the stack of papers, for a moment forgetting his manners. Buck turned to the newspapers and pretended to read.

"I missed you last night," Richard said to Rebecca.

"How did it go with India?" she responded lightly and turned to Buck.

"Oh, I didn't see you sitting there behind that stack of newsprint," Richard said. "What do you think about our press?"

Buck searched his mind for something intelligent to say about an article but nothing came. "Sir, is India already being trained in some way? I feel responsible to her family, and I ..."

Richard shook his head. "Buck, you *must release* her. She's a grown woman making her own choices. India told me she explained to you that she came here to devote herself to God and to experience her rights as a woman. Is it fair to judge her when you yourself, against your own conscience, allowed Sonja to be intimate with you last night?"

Rebecca laughed in disbelief. "Have the end times truly come, Richard? You seem to be going very fast with these two."

Richard waved her off. "Not now, Rebecca. Not now."

"Sir, you seemed pleased with me only a few hours ago," Buck said.

"And so I was. Realizing how little control over your body you actually have is the first step in becoming a better man. Only if you recognize your weaknesses are you ready to work on them and put them before God."

"Forgive me, sir, but I'm completely confused."

"You are forgiven by me and God. In our fallen world—the one you've come from—good men must protect women like India, so you only do what you know. But here your behavior stifles another's soul. India has nothing to fear here, and she is embracing it fully as you did last night. Would you want her to judge you?"

"No," Buck said, but still couldn't help judging. "The idea of everyone living in peace and ridding themselves of selfishness sounds so like what Jesus taught, and these papers confirm your many years of fighting for the kingdom and everything, but I'm just having trouble imagining loving everyone equally—especially physically."

"I don't expect you to understand everything in two days, son. Of course not. But the part that you worry about is where the greatest joy and unity with God come from. To deprive yourself and others of that joy is the biggest sin. God has given me a gift in that area — to be an inspiration for others. A woman's body is a musical instrument and man creates the music for God's pleasure, and in return love is spread and given back to the man."

"I've been taught that it's sinful to think that way," Buck confessed.

"You think of physical love as an act of human pleasure or human sin, but it is the holiest of the sacraments. Why is there an entire book of the Bible devoted to it? When you think of it as an act that gives you pleasure and you alone then you have the selfish spirit about it, and then it is terribly wrong. But when you are trained and disciplined to do it only for the pleasure of God and the other person, then you have attained pure enlightenment and unity with God. Think of how Mary must have felt with the Holy Ghost."

"I can't imagine that *at all*," Buck said emphatically. "It bothers me to think of it."

Rebecca smiled. "Richard, you've found yourself the perfect specimen. An outsider who is pure."

"Your cynicism is very unbecoming, Rebecca," Richard said. "Obviously Buck here is trying very hard on his own to live a moral life. That should be commended no matter how off the mark he is. In his world Buck's values make sense. Here they harm him, but we'll help him along. I feel a deep kinship with him. God has placed it on my heart to guide him so my soul can rest when He takes me to be with Him."

Rebecca looked deeply into Buck's eyes and pulled him to his feet. "Richard, you see that this young man has scars that you can't heal? I advise you to be careful with him."

Buck didn't like her depiction of him. "I'm completely healed of my injuries. It's something that happened in the past. I want to forget about all that."

"You must remember every time you look in the mirror," Rebecca said.

"These scars are the punishment I deserved for the things I did wrong. I've made peace with them."

She sighed. "Richard, you know I trust your judgment completely, but don't push him too fast. He needs a lot more love before he's ready."

"I don't need more love, ma'am," Buck said. "I just need a chance to get started at something and not to be looked at as some sort of weakling. I'm fine! I want to work for God no matter the cost! And He takes the weak and makes them strong—isn't that so?"

"You see, Rebecca. This man has my passion, and I know he was sent to me. There are no coincidences," Richard said. "Now, Buck, it's time that you get some air. The first part of being a true follower of God is to relax and enjoy the life He has given you. Remember what I told you this morning. I will be disappointed in you if you don't do at least one thing that you think is a little naughty."

"*Naughty*, sir?"

"You're too fraught with nerves, and it does you no good." Richard pushed him along and out the door.

Buck turned back once on the path and saw the shadows of Rebecca and Richard embracing. He found himself wondering again what Fred would think. He'd love the idea of everyone sharing themselves. Maybe Buck had always been too prim, and all it had ever gotten him was trouble. Further along the path he saw the round little form of Sonja walking two small dogs. Before Buck could decide if he really wanted to talk to her, she spotted him and waved enthusiastically. Poor soul, Buck thought, there really wasn't an ounce of natural beauty about her. Buck's heart went out to her as he quickened his pace. He couldn't help smiling at her happiness and the two Pomeranians bouncing and yapping at her feet. She spread her arms wide, inviting embrace. Buck complied easily, kissing her forehead lightly. He couldn't sort his feelings easily and tried not to—thinking of Richard's orders.

"How was your morning?" she asked, trying to make her pups sit.

"Fine," he said but felt protective of her feelings so didn't elaborate. "Growing up we had toy spaniels. My mother and her friend were always in competition for the best ones." He crouched down to pet them as they eagerly jumped up to lick his face.

"The competing spirit is one of the Devil's greatest tools to work against women." Sonja sighed. "Did you see my husband at the printing press?"

He stood. "Only briefly."

Sonja rolled her eyes in a vain attempt at hiding her obvious hurt, but quickly distracted herself with one of the misbehaving dogs.

"Richard told me to do something fun today and a little sneaky. I'd like some company at it."

"You mean *me*?" She laughed. "What do you have in mind?"

"Food, first off. I'm starved. Can we steal some from the pantry? Not vegetables, but real food—a sneak feast—then maybe row out to someplace quiet where we can eat in peace."

"I don't know. I do have window washing and a meeting with the finance committee ..."

"That sounds dull as death," Buck said, now really wanting her as company. Sonja seemed so sad and alone, and he wanted to cheer her. "Richard said the first way to knowing God is to not take things so seriously and to accept what He offers."

"Did Rebecca say anything about me?" she asked, her mouth grim.

"No, but why talk about her? I need your help."

Sonja looked past him obviously thinking about Richard and Rebecca. "You're right. I need to follow Richard's advice once in a while, don't I?"

"Why should you be the responsible one all the time?" His excuse-making for doing wrong came back to Buck like an old friend. But here it promised happiness, if briefly, to this kind, older woman.

"I'll just put Jacob and Jonah away and meet you by the cherry trees in an hour."

Buck smiled and kissed her cheek. She skipped off, giggling, and Buck considered all the things he was learning. He in no way felt sexually attracted to her, but their night together had indeed made him more sympathetic to her. He felt a sort of friendship with Sonja that he would never have entertained in the real world. He thought he felt a Christian love for her well up in his heart and excitement that this could truly be something special here—a new way of living where one really did want to joyfully serve others—even the plain ones! The smallest bit of self-satisfaction in the thought that he might be a quick learner took hold. He walked back toward the main house, admiring the rhododendrons and azaleas in their just-past-peak brilliance as he sucked in the cool air. His throat didn't pain him today, and he wondered why. Was it the awful sage tea or had God begun to really heal him?

"Buck!" India raced up.

"India." Buck suddenly felt embarrassed and afraid that India would see Sonja and him together, however innocently. "I'm in a hurry, sorry."

"What? Where are you off to?" She was flushed and seemed surprised that he might actually have made plans without her.

"Richard has some work for me to do."

"Oh, isn't he so amazingly wonderful?" she gushed.

"I don't know, is he?"

"What's wrong? You seem angry with me."

"So how was *your* night with Richard?"

India looked at him sideways before speaking. She held her head high then. "We talked into the wee hours about God and His plan for the world and the part we play in it. It was the first time I've *ever* felt valued for my intelligence."

Buck snickered.

"How was your *therapeutic* massage, Buck Crenshaw?" India asked pointedly.

"Fine."

India stood a while, trying to figure out his mood. "So ... you've started your training ..."

Buck's stomach churned.

"I saw you heading toward the printing shop this morning. Richard told me he'd send you."

"Oh, yes." Buck replied in relief.

"Has something happened between us?" she asked. "You don't seem at all happy to see me."

Her hair shone and her eyes invited him closer. Buck pulled her behind a tree and kissed her at first hard and aggressively, but remembered what Sonja had said she liked last night and kissed India gently then before pulling away.

"Land sakes, Buck," India sighed. "Do it again."

*"Really?"*

She pulled him closer and kissed him first. "You are adorable."

"Richard told me to do something fun and a little naughty—I don't think I've heard that word since childhood. Do you think this qualifies?"

India looked disappointed for a second. "Richard told you to do this?" but then brightened. "Well, it's very nice anyway."

Buck tried to explain, more for himself than her. "It's that we're not courting or anything, and I didn't ask permission to kiss ..."

She kissed him again. "You're such a surprise. But if you stay here we'll never court ... we will be each other's but everyone else's too."

"I don't think I'd want to share you." He tried to kiss her, but she stopped him.

"This is why we're not ready. Richard has explained to me in great depth the evils of selfish love, and I'm convinced that if I allowed myself to give in to those desires I'd devote myself completely to you."

Buck smiled.

India stepped back. "But I must be for God first."

He felt annoyed and chastised, but maybe she was right. Not for a second while kissing India or being "massaged" by Sonja did he think of God. Perhaps he was even more sinful and not really as saved as he thought? Buck wanted to immediately run to Richard for explanation and help.

"I understand," he said. "Maybe you're right. I think I like you too much."

"Don't say it like that," she said with a winsome smile. With her hair pulled back one would hardly know she had cut most of the length off. "It sounds sort of sad and pathetic. Just imagine that one day we will be in each other's arms with clear consciences, pleasing God and each other."

Buck felt a rush of desire at the thought. "Do you really think so?" He took her hand, wanting one more excuse to touch.

She squeezed his hand warmly. "I know it! How could it be any other way? Here we are, and we both like each other so ..."

"Well then I hope to be spiritually ready very soon and will study very hard for it."

"Fred, you're so funny." India laughed.

"What did you say?"

"What *did* I say?" She grabbed his arm.

"You said *Fred*."

"Oh gosh, Buck! It was just a mistake." She blushed. "I'm sorry. It's just I've known him a long time and you only a few days, and sometimes you remind me so much of him ... you are twins after all. I bet this happens all the time."

"No, not really. People think we behave very differently."

"Oh, of course! You do! Fred is a brute, and you're adorable."

"Can you please find another word to describe me? I'm not a puppy." His shoulders slumped ever so slightly.

"I know you two are at odds, but Fred only has what's best for you at heart."

"I think I know my brother a sight better than you, and I really want you to stop defending him. I have someplace I have to be."

"Where are you going? I was hoping we could go boating before afternoon chores."

"I'm already going boating with someone else," he said, turning swiftly without thinking and catching his forehead wound on a rose thorn. "Sakes alive."

"Oh dear! Did you hurt yourself?" India called after him as he stormed off, wiping his sleeve over his eye.

He didn't have time to clean up because there was Sonja on the front porch waving him on silently, her dark eyes darting about checking for witnesses to the crime they were about to commit. He laughed to himself at the sight of her and trotted up.

She pulled him in through the servants' quarters. A hasty mental note about equality came and went through his mind. Once inside a small pantry hidden from most people, Sonja gasped. "Buck, your head!"

"Father says I have a condition of the blood."

"Richard said that?"

He laughed. "No, my real father. Let's not worry about it now. Who does all this food belong to?" The dimly lit room smelled of yeast and sweets and savory things too.

"It's mine," Sonja whispered. "I love to bake, and Richard said it was making me prideful when I put the compliments people gave me before my duties to him and God. I don't know why I'm confessing this to you. I've been feeling so guilty for so long."

"Well ..." Buck really didn't know what to make of it all. "Well, who eats it? It does seem a sin to waste it. You couldn't possibly eat it all."

"Oh, no. Gluttony is not my struggle at all. Do you promise not to tell?"

"Of course."

"I give it to a servant girl. She sells it all and donates the money to an orphanage in New London, Connecticut."

"That sounds mighty saintly to me."

"No, I'm prideful like Richard says. I believe he *is* inspired by God. Richard has healed people with worse scars than you have, but as I get older, I feel ... forgotten by him. I've confessed this many times at the Circle of Improvement, and people have lovingly criticized me when they see me holding Dick too close, but I can't seem to stop."

"Do you believe in *sharing*?"

"Yes, Buck, very much. I believe it's God's plan, but sometimes ..." She covered her eyes.

He stiffly put his arms around her, and she fell into them. "Um, there, there. Enough of this, Sonja. Today was supposed to be all frolic. Let's both try again."

"I'm sorry. Maybe we should plan it for another day," she said, blowing her nose.

"Are you joking? I'm not going anywhere without you and all of your marvelous confections!" He tugged at her playfully. "Come now, you'd be helping a fellow out. I need your friendship."

"That is the kindest thing anyone has said to me in a long time." Sonja sniffled but perked up. She glanced around the room deciding. "Now, how about some mince pie? I season it with just a little rosemary and some strawberry muffins and ..."

Buck grabbed a handful of cookies and shoved them into his loose pockets. "Let's just take whatever strikes our fancy."

They laughed—almost hysterically—and Sonja, though more thoughtful about her preferences, began stowing meat pies and cookies into the pockets of her skirt and even up the sleeves of her jacket.

"I'm not sure I can move with all of this treasure," Buck whispered.

She took his hand with muffled laughter and led him out and down a new path to a private dock where a small row boat awaited them on the stream that washed into the common pond. He helped her in. She habitually took the oars. He settled himself and leaned in to take them from her. "Let me ..." He stopped when he remembered his useless hand, embarrassed. The thought of India seeing him being rowed out by a woman was provoking.

She smiled. "You have very good manners, and I'm charmed that you'd like to row for me, but it's not unusual here for women to do things for themselves."

"Maybe so, but I wanted to."

"Here's an idea—you take one, and I'll take the other," Sonja replied and placed an oar in his good hand.

They laughed all the way into the pond as they tried to synchronize their movements. The pond sparkled, full of small vessels, and much to his relief plenty of women were rowing. India was nowhere to be seen. They rowed across and out further than all of the others to a shady spot beneath a stand of willow trees. Buck jumped out before Sonja could stop him and sloshed to the shore dragging the boat with his strong arm. She watched him adoringly, and Buck's pride surged. The air and water renewed his vigor, and he thought he was on the right track spiritually—finally! He helped Sonja find her footing and pulled the boat in under the willow. It was a perfect day—no bugs and a cool breeze lilting off the waves. The shade softened Sonja's rugged features as did the smiling and laughing. They ate then, Buck complimenting everything he tasted. Sonja mainly watched, enjoying his pleasure more than the food.

"We Crenshaws have big appetites," he said between bites. "Maybe it will catch up with me one day—but not today!"

"You're tall and well-built," Sonja said.

Buck shrugged and finished a mince pie. "These are as good as my mother's, and her cooking is well known in Englewood."

Sonja didn't seem happy to be compared to his mother.

Buck wiped his mouth. "Sonja, what can I do for you to bring you pleasure? You've already helped me a lot."

"I'm happy that you like my cooking and won't tell Richard or anyone," she said apprehensively.

"I promised I wouldn't. Now, don't worry. But what about something just for you?"

"I love serving."

"No," Buck interrupted. "I want to be trained. My father never knew how to please my mother. I want to know the right way, and I want to make you happy right now." He took her hand and kissed it.

"You won't laugh will you?"

"I promise I won't," Buck said, but worried.

She sighed. "If we lie back, and you hold me in your arms—I'd be grateful for it."

"Grateful? I want you to be happy! You know, you don't give yourself enough cred-it. I wouldn't have guessed I'd meet a friend like you, but you're fun and nice and ..."

She kissed him. Last night, what she did to him was purely for him and rather clin-ical, but this was different. He pulled her to the grass.

"Hold me like you care for me," Sonja said.

"That's too easy because I do." He put his arm beneath her head and ran his fingers through her soft hair until she closed her eyes and was quiet. He kissed her forehead again and she sighed and reached to touch him like she had last night but he stopped her. "No—just for you, remember?"

She smiled and fell asleep in his arms. Maybe being a Christian was this easy.

His mind drifted at the sound of lapping water on the shore and the distant banter of other Middlemayers on the pond. His limbs were heavy and a happy laziness dulled his mind's restless meanderings. No worries, he thought as his eyes slid shut.

When he awoke it was to the sound of very close whispers. Someone nudged his side with their foot. He blinked awake as did Sonja to find India and Edmund staring down at them.

"Aunt Sonja, what a surprise," Edmund said lightly, but Sonja jumped to her feet and straightened her hair, her eyes scanning the area for damning evidence of their theft.

Buck rose up more slowly, red-faced and unable to meet India's eyes.

"We just fell asleep. Nothing more," Sonja assured the two newcomers. "Isn't that so, Buck?"

"Of course," Buck said, watching Sonja rush about. For a moment he felt embar-rassed in front of India, but then he was only caught doing what India said most im-pressed her about Middlemay, sharing—in a very small way—a bit of himself. "India, I see you've met Edmund already."

India blushed. She read something in Buck's tone that caught her out. "We're all adults here, I hope," she said, recovering herself. "Father Richard believes, for your in-formation, Buck Crenshaw, that I've done so much study and prayer on his teachings before coming here that I'm further along than most women twice my age—spiritual-ly—and ready to become a full and active member, under his guidance of course."

Now Sonja sighed. India took no notice but kept her eyes on Buck.

"I'm very happy, Buck, and I hope you are too—with whatever Richard has in store for you."

Edmund chuckled. "I believe Father has his sights on Buck as his successor or un-derling."

"That seems rather quick, don't you think, Edmund?" India asked. "I was aware that Father had plans for Buck, but his successor?"

Edmund shrugged and looked bemused by his two new friends.

"Father Richard sees something in us all, I guess," Buck said smugly.

"I have such a terrible headache," Sonja said now. "India, will you please row me back to the other side?"

India hesitated.

"I'll take you," Buck said.

"India will be quicker, I think," Sonja said.

They stood for an awkward moment until Sonja headed for the boat. The men looked at India, who with red face and set chin turned and followed the older lady. Buck and Edmund silently admired India's strong silhouette and broad backside. When they turned to each other they were both smiling and laughed knowing what was on the other's mind.

"Some pumpkins," Edmund said.

Buck laughed some more. "Indeed." He still had some cookies in his pockets and popped one in his mouth.

"Now where did you get those?" Edmund asked.

Buck tossed him one. "I have my ways."

"Did you have your way with Aunt Sonja?"

"God, no."

"That's a shame. She needs some refreshment now and then, poor thing."

Buck swallowed hard. A crumb went down the wrong way. "That doesn't seem the right way to talk."

Edmund raised a brow. "Oh, come now. You're not really a prig, are you?"

Buck didn't know what to say. He wanted to impress his new friend, but wasn't sure if he was being spiritually tested or being talked to by a normal healthy young man—the way they talked in the real world. He decided to be honest. "I like India."

"And that's your news?" Edmund laughed. "Obviously so does every other man here. I don't know her well enough yet, but is she truly a spiritual giant?"

"I couldn't say. How would I know? I'm still on page one of the Middlemay manual," Buck said, handing Edmund the rest of his cookies. "Sonja came to my room last night, and we struck up a friendship. She's nice, I think. She makes me laugh."

"Aunt Sonja?" Edmund adjusted his spectacles. "My father has no time for her. He believes that God sent her as his thorn. Of course he doesn't mind her money."

"That sounds very cynical."

"No, it's just complicated here. It's all well and good that God has given my father the privilege of training all the young girls first and with good reason—he is after their best interests, but it does leave Sonja in an unhappy position. She believes Father is inspired, but she also believes that she's been cursed by God. No one really finds her attractive, and Richard sends the young men to her for training. One night at the Circle of Improvement a young fellow who has since left the society was quite cruel about her lack of finesse—it was excruciating to listen to."

"Well ... what do you think of her?" Buck asked.

"She's sour, but I was never trained by her. Rebecca took me under her wing."

"This all sounds dangerous to me."

"I've grown up in it. It's what happens when there's people involved in God's plans. I part ways with my father on perfection. I don't think it's possible in this lifetime. Father thinks he's already attained it. I think he may be close. Most of what happens here is for the greater good, but it does hurt people like Sonja who aren't gifted with brilliance or looks or anything. Father says he doesn't want brilliance but happy mediocrity. But then there's nothing mediocre about India."

"So Richard has a blind spot."

"Yes, but how can I be hard on him? Don't we all have them?" Edmund replied, taking a bite of a cookie. "Sonja made these, right?"

Buck nodded absently. "I'm not sure how Middlemay is doing anything for the greater good. Whose good are we talking about?"

Edmund laughed, brushing crumbs from his vest. "You think too much, but I'll tell you, in my experience most people here are much happier than those on the outside. I know I'm happier here. Work is pleasant and there's very little materialism, which on the outside leads to great poverty. If only the leaders of the world could see our little experiment. Things would be so much the better."

"But what about shirkers?" Buck asked, licking his fingers after finishing a strawberry tart pulled from his pocket. "The Bible says the poor will always be with us. My father says if you give a poor man a million dollars, he'll be back in his hovel within a year. You must have some lazy people here."

"Father is so good at coming up with ways to keep people happily employed, I've never met a lazy person yet who stays."

"Well, in the real world there's no place to send the shiftless people or the cripples ..."

Edmund checked his watch. "I need to get back to the field and help with the plantings."

"I'd like to come if you don't mind. Your father suggested ..."

"If you stay," Edmund said, "he's *our* father—I have no special attachment."

"Yes, of course," Buck replied, not believing it. "Anyway, he said I should walk about and see the work being done."

"Come on then." Edmund slapped Buck's back heartily and off they went.

# Chapter Twenty-One

Peepers sang in the low, wet places at Middlemay that night as the community readied itself for their Circle of Improvement. The stars twinkled and the mountain breeze brushed Buck's sunburnt face. Tired but happy, he strolled toward the open fire surrounded by the rustic chairs and benches made by the industrious Middlemayers. Although Buck detected smiles in the shadowy faces, loneliness hung over him until Edmund found and led him to where most of the young men congregated.

"We were just praying for you, my friend," Edmund said.

"Really?" Buck laughed.

"I'm quite serious. The Circle of Improvement can be a hard thing for new people. It will test your confidence."

"Oh." Buck resolved to show restraint and aplomb. What could people say about him so soon? Leaning back with a sigh, he gazed up at the stars, listening to Edmund and his friends converse with a distinct lack of peppery language.

The community members sang a song written for the occasion:

*God is great*
*We can't wait*
*Mold us now*
*In this we vow*
*To let your pruning turn weed to rose*
*To criticize the perfect dose*
*In love and friendship thus improve*
*Whomever in your grace You choose.*

Buck turned to Edmund with a cynical smile, but Edmund sang with the others. Richard briefly lectured on cleanliness and the problem he sensed in some members spending too much time worrying about germs, sprinkling his lecture with a few humorous examples to make the community laugh. It all seemed silly to Buck, and his mind wandered until Richard said his name.

"As most of you know," Richard said, "God has sent us two lovely young people. We at Middlemay have prayed for this and welcome Buck Crenshaw and India Van Westervelt to our little heaven on earth."

Polite applause.

"The Circle of Improvement has done such wonders for each of us in our walk with God, and we consider it sacred. Remember that any words that hurt are said in love and a commitment to bringing out the true richness of your soul for God's glory. Will you allow us to help you?"

Buck spotted India nodding with a nervous smile as she sat with Parmelia and the other girls.

Someone rang a tiny bell. Edmund had one in his hand. Edmund pointed to one under Buck's chair and he picked it up, smiling at how quaint it was.

"Before we critique our new members," a small, middle-aged woman with big teeth began, "I wanted to mention that Annalee Dobson has been more than a little critical with the children at Sunday school. She means well, but seems to single out *certain* children brought into this world by *certain* people to be especially harsh with. What would our Lord have to say about that, I wonder?"

Richard spoke. "Annalee, you are one of our most esteemed elders. We've discussed this before. The children we speak of carry traits, both good and bad, of their birth parents, so it is incumbent upon us to discipline but not denigrate these children. Edmund's children are showing quite the spiritual side already and hardly ever misbehave, but for now they are the exception. The importance of subjecting your desires to the guidance of the elders before considering a pregnancy cannot be emphasized enough. The elders, with their great experience and wisdom (from God), perceive those who are truly meant to bring fit children into the world. Annalee, it's difficult for you to look at these specific children without recalling your own relationship to the father, but specific love brings this sort of pain, and I believe it will cause you to think twice before being led down that path again. In the meantime, you should turn over your work with the children to another and help in the kitchen."

Annalee tearfully nodded her assent.

Everyone paused a moment. A bell rang. The thin man, Arnie, stood now. "I don't mean to be harsh, but Buck Crenshaw was rude to me twice in the last two days. He has a lot of pride and superiority about him despite his appearance and doesn't take our food seriously, and many of us have put enormous effort into getting it to table. Mr. Crenshaw also showed me no respect setting out the silverware."

Buck opened his mouth to respond, but Edmund shook his head no.

Richard's voice rose again, his features animated in the glimmer of the fire. "Buck has already confessed to Sonja and myself that he has difficulty controlling his appetite. The young man has agreed to follow a strict vegetable diet for the time being as a way of fighting off the Devil's temptations. If it wasn't for you, Buck would never have realized how food controlled him. Thank you for bringing this up so we could use it as inspiration for others—God does work in mysterious ways."

Buck nudged Edmund to explain himself, but Edmund shooed him off with a warning look too late.

A bell rang and a man sitting next to Buck said, "I can see as he complains to Edmund that Buck is filled with a prideful spirit—he's defensive."

"Buck, you may speak," Richard said in a fatherly tone.

Buck cleared his throat. "I'm not defensive, but I don't recall saying ..." He looked around at everyone's serious faces. "I don't believe I agreed—about vegetables—well, I'm sorry if I offended anyone over the food, and I'm sorry I didn't mind what you said about the silverware. I was distracted by Parmelia and ..."

A bell rang and a person spoke. "Buck is expressing a specific fondness for Parmelia, and it was agreed upon by the elders that newcomers had to go through even more rigorous training before they could share with others."

"Parmelia." Richard's voice dropped an octave and his tone was grave. "You agreed at our last circle that you would not flirt and give false hope to any of the younger men. I am surprised at you—a product of two elders and set to be one of the top breeders here—that you would squander your time on the young and unproven."

Parmelia, with a self-satisfied smirk, rang her bell. "Rebecca still hasn't cut her hair, Father Richard. What shall we do about that? It leads to sexual sin."

Richard ignored her and moved on, obviously ruffled. "Tonight will be devoted to our newcomers."

A bell rang. "Father Richard, I saw Buck Crenshaw gorging himself on all sorts of confections the kind we haven't seen the likes of since we decided to rid ourselves of excess. He was on the island and lured Edmund into eating cookies with him."

"How did you see us?" Buck burst out.

"Edmund, where did you get the cookies?" Richard asked.

"Aunt Sonja made them."

The bell ringer spoke. "I've heard about and seen myself in the last two days, Buck Crenshaw kissing several young girls, and I saw him sharing with Sonja."

"We didn't share!" Buck said.

Richard laughed. "Buck, it's all right. You don't have to be ashamed. Many of the young men are sent to Sonja."

Buck scanned the crowd and saw Sonja crying in the shadows.

"I'm not ashamed. I like Sonja, and while she may not be breeding material, she has a pretty soul, and it's true she let me have a few cookies because I was hungry. Richard said I should do something *a little naughty*—those were his words. Sonja shouldn't be punished for generosity, and no one should make a joke of her because she has already taught me a lot about Christian love. I shall be happy to be trained by her and to be her friend."

Richard stood silently for a long moment regarding Buck's demeanor, but recovered. "Young man, I'm proud of your misdirected loyalty to Sonja. It takes spunk. What worries me is the news that you've been sparking so soon with the young. One day you will be in my position, but not yet."

There was a murmur through the crowd as most had not yet heard of Richard's hopes for this untried newcomer.

Buck rang his bell. "What about India and Edmund? They're both young, and India hasn't been here long either."

Another bell rang. "I'm sensing Buck has a thin-skinned spirit and needs to see it's immature to make comparisons. God wants you to worry about *you.*"

Edmund spoke up without the bell. "I like Buck. But I'm sorry, friend. Honesty is important here for everyone's good. Sonja didn't just give you a few cookies, did she?"

"Why are the cookies so important?" Buck asked. He let his bell sound only once. "I'm afraid Richard forced Sonja to give up cooking because he worried she might gain confidence in herself! I stole the cookies myself. Sonja did nothing wrong. Forgive me, Richard."

Everyone hushed and waited to hear Richard's response.

India rose to speak, tinkling her bell softly, endearingly. She glanced around the fire. "Buck means well. He truly does, but he's terribly awkward. We must all remember that what Father Richard does in this community happens through the direct inspiration of God. It's why all of you are here tonight and why I've given my life over to the cause of communism and this godly community. Sonja must answer to God through Richard, who is her better and knows what's best for her. I've heard that she struggles with prideful talk, deceit and selfish love, and I'm sure she wants help in gaining victory, or she wouldn't be here. I know that she not only gave Buck cookies but has a private stash of supplies—held back from the community—for her own amusement." She walked over to Sonja and sat at her feet, taking Sonja's hands. "I am devoted to your cause and I hope you forgive my honesty—for your own good."

It may have been the flames in the pit, but a brief fire reflected in Sonja's dark eyes as she looked down upon India. By the time Sonja raised her head and met Richard's gaze it had vanished and her deference to him returned. He walked to the two women and prayed over them.

Buck shook his head and sighed.

Edmund leaned over. "Nice try, Buck. You'll soon learn the ropes though."

"Thanks for your *help.*"

"Don't be sore. You *are* defensive and very naive, but so what? Your problem is that you don't submit your will to God's. You still want to carry on a fight all by yourself. Isn't it a heavy load?"

"I don't like to see innocent people suffer," Buck said sourly.

"Sonja is no innocent. She knows Richard longer than any of us—and she still cheats and steals."

"I hardly think baking nice things counts."

"You live on a slippery slope, Buck Crenshaw, if you can make excuses so easily," Edmund said in such a good-natured way that Buck could not take offense.

"Maybe you're right. I don't know, but I've never met people like you, and I don't yet know what to make of it all."

"Buck, consider me a true friend. I'm never wrong reading people, and I've a feeling you and I are going to be best chums."

Buck laughed dismissively, but his eyes lit with gratitude. It had been years since he had a friend.

There were a few more bell ringers, but they mostly focused on India's surprising maturity and bravery before the crowd— with only small hints that she seemed a tiny bit vain in her choice of outfits so far. India agreed with eager eyes to be re-dressed by the elder women who knew the best things to do to cure the vanity spirit.

Buck sighed in annoyance yet realized his jealousy of her approval.

Richard always decided the best time to end with a song. Buck listened and prayed he would be given guidance. People began to file out. Some said good night to Buck and Edmund and some did not, caught up in their own private conversations. Sonja left quietly, but India stood next to Richard, chatting with other members who gave her warm embraces before leaving. Richard took India's arm and kissed her head lightly. Buck moaned. Edmund stared but said nothing. Richard spotted the two young men and sauntered over with India at his elbow.

"Buck, I'd like to speak with you in private. Say, in an hour. Does that suit you?" Richard's tone made clear this was more of an order.

"It suits me," Buck replied, getting no read from the man's expression.

"India tells me, Edmund, that you were very helpful to her today. Thank you," Richard said, with an uncommon stiffness, Buck thought.

"You're welcome, Father. Anytime."

Richard's eyes narrowed at Edmund's obvious admiration for India. The old man turned to her then. "Shall I escort you back to the house? I have many fine books to lend you that will help free you from old morality in favor of God's true plans for you."

India smiled extravagantly. "I want to give myself completely and to know exactly how to do it."

Buck cringed. Edmund stood in silence. After India and Richard walked off, Buck turned to Edmund. "It's like you and your father hardly know each other."

"Well, we quarreled earlier, but we've never been close."

"Oh. I'm sorry."

"Don't be," Edmund replied. "Dick's a great man and very busy. This life has given me a lot of freedom."

"But doesn't it bother you at all?"

"I remind him too much of my mother—the loss still pains him."

"But I thought Richard was opposed to loving only one woman."

"He didn't love only her—Dick just loved her best. They both shared extensively with others, or I wouldn't have so many half brothers and sisters here."

"My sister had a baby with a soldier. They were to be married, but Fahy died before ... so my parents made Thankful give it up."

Edmund pursed his lips at Buck's admission. "Even mistake children are treated with love here. On the outside we're all considered bastards. I never let my offspring mingle with outside children for that reason. I want them surrounded by godly people like I was."

"So you think the sharing is a good thing?"

Edmund laughed. "The young girls already fight over you, and our father says you are of highly spiritual material. That means in time you will have your pick of partners every day of the week. How does that sound?"

"Too good to be true," Buck replied, his heart racing at the idea of being with India.

"But mind you, there is a big difference here. Here the women have a say in how things are done, and you must learn to really please them. It's not as bad as it sounds. I've had times when intercourse attained something quite spiritual."

"That sounds ridiculous." Buck laughed, though the intensity in his demeanor betrayed how serious he took it all.

"I like you, Buck, but you're such a cynic."

"No. I'm not. I just want to understand things and not just follow like a sheep."

"Jesus liked sheep."

\*\*\*

Buck dreaded the looming talk with Richard as he washed up in his room and sat a minute trying to gather his thoughts. India walked in glowing after a quick knock.

"What did you think tonight?" she asked.

"About what?" he said, not wanting to give her more praise than she already got at the Circle.

"I worried you'd lose your temper."

"The only person I'm in danger of losing my temper with is you for having so little confidence in me."

"Oh, there you're wrong. I have the greatest hopes for you. Richard is sure you're the one to take his place when he dies."

"This is crazy. I have no ability."

"If you're anything like Fred, you're a natural leader."

"I'm *not* like Fred."

"Listen, I know you have to go see Father," India said.

"You mean *Dick*."

"Yes, but I have to ask you something." She leaned in close. "Have you really begun training with Sonja?"

"Why?"

"Because just now I had my first sharing with Richard, and he was so ... gentle. He made me see how sacred it all is. It was fantastic! Dick touched me ..."

Buck grabbed her hand. "Please stop. I don't want to hear it."

"But there's no shame," she said expansively.

"So he was your first?"

"Yes, of course," India replied with pained expression. "What kind of girl do you take me for?"

"A foolish one."

"Buck Crenshaw, that's not fair! I don't do anything by halves. I'm committed to this community and God forever. Richard and I feel I was given such pleasing features to make men happy."

"Richard is using your vanity—the very thing you said you wanted to be rid of—against you!"

She shuddered. "Do you think less of me?"

He hesitated. "Sex before marriage is a sin."

"I'm married to God and His true followers," India said. "You're here, but you don't believe. Maybe someone should tell Father."

"You've known him for a few days, and he takes the place of your father?"

"God has placed it on my heart that I've known Richard forever. Buck, I've been reading everything he's written and *I know* he's right about God's plan. What if the world ended tomorrow, and you were on the wrong side?"

"I don't know the *right* side."

"I'll pray for you. When you get to my level of enlightenment you will be so happy. I love you, Buck. I can say that with a true heart because I've let go of any expectations of you. You can come to me, just as you will in heaven, and I'll embrace you and share with you—once I learn the best ways to be—to please you and God."

India kissed Buck with passion. "I was imagining you when Richard kissed me ... my old selfish side ... but I'll learn not to have any ties to you but as one of the family."

"I don't know if I want that," Buck confessed.

"You wouldn't want us to share?"

"Oh, no, I'd want *that*—or at least I *did* want that before ... I want it to be the girl's first time ... I'm sorry. I'm just not as advanced as you are yet. Forgive me. Maybe one day ..."

India stood up, sulking.

"You and Sonja did it first," she said.

"No. We haven't done anything yet."

"You lied for her too, as if she played no part in the cookie debacle."

"It was only a little lie, and it would have been nice if someone besides me had stood up for her."

India tsk-tsked like an old schoolmarm. "I'm not like you—you have lying in the blood."

"What's that supposed to mean?"

She hesitated. "Well, Fred's the biggest liar I know."

"I'm not Fred, and really he's the only liar in the family. Anyway, Sonja is a nice lady, and she gets treated in a very subservient way. I thought you'd be opposed to that."

"I just don't think she's all that *spiritual*."

"What does *spiritual* mean? Sleeping with every young girl who comes along like Richard? Sonja secretly gives to the poor. Did you know that? I bet you didn't. Yes, to an orphanage in Connecticut. I want to be a good Christian. Is that spiritual?"

"Richard says you have the makings of a great Christian."

"How can he know that?"

"How can you say you're a Christian and not believe in the supernatural power of God? How does your throat feel today?"

Buck ran his fingers along the scar. "It feels like nothing ... no pain whatsoever." He swallowed to make sure. "No pain."

"Guess who has been praying for you since we first got here?" she said triumphantly. "And your voice is already much stronger since we've come."

"Do you really think so?"

"Yes! Oh, Buck, Sonja and Richard both believe you are here for a special reason, and they have so much experience in reading God's signs. Your voice will be used to glorify God! It's so exciting. And I will be here to help you when I become an elder. Imagine one day we will be old and the best of friends and lovers."

He stared at her. India's imaginings were nothing like what he imagined for his future. Was he being healed by prayer? He wanted God to prove Himself and maybe He was. Maybe Buck was being too stubborn to listen. India imagined them together in the future ... maybe they'd have children ... to give to the community. After all, he wanted children only to prove that he'd been intimate with someone—he was lying to himself here. He loved children and imagined himself a good father (in the traditional sense).

"Wouldn't it be interesting if we bred together?" he asked, trying to make peace with community terminology.

"I bet they'd be quite handsome, Buck. I don't like children, but they are a necessity. I'd do it for God. At least here I could have other people raise them."

He swallowed hard. Did it matter if she liked children? Women should be just as free as men to decide ... but it disappointed him anyway. He sighed. "I have to go speak with Richard."

"Yes, you should. Please do me a favor," she said blushing. "I'd love it if you really put your best into your training. I so want us to be matched up occasionally. I didn't realize how wonderful sharing could be!"

These words both sickened and pleased him. India kissed him and left. Time raced by here with everything a blur. Questions came and went. Emotions bobbed to the surface only to be submerged by new events and the people surrounding him. Buck wanted to retreat to his bed and write things down, but could find no pens or paper so moved toward the door. He glanced in the mirror and saw a healthy face glance back. It stopped him and he looked again. There were the scars, but the dim lighting made them fade just a little. Something was happening here, but he didn't know what.

Richard appeared in the hallway just as Buck closed his door. "I thought you may have gotten lost," he said breezily. "Let's go for a stroll. The moon is out in all its glory tonight."

A grey-haired man with Burnside whiskers was just slipping into one of the girl's rooms.

Richard smiled and whispered. "Good luck, Herman. We're praying for you."

The man glanced at Buck with a weak and pathetically sheepish grin, shoulders slumped, hands in pockets.

Once out in the night air, Buck braced himself for the searing pain which usually came when the air temperature changed in his throat. It did not come.

"Well, son, how do you think tonight's circle went?"

"Awful, sir. I didn't make a good impression."

"Oh, don't be too hard on yourself. A good leader grows a thick skin."

"I'm very uncomfortable at the thought of leadership when no one knows me."

"Coming to an old lady's defense will make you popular with the elders. Sonja was wrong to lure you into her bad habits, but that's not for you to worry about just yet. I'm pleased that you stood your ground at the pettiness of some of our members."

"I feel like I'm losing my footing here, sir."

"It's called surrendering." Richard flung his arm around Buck's shoulders in a way Buck always longed for with Graham. It used to bother him that William took his father's easy affections for granted.

"My family would be very surprised to think that I possess leadership potential."

"We are your family too. Remember Moses and the doubts he had when God called him. He stammered and was afraid. You spoke from a pure heart tonight."

Buck puffed up at the comparison. "But I don't even know what I'd be leading about or preparing for ..."

"Middlemay is a disappointment for me," Richard said. "The end times are taking a little longer than expected, and while most of the old folks hold the same enthusiasm for the kingdom, the young question my relationship with God. It's Satan testing. It was a mistake to ask my first son—a misguided product of sharing between Sonja and me—to be my apprentice. He was too attached to his mother who, God love her, has been a great help but also a hindrance in my work. Wilbur became too attached to the world. His grandparents exposed him to many worldly enjoyments—including the haberdashery business which Sonja's father owns. Of course I have nothing against hats and nice suits, but it was my son's dream, even after the community paid for his education at Yale, to make hats with his grandfather! Now having a God-given skill is a blessing, but pursuing the perfection of that skill brings pride—like Sonja and her baking." Richard stared long and hard at Buck in the moonlight pressing him to respond.

"I have no grand talents to pursue," Buck assured him. "I think they were left at the academy."

Richard laughed. "Now what a coincidence that you come to me with no home to speak of, no motives, and no direction, stripped of your old identity before God and man! You, my son, are an empty vessel waiting to be filled by God through me! Isn't that extraordinary? Everything you may have thought was a disadvantage has come to be the very things I need to advance communism and the true love of God. God in all of His wisdom lured you in on the bustle of a pretty girl, but He has been preparing you, sharpening you, for a great role in His plans."

"But ... what are the plans? Your newspaper says you want Middlemay to be an example for the world on how to live like the apostles and Jesus, but how can *I* help?"

"Does a lieutenant in the army decide what the general will do with him? Does he even have the right to ask?" Richard was stern now.

"I'm sorry, sir. I didn't mean to be offensive ..." He wasn't sure why he was apologizing.

"No, Buckie, I'm not in the least offended. I mean to love you as you are and to be a humble teacher to you. I am your servant—for as the Lord said, the greatest will be the servants. I feel God's call upon me, and I won't be long for this world, but I will not rest until I have installed someone to carry out God's vision for this place which has brought so much joy to so many. Are you willing to let me guide you in God's pleasure?"

"Yes, I'll try to please you—and God," Buck replied, surprised at how easily the words flowed. This man saw something in him that was good. What a relief!

Richard's eyes welled with tears. His tears satisfied something in Buck. "From this day forward I will consider you a son—mine and God's. It's as if the Holy Ghost will birth your true nature through me."

Buck shifted his weight at the heavy words, yet an excitement and wonder at the grand turn of events in his life flooded his emotions. Only God could create such a surprise.

"Well, enough for tonight, young man. I'm proud of you."

"Thank you, sir," Buck said as he turned toward his room.

"But Buck, one more thing—God has nudged me to mention that in light of your theft of community food—you do have an unhealthy desire for a rich diet."

"My mother fed us well. I suppose it's a comfort somehow."

"God is your true comfort, my son. It might help you along on your journey to fall in with the others who abstain from meat and sweets—for the present."

Buck's appetite was on high alert at the moment and rebelled, but he checked it, realizing his fleshly rebellion was a sin against God. "Sir, I trust you're right, but I get terribly hungry with just breakfast."

"Discipline and prayer, Buck. It's up to you. Your heart will lead you, but I share what I'm being inspired to say because I care for you."

Buck had practiced discipline at West Point and figured he could do it here too, though he dreaded vegetables. "Good night, sir." He turned again, but Richard tapped his shoulder.

"Buck, it would mean we've turned our first corner if you could honor me with the name Father." Richard said this in such a tender way, Buck could not disappoint him—and didn't Catholics call their priests father?

"If it pleases you, *Father*, I'll do it."

Richard smiled and waved him off to bed.

# Chapter Twenty-Two

The days flowed into each other in a soothing monotony of study, chores, and meetings, always in preparation for a vague but glorious battle with the Evil One. Buck suffered great hunger at first, but soon a peace and focus fell over him. He had no desire to fight or win or worry too hard. A mellow devotion to all things Middlemay smoothed his natural intensity.

The mornings were spent in prayer and study of the Bible and Richard's writings. In the afternoons he worked at the press or occasionally in the hot fields weeding carrots or trying other small manual labor requiring only one hand. He pushed himself harder when a member at the Circle of Improvement hinted that he was not pulling his weight and using his amputation as an excuse and that he'd ruined an entire row of carrot seedlings. How was he to know that the frilly, tiny plants were the carrots and not the weeds he'd tossed aside when he'd never farmed before?

Richard, Sonja, and a coterie of elders swallowed him up. Only occasionally did he get to spend time with Edmund and the other men his age. Aside from Edmund they all claimed to enjoy vegetables, which made them suspect in his mind (and they were mannerly in a way Buck considered effeminate). Edmund had tasted a good steak from the real world, was rakish with the girls, and possessed a Christian heart. He made no demands and gave everything of himself. Constantly organizing events, he included Buck in everything, assuring Buck's place in his crowd and casually overlooking and making up for his handicaps. Edmund illustrated the truth that service leads to greatness.

People here smiled while working and sang godly songs (Buck missed a salty song once in a while). Middlemayers smiled all the time and played virtuous games of cricket and badminton. At first Buck assumed this was a false and overly pious sportsmanship, but he had come to see that these people were as virtuous as their games. One day he would be their caretaker! He looked forward to presenting Richard with the first of many donations and wondered when money would come, as he had sent his father a letter explaining his plans a week ago.

But the one thing Buck couldn't give yet was his body. Unlike Richard, who bristled at Buck's reticence, Sonja in her patient, matronly way assured him that sharing himself physically with the community was not a sin.

"It's why we call this training, my little dear," Sonja said one night, when his old conscience stood in the way of experiencing certain earthly pleasures.

"Everyone here seems so happy and at peace with each other," Buck said, "and if you hadn't come in here that first time we wouldn't have become such good friends.

But my father was a bastard, and my sister gave herself to a man before marriage with terrible results. I wish Middlemay was normal in this one respect."

"Oh, never wish that upon us!" Sonja said. "Communism can't work that way. Special love brings special attachments and gifts to some and neglect of others. If people kept their own children close, they'd leave others out. Men would fall prey to grasping for funds to keep their own a little more comfortable than the rest. Women would compete with other mothers. I learned this lesson the hard way, and now my only son is a worldly haberdasher who never comes to visit me. It's a sorrow I must bear for as long as God wills it, and every moment is like an eternity."

"My father worked so much we never saw him, and my mother was very competitive—maybe I'm supposed to be a celibate."

Sonja laughed. "Celibacy is one of the most selfish attributes of a spiritually weak person. God calls us to love and give pleasure. How you love others is how you love God."

"I guess India loves God a lot."

Sonja shook her head with a sad sigh. "Let her go, Buck."

"But you and Richard ..."

"Yes, and look how my special feelings have brought friction and suffering. Think of your parents suffering. You were called to something better."

"My mother read me fairytales with happily married princesses, and my father *tries* to be good to her. I used to think they were happy when I was young."

"Are you sure you aren't Irish with such a melancholy soul?" Sonja said with a kiss as she smoothed his hair.

Buck smiled falsely, kissing her forehead with eyes closed. He wanted to transcend his attachment to the idea that sharing should be only between two young people who found each other beautiful. Richard and Sonja espoused sexual union without the confining and deadening element of monogamy as the greatest gift of God — even mirrored daily in the acting out publicly of farm animals and birds and such, but Buck still hesitated, wrestling with guilt for wanting beauty.

He was unskilled and mostly afraid to take this final leap into a moral terrain that on the surface made so much more sense than the games people played in the real world—this was his *real* world now. Sonja was here to teach him how to please a girl without getting her pregnant. If only Lieutenant Fahy had been so trained. India and Parmelia came to mind. One day in this world he could love them both. This sickened him slightly—a remnant of the old Buck. He sighed and let Sonja help him get in the mood. She was his mother's age!

Sonja caressed him as he ran his good hand over her hips half-heartedly. She stopped him and sat up. "Buck, you're not attracted to me, and it's all right."

"No, no ... it's not that ..." he lied. Would it be foolish to say he had a headache?

"I'm recommending that you continue your training with Rebecca," she said, turning away. She slipped from the bed and pulled a sheer gown over her head.

A flood of inexplicable resentment at her rejection rushed over him, an emptiness and fear came too. "No, I couldn't with Rebecca—she's with Richard."

Sonja turned on him. "No! She shares with others too!"

"I know that. You don't have to yell at me."

"I'm sorry." She sank into the chair by the window, her eyes filled with emotion as she scanned the dark countryside. "Richard found my little pantry and threw everything to the swine and chickens."

"Dash him. That's awful mean. When I'm in charge, I'll let you cook all you like," he began, but something new took over. "Sonja, the cooking led you to lie to Father—like it led me to get you in trouble. Maybe it's for the best."

"Buck, I'm so happy you're here, but it's sad that you're changing so quickly."

"I haven't changed a bit," he said with a touch of pride. Someone had noticed his changes! "I hope you aren't taking my feelings about sharing personally. If you imagine I've changed so much that I'd want to go with Rebecca, who seems a selfish pleasure seeker ..." He looked up at her. "I've said too much."

Sonja's severe brow softened, and she hid a giggle behind her big hands, joining Buck on the bed again with girlish enthusiasm. "I don't like Rebecca either. It's our secret." She laughed.

"We should go to Father and tell him how we feel," he said earnestly.

"We don't need to worry him about *that*." Sonja stiffened at the touch of his hand on hers.

"Did I say something to offend you?"

"No. I suppose you're just getting closer to what Richard prayed for."

"And that's a good thing, isn't it? Aren't you happy for me?"

She held his thin face in her hands. "I'm selfish, remember? Training the other young men has been easy because I did it to prove something to Richard, but he never noticed. With you—it's hard because I love you."

Buck's stomach turned. "I don't know what to say ..."

"I love you as a *mother* loves a *son*," she confessed. "You remind me of my son, and I hate to see your innocence and independence go—even if it's for the best. Watching someone grow up and give their very essence to God is painful for the ones left behind."

"I'd never leave you behind."

"I'm not *attracted* to you in a *physical way*, Buck. It feels wrong, and it's a weakness in me."

"No!" he said with a sigh of relief. "I'm happy you told me! I'm not ready to learn ... about how to prevent babies. Suppose we let people *think* I'm advancing? Let Richard *think it* ... until I'm ready. If you just tell me what to do instead, we could just meet as friends because I do love you that way—like a mother."

"*Really?*" Sonja cried. "Thank God. He always finds a way! I've been feeling so uneasy about touching you."

They both laughed and grew silent.

Buck pulled on a shirt. "I'm angry that Father doesn't love you best."

"You're such sensitive soul. It's refreshing, but it won't do here. You must follow Richard intently. He's stronger than me, and you'll see one day the advantages for a man to be free of monogamy."

\*\*\*

The persistent racket of chipmunks and squirrels defending their territories outside Buck's window had at first been charming. Now the creatures interfered with a few extra minutes of sleep, and Buck cursed them—and then himself for finding fault with God's creations. Sonja was gone. She had laid new clothes on his chair. Only yesterday he complained of slipping out of his old things as his weight plummeted. Not since early childhood, when the Crenshaw housemaid Lucretia was assigned to care for him, had he been doted on so much. He thanked God for his luck, surveying his future kingdom as he looked out the window wiping sleep from his eyes. God was lavishing him with riches—a sure sign he had found the path to righteousness.

Before breakfast he picked Sonja some roses, just opening their pale yellow petals. At breakfast he slipped the roses to her and she looked happier than anyone had seen her in years. Tongues didn't wag, but knowing looks were exchanged. He didn't notice. A heaping pile of aromatic sausages tempted him, but he offered this sacrifice to God, took a piece of toast, and felt all the better for it once he filled himself with enough tea.

Richard sat with the elders but got up to greet different diners with a relaxed and satisfied air. He joked, at ease with everyone as he got his breakfast. Richard's plate nearly toppled under the weight of sausage after sausage. Buck perceived that the Middlemay leader took no special notice of his food and hoped one day he would be spiritually sound enough to do the same. His early doubts about Richard, he realized now, were symptoms of his experience in the corrupt world. Day after day he witnessed peo-

ple full of health who had once been sick and lapped up the many methods the group
had to improve themselves. He looked forward to the Circle of Improvement now as
a time when his hidden flaws might be exposed and rectified. Only on rare occasions
did he fear a rival might come and impress Richard more.

Buck imagined himself doing heroic things to hasten the full blooming of God's
kingdom. Richard's rare compliments kept him floating for days. The community liked
the new Buck, or at least deferred to Richard's judgment about his special place there.
Of course some people—the spiritually inferior—grumbled when he gave testimony
of his conversion, and others hinted that he worshipped Richard too much.

This morning Buck recalled how weak he had been upon arrival and thanked God
for his renewed vigor while scaling the steps up to Richard's office two at a time. He
knocked and entered, finding Richard at work at his desk. The old man glanced up at
him through spectacles at the tip of his nose. "Buck, good morning to you."

"And you, Father," Buck said easily, taking his habitual seat across from Richard.
Buck's thin limbs jutted out like an awkward colt's. "I finished reading everything you
gave me, Father. I confess I was skeptical of your theory that we're entering a new ice
age, but the evidence you give and the way you tie it into Scripture is very impressive."

"Yes. Buck, I saw you gave my wife flowers this morning. You realize that there's a
rule prohibiting cutting flowers from the new garden."

"No, Father. I'm sorry."

Richard removed his spectacles and ran his thumbs along the insides of his suspenders. "I'm afraid you may be kindling a special love for Sonja."

Buck laughed nervously, playing with the prosthetic strap at his wrist. "No. Not at
all."

"How is the training going?" Dick asked.

"Splendidly," Buck replied with far too much enthusiasm.

Richard waited for the truth with an intense gaze.

"Well, not *really* splendidly," Buck confessed, looking into his hands. "I'm afraid I
haven't been able to submit to the notion of sharing as easily as I'd hoped."

"So Sonja is too unattractive for you," Richard said with satisfaction. "I understand."

"No. I quite like her," Buck insisted, not wanting trouble for Sonja, yet yearning to
confide in Richard. "She's sweet and gentle, and I wouldn't want to be trained by anyone else."

"So you find her *special* in a way."

"Not special, exactly." Buck squirmed. "I'm ... I've been shy about such things before coming here. She's patient."

"Really?" Richard tossed his head, his fingers tapping his desk. "What has she said about me?"

Buck swallowed hard. His neck hurt. "She said that I should put my trust in you because you're stronger and better than she is."

Richard's shoulders relaxed as did his expression. "You, my son, are progressing in leaps and bounds. I wouldn't want anything to interfere with God's will. Would you?"

"No, Father," Buck said, sitting at the edge of his seat. Each day he grew more protective of Richard's vision for him, even stopping any correspondence with the Crenshaws for fear they might spoil it somehow.

Richard paced. He opened a desk drawer, pulled out a caramel crème, and popped it into his mouth.

Buck watched Richard's tense muscles as the old man chewed and thought. The sweet, sugary smell annoyed him. "Sonja and I have a complicated relationship, but one God has confirmed to me is necessary and profitable for God. My experience with Sonja is that she can grow too attached to a young man and derail his spiritual advancement."

"No, it's not like that," Buck said, wiping his sweaty palms on his trousers

"Will you follow Sonja's advice and choose her over me?"

Buck stared in confusion.

"Listen to your closest advisor and follow me. Your training with Sonja is over."

"But ... we haven't gotten that far, sir. I'm untrained! Sonja did her best. I ..."

Richard sat on the edge of his desk, looking down on Buck. His masculinity was imposing. "Those flowers tell a different story. I saw the way she looked at you, and it's a spiritual danger for the both of you to continue."

"I can assure you the flowers meant nothing. Yellow roses are for friendship—or so says my sister ..."

"Buck, it's time for you to make friends with girls your own age. You and Edmund have become friendly."

Buck hesitated. He feared Richard would forbid their friendship too. "I like Edmund well enough."

"Good, he's an influence you need now."

"Thank you, Father," Buck said in relief.

"Edmund can make you more comfortable with our breeding program."

Buck looked up with pained expression. "I'm ... not trained."

Richard laughed. "You needn't be as careful about it if we're helping to match you with girls who want a baby for Middlemay."

"I think I should stay with Sonja a while."

"Buck, fear is the opposite of love. If you have fear you don't have God. The Devil has set up an obstacle in your mind. Are you going to let Satan rob you of your rightful place in the community? Didn't you realize you'd be called upon soon enough to prove your commitment to us by producing offspring?"

"I didn't think ..."

"Well, you *should* think," Richard lectured. "You enjoy children. I see how you are with them. The elders love that about you. It swayed their decision to back you as my heir."

"It did?"

Richard shook his head with a grin. "In some ways you are so boyish, and I guess it's why everyone wants to protect and coddle you still. I'm very satisfied with how thoroughly you've digested our values and the way you whole-heartedly have thrown yourself in with the others. You are more of a man than anyone else here your age."

Buck sat a little straighter. "It's easy when everyone here is so nice."

"I will tell you that there's nothing like offspring to keep you from running when times get tough."

"Father, I have no intention of leaving. Where would I go?"

"There was a mistake at the post office," Richard began. He handed Buck a few envelopes with familiar handwriting.

Buck opened his father's letter and found a bank check, the same as usual. Buck smiled and handed it to Richard. "I hope we can use this to help people."

Richard took the offering with a grateful bow of the head and a quick glance at the amount which caused him a small gasp.

"Is it too little, sir?"

"Your natural father is a generous man," Richard said, folding the check and putting it in his vest pocket. "We were considering a new printing press ..."

"Father, if I may suggest that we use some to help the less fortunate—those sufferers on the outside maybe ..."

Richard folded his arms and thrust back his head as if annoyed, but rethought his position. "Buck, you're right. I still have a small bit of selfishness to rid myself of. Your Christian impulse was greater than mine on this one—and an old man must finally pass the torch."

Buck held back a smile of superiority. It proved his progress. "We could donate to an orphanage."

Richard's enthusiasm disappeared. "Why an *orphanage*? There aren't any close by."

"Sonja mentioned one, and I thought it would be nice."

"No, no," Richard said. "That won't do at all. There are plenty of local hardscrabble people." He rubbed his chin. "It's been on my mind to hire on more help to clean stables and do the more menial work. It seems a shame not to offer the opportunity to a few outside young women."

"But, sir, in your writings you insist everyone must take on their share of the burdensome work ..."

"Yes, but a careful reading of the Bible proved me wrong. At the time I wasn't presented with the full revelation of God. I see now that the kingdom could take more than a generation to blossom forth, and while I once supposed that even the undereducated would flock to our call I now understand that most are not convertible (who am I to question God's sovereign will? Some people must populate Hell) ... but working here, attending our concerts and being treated with fair wages—some may still be saved (God willing) or their children may—and we will in a tangible way give back to the locals. The more backward thinkers in town have expressed concern over our practices. A little money in their pockets might quiet their consciences."

Buck's throat hurt. His brain hardly registered it, but his hand fingered the scar. "Sir, excuse me for suggesting it, but wouldn't people consider quiet money a form of bribery?"

"In my pocket is a sum of money. The person who sent it—was he manipulating you?"

"My father? I mean, my *natural* father. No, I don't know for certain, but ..."

"He sends you money because he cares about you. Am I right?"

"Yes," Buck replied, doubt clouding his thoughts.

"So as Christians we send money out because we care. We love even the ignorant, but we must realize that we know best. It's not their fault they're backwards. To love at a distance—say orphans in New London—is far easier than the spiritual practice of loving the locals who may annoy us with their foolish ways. We will use this money to hire on more service workers. You may go to town and choose them yourself."

"What would I say? And to whom?" Buck imagined himself tapping people on the shoulder and asking them back to Middlemay.

"I will send you to Beatrice Slayer. She's the town busybody, but a good judge of character."

"How many people would we hire?"

"Think of it as helping, not hiring, son, and I would say we need about five girls."

"What about men? Wouldn't they be more useful in the barn?"

"Outside men, you should realize this yourself, are far too rough in their manners. We must keep cussing and leering out of our women's sanctuary. A few of the girls and boys raised here have a small, rebellious spirit. Because of your age it will be easier for you to quell such things as long as we keep worldly influences in the shape of virile young men—brutes—from entering. Always remember that while we insist on treating women as equals, they are just that small bit less capable than ourselves. We want them to flower in safety."

"Like hothouse flowers?"

Richard pursed his lips sourly. "God has made it so. We protect and admire women here. Do you find me amusing, young man?" Richard had a way of changing expression quickly and dramatically.

"No, sir!" Buck replied, timorously. "I-I was imagining what my sister would say."

"This is the sister who traipsed across the West by herself and gave herself to strange men? I don't recall that ending well."

"No, sir, it didn't ... I wouldn't say exactly *traipsed*."

Buck still worked at not resenting the manner in which the old man sometimes stared at him as if waiting for one of the sage's great truths to settle into his small brain. Buck resolved to pray more for humility.

"I will have a car readied for you at three for town," Richard said, as he gave Buck a final once over with concern. "There is something in your manner today that suggests your health is precarious. I'd like for you to consider a sabbath."

"But it's Tuesday."

"No, I mean a rest from study and mental stimulation. Take a walk in the woods and contemplate what thoughts you may be having that are causing the pain in your throat."

Richard was all-knowing. Buck silently doubted he would ever being so sensitive toward others. He grabbed a book he had begun the previous day to take with him, but Richard put his hand upon it and shook his head. This annoyed Buck too. Maybe the hunger made him oversensitive.

"Father, I wonder if it might be all right to have just a small bit of sausage in the mornings again."

Richard raised his brow but said nothing. He flipped through a stack of papers.

"Sir, it was uplifting for a while to free myself of meat. There was a certain lightness of being, but now my body craves something. I dream of a steak." Buck let out a small laugh.

Richard continued his search through the heap of papers.

"Sir?"

"Buck," Richard said, his eyes full of intense annoyance, "take your freedom seriously. God has blessed me with great patience, but you do exasperate me at times."

"I do?" Buck recoiled at the insult.

"When you're leading our family who will you ask about sausages? Do you see how legalistic you can be? Only you can determine if dreaming (or being tempted by the Evil One) is a good enough reason to cave into your bodily desires. Eat sausage if you think it's best. I eat sausage and steak and mince pie ..."

Buck's mouth watered.

Richard continued, "But I don't *ever* dream of sausage. Contemplate it this afternoon. Ask God for inspiration. You decide."

"Yes, Father," Buck said, glumly shoving his hands in his pockets.

"Buck, I'm proud of you and consider you the greatest gift God has rewarded me with so far."

Buck sensed a falseness in Richard, but then he smiled so generously that Buck felt guilty for his cynicism. Richard had touched upon his inability to trust people many times in the past few weeks, and Buck had been surprised at how often his mind determined not to trust God. Richard explained that many people's experiences with their earthly fathers colored their imaginings of their true father in heaven.

Richard's supreme gift of discernment and extensive knowledge of scripture convinced Buck that God had given him a grand opportunity to learn and serve under Richard's wing. Buck sighed to himself. He still had a long way to go before he could trust completely. Why couldn't he be more like Edmund, who seemed to float through life without a care? Or even India, who had taken to the sharing quite easily ... oh, but now he could have his chance with her! Buck's elation lasted briefly. India would be more experienced than him, and he'd look foolish! Better to go with someone else the first few times. Was he really ready to go with a few girls when he'd already determined that one (after marriage) was all he could handle? Maybe his old skin finally began to shed.

"Father, I'm happy to begin—with the girls, I mean."

"Of course you are," Richard said with a sly grin. He saw that Buck was serious and became serious as well. "The act is natural and more uplifting when you understand that you are participating in one of God's miracles. Sonja, I'm sure, has done her best, but her time is done."

"I've enjoyed her company, sir." Buck said with a cough.

"I will ask you to refrain from spending too much time with her. She has such trouble letting go of favorites. For her own good, let her alone for a while. The elders have decided that Parmelia may be ready for you. I've tried with her many times now, and she's a young colt in bed. A truly untamed spirit."

"She might be a little much for me after Sonja." His face burned at his words.

"Exactly. You have to experience the ones with a pulse, my son. Sonja says you are a superior lover—as I'd expected. Parmelia is a project I'm willing to hand over to my protégé. Two of my other girls are with child, and it would be unfair to the rest of you boys if I took them all out of commission."

Buck laughed nervously. "Excuse me, Father, but things are just so different here. It still amazes me."

"I'm glad you see how special this place is since you will one day be responsible for it. God has blessed us. He truly has." Richard let the tear in his eye trickle just a bit before wiping it away. "Now off with you. Enjoy the day, and tonight Parmelia will be your partner and carrier of your seed."

Buck gulped air, his throat paining him still.

# Chapter Twenty-Three

Buck had forgotten the other letters from home in his pocket until he was half asleep under an oak tree dreaming of Parmelia and children. A horsefly startled him, and he stood. The letters peeked out from his pocket.

*Dear Buck,*

*The note you sent home meant so much to me you cannot know. Of all my children you were the one most inclined to spend time with your dear old mother, and I often found it a nuisance how clingy you were, but now I miss those days very much.*

*I wanted to apologize to you for something we never talked about when you were young. I am sorry that I broke your arm when I was scolding you and then did not believe that it was broken. I asked you to not tell your father and to lie if he asked you anything about it. Thank you for keeping that secret.*

*I've opened the piano quite a lot since your letter, and I think I may offer my services at church or maybe give lessons again. Thanks to you, my son. Be safe.*

*Your mother,*

*Margaret Crenshaw*

Buck reread the letter multiple times wanting more from it.

He couldn't wait for this evening— not so much to see Parmelia undress or to kiss her where he'd fantasized about but more to claim his spot here through the making of a child. He *must* know a few of the girls and right away! He'd tell Richard he wanted them—not to *own* them—just experience them and make up for lost time. What if Edmund suddenly impressed his father as the true heir? Edmund already had a few offspring, but no, Richard was not as small-minded as Buck still tended to be. God Himself had told Richard it was to be Buck!

He hurried to the mailroom and handed a letter to the smiling clerk—a girl he hadn't noticed before. He wondered if she was spiritually sound enough to share with. He grinned back and found it easy to charm her with small compliments until a rumpled Edmund came in.

"I saw you jog off this way, Buck."

"Well, you've found me. What's new?" Buck asked, still grinning at the girl.

"Everything's new," Edmund said with an odd look of confused excitement. "Won't you walk with me to the falls? Are you busy in study?"

"No, Father has given me orders to amuse myself till three. I'd love a walk."

They said goodbye to the girl behind the counter, with a few lingering glances on Buck's part. The two men strolled on a close path through a manicured woodland garden. He breathed in the cool air. "When I'm in charge I'll order all of the forest to be done just like this," he said.

Edmund flashed him a look of horrified wonder. "Don't get ahead of yourself now. Father has a good many years left in him."

"Oh, I didn't mean to offend you. It was more a compliment to the gardeners," Buck said, chastened. His expansive burst checked.

"You sounded downright prideful." Edmund flushed with anger.

"I said I was sorry," Buck said with a hint of aggression. "It was stupid of me. Are you jealous of Father's relationship with me?"

"No. I pity you."

"This is not the walk I expected, Edmund." Buck took on a tone that was Richard's.

Edmund laughed derisively. "I hoped you'd give my father a challenge, but I see now I was wrong!"

Buck didn't take a step further. "What's this about? I haven't done anything wrong but talk about a silly garden in the future. I didn't think I'd be attacked in such an unchristian manner by you, of all people."

"Buck, are you still in there?" Edmund asked. "Stop all the Christian bunk. I need to talk to you as a friend."

"Well, you're doing a fine job so far!" Buck replied, tossing his head.

Edmund relented then. He sighed and grabbed the spectacles from his face. His eyes always looked soft and wayward when he did this.

"Edmund, I'm truly sorry if I've angered you."

"No, it's not you who should apologize. It's me. I'm taking out my frustration on you, my only trusted friend."

"You have so many friends," Buck said in awe.

"I don't trust them with what I need to talk to you about. You will understand me—coming from the world outside."

"I'll help you in any way I can, but you're the natural at all this."

"Until now. Buck, something's happened to me, and it's from the Devil, but it feels so good."

"You haven't taken to drinking?"

Edmund rolled his eyes. "That I could understand and just stop ... but it's India Van Westervelt! Even her name ... she's nearly perfect, isn't she?"

"No. Not perfect. Very attractive, yes."

"Buck, how do I quell a special love?"

"You can't be in love—not *that* way," Buck said, a rush of annoyed jealousy rearing its head. "India's against that sort of thing, and Father is very right— it's selfish and dangerous."

"I know, I know!" Edmund laughed miserably and waved his arms in exasperation. "But I can't stop thinking about her. When we talk it's like I've known her forever, and I want to keep her to myself. I'm being tested and bound to fail."

Buck's hero was falling from grace with India! "Have you and her shared yet?"

"No. Father has her so bewitched by his ideas that she gives herself freely only to the older, wiser fellows. But soon she'll be set aside for breeding, and then it'll be too late."

"Does India feel the same way?"

"I don't know." Edmund slipped his glasses on clumsily. "I act like such a fool when she's around. Maybe these feelings will pass, but for now they're torture."

"You should avoid her altogether. Father would agree."

"I'm tired of Father having any say in it," Edmund complained. "What about me? I've done all he's asked of me, but this curious loneliness crushes in on me even in company ... except when India speaks to me."

Buck laughed, trying to convince himself of Edmund's silliness. "A schoolboy infatuation. Besides she's too free and easy."

Edmund leaned back regarding Buck critically. "I hope you don't judge India differently than you judge me. And what about you? What have you been doing all these weeks with Sonja?"

"Nothing." Buck couldn't lie to Edmund. "We both agreed that it wasn't right for us."

"There's no spiritual greatness in celibacy, you know."

"I agree. Father does too, and tonight will be my start," Buck said sheepishly.

"Do you mean he wants you to share or to *produce*?"

Buck cringed at the terminology. "Produce."

Edmund shook his head sadly. "I wish you the best." He pulled at the leaves of a low maple branch as they strolled to the falls. "What would you do if you fell in love here, Buck?"

"I would go to Father and pray for it to pass," he said with great resolve and earnestness.

Edmund sighed in disappointment. "I had you for a romantic. Pity that. Somehow the idea of endlessly knowing people lightly seems unbearable to me lately."

"Why *lightly*? Everyone is so much more friendly here than the real world. You're cared for from cradle to grave."

"That sounds more like security than love," Edmund said. "I never dreamt love was this real and painful ... but it's also thrilling ..."

"Don't waste your time on India. She'll devour you."

"I'd like that very much." Edmund laughed. "I intend to tell her. Maybe it will help me to get on with life."

Buck sighed. Richard was right not to let Edmund be in charge. Caving in to especial love made it impossible for Edmund to see clearly. Already Edmund had been short with him. Their friendship would change. Buck remembered the competitive spirit stoked by Rose Turner when Fred stole her.

Now in hindsight, he was happy to give way to Fred. If he had settled with Rose he'd have been bored by her lack of intellect, just like his father was with Mama. God was miraculous. Most people here were satisfied with the arrangements, and few had the need for special love.

Parmelia scared and excited him, but he did not love her especially. The idea that his sexuality would suddenly have no negative consequences made him giddy. How could anyone be lonely here? There was so much to do and people who really liked him. He tried not to smile at his luck.

"Edmund, see how Sonja suffers under the sort of love you think you want?"

"That's not a fair comparison. Richard used her from the start for her money—you realize that, don't you?"

"He explains it as a mutual decision. She knew full well ..."

Edmund laughed. "And you're the worldly one? Sonja was in love, and Richard wasn't. I would only want India if she loved me back. I'm no Sonja, and it's a rather annoying comparison."

"Point taken," Buck said. "But infatuation is different than love."

"How many times have you been in love?"

"Never," he said with pride.

"Never? What were you doing out there?"

He considered a moment. "I guess I was too busy trying to beat out Fred. I never had time for girls though I liked a few from afar."

"And then you come here and are crowned prince and provided with as many women as you want! It's almost Biblical." Edmund laughed.

"I don't understand you sometimes. Do you believe in this place or not?"

"Until India came along I half-believed my father was a god, but being in love makes me question the whole setup."

"Have there been others who've fallen in love?" Buck asked, unable to suppress a wave of melancholy longing.

"Yes, and they usually leave," Edmund said, working his jaw. "A few come back when they get tired of it I guess, but most we never hear from again. I care deeply for everyone here so I don't know what I'd do." He turned to Buck in open panic, begging for an easy solution without saying another word.

"Keep away from India is what you should do. Have fun with the other girls."

"You do realize this is supposed to be a spiritual thing?" Edmund said in annoyance.

"Of course, or else I'd feel guilty—but I'm almost certain I've conquered that."

Edmund smiled but with a look of sad concern. "Father has really changed you. I hope it makes you happy."

"I *am* happy," he said, waving his arms expressively—but it did not come naturally. "Happier than ever. There's a plan for me after all."

The path narrowed, and Edmund pushed through the undergrowth first, squinting as the glare off the falls hit his face. He stopped and Buck glanced over his shoulder to find India and the girl from the post office immersed in the pool below the falls. Their clothes lay in a rumpled pile a few yards away as they talked and laughed.

Edmund stood in adoration. Buck enjoyed the scene as much as Edmund but not as respectfully. He admired the girls as objects, not as equals, and in this he didn't care. Even Richard admired the female form as a work of art.

Buck waited breathlessly for one of them to expose themselves—any part would have been enough for him. He tried not to laugh at his excitement. Edmund elbowed Buck to shush him and stared at India as if willing her to come up. The postal girl stood now, exposing all but her shins in the shallow water. She had a soft round belly beneath small breasts and was delightfully pink. Buck wanted to share with her right this minute, but he'd ask permission later from Richard and the elders.

India stood next and in every way surpassed her friend in beauty and form. Her red lips shivered as she reached for a towel, and her blond hair, slightly grown out and tousled, shone in the golden afternoon sun. She looked rounder than when Buck and she had arrived, but maybe the corset and bustle made her slim. Buck wondered if she was pregnant yet, and a sudden and surprising possessiveness came upon him.

Edmund whispered more to himself. "She is the loveliest creature. I want her as my wife alone." He glanced at Buck, but Buck's eyes were fixed on the girls.

India turned her head, spotting the two. "Hey you boys! Show yourselves this minute!" she yelled, wrapped neatly now in her long shirt.

Edmund readily stepped forward, and Buck happily followed. "We weren't expecting anyone here at this hour," Edmund began.

"What's a good hour to come to the falls, Edmund?" India asked playfully.

He offered no witty retort. Buck was disappointed.

"Buck, you're just the one I wanted to see this afternoon," India called. "We never see each other anymore."

"How are you, India?" Buck asked, but her happy face answered the silly question.

She waded across the shallow part of the pool, stepping on rocks, nearly losing her shirt a few times and laughing all the way. She was a transformed girl here—so relaxed.

"Buck, I need to talk to you for a private moment about the home folks—in the trees over there," India said with unexpected seriousness.

Edmund stared at India too eagerly, and Buck cringed at the sight of it. "The home folks?"

"Not to worry, but I've got news about your family."

He followed her into the trees with a shrug toward Edmund, who wore a pained expression.

India walked Buck a little further and put her finger to her lips when he tried to speak. She dragged him behind a large boulder.

"There's poison ivy," he began, but she pulled him close and kissed him with her soft, lovely lips.

She let her shirt fall in the ivy, and Buck picked it up worrying about her skin. She giggled and stood, naked but unashamed. "I heard that your training is finally done. Let's share right now."

"India! We can't! The elders have decided for me and Parmelia."

"Yes, I know all about that. I don't want to have a child with you yet. I think I may be pregnant with Richard's baby. I feel different."

India's physical proximity made proper thought impossible. "I'm not trained that well ... I ..."

"Everyone knows Sonja makes men impotent," India whispered against his neck making his hairs stand on end. "I can help you so you don't embarrass yourself with Parm."

He froze.

"You're so handsome, and I've been dreaming of you since our first day together. I'll show you what pleases Parmelia because all the girls talk."

"What would Father say?"

"Why does he have to know?" India asked, playing with his suspender.

"But you worship him." Buck's palms sweated.

"I worship God, silly, but this may be our only chance for a while, and why not? It won't hurt anyone. I'm already pretty sure I'm with child, so even if you make a mistake nothing will happen."

"Richard says Parmelia and I will make superior offspring ... I ..." Buck stammered.

"I agree. I can't wait to see them, but now let's do something before someone comes looking—where's that annoying Edmund?"

"Don't you like Edmund best? All the girls do, don't they?" Buck fended off her exploring hands—briefly. "We should find him ..."

"No. I'd never share with anyone who has no future here. What kind of children would we have?"

"Edmund has a good heart, and he's tall."

She laughed. "Crenshaw men are so stupid." She kissed him and unbuttoned his trousers. She touched him, with much more enthusiasm than Sonja. Buck couldn't resist her skin. He couldn't keep himself in check at all. He tried to. He tried really hard, but nothing worked, and when she pulled him close his mind surrendered consequences and loyalties. It happened quickly and ended happily for both of them. Buck leaned back on the boulder, amazed at the superior quality of the experience.

"India, I ..."

She covered his mouth with her hand. "This is our little secret for now," she whispered. "You don't want to ruin your chances here. You'll do just fine tonight. It was better than I expected."

She wrapped herself up and helped him pull his braces over his shoulders while he stood in bewilderment. He pulled out his pocket watch to find that if he didn't run he'd be late for the carriage to town. "I have to go! Tell Edmund I'm sorry, and I'll see him later. Won't you?"

"Of course, but what's the hurry? Didn't you enjoy it?"

"I loved it." He didn't want to say that. He didn't want it to be true. Poor Edmund! His only real friend here, and he'd gone against him. Buck thought of virginity and how he had saved himself—for nothing—and ran down the path toward the real world again.

# Chapter Twenty-Four

The sleepy driver led Buck past a small grocer, a tobacco store, a rough saloon, and a trinket shop selling books and maps with pamphlets advertising Middlemay's generous donation of funds for the first new street lanterns in years and a Civil War monument at the circle. Weeds covered the lot, choking out a few sad tulips past bloom, and three thin daffodil blooms surrounding the base of the yet-to-be-finished monument. Most people must have been napping, fishing, or haying by the looks of it, and he wondered if he'd find anyone interested in working.

He pulled the woman's name—Beatrice Slayer—from his pocket as his driver stopped before a narrow, weather-bleached building with a tin-roofed porch hanging to the front. A few neglected pots of flowers stood in as décor. Fishing flies hung on a wood-framed screen propped up on a bench that shaded buckets of worms for sale and soda pop of country make.

Buck had imagined the town gossip as an overweight dowager in a house of quiet respectability, so it came as a surprise to find her middle-aged and trim with a tobacco-stained smile. Her starched dress, though plain by city standards, caught his attention. Even in the country, women competed over bustles and fabric, and this woman was not above or beneath that.

She nodded as Buck mumbled a tentative good afternoon. Guilt oozed from his every pore—could she tell he'd slept with his best friend's girl and acted on animal impulse instead of godly service? All the way to town he had relived the few exciting moments.

"What does Sir Richard want now?" the woman asked with alert eyes and no hint of malice.

"How did you know Richard sent me?"

She laughed. "No self-respecting farmer would wear those trousers."

He blushed with a sigh. "I was wondering ... if any young girls would be interested in work at the community. They wouldn't be members or anything ..."

"Of course not *members*," Beatrice said with a tolerant grin. "What would they be?"

"Oh, nothing bad ..." He shifted around and glanced at the ceiling.

"Who said anything about badness, young man?" Beatrice found a feather duster and stayed busy shooing a thin layer of road dirt from the glass counters. She pulled writing implements from a box and refilled a cracked cup with them.

"Ma'am, I'm just sent as messenger," Buck said as she climbed a ladder to retrieve soap for the toiletry counter.

She seemed to note how her silence discomfited him as she placed the soap in a dish. She picked up a pencil and took out a knife to sharpen it. "You're the new man Richard is bent on making a saint, correct?"

He met her eyes with an embarrassed smile. "There's no hope of that, ma'am."

"Oh, you're a humble one? That's a first. Not like the ones before you, then. Not like Sonja's son."

"Ma'am, I know nothing about that— only Father, I mean, Richard sent me to see if we could employ some girls ... they could come to our meetings if they liked."

"Could they, now?"

"And they'd be paid well."

"How much?"

"Well, I suppose a decent bit." Buck glanced around the shop, picked up a confection, then, on second thought, returned it to its place on the counter.

"Son, the girls here are afraid of you boys up there at Middlemay. People talk. Plus it's a long walk up that hill. And if I get them for you I'd need assurance they wouldn't be taken advantage of."

"Of course not!" He puffed his chest. "What do you take us for?"

"Richard is a kind man, but his lofty ideas sometimes blind him to the needs of real people. It's nice that he lets the town folk come to his entertainments and imagines he's uplifting their souls because they couldn't possibly do it on their own, but these are real girls who have families and problems and babies and poverty. I'd want a fair wage for them and something for my troubles."

"I understand," Buck said with a smirk. Things never changed in the real world.

"Is it wrong to ask for something myself?" she asked.

"No, ma'am," he lied.

"Without my good word there's no way the girls would go off with you."

"I don't want them to *go off with me*," he said, unsettled. How easy it was for India to arouse him! "I'll keep my distance altogether."

"That's what you folks do. You keep a cool distance while you spout off about the poor, stupid, country folk, and then you condescend to employ them with tasks you have no stomach for. Chamber pots and such."

"Yes, it bothers me too, and it doesn't quite fit with our ideals. I've been meaning to talk to Father about that."

She laughed. "Good luck."

"Maybe when I'm in charge I can do something." He blushed again, pulling on his ridiculous suspenders. "I'd like to help people and ... I'm just as sinful as any poor man and have no call to judge or lord over anyone."

"I thought you were all perfected over there."

"Not me. Not yet." He absently tapped his prosthetic against the counter.

The woman warmed to him then. "I like you for some reason, and I'll get you those girls on the one promise that you will answer to me if anything goes wrong. You seem normal."

He laughed. "Ask my family." A fly passed his face, and he swatted it.

"Hmm, how'd you lose your hand?" Beatrice asked.

"I was in a fight."

"With something sharp, I guess. Hope you won."

"I'm here so I guess it worked for the best."

"The jury's still out on that," Beatrice said. "I'm curious to see how a gaunt, beat up young man will fight the big bugs in the churches down here who want Middlemay shut down. What are they feeding you—turnips?"

"I'm in *perfect* health," he said defensively, "thanks to God—and Richard's advice. And I'm just sorry for the people who don't understand God's will the way we do."

The woman laughed. "Oh, Richard really has you doesn't he?"

"No, *God* has me, and if he had others as willing the world would be like a heaven on Earth."

Beatrice laughed again. "Youthful enthusiasm leads to such comedy. Come again and tell me all about the plans you have for when and if Richard finally floats away in the clouds. For a while he was sure he would never die, poor man."

"You shouldn't speak so disrespectfully of a man who has such a close relationship with God."

She hesitated and composed herself. "Yes, it's unchristian of me to dampen your spirits. I wish you great luck, young man."

"I don't need luck when I have God."

"Well said," she replied. "Take a soda pop on the way out—my treat."

"Thank you." He walked out but denied himself the pleasure of the sweet drink.

All the way back to Middlemay, the hired driver droned on about his spiritual quest. Buck clenched his teeth in no mood to educate the man.

"You folks up there is mighty pious to be sure, but we're the salt I tell you."

"Yes, certainly," Buck said.

"My wife tells me it's very simple. Keep yer eyes on the right road and don't let yerself be strayed by the Devil in all his guises."

"True," Buck said, checking his watch. The sky would be light another few hours at the height of this northern summer. He hoped to avoid Edmund—and Richard and

India. Should he confess immediately to Father? No. He needed to protect India from herself. And Edmund would be crushed if he found out.

Poking India was a blunder, but land sakes it felt wonderful! He smiled a secret smile and longed to tell someone—Fred. Buck missed him just now and remembered the good times— carousing with the boys back in Englewood. They only did the occasional *bad* thing— just teasing and sipping applejack and stealing small bits of things from Demarest's store. Poor old Demarest! He surely hated teenaged boys. Cadet Milford Streeter's frightened face on that snowy, terrible night at West Point—the night Buck nearly killed a man—flashed before him.

And now Middlemay came into view. The willow trees swayed at this hazy hour with the crickets purring, the birds flitting, and the sun making a golden archway of glistening elm over the long driveway. "I'll walk from here," he told the driver, eager to be rid of his stupid chatter. He jumped down, weak in the knees when he landed. Pushing the elaborately decorated gate open took effort. A nap would be just the thing. With great relief he found his way to bed with no chance meetings.

He fell asleep, too tired to dwell on the future or the past.

# Chapter Twenty-Five

The reprieve was short. Buck awoke to a polite knock as Richard entered the room. "Son, it's time you readied yourself for Parmelia."

Buck had been far away in his dreams and took a few moments to understand fully the meaning of Richard's words. "Oh, yes. I was just so tired."

"I'm glad to see you heeding my advice. A good nap will make you more powerful tonight. Parmelia told me this morning she's ready to open herself to you."

Buck's face reddened at the words. "What should I do?"

Richard chuckled. "Follow the impulse God has given you and fill her with the holy spirit of selfless love. Remember, your seed is precious to Middlemay and God. I am so awed that God sent us such a pure young man. I didn't think there were any left on the outside. Sonja has given you the highest marks in self-control and decency. Parmelia comes from the ranking elders, and like a thoroughbred filly she has refused to share with anyone. I've been eager to have her a parent for years. Only because of her family line have I put up with her tart personality, but she will be tamed yet, and you're the one to start the process. A young lady with child becomes quite a dependent creature which will teach her a lesson."

"I don't know how I feel about teaching her a lesson," Buck said. "Parmelia seems to have some doubts about your divine inspiration but ..."

Richard stared at Buck as if he'd been stabbed. "Does she now? Did Parmelia tell you that?"

"Yes, but she's young and coltish like you said. I didn't take her seriously." He scratched his neck, trapped and squeamish.

"You should. That girl has many young followers who begin to be persuaded that the elders should not be their mentors. They want freedom to choose their own partners in union."

"Why is that so wrong?"

"Why?" Richard's eyes bulged. "Have you not been listening to me all these weeks? God has given me the ability, and it can be a great burden at times, to make sure that the girls are taught properly and handled with delicacy. The elders have so much experience emotionally. Young girls are unstable and bring all sorts of trouble if they are not guided first to the more spiritually advanced men. You are an exception, and Edmund too. You possess the maturity to love with detachment. Young lovers have no brakes. If it wasn't for the fact that you shared with Sonja without protest I would have suspected that you could not handle love with a young and pretty girl. If you could bring pleasure to Sonja then you truly are seeking after the greater good more than the average young man with blue balls."

Buck caught his breath. He coughed and wiped his mouth with a handkerchief made by Sonja. "Father, you give me too much credit. I hope you can guide me through any storm of emotions I may have in future for a girl. I'm devoted to your cause."

"God's cause, son."

"Yes, God's cause. Are you sure I shouldn't hold off longer? Edmund was nearly a saint until today …"

"What about Edmund?"

"Nothing."

"God hates a liar, Buck, as I do."

"It's nothing really. It will come to nothing." Buck's thoughts blurred in panic. He mopped his forehead.

"What will come to nothing? What are you hiding from me?"

"Edmund confessed to me … he has special feelings for India, but India told me she doesn't share in those feelings and would never act upon them."

Richard's eyes always scared Buck, now more than ever. "I am angry at you for covering for the two of them. It has been brought to my attention that someone saw India in the woods with a young man near the falls. It was from a distance, and they couldn't make the boy out, but it must be Edmund since he mentioned the falls to me today. I had already told him that India was my project, not his."

"Sir, I don't think a girl should be a project, I …"

"Edmund will be made accountable for his actions."

"But, sir … what if it was someone else? Maybe it was India who started it. I know she wants a child with you and thinks she's carrying it right now. Isn't that good?"

"Why are you defending actions that go against my authority and God's will? I begin to think you do need to be kept a while longer from the young. They are corrupting you. My intuition told me that God wanted you to be protected a while longer, but I was too eager. Buck, accept my apologies for sending you out a babe in the woods."

"Please don't apologize and please don't punish them. You've got it all wrong," Buck said, taking a deep, panicked breath. He lied now. "God has placed it on my heart to tell you that through the mouths of babes sometimes comes wisdom, and the *Holy Ghost* is telling me that you should leave rumors alone for the time being." He licked his dry lips. "Edmund has been nothing but a loyal follower, and he came seeking advice in how to get through this temptation. He means to fight it."

Richard played with his earlobe a moment then sighed. "Buck, you are a gift. A salve really. Sometimes being in charge is quite lonely. You're right. Jumping to conclusions is not what God would have us do."

Buck lay back in bed heavily.

"Son, it sounds as if the young ones begin to trust your wisdom and seek you out for guidance. That is a true sign of God's hand on you," Richard explained. "For now you should avoid India and Edmund and let me handle them."

"But what about Parmelia? I don't feel up to it tonight."

"Stuff of nonsense!" Richard pulled Buck from bed. "Parm is the perfect reward for you after having such a productive day. I hear that Beatrice will send five girls our way in a day or two. She and I had a falling out a few years back so I was wondering how she would take to you, and her response confirms again that you are from God. One day I will meet my maker perfectly secure in how I left Middlemay," Richard said with a warm and comforting grin that did nothing to untangle the knots in Buck's stomach. "Now rise up, young man. There's God's work to be done, and you are his glorious instrument."

Buck fatalistically followed Richard's orders. He combed his hair drearily in the mirror noticing how thin his face had become. The shadows of evening deepened the circles beneath his eyes. He remembered the soda pop he had deprived himself of earlier and wished he had it now. He was so thirsty for something sweet and fortifying. "Father, what if this is all wrong?"

Richard frowned. "Don't let the Devil twist what is good. You should be stronger than that by now."

Buck averted his eyes. Richard took him by the shoulders. "Tonight you will be the tool God uses to bring Parmelia back into God's kingdom. Think of that. Don't you want to help others find God?"

"Yes, but ..."

"Parmelia is waiting."

***

The girls' wing lay down the hall after a quick left at an amateur artist's imitation of Raphael's *Madonna of the Meadow*. The shoddy workmanship of the piece annoyed Buck's sensibilities every time he passed it. His real mother at home always brought them to see great works of art when they were exhibited in Manhattan, and he had often found it boring, but now he appreciated the masters. A few days ago he had commented on the painting, and an older lady reproached him for finding fault with mediocrity. She reminded him that it was the community belief that brilliant talent in some, if left unchecked, would bring inequality to Middlemay and an attitude of pride so evident in the outside world. Buck sighed now and walked on.

Richard knocked at Parmelia's door when Buck hesitated, and they let themselves in. Parmelia sat at a small desk, looking impatient with their tardiness, but stepped over to Buck and kissed him as if she'd been made to do it, then stared at Richard in rebellious silence, her nostrils flaring. Richard did not notice and smiled. Two of the elders entered. One with white flowers and the other with a cigar for Buck.

Buck and Parmelia posed before a camera, its brilliant powder flash momentarily blinding them. The elders prayed and congratulated them for their entry into the breeding program. Until Parmelia became pregnant they would only share with each other to keep pure, but they should pray ceaselessly to be released from any selfish feelings of possession. The photograph would tell the world a rather grim looking story. The elders left, and the two were alone in the half dark of a few lit candles and a dimly flickering lamp.

"The lilies are pretty," Buck offered.

"Did you pick them?" Parmelia asked.

Buck shook his head. She tossed the lilies on the desk.

"Parmelia, if you're not ready, I won't make you ..."

"Of course you can't make me!" She glared at him. "Even dear old Father can't make me do anything. I'm the only girl here who takes rights seriously."

"Richard told me you wanted it to happen between us, but you seem angry."

"Why did you have to go and ruin everything, Buck Crenshaw?" Parmelia sat on her bed waiting for an answer.

"I don't know what you mean," Buck said, mopping his brow.

"I was saving myself for someone special—someone not so used up and blasé about the whole thing. Richard thinks everything is mechanical and learned like playing the piano, but I know in my heart it's about feelings. I hoped you might still have some humanity left in you, but I was wrong, and now I'm stuck with you."

Buck opened his mouth to say something, but she waved him off.

"I know what happened this afternoon."

"How?"

"Viola, the post girl, told me. India told her." Parmelia waited for a reaction but none came. Buck stood in silence. "Why do you all love India so much? Of course she's pretty, but she's a sensualist and a fake. There's no point in telling Father because he's bewitched by her and is so insecure about his aging sexuality. It's ridiculous for a man his age to force himself upon sixteen-year-olds! I hate that about him."

"He protects them," Buck said uncomfortably.

"Oh, really? Then how come he protects only the lovely ones?"

"I don't believe that. Girls are always so mean about each other's looks. I thought you'd all be different here with the short hair and modesty."

"Did you notice India's short hair?"

"I didn't mean for it to happen. Edmund loves her, and she said she wanted to talk to me! I don't know how it happened, but now I wish it hadn't! I wish I could take it back. I was so looking forward to you," Buck said, sitting beside Parmelia. "I thought we weren't supposed to get feelings hurt here when everyone is supposed to love each other. I didn't mean to hurt you. I'm so confused, and I've hurt Edmund—and he's so decent."

"He's so soft-hearted and so ridiculously trusting. Edmund's like a child. You know he's my real half-brother?"

"What should I do now?" Buck asked.

"I won't tell anyone what happened. I don't want Edmund hurt. But be a true friend to him. Keep him away from India."

"I told him that already."

"Lead by example," she said.

Buck nodded. After a few moments of quiet listening to each other breathe Buck leaned over and kissed Parmelia, but she pulled back.

"No, Buck. I won't do it. Even if I have to wait forever I want someone who's waited for me."

"But that's not the way it works here! I don't understand why you stay." Buck panicked. How would he explain it all to Richard?

"Boys are all the same. Middlemay isn't about free love. It's about *real* love. Uncle Richard's own appetites have caused what was once holy to be tarnished by plain old desire. I thought you were different because I do believe God has a plan for Middlemay. My parents believed it too."

"Parmelia, I am different. I want what you want."

"Well, now you can't have it. You've spoiled it."

"Parm, I couldn't do anything with Sonja because it didn't feel right. I wanted it to be something special, but Richard and Sonja said I was wrong." Regret flooded in where this afternoon's excitement once was.

Parmelia shook her head sadly, twisting her hair around her finger. "Every girl was infatuated with you because you were being so good about Sonja. We imagined you being nice to us when we're old and ugly."

"But I have been nice!"

"You've been lying to everyone. And to so quickly drop your trousers for India!" she said, eyeing him suspiciously. "Unless you were a couple before you arrived ..."

"No! I hardly knew India back then." Two months seeming an eternity.

"Well, you know her now," she said in disgust.

"What will we do? Father expects us to have a child. What will we say?"

"What will *you* say ..." she corrected. "I've done nothing wrong."

Buck's temper rose at her smug attitude. "All I've done is take what is rightfully mine after giving up everything of myself. I study all day and work in the fields and do everyone's bidding. I've been put in the children's rooms most nights when nobody else has the patience for them—when all the rest of the young people dance and play! I deny myself even a soda pop!"

"Where did you get soda pop?"

"What? Why does it matter? I didn't ask to do any of this. It's the will of God! I wanted a wife and children of my own, but I've given up that hope to lead this place. Now tonight you undermine me—like all girls do."

"I didn't know you were such a spoiled baby!" Parmelia cried.

"That's funny coming from you!"

She laughed. "The only person undermining you is *you*. What would it have taken to say no to India? What would it have taken to think of Edmund's silly feelings and be a friend to him? You're just like Richard. He's a callous, proud dictator with a pleasant smile fooling the foolhardy! Poor you, with your cuts and scrapes and false hand. We fell for your puppy dog look, but beneath it you're all pride and lust!"

"How dare you talk to me this way!"

"Look me in the eye and tell me it's not true!" Parmelia said as calm as could be.

Buck looked at the low-burning gas flame.

"Please leave my room," she said.

"I'm not what you say ..." Buck's voice trailed. He lingered a moment before running outdoors to the deserted fields. He stumbled up through thickets of thorny blackberry brambles and wild roses until his body gave out. He sat beside a trickling stream in the dark of a moonless night.

"God!" he called out loud, but stopped suddenly realizing that he hadn't spoken to God in weeks. He hadn't prayed in weeks. He studied divinity and morality and sex, but there was an absent quality about Middlemay prayer. "God, tell me what to do! Why did you bring me here? I thought this was what you wanted!" he cried out, only hearing water against stone in the stream as response.

# Chapter Twenty-Six

At the first tinkling music of the bellwethers rising up through the pastures with their flocks, Buck scuttled down out of the woods and into his room, changing into the fresh clothes washed by the outside helpers. Maybe Parmelia would stay quiet, but what of the others? He decided he'd confess to Father, hoping the scene from the prodigal son would replay itself.

Skipping yet another breakfast, he dragged himself up the stairs to Richard's office and stood on the dimly lit landing gathering his thoughts before knocking at the door, which opened immediately. The smell of bacon, eggs, and coffee filled the enclave. Richard sat eating, and a new young girl closed the door behind Buck with a shy smile. She looked hungry too.

Richard beckoned Buck to take a seat. "You're a bit early this morning. Well-rested?"

Buck's eyes were bleary. "No, Father. I've come to beg forgiveness."

Richard put his fork down, removed the napkin at his neck, and leaned back to give Buck his full attention. "What's this about? Don't worry if you were impotent last night. I always try to explain that bedtime is not the place for talking, and I imagine Parmelia talks a lot."

Buck's words were lost.

"Son? Tell me your troubles. I'm here to help you."

"Father, yesterday was a very low one for me. I lied to you and have suffered all night thinking about it. Please forgive me."

"It was Jesus who said forgive seven times seventy." Richard popped a chunk of sausage in his mouth and licked his fingers.

"Yes. Well, I didn't mean for it to happen, and it's no one's fault." Buck shifted uncomfortably and rubbed his nose. "Well, it's my fault because I was so ill-prepared."

"Is this about Sonja's methods?" Richard asked, motioning the girl to pour him more coffee. "I must speak with her again and this time tell her she's finished at training."

"No! It's nothing about Sonja," Buck said. "She's the only one who understands me. Sir, I was the one in the woods by the falls."

Richard took a sip of his coffee and looked over the cup at Buck. He put the cup down, rattling the saucer. It seemed a very long time before he spoke. "Then you saw Edmund with India."

"*No*, it wasn't Edmund. It was me."

Richard stood up. Buck felt himself cringe back.

"Why do you look like I'm going to hit you, son?" Richard asked in a voice lacking any clue to his emotions. With one hand on his hip and the other at his forehead, Richard sighed. "Son ..."

The very word relieved Buck's anxiety.

"I am very hurt that you would lie to me."

"I was ashamed, and I didn't mean for it to happen. Edmund is a good friend, and he had just told me he loved India."

"Edmund is a silly fool. India has no interest. I'm telling all of the young ones to shun Edmund for a week. The girls are not to be with him."

"But why is *he* punished?" Buck asked, wiping his forehead. The room was close and humid.

"It's not a punishment," Richard explained. "He needs some time to reflect, and his social nature does not allow him to do that, so we will help him set the time aside until his lust passes."

"It's not lust, sir."

"And this you know how?" Richard asked, adjusting his glasses.

"Edmund is a good fellow. Gentle and kind, and I saw the way he looked at India."

"Before you had sex with her?"

"Yes." Buck slumped in his chair, looking despondently toward the window.

Richard sat on the corner of his desk. His eyes were the yellowy eyes of an old man. Up close Buck could see Richard's long grey nose hairs and small tufts sneaking from his ears. "Buck, I think you did us all a favor. Once Edmund sees that India is everyone's goddess, his personal feelings will pass. You must be an example for him. Do you feel any special attachment to India?"

"None whatsoever. I don't think I like her very much *at all*. I don't know why I did what I did."

"I do," Richard said with authority. "The Holy Ghost led you. You were saving your friend from a terrible mistake."

Buck sat in wonder. He didn't know what he felt except relief that Richard wasn't angry.

"You must tell Edmund what happened," Richard said, pounding his fist into his hand in that determined and annoyingly dramatic way he had, "and further tell him that you will no longer speak to him. It will be for a week, but do not tell him that. Let him wonder."

"But, Father, that sounds cruel. I can't."

"God has made you a leader, now behave like one, son," Richard ordered. "Make me proud."

"Father, Edmund needs sympathy."

"Sympathy comes *after* repentance—read your Bible."

"Father, I'm sorry."

"Son, I have grown to love you—almost too much. I want to help you in every way and in my enthusiasm I asked you to breed with Parmelia after she begged me—what happened?"

"Nothing. She doesn't want me now because of India."

"Parmelia always creates new wrinkles," Richard fumed. "If her parents weren't such saints I'd think she was from the Devil."

"She wanted it to be special."

"She wants *to be special,* but she's not. She is ordinary like the rest of us and must be made to learn this, or she will forever miss God's grace and joy. This is the hard part of leadership. You will one day take care of their needs, and they won't always love you for it." Richard snapped his fingers at the girl hanging about listening with fascination at the men talking. "Take these dishes. The meal's gone cold, and remember we don't pay you to gossip."

"Yes, sir." The girl kept her head down as she cleared the desk and carefully balanced the tray hesitating with hands full before the door. Buck rushed over and opened it for her. The girl smiled gratefully.

Richard shook his head when Buck turned around. "No, Buck, you can't sleep with the help."

"I wasn't thinking of it," Buck replied angrily. "I was being polite."

"Beatrice will be watching for any reason to take the girls back to their lives of squalor. These poor girls are not smart enough to know the difference between a flirtation and manners. Leave them be."

Buck felt the pulse of his heart in his temples.

"Now, son, back to the order of the day. Talk with Edmund. India will be restricted in her sharing to just me which is how she wants it until she is with child. She told me last night that she did it with you because she was afraid that Sonja had not prepared you well enough. I think she's correct, and it's one of the reasons I admire her spirituality."

"So you knew before I told you ..."

"Yes. Of course. She was sent to help me with my sadness over aging. She makes me feel young again—like I could go on for another fifty years."

Buck was shocked to find that for a second he was angry at the thought of having to wait that long to be in charge. He immediately felt guilty.

"I think for your own good we need to have a Circle of Improvement tonight—it will cleanse you. Also, I will send Verlinda Beecher to be your new teacher to get you on the right track."

"I don't know her."

"She usually works in the kitchen."

Buck nodded eager for the abuse at the Circle of Improvement. Maybe it would help relieve his spirit.

Richard gave Buck a few of his newest writings to bring to the print shop and bid him farewell. "These are all just growing pains, my most precious son."

Buck left with an aching hunger and considered working in the fields where the last of the cherry tomatoes were ripening, but at the bottom of the stairs he found the town girl crying over spilt food. She looked petrified at the sight of him. "Sir!"

He knelt down and helped her pick things up.

"No, sir, don't."

"It's my pleasure. Don't worry, miss. I won't tell. We all make mistakes."

She looked skeptical and very young.

"Miss, how old are you?"

"I'm seventeen."

"You're lying," he said with a smile.

"I'm not very religious, sir. Please, I need this work."

Buck sat Indian style on the floor. "Don't be afraid. The first day is always the hardest. Do you know how many times I drop food with this hand?" He showed her his prosthetic.

She burst into tears. "My daddy came home from the war with only one leg, and it was all right until my mother just died having a baby! I'm so lonely, and my daddy wants to give the baby away."

He put his arm around her like he had so often done with his own little sisters at home. "There, there. I can talk to your daddy, and maybe we can help him."

"Do you think so?" she asked. "I've prayed about it—in my own way."

"I think that's the best way to talk to God," he said. "Now you run along, and I'll bring the scraps to the pigs on my way to the printing office."

She smiled and wiped her nose on her sleeve. Buck pulled out a clean hankie and gave it to her. Buck watched her walk off toward the kitchen and disappear behind the door before shoving the cold eggs and sausage in his mouth.

As he stepped out under the long porch a chill went through him as he saw Edmund sauntering across the grounds and up to greet him with a generous smile. "Buck, you deserted me yesterday! How was your night? I was thinking we could meet around noon so I could help you with your Greek."

"Edmund, we need to talk."

"Of course. What's the matter?" he asked, sitting easily on one of the homemade Adirondack-style chairs that lined the porch.

Buck slid into the chair next to him. "It's about India. She's all wrong for you."

Edmund laughed. "I'll be the judge of that."

"No, as a friend I have to warn you that—she has no special feelings for anyone."

"Did she tell you something?" Edmund asked.

"Yes, she told me she didn't feel anything for you. She only wants to be with the elders," Buck said, avoiding Edmund's eyes.

"Did you tell her something about me?"

Buck turned to him then. "What could I tell her? I think she's a fool. You're too good for her."

"No, she's supremely good. I've seen her with my children—and she's so kind."

Buck moaned. "That's faking. She doesn't like children. India only wants them to please Richard."

"Why are you so concerned about all of this? Don't you have your own worries?" Edmund stretched out his long legs and pulled at a badly sewn patch on his trousers.

"By mistake I told Father about your feelings for India."

"You're joking!"

"I was concerned about you, and it just slipped out. Now he wants for the young folk including me to shun you for a week so you'll have time to think clearly, and maybe it's a good idea."

"You're seriously considering shunning me?" Edmund's fair skin rose in color.

"Father thinks it will help you. I only want to do what's best, and it's only for a week."

"Why are you so afraid of him?" Edmund asked, his strong voice full of resentment. "Now you're his stooge! I thought we were friends."

"We are, but there's more that I have to tell you."

Edmund stood up and adjusted his glasses, which were fogged from the dewy air. "I don't want to hear it. Start your shunning, Buck, you ass-lick!" He stalked off with hands in pockets.

Buck spent the rest of the day in the truck garden, half-heartedly picking tomatoes for market until the evening vespers bell rang out. He felt rank with the residue of tomato plants staining his hand and arms, but there was no time to clean up since he had forgotten to deliver Richard's writings to the press and had to race over before they shut their doors.

Buck could see the first of his peers arriving at the circle as he came up. The days were beginning to shorten more noticeably now, and the gardens looked past prime, with goldenrod beginning to invade the wild spots. Buck took a seat and bent his head, pretending at prayer to avoid people's glances. He felt Edmund sit beside him heavily. Buck closed his eyes. More people came in quietly, and soon Buck was surrounded by his community. They sang their usual songs, and Richard stoked a small fire with the help of a few hired hands. "Friends, let us pray for our dear Buck tonight. May the Holy Ghost illuminate all of our souls with love and helpful advice."

Three people rang their bells. "Yes, Harold, you may begin." Richard sat down as Harold stood.

"Well, I noticed today that Buck wasn't working as hard as the rest of us picking tomatoes. I said to Milly, 'He ain't pullin' in his share.' She said yes he ain't. All I have to say is maybe he should come and do his share more often instead of spending half the time popping cherry tomatoes in his mouth."

Richard spoke. "Buck, as you all know, is still trying hard to conquer his gluttony. Please pray for him and hold him accountable."

Another bell rang frantically, which aggravated Buck.

"Sometimes Buck is late for Bible study."

"I was only late once!"

"And he was late bringing in your writing to the print shop, Father, so we have to work earlier and later tomorrow."

"I said I was sorry about that!"

Another stood up, "I think Buck has a superior attitude about work and too much pride in his looks."

Buck laughed.

"Buck doesn't take his peers' observations seriously ..."

"And he's too defensive and uses his hand as an excuse for not working."

Edmund stood up now. He looked around. "What's wrong with all of you? Is Buck really a glutton? Look at the state of him! Father has made him a scarecrow. And who *wouldn't* struggle without use of your good hand? How unchristian you all are! I'm ashamed right now to know any of you. How many of you actually even go to Bible study anymore? Since when do we hire out to start a fire? Are we that special? Are we communists like the Bible? It didn't even work back then."

Richard stepped forward and raised his hand before Edmund. "Son, I told you to stay in tonight, but since you're here I think Buck has something to tell you."

"Sir?" Buck's stomach dropped.

"Your friend Buck did a very noble thing for you," Richard said. "He shared with India yesterday at the falls."

Edmund turned to Buck.

"It's true. I tried to tell you ..."

Edmund sat back down quietly and stared into the fire.

Buck tried to talk to him.

"Buck, I'd rather you shun me right now."

Richard addressed the Circle. "Children, Buck has done a truly noble thing. He was supposed to have his first experience with Parmelia last night and had wanted to please her with a child, but only God knows the future and the plans He has for us. Aren't they always for the greater good?" He glanced around for emphasis. "Everything Buck does is monitored by me, your servant in Christ. Buck saw that his friend was being tempted by the marriage spirit and intervened. India Van Westervelt has stated her intentions of staying under my tutelage until we feel she is mature enough to handle multiple partners. Her experience with Buck has made her realize that he still needs more training too. India said that he wasn't as giving as she would have liked. I have determined to send Verlinda Beecher to Buck this very night."

Buck noted the younger set whispering but couldn't see their expressions. A few more words were said, and the final hymn sung. Buck looked to Edmund, but Edmund refused to acknowledge him so he went to his room.

The new moon left the hallways dark. Buck felt along the wall for the little gaslight in his room, but someone's hand was there before his, and he started. The light slowly rose in the room to reveal a woman of gaunt expression. "Can you smell it, young man? It's the smell of the Holy Ghost sanctifying our time together."

Buck stood still, watching the old lady lighting another candle.

"I think it's the flowers on the desk that you smell," he said, looking at the woman in horror. "Ma'am, I don't think tonight is a good night."

"Every night can be a good night with the love of God and all of the saints looking down on us."

The idea of people watching only disturbed him more. He thought of Fred. How he would ridicule Buck if he only knew!

Verlinda smiled at him to reveal a missing tooth just off to the side of her two tiny front teeth. There wasn't a sign of feminine curve anywhere. Her intensely ravenous eyes repulsed him.

"I've heard that you aren't very good in bed yet, but we'll get you there. Richard tells me the reason he only sends men to me but rarely is that my love is too strong for most, and they'd get too attached. I want to keep my freedom. I tell Richard that he has to protect me because in the past I was bothered by too many suitors with ungentlemanly ideas—that was before Middlemay, of course. Here I notice a definite increase in impotence among the men. God's way of chastising all the men for their behavior on this earth."

He still hadn't moved. Was Richard punishing him? Buck tried to give him the benefit of the doubt. Maybe this hideous woman had some rare gift Buck couldn't see. She came to him suddenly and wrapped herself around his middle, rubbing her frizzed hair against his chest and looking up at him with fluttering lids.

Her nose was long and straight, and her eyes had a sunken quality, but her skin was surprisingly wrinkle-free. He searched in panic for something endearing or even just likable about Verlinda. She ran her fingers over his buttocks while humming and still staring up at him. He backed away, pushing her off, at first gently. When she clung to him still he used more force.

"I'm sorry, ma'am. I just can't."

"Don't be ashamed. I'm here to help. It's what God created me for."

Many doubts about God flooded into his mind at the moment.

Verlinda stripped out of her clothes so quickly he hadn't time to stop her. She sidled up next to him again. He kept his arms folded, not wanting to touch her anywhere. She reminded him of the pictures he had seen of prisoners of war. His mind raced for excuses, for some Christian word, but nothing came. He stood speechless and horrified.

"Saint Paul says it's better to marry than to burn with passion," Verlinda said. "Let your passion be extinguished on me."

"Verlinda, I really don't want to hurt your feelings, but I don't feel any passion at the moment, and I really want to be by myself. I'm sure you've been a help to some, but ..."

"Let me touch you."

"No, I'd rather you didn't." He felt a surge of anger and then guilt about it.

Verlinda knelt down in front of him. "Lord, send your healing spirit to Buck. He's afraid of sexual intercourse and has trouble in his private area. Middlemay needs you to free him from his problems so he can become a real man and fulfill his duties to women." She grabbed his trousers and opened the top button.

He shoved her off. "Stop! This can't be right!"

"Confess it now," Verlinda screeched. "Do you struggle over your manhood? Ask God for healing, and let me just stroke you."

"For God's sake, *no*! I just can't do this. I'm sorry but I'm filled with repulsion! You're old and ugly and pushy. It disgusts me! Please just leave. I need time to figure this out! Please go!"

Verlinda picked up her clothes, bending in ways that most accented what Buck was sickened by. "You missed a great opportunity to expand your capacity for love."

He turned toward the window, praying she would just leave. Finally, after feeling her lingering stare on his back for what seemed an eternity, he heard her go. He threw himself into bed, his head spinning. He tried to remember the constructive criticisms at the Circle but only recalled how Edmund had defended him.

He didn't bother to undress, just lay across his bed staring at the cracks in the ceiling. He heard footsteps in the hallway and prayed they'd pass his doorway, but when Richard stepped in he sat bolt upright.

"Father, I tried, but I just couldn't!"

Richard sat beside him. "I have presented you with all of the riches of Middlemay, and you squander them."

"I couldn't feel anything for Verlinda. My conscience is sore over Edmund! He's the true follower of Christ."

"No. He is weak and emotional like his mother was. You are cut of better stuff. I sent you Verlinda as a reminder that I'm not dead yet, and Christ has not seen fit yet to give over the reins to you."

"I never hoped for your death ..."

"You defied me with India."

"I didn't know she was your property."

"How dare you suggest that I enslave her!" Richard's voice shook.

"No, she's willing—but what about special love?"

"This is how God ordained it. The elders train the young. India is too young and foolish to be left to the likes of you and Edmund."

"She's too pretty," Buck said.

"I am here to tell you, young man, that if you want your share of the younger set then you will do well to obey me. There are plenty of women like Verlinda anxious for any scrap God sends them. I know best. Maybe that's your mission—to please the elderly and infirm."

"Is that a *threat*?"

"No, son. I can't believe you would imply that. But I know what's best for you and this community. When was the last time you can say you received direct revelation from God?"

He couldn't say.

"Exactly. Now go to bed, and we'll act as though this night never happened." Richard patted Buck's head and left him to stew.

# Chapter Twenty Seven

Verlinda's shriveled limbs and toothless mouth haunted Buck as he lay awake in bed. Sharing promised to be nice even with a few of the older ladies here, but to be put to bed with an ugly stranger seemed a punishment, and it galled him. He prayed God would send him a contrite heart as he fumed. Everyone here loved Richard, but Buck could not bring himself to that. He admired Richard sometimes and ached for his approval—but love—that was different. Buck missed his real father in New Jersey, and even surrounded by people who quoted Scripture and smelled the Holy Ghost he found that he missed God.

Buck jumped at a bang on the window, a bat maybe, but then it came again.

"Hey ass rag, open the window before I fall!"

Buck ran to the window, and Fred tumbled to the floor, his face scratched and thorns sticking in his fine clothes. Fred had always been the more solidly built of the brothers and carried a few extra marriage pounds. His handsome face was red with effort, but he laughed.

"What are you doing here in the middle of the night and how did you find my room?" Buck whispered, pushing a chair against the door.

Fred sat on the floor hands behind him with a look of concern and mild amusement. "A poor young girl taking out trash by the kitchen told me where to find you. I was hiding back there all damned day. On a diet?"

"Richard says ..."

Fred rolled his eyes. "Oh, please don't tell me you've really been taken in."

"Why are you here? I don't need a lecture from you right now."

"Mama's worried about you. I knew it was just a matter of time that I'd have to come rescue you from yourself."

Buck sat on the chair blocking the door. "Actually I'm having quite a bit of success here. Richard wants me to lead after he's gone."

Fred laughed. "Or until your money runs out."

"It's not like that. The money goes to good causes."

"Like hiring young girls as harlots?"

"What the hell are you talking about? The girls we hire get a decent wage, and they only do menial labor. You have to be a full member to share."

Fred got up, amused by the rustic furniture. He picked up a framed picture of Richard and Buck and shook his head. "I spoke with a woman from the general store in town, and she said you had fallen under the man's spell. I told her I wasn't surprised."

"How do you corrupt everything you touch?"

"There's nothing new under the sun if you'd only study human nature instead of the nature of the gods. I've done some reading on Middlemay. I'd have come myself a few years back for the free love, but this can't last. One day Richard will get himself into trouble."

"Are you talking about him or you? Richard has created a society where women and men treat each other with respect. Everything is open and honest. India tells me you've already been unfaithful to Rose."

"So?" Fred replied dismissively. "How is India? Her father asked that I bring her home."

"What are you going to do? Steal her away in the night?"

"No. I just didn't want any nosy people seeing a future senator for New York coming into this place," Fred laughed. "Plus it's like old times sneaking around."

"India won't go with you. She loves it here."

"Her father is a powerful man, and I aim to impress him," Fred said, sifting through Buck's things. He laughed again. "Look at you in that get up. Did I tell you Mama is back at piano and even taking on little ruffians as pupils? Seems happier than ever. I'm glad Father gets to see how happy she can be despite him ... bastard!"

"I'm glad for Mama. I miss her," Buck said, grabbing a clay figurine Fred bounced in his hand and placing it back on his mantel (a child had made it for him—a tiny buffalo).

"Buck, why is there a chair blocking the door? What are you afraid of?"

"It's just there's no locks. I want a little privacy. Leave it to you to break in." Buck couldn't help laughing. "Remember when we robbed Mr. Lodgsen's guns, and you shot your toe? I don't know how you kept that from the parents."

"It was only the little toe ... I miss those times too. I wish I could keep you near, but you've turned so queer in your ways ever since West Point, and one of us has to bring success to the family. I suggested India take you along that weekend, and I hoped you'd stay. It's fine that everyone regards you as some kind of hero saving those girls from Indians, but I knew you'd end up saying something pious and embarrassing, so a little time away ... I'm sorry."

"No need to apologize. I *know* you. There was a time I wanted to compete with you—by going to West Point, but I don't want it anymore. I've made my own way here, and I'm happy. I hope you are too—with Rose."

Fred's face darkened in disappointment and frustration. "I should have let you have her. I don't much like her anymore, and if I'd have waited ..."

Someone turned the knob at the door and tried to push through. "Buck, let me in! I need to talk to you." It was India.

Buck turned to Fred for guidance. Fred's eyes lit up as he shoved the chair away and opened the door. India froze at the sight of Fred, but he dragged her in and barricaded the door again. "Your hair!" he said with a grin. "You've ruined yourself."

Fred hugged her close then. When they separated she was crying.

"Fred says your father wants you, India, but you don't have to go."

India hardly listened, her attention on Fred.

"India, I'm here as a favor to your father," he explained.

"You didn't come for me on your own?" India's voice trembled.

"Of course not. Now, India, how could I do that? I'm married. I wish it weren't so, but I can't have a scandal. Don't cry. I'll always love you best, but ... dash it! Why couldn't I have met you first?" He hugged her again, and she burst into heartbroken tears. "Buck, get her a hankie or something," Fred ordered. Buck handed him one and stood gawking. Fred smoothed India's hair. "I'll always love you best. Didn't you hear me?"

India wiped her face and sniffled. "I did hear you, but it's only words. I was done with you and your lies and your charm. I even shared with Buck who has very little charm, but a much bigger heart and ..."

"You had relations with Buck?" Fred said angrily. "That's a cruel thing to do!"

"At least we both weren't promised to others—and now I'm having your baby."

"What? Are you certain it's mine?" Fred asked. "It could be Buck's or ..."

"I knew before I came here. It can be raised here and no one will know."

"So that's why you needed to share with me ..." Buck said.

"No, Buck ... well, partly, yes," India cried. "The baby may look like you Crenshaw boys. How would I explain it? You're very, very dear, Buck. The only nice Crenshaw—and I'm sorry I took advantage of your innocence, but you understand why I can't tell Richard. I need to stay here. How else will the baby be taken care of? Imagine Rose and her friends whispering about my family. My parents would be so ashamed."

Buck thought of Parmelia, and how he'd ruined his chances with her by giving away the one thing that made him special in her eyes.

Fred shook Buck out of his head. "Buckie, you can't tell a soul! I'll be ruined! You have to promise me!"

"What would I say?" Buck asked half dazed. "I liked you at the beginning, India. I believed we were friends."

"We *are* friends," she cried. "I imagined you'd be just like your brother, but you're decent and sweet. If we had met anywhere else ... at any other time ... but I already decided what I had to do."

Fred jumped in. "Don't drag Buck into this. How dare you play with his feelings when I told you how gullible he is!"

"And you're the one who wanted me to bring Buck here, to *hide* him! I at least care for him." India grabbed hold of Buck's wooden hand.

Fred pulled it back and because Buck kept it loosened during the night it fell off into Fred's hand. "For God's sake! Buck, what will I do with you! You break my heart!" he cried. "I'm sorry ... for everything."

Buck took his hand back and placed it on the bed, sitting beside it.

India and Fred stared at him in silence. Finally, India came to Buck and wrapped her arms around him. He shoved her. "I'm fine, just leave me alone."

"I didn't mean for any of this to happen, Buck. I was desperate. Please forgive me," India begged.

"I forgive you seventy times seven," he replied, because he had to. "But please leave me alone. I've lost all of my chances because of you. I lost Edmund as a friend."

"He'll forgive you. I know he will. Just promise not to tell anyone! Please."

"You're so selfish," he said in awe. "What will Richard say when the baby looks like us?"

She stroked his hair from his face. "Richard already knows we shared. He'll just assume it's yours and get over it."

"But I'll carry the truth. How will I face my family? How will I be able to see the little one and not love it as a family member?"

"Buck, you can pretend it's yours. I don't mind," Fred said solemnly.

"Of course you don't! It gets you off the hook, and I have to carry the burden of your sins!" Buck's words caused his throat to catch. *Maybe that was it.* He was supposed to carry the burdens of others—like Christ. Nowhere in the Bible were there promises of an easy life. God was calling him to lead and care for others. Self-pity was sinful and a barricade to God's grace. His pride and recklessness, his loneliness even, exposed how he had not put God first in his life. If he had, he would still be friends with Edmund and in the arms of Parmelia.

Was any of this the fault of an unborn child? Buck shared with India knowing what could happen. His father had always suffered under the burden of being a bastard child. Here there was no such thing, and what good would it do to tell Richard the truth about any of it? Buck knew he had to rise above his own hurt feelings and disappointments to protect India and the unborn innocent.

For a moment he was powerful, like a spiritual giant. "Fred, go to Rosie and make things right with her. See this as a lesson to you. In the world out there, marriage in the conventional sense is the only right way."

Fred accepted the lecture. "Of course, Buckie. Of course."

"India, please go to Richard and let him care for you. I'll see to it that the child is taken care of, because I will love it as my own."

Fred bristled at Buck's lofty tone but said nothing. India slipped off the bed and cried at Buck's feet. "Buck, I'm so blessed to have you as my inspiration. I hope one day to be as good as you! God has chosen rightly!"

Fred rolled his eyes, but Buck basked in the short-lived adoration.

A cock crowed. Fred jumped at the sound. "I need to be going now. India, I'll tell your father anything you want me to."

India twisted the damp hankie in her hands a long while as Fred impatiently watched the sky turn bold orange in the east. "Tell him the truth," India said. "Tell him I've disgraced myself. I'm with child and giving myself freely to all men because the one I truly loved abandoned me for another."

Fred said nothing. He helped Buck strap his hand back on and left the way he came. India stayed for a while longer, petting Buck's hair. He didn't stop her because he didn't feel her fingers. Somewhere inside his anger burned, but it raged deeply as if inside a faraway soul. India left him finally. He sat in a room of small comfort. God was supposed to provide for that. The yoke was supposed to be light. He felt lightheaded. Was that it?

Framed copies of famous engravings hung on the wall ... peasants working fields with strong arms and heavy bodies. Buck was as light as air, and his hand was useless. How long did it take just to pull on his boots? He missed tying laces and writing letters that were neat and in his familiar scrawl. His words were weak, his left hand wrote unsteadily, and his limbs were unfit for even the simplest task of picking tomatoes. If God wanted a hollow vessel, He had one for the taking.

Buck wanted a wife, a good steak, and his own children. He begged God to take away these selfish, sinful desires and prayed to be more like Christ—detached and amused at human folly. He hated this distant Jesus. What kind of man didn't want a pretty girl at his side? The martyred saints came to mind, and he hated them too for their supposed goodness. They mocked him for his attempts at sainthood. They threw God's blessings away to prove how wonderful they were! Buck hated how they made being decent seem so trivial. Hadn't he suffered enough trials for a while? Self-pity was for the spiritually weak, but right now he didn't care.

# Chapter Twenty-Eight

India announced her pregnancy later that day. Buck listened to the women gush over her at the summer porch Bible study under his window. She spoke of God's grace and how she looked forward to giving Middlemay the gift of life just as Middlemay had given her new life. Whisperings filtered up on the breeze. The child with India's beauty and Richard's spirit promised to be a spiritual giant.

In a few months India would cradle a Crenshaw baby. Wouldn't the community bristle at the betrayal? Yet mistakes had been made in the past, and the children thrived as well as the others.

Having renounced his right to any possessive feelings for a wife and child, Buck resented Fred for giving it up so easily. But still he missed his brother and wished he had not been in such a hurry to leave. Buck hoped Fred might one day understand him, and they could be close again. Edmund had been the closest thing to a friend his own age since his first year at West Point. So much time here was spent with Richard. Buck skipped his morning meeting and waited for the inevitable knock at the door and rude entry. It came at half past nine.

"My son, are you ill?" Richard's face was aglow with excitement. "Have you heard the news about my little India? I was secretly afraid God wouldn't grant me this final child. I'm young and alive again! God is good. We're going to celebrate with an afternoon picnic by the lake. You must come."

Buck sat up. His sore stump rubbed against his prosthetic. "Sir, I'm so confused. I feel ... I feel God has abandoned me again."

"God never abandons us. We abandon Him. He wants what's best."

"I need to eat meat, sir. I'm terribly weak," Buck said, his voice full of pent up frustration.

"If you're being guided in that direction, then by all means ..."

"I don't know if it's guidance or hunger, sir. I just want to," Buck grumbled, almost hoping for a fight.

Richard looked at him with concern. "Son, you are so like me when I was young. So high-strung. I understand your pride is hurt over Parmelia and Verlinda, but your functioning will come back."

"My functioning is fine! I wish this wasn't everyone's business!"

"India told me that your sharing was very brief and fumbling."

"She forced ..." He stopped himself, suddenly imagining his life if he gave vent to his emotions. If he said he doubted everything and resented Richard's relentless guidance, and that he considered Edmund the only sane person here, and that he had compromised himself and his faith in exchange for the promise of power and comfort, what would he do then? "Sir, I fear I'm under great spiritual attack."

"It's to be expected, son. Remember how admired and loved you are here. These are growing pains."

"I'm very sinful."

"Buck, I'll be honest with you, and it hurts me to suggest it, but these last few days I've noticed your selfishness in the area of sharing. Think about it. Ever since you've defied me and been resistant, you've been miserable. I remember only a short while ago a young man lit up for God and excited about his opportunity to serve me. You must tell me the truth now—are you in love with India?"

"No! This has nothing to do with her."

Richard looked relieved.

Buck's anger surged. "Sir, some say you don't follow the same rules as the rest of us."

Richard threw his head back. The whites of his eyes grew large, and his face colored. "Someday you will understand that Christ has many rooms in his mansions. These rooms are different sizes. Those with more capacity for God's grace get bigger rooms. Earthly people resent that, but in heaven everyone will appreciate the justice of it and be happy with what they get."

"Father, I think I've made a mistake here."

"No, son. Don't turn your back on God. Where would you go? India told me your family is ashamed of you and happy to send you funds to keep you away. You couldn't go back to them. There are still so many crippled veterans of the war with families—of course they will find employment before you. How would you support yourself? Even the menial laborers here have to help you live a normal life. No, Buck. This is where you belong. Maybe Verlinda was a little too much of a challenge for you. I wanted to get your attention. The yoke you're under is of your own making. Jesus beckons you, but something in you still resists."

"I resist because people aren't who they say they are."

"Who do you mean?" Richard asked.

"I, well, I mean ..."

"Luther." Richard slapped his knees.

"Sir?"

"Martin Luther suffered under such nervous prostration before the Lord, and then came his enormous breakthrough to God's grace! You, my son, are on the verge of greatness! Have faith! A dark night of the soul is all."

"Sir, I've had a dark night of the soul for almost my entire Christian walk. *When will it end?*"

"When you finally submit. *Submit*!! You are still so timid in the faith. This isn't about others not being who they are! It's about you! God sent you here for a purpose. Now finally live it! Take courage, and let small minds think what they will."

"How many times should we forgive a girl who lies? What if a girl is overcome by the special love and has a child the elders didn't sanction?"

Richard sat on the bed again and put his arm around Buck. He sighed. "I know India troubles you somehow. It's very admirable of you to want to protect someone from home, and you may think I've disappointed you by not asking the elders, but remember Job? All of his friends had their theories about Job's misfortunes, but they were wrong. God has appointed me here, and only He knows why He inspires me to certain actions like taking India under my wing because she has been hurt by men in the past—just a feeling, but one that I know is from God."

"So, *no matter what*, a girl should be forgiven."

"Of course. India may have done things she's not proud of, but I trust her loyalty and devotion completely, and I feel God may be changing his mind about sharing here."

"What do you mean?"

"I'm not sure yet, but maybe in special cases God sees two people who complete each other—not in the old sense—but as a way of bringing new life to the old. India may be my fountain of youth—maybe a reward for obedience."

Buck shook inside. "You mean to keep her then?"

Richard's look turned severe. He let Buck stew a moment. "This is nothing for you to worry about. Worry is not from God. The Lord has not yet fully revealed Himself on this. It's more an informal dialogue we're having. I trust He will make things clear eventually."

"But that would change everything here! No, it can't be done!"

Richard patted him on the back with a look of pride. "You will be the defender of our noble institution, and I am so happy to see you have finally come to believe our way is best. Of course the old morality of the world beyond our gates is not for us—especially not for the women and children, who would be judged more harshly than the men. Everyone has too much invested to ever give up our communal society, but I'm old, and everyone will understand my taking India as a symbolic act of unity of the men and women as a whole here. God has begun to tell me the young find sharing with me to be a burden. My sexual energy is intimidating. I've seen the girls shrink away from me on training nights, and I would be lying if I didn't say it breaks my heart that they will never experience the things I know. But I will be satisfied knowing you and Edmund and some of the other young men will do your best while I work on my final project in India. Her loyalty and honesty have taken my breath away, and the fact that she would share with you, knowing your difficulties, to put my mind at ease about you gratifies me. Maybe Sonja's training was in God's will for you after all. Frankly I don't know how you managed to control yourself with India."

"I didn't," Buck said, but he didn't elaborate because it was obvious that Richard did not want to hear. Buck was afraid that a full confession now would do harm to India and the baby. Maybe the baby wouldn't look like Fred. Or maybe it would, but Buck wanted to believe Richard. God could turn all things to good for those who loved Him. Buck must submit the future to God. "Father, forgive me."

"You're too hard on yourself. Now come and enjoy the gift that God is giving our community. A new little one."

"I'll be down in a while, Father. I just need to clean up."

"Of course."

Richard left, and Buck sat at his desk to write a letter.

*Dear Thankful,*

*I miss you so much. I wish I had you to talk to here. I have met some very nice people, but they do not know me the way you do. Here there are so many expectations for me. I thought I would like that. God is very good to me, and I am ungrateful as always. I need your clarity. I am alone in the world. Things spin, and I have no focus.*

*I wish I could have saved you somehow.*

*By now I am sure you know that Middlemay followers believe in free love. On so many levels it makes sense, but I'm more lonely and hopeless than ever at being able to break myself from craving a special love. Thankful, I confess to you that now I am no better than you. I let myself be convinced that somehow physical affection would heighten my love for God! I am not even sure I thought this nobly at the time. I believe I was just seduced by a beautiful girl and was too undisciplined to stop. Did you know Fred is unfaithful to Rose already?*

*Richard assures me that God is at work in me, but I keep waiting to feel something. The only thing I feel is a terrible sense that God has given me a great chance at success, and I repel it at every turn. I thought when I first arrived here that Middlemay was an expansive place, but it feels so contracted now. There is always someone in my room bothering me, and I have no time to think my own thoughts.*

*Maybe God knows that if I thought too hard I might be afraid of all that He wants me to do. Thankful, I confess that I struggle under the burdens of others. Secretly I do not want to help any of them. I resent their troubles, and how they affect me. I feel petty and* selfish when I find that I am angry with a person for sinning because I have to pick up the pieces. I am not a good Christian yet. I am ashamed to admit that I am angry at God for taking my hand and my face and West Point and even Rose. I want to believe it is all for a purpose, but when I look around I see others taking just what they like and suffering no consequence. God has every right to be unfair if He wants to, but it hurts me to think He wants so little joy for me.

I am being summoned now to celebrate. Please pray for your foolish brother.
Buck Crenshaw

\*\*\*

Dear Buck,

You have always had such a flair for the dramatic. I love you dearly, but you put yourself as the lead in a theatrical when you are just a bit player like the rest of us. God didn't call you to Middlemay, a pretty girl did. It seems that like always you fall under the spell of authority and lose your footing. Why must you always be led? Why do you not lead yourself for a change? Whenever you defer your intellect to another's you make mistakes. Why do you not have some confidence in yourself?

I do not want to hear you talk about your face and hand any more. You are handsome enough. You have enough money that your hand is of little consequence. You say that you want to serve God. Do you need a title or a leader to do that? I do not know why you joined this silly group, and I am sorry that you have allowed your one moral stand to be undermined, but as a man you will have other chances. I do know that a self-pitying man is repugnant to most women. You should stop. I know this is a harsh letter, but I am so tired of watching you sacrifice yourself for mistaken loyalties and a very weird sense of God's will. God is a loving father. The mistakes and missteps are our own. Think upon that, dear brother.

As always with love,
Thankful

# Chapter Twenty-Nine

Buck did not celebrate India's pregnancy. There had always been a resentment among his siblings against his parents over abundant procreative tendencies, but Buck had never shared in it. He loved a full house and big meals and shoes of all sizes tossed around the mudroom. He missed his little sisters the most when watching the young folk here play so innocently.

That Fred's child—a Crenshaw child—should be thrown off by his brother maddened him. Buck didn't blame India because he knew how charming Fred could be. Unlike the women who were born here or came by their own free will, India had come in desperation. Maybe she wanted to believe in the theology too, but the baby and Fred drove her to abandoning all say in her personal life. Buck almost admired India for finding a place where her child would not be tarred a bastard. When he glanced out the window and caught sight of her walking to her work at the press she looked more handsome than ever.

He hoped she'd be happy in her security forever and vowed to protect her and the baby, but from the distance of a cordial friendship. If the child aroused no suspicions, he might be good friends with it—like a true uncle.

India's news kept Richard in joyful preoccupation for weeks until he sailed off to England to study spiritual gardening. The pressure to train for future leadership receded, leaving Buck time to concern himself with small, pleasant things like talking with Sonja about cooking or helping Parmelia with her Latin. Sonja convinced him that his fasting had gone on long enough (not that he needed prodding), and Parmelia laughed at him when he took Latin conjugations too seriously. For a brief interlude God's hand wasn't around his neck. Between bites of Sonja's flaky-crusted shepherd's pie—the best he'd ever tasted—he noted a clearness of thought and a resurgence of strength—now with a purpose—to make sure the baby would be treated well.

\*\*\*

Frost glistened on the windows now each morning, and the voices of shepherds coaxing the animals up the meadow sounded cool and hollow without the summer birds singing. The floors creaked as the wood shrank in the drafty rooms before fires were lit in the stoves. Buck's throat always ached in the fall, and without Richard's prayers the pain had come back strong like an old part of himself. He wrapped his neck in a rustic scarf knit by one of the children and went out for a walk in the jewel-toned woods listening to the wind brush against the dry, old leaves.

A call startled him. He turned to India and Edmund, surprised to see them together this early in the day. India looked green with morning sickness, but happy.

"Buck," she said, "I've been meaning to talk to you for weeks but was too ashamed. I never should have used you the way I did."

Buck glanced at Edmund.

"Don't worry. Edmund knows everything. I told him all about Fred and you," India said.

"Was that wise?"

She shrugged, her round face rosy in the cold. "I'd hate for my actions to destroy your friendship. I'm so grateful that you haven't snitched to Richard yet."

"I will never say a word." Buck turned to Edmund. "I've regretted what happened that day by the falls so many times. I don't know what came over me."

Edmund smiled. His glasses were frosty. "Your manhood overcame you. I was angry, but I have no claims on India, and now I understand why she needed to be with Father. I can't pretend to understand what it's like for a girl out there on her own. It convinces me that sharing here is so much better for everyone. I prayed and prayed for the marriage spirit to dissipate in me, and now it has. Father was right. You saved me from a grave mistake. India is set aside for Father."

Buck smiled and shook Edmund's outstretched hand, yet it troubled him that Edmund had given up so easily. "Richard shouldn't be excused from the rules."

India shook her head. "Richard has shared with so many and taught the girls for so many years. Can he really be expected to keep that sort of thing going forever? I can give him peace and rest. It's a small sacrifice to pay for the child's security. It's not as if other young women want to be with him anymore. This saves the poor man's pride."

Edmund still looked at India adoringly. "This unbelievable woman has taught me so much about sacrificial love."

Buck's stomach turned, but he agreed that for the child this was best. He left them and wandered over to the children's room. With Richard gone he had mornings free. The young pupils sat drawing pictures of the Good Samaritan when he arrived and seated himself in the corner on a small chair. Lily Johnson, a middle-aged and mild-looking woman ran the school while other adults filtered in on a weekly basis to help out. Buck enjoyed the old familiar smells of chalk and the ink-stained desks and blotters. Apples lay toppled on Lily's desk, and her perfume mingled with the yeasty scent of children's snacks unfinished and thrown into the bucket set aside for pig slop. Lily smiled at him but continued to talk about the Samaritan, wandering around the room, occasionally patting a distracted child's shoulder.

Buck scanned the faces of the children, trying to catch resemblances to the adults at Middlemay, but except for a few they all looked average and unfamiliar. Would Fred's child fit in? Buck vowed to stomp out any of Fred's ruthless tendencies. No point in raising another spoiled child. But then Buck would not be raising the baby.

The elders continued to insist Buck produce a baby of his own too. He could not lie to himself. That Fred's baby would come first galled Buck. What was he waiting for? Lily came over now. "Buck, are you here to help? Joan is supposed to be here in a few minutes."

"I just came to visit, if that's all right. I wonder how the children feel about living here."

"It's all they know. Most of them do just fine, but I suspect even on the outside some don't like being separated from their mothers."

"I was afraid to leave my mother's side. I thought she'd die," Buck confided. He kept to himself that on some occasions he hoped his mother would die.

"Veronica is the little girl with the black hair over there," Lily said. "She's having a hard time sleeping in the children's wing. She was a mistake child, and the mother should never have had her. She's a wonderful woman but so needful of affection and has handicapped poor Veronica. The girl misses being doted on and has been pining for her mother all day long—poor thing. See how she stares out the window? She's been like that for an hour. I told Richard that we should have taken the dear little thing earlier, but Richard's heart for the mother is too big, and he let it get the better of his judgment."

"How old is Veronica?"

"She's five years but precocious. The smart ones take it hardest leaving their mothers," Lily said. "Why don't you talk with her?"

Buck walked over, grabbing a small chair and motioning for the prim girl with the pointy chin and frown to slide over. Veronica did so grudgingly.

"I miss my mother sometimes too," Buck whispered, "but you'll get to see her again."

"It's not the same for you because you're a grown-up, and you can do as you please," Veronica said with great bitterness.

"No, I can't do as I please. God has rules for adults too."

"God is stupid then, and I hate Him."

"Never say that," Buck said, but stopped. "Maybe we just don't understand everything."

"I don't want to understand God if he takes away my mommy and makes her cry."

"Special love is problematic," Buck said, feeling a fraud.

Veronica looked at him as if he had three heads.

"Special love keeps you from loving others," he added.

"I never used to hate everyone, but now I do," the girl said, scribbling on a piece of paper.

"Oh, don't say such ugly words. You're too pretty for that."

"Mother said I should never trust a charmer." She didn't look up, just kept doodling.

"Are you really only five?" Buck laughed but saw how serious and sad the girl was.

"Yes, Mother says I'm smart like my father, but Edmund seems stupid and doesn't care a bit about me. I want to go to a real home like in the books," she said, studying him. "What was your house like when you were little in the world?"

Touched by her thirst and yearning, Buck leaned in closer. "My house was full of noise—never a moment's peace. Everyone fought and climbed the curtains. Not like here." He took her pencil and sketched a shaky drawing of the house on Chestnut Street in Englewood. This made the girl smile. "We had two cats and several dogs. My favorite one was a retriever who was awful to everyone but me."

"Special love," Veronica said.

Buck laughed. "Caught, I guess." He continued drawing and warmed to his subject. "We had horses—grand Percherons—and we weren't allowed near them, but my brother and I disobeyed. One time I got kicked in the head."

"Is that how you got beat-up looking?"

"No, that scar's hidden by my hair, you want to see?"

Veronica smiled. "Yes."

He leaned over to give her a view of the place. She touched it and giggled. "Tell me more."

"Hmm. Let's see. We used to play this game on the stairs like we were sledding on our pillow cases, and Fred, my brother, knocked his teeth out when he hit the banister. Oh, and once we told my sister Meg we wouldn't let her in her room until she sang a bawdy song at the top of her lungs in the hallway so my parents could hear her. Meg got in so much trouble. My mother spanked her, and then we got spanked too." He lingered on the memory. "But Mama tried her best after all. We were rambunctious. We broke everything valuable she owned.

"And I'd often wait for my father to come home from work. Just wait for hours. When he came home he'd make such a racket on the stairs because he was heavy and tired. I'd jump from bed and say something to make him smile. Sometimes he'd take me to his study and tell me all sorts of things I didn't understand, but I didn't care. I just wanted to be near him. Even the smell of his cigars soothed me. Funny, I remember my mother sometimes joining us when I was younger than you. Mama would sit near Father too. Sort of in a shy way, but I believe she cared for him then."

Veronica leaned her head on his arm. "And what else?"

"And there was the time at West Point when everyone hated me, and my parents came to visit. I was so happy to see them. My father gave me an expensive watch that belonged to my uncle who died in the war." Buck stopped when he noticed that the other children had stopped working and were listening to him. "I'm sorry, I don't know why I'm telling you."

"You're so lucky," Veronica said.

Buck caught the annoyed look on Lily's face and stood up. "I'm sorry. Veronica, this way is better. You'll have a ton of grand memories of your brothers and sisters here."

"They're not my real brothers and sisters!"

The teacher grabbed Buck's arm. "Say good bye to Mr. Buck. He has an appointment now."

"Won't you come back?" Veronica asked.

Another boy raised his hand and spoke at the same time. "You were a soldier? That's what I want to be. Did you kill Indians?"

"I fought them only once," Buck began.

Miss Lily interrupted. "Here at Middlemay we believe in peaceful ways to resolve conflict. No one from Middlemay has *ever* been a soldier. Mr. Buck has changed his ways since coming here, haven't you, Buck?"

"I've known many brave soldiers who fought to free the slaves."

Another young boy jumped in. "Why'd you fight an Indian when they're so innocent and noble? That's what Father Richard says."

"I was walking in the desert when a coach headed for the fort was taken by Apache men. There were girls inside so I tried to help. I didn't mean for any of it to happen, but they got me in the hand." Buck pulled up his sleeve and showed where his prosthetic ended and his real person began.

A few of the boys ran up to get a better look and to run their fingers over the wooden hand. Buck smiled. Children were so unlike adults who cringed and looked away from the grotesque. The boys smiled up at him, peppering him with further questions, and the girls, though shy, gathered round too. Veronica took his real hand in hers. "You're like a hero in one of my mother's books," she said.

"Children, this is quite enough," Lily scolded. "You're embarrassing Mr. Buck."

"No, it's fine. I miss my little brother and sisters, and please, children, just call me Buck."

Lily ordered the children to their seats. "A moment of silent prayer now while I speak with Mr. Buck outside." She gave them a long, stern look until all of their heads were bowed in prayer before leading Buck to the door. Veronica's little head popped up, and she waved to him as he left.

Once outside, he looked at his shoes and then out over the fields, waiting for a lecture.

"My, you have a way with children," Lily said.

"I like them."

"But, you must understand that one day you'll be an authority figure to them. Your familiarity was inappropriate."

"When I'm in charge I want the children to feel they can talk to me. I hate intimidation."

"Richard has been very supportive of Indian rights. What do you think of that?"

"That's fine, but I'm not going to lie to anyone about the world, especially children. I'm not ashamed of the military. It's natural for little boys to have an interest."

"Maybe boys on the outside, but here we intend to raise men who can rise above animal instincts."

"I resent your characterization of soldiers as animals."

"I didn't mean to insult you," she replied unconvincingly, "but we follow Jesus here."

"Jesus never told a soldier to stop being a soldier, but he endlessly lectured hypocrites."

"Are you insinuating that I'm a hypocrite?"

"No more so than any of us, I suppose, but yes," he said. "We live in this false and safe world. It's not so safe or idyllic out there in town. Pacifists get to shirk responsibility yet benefit from the law and order of the regular folk who never have the chance to live in a community like this. If property rights weren't respected and upheld by soldiers and law we couldn't stop anyone from invading the land and taking our mansion."

"One day everyone will live in a place like this," Lily said, her voice full of hope and sentiment. "God promised mansions for everyone—we're just the vanguard—so says Richard."

"The mansions are heavenly mansions—so says the Bible," Buck said. "Here we are promised troubles and persecution for our faith in Jesus. I wonder sometimes if we've buried our heads in the sand. The young girls we've brought to work for us—have you noticed the hunger in their eyes?"

Lily thought a moment. Her shoulders sagged. "I'm ashamed to say I hadn't taken any notice of the girls. So they are hungry you say? Hungry for knowledge?"

"Lily, you know I mean food. Shouldn't we put ourselves out a little at least? I think about the goats and sheep—will we be on the right side? I worry sometimes, don't you?"

She gasped. "Such a lack of faith worries me about the future! A leader must assure his people. Richard has done that. Don't you believe we're ushering in the last days and the coming kingdom?"

"Why are there no uneducated people here except the help?"

"One day we will convince them we have a better way for them, but right now they are so stuck on their simplistic traditions."

He smiled. "You're just another snob."

"And you're an infidel!"

"Now that's extreme language," he replied. "The kingdom of God is for everyone even if they never understand the joy of learning Greek. The first thing I will do when it's my time is to let anyone who wants come and join."

Lily laughed now. "Richard tried that already. There's nothing original in what you say. For about five years we let the poor and hungry take refuge here, but they could never be convinced to work or learn. They stole from our funds and didn't take our walk with God seriously. It was impossible to convince them of anything. It is true what Christ taught us—the poor will always plague us. As long as useless people have offspring.

"It was finally decided that it was cheaper to buy them off with a little money than to keep them here sapping the life out of everything. Two were sent to prison even. Richard says that it's not for us to solve problems that the fallen world creates. We can only be a beacon for those who are ready for change. It's why the breeding program holds so much potential. If anything, we need to be having more children here."

Buck looked across to the apple orchard where the last of the fall apples were rotting on the ground. "I wonder if maybe you'd like to be courted."

"Pardon?"

Buck hesitated. "Well, it seems rude to ask if you're still able to—have children, but ..."

Lily blushed. "It's still a possibility for me, but I've never been asked to have children."

"Why not?"

"I suppose because in the beginning when I was young Richard opposed procreation because he believed the end was near, and then upon further revelation God changed his mind. By then there were younger, prettier girls."

"You're handsome and refreshingly opinionated. And you don't look all that old."

"Thank you, *I think*," Lily said, but her eyes sparkled. "There is something nice about you though. Did you really save girls from Indians?"

"I was just at the right place."

"How do you mean to court me? That's not done here. Will you go to the elders or shall I?"

"No, I told Richard that I must begin to lead myself."

Lily sighed.

"Just meeting in a room seems unromantic," Buck said. "Let's not share right away. I'll send flowers first, and we could stroll out to the rye fields. Everything looks so golden this time of year."

"You've taken me so by surprise. I don't know what to say."

"I'll let you get back to the children." He kissed her hand.

No monumental thrill of attraction came, but neither did the sickening feeling of rejection. He watched her as she turned back toward the children. She glanced over her shoulder once with a funny smile and closed the door behind her.

Somehow making this small decision on his own heightened his excitement at the prospect of sex with this average-looking woman. Maybe they wouldn't court for too long.

As he walked past the vegetable garden he averted his eyes. Picking pumpkins with one useless hand was difficult, and after much frustration he'd lagged behind even the laziest of workers earlier in the week. Richard left him a full plate of studies and themes for articles to be written and published in the paper. He was also to oversee the workers at the print shop while Rebecca traveled (which was unnecessary—Rebecca had their hearts and minds wrapped around her finger). A small controversy had ensued when it was announced that she would be traveling to Europe with Richard as his assistant. India begged to come along, but Richard insisted she stay put for the baby's sake.

Some questioned the necessity of this trip. Richard explained that only the best cheeses were made in the Alps. Would it not serve Middlemay well to make special cheeses for the outside world? Buck liked cheese well enough but wondered if the trip was self-serving when no one else had the possibility of such sightseeing. Buck did not have in him a real sense of wanderlust, but recognized in some Middlemayers a jealousy over the trip—did they nurse a secret urge to escape sometimes? Buck understood why Richard had hotly argued against the fencing of their lands. A visual reminder of their entrapment might arouse a conflicted spirit. The gate as picturesque entranceway and Richard's strong personality were enough. Buck reminded himself that this was a *holy entrapment*.

Before climbing the stairs to Richard's study (which would one day be his own), Buck slipped into the kitchen to make himself a small meal. He wasn't really skirting the rules if he wasn't taking advantage of women, was he? He buttered a slice of bread and spread Richard's delightful jam over the top. Verlinda stood at the door scowling with arms folded. "That bread is for the bread pudding I'm making for tomorrow's breakfast."

"Oh, there's plenty more. This won't be missed," Buck said, trying to move around her, but Verlinda blocked the door. If Verlinda were a man he would have shoved past her. "Verlinda, I have studies to do. I'm sorry I took *two* pieces of *stale* bread. I'll never do it again."

"I'm sure you won't when I get done with you at the next circle. This isn't the first time you've stolen from the community."

"All right, I do occasionally take a snack, but I get hungry. Is it a sin?"

"It is if you steal and if it's already been noted that your weakness is gluttony."

Buck tossed the bread on to the clean counter. "Here, take your stinking bread. My money probably paid for the flour! And, you bitter old hag, I am part of the community and have a right to eat."

"People who work have a right to eat," Verlinda mumbled.

"What did you say?"

"You heard me, you son of Satan!"

"I work for Richard!"

"It's always the same—men with scheming brains—the smart ones—convince the rest of us who sweat and slave that their big ideas will change things. Looks like Middlemay is no different than anyplace else. The little people always get used by the big bugs, and we're stupid enough to buy into it. Richard makes a fuss over you because you came with money and pedigree. I lost all faith in this place once we brought in poor folk to work for wages instead of God's glory. Everyone here is too good to do their own dirty laundry, and we have an invalid little prince awaiting his turn at the throne. This is not what I signed on for!"

"Not everyone is made for manual labor ..." Buck replied shakily. Her thoughts were his own. "But someone has to be in charge, I suppose."

"Yes, but it's never a working man."

"Intelligence counts for something, doesn't it?" he asked. "I wouldn't want an idiot as a doctor, for instance."

"No, but the people who build and plant and wash up get no reward."

"Verlinda, I agree with you, I think, but I'm not sure what can be done about it. Some people are just better than others—at things. If I ever do take Richard's place I'll try my best to treat people fairly."

She snapped her towel. "I have real work to do. I'll believe it when I see it. For now just stay out of the kitchen."

# Chapter Thirty

On his way to his room to grab a book he'd left behind, Buck met the little girl with the war veteran father. Lorna carried a basket of sheets to be delivered to the rooms upstairs. He took the basket from her, cradling it between his good hand and his left arm. "Let me help you."

Lorna smiled and followed him down the hall.

"So, how's your daddy?" he asked. "I've been meaning to ask, but I've been awful busy with studies."

Lorna shrugged.

"What is it?" he asked.

"The little baby—Noah—is so good and cute, but Daddy can't love him. It's not Noah's fault, and when I'm here I feel like I should be home, but when I'm home I worry over money so I'm always mixed up."

How long ago had Buck promised to visit? He checked his watch and sighed. "What do you say we go home right now?"

"Am I fired?" she asked with tremulous voice.

He set the basket at the bottom of the stairs. "The laundry can wait. I made you a promise, and I'm going to keep it, but first let's get some supplies." He took Lorna's hand and bypassed the kitchen for the little closet where Sonja had moved her baked goods. He had one of the two keys. Lorna's eyes lit up at the sights and smells. Buck found a canvas bag and piled it with assorted items. The two raced to the barn now, and he took a horse. The girl helped him saddle it. They hopped on and cantered along the main path to the gate.

Buck hadn't ridden since losing his hand, but it came back to him easily, steering the horse with his weight and legs. The girl sat in front of him, laughing and talking as they traced their way through the lonely woods, but quieted as they trotted past town onto a dirt path that led to a tin-roofed farmstead neglected for years by its crippled owner. The girl looked back at Buck embarrassed, but he pretended not to notice.

"I hope your father likes mince pie."

Lorna smiled, but not without worry.

He jumped from the horse and helped the girl to the ground. She led him to the front door and into the darkened front room where only small shafts of sunlight penetrated the gloom behind thick canvas curtains covered with months of soot and spider webs. At the sound of their hushed voices and the creaking floor, a large man with grizzled beard and sunken cheeks joined them, adjusting his suspenders. "Lorna, what are you home for?" he asked, ignoring Buck's extended hand.

"Daddy, this is Mr. Crenshaw from the place I work."

The veteran glanced at Buck and then back at his daughter tenderly. "Did you get yourself in trouble, Miss Doone?"

Buck answered. "No, she's a good little worker."

"She's a tough one," the man replied. Keeping his eyes on his girl, the man lit a pipe.

"Yes," Buck said, clearing his throat. "Well, I came to check in, sir."

"What did you imagine you'd find here?" the man asked, taking a seat without offering one to Buck. "I don't drink or beat the children. I appreciate you giving her work, but I don't need interfering from you—I'm a Methodist."

"I'm not meaning to interfere, sir. It's just sitting up on that hill sometimes it's easy to forget that God wants us to help others."

"I didn't ask for help from you or God."

"Sir, I just wanted to bring you a nice meal," Buck said, "and to talk about the baby."

Lorna's father puffed on his pipe. "The boy'll be picked up in a week to go with the orphanage people. Truth is I'd send Lorna away too if I wasn't so selfish."

"Lorna's your own flesh and blood. That's not selfish. And it's hard not to resent a baby who took your wife."

"You should leave," Lorna's father said, running his hand over the clean but bare table.

Buck pulled the mince pies and apple tarts from his bag. "My father back home was a doctor, and I went with him all the time to deliver babies. When the women died he always tried to keep in touch with the men because they'd get so lonely and keep to themselves. It must be hard working this place with your injury." Buck rolled up his sleeve, exposing his prosthetic. "I lost it when I was still in the army."

The man looked up, still chewing the end of his pipe. "I thought you were a religious crazy."

"That I may be, but I was once a soldier and wanted to be an officer, but it didn't work out. Lorna tells me you were a hero during the big war."

"Lorna's a young thing and much impressed with stories," the man said, scratching his beard.

"Oh, she's very clever and worries so much about you ... and Noah."

The man's face shadowed in the dim room. "Lorna thinks I hate the child, but I'm at wits' end what to do with him. He was unexpected, and I was happy with the way things were. This place was never much, but my wife made it nice with flowers and such. I knew her since our schoolhouse days and never imagined life without her."

Buck sat quietly, praying he could come up with something to say. A few children a little younger than Lorna lurked at a door to another room. Buck waved them in and handed out tarts, but they waited for their father's permission.

"What do you say?" the father reminded them, and they all thanked Buck.

"Sir, I'd like to help you if I can, though I have no idea how."

"Son, just tell me, when you were with your father ... with those women who died ... do you believe we might meet them again?" The man had a hungry look behind years of weathered skin. Buck imagined him as a young soldier going to fight in the glorious war with his sweetheart waving him off and there waiting for him when he returned.

"Father says the dying forced him to believe in eternal life," Buck said. "Sometimes we felt as if the spirit floated in the room before leaving. It scared me as a child." He glanced out at the darkening sky. "Sir, what would best help you get through the winter?"

The man stared into the fire. For a long time Buck thought he might be thrown out, but then the man looked at him as if daring him to find fault. "I have no time for the small child. I have wood to chop for the cold, and the pigs need slaughtering and smoking. The baby is more than I can bear right now so I've arranged for him at an orphanage—before the other children get too attached."

"Sir, you might regret that. Lorna *already* loves Noah." Buck stood up and went to the quiet cradle where the baby napped. The child was small and thin. Buck picked him up with a smile. "What if I took him back to Middlemay for the winter? Lorna could visit him every day, and he'd be well cared for while you get things in order here. In the spring he'll be much sturdier and walking I bet."

"I've heard stories about you folks—I don't know."

"I will personally care for Noah. I give you my word. Take time to mourn, sir. It's the nicest thing—the devotion you have to your wife. It must have been great to love like that." A sudden yearning crept upon Buck, but he stifled it with heroic resolve—selfish love was not for him. Self-denial would be his spiritual strength.

"My wife was the greatest thing I ever had." Lorna's father spoke to his daughter now. "I don't want you to be Noah's mother when you're still so little yourself. Noah can go with your friend here—we'll see how it goes. Then you can keep an eye on him for us, and we can visit him on Sundays—if that's all right."

"Of course. You can come any time you like and bring everyone. There's nice things to do for children, and in the spring ..." Buck rocked the baby in his arms, missing the years long ago when he cradled his little sisters. "I'm certain things will feel different."

"Yes, I hope so," the man said, touching the little boy's tiny hand as if it pained him.

"Sir, one last thing. Would it be all right if I sent down a few boys to help you chop that wood? The young men get restless up on the hill sometimes, and it would be good for them to experience something of the world. You'd be doing our community a favor."

The man nodded. The sky was aflame against the dark woods. "If you don't mind I'll just ride you and the baby to the gates." His stoic veneer threatened to crumble as he left for the barn.

Buck didn't feel proud of himself—that would be prideful, but he couldn't help grinning—God used him for a good thing. He pulled Lorna aside. "Land sakes, what's your father's name? I was awful rude."

"Jack Fellows. You sure you can take care of Noah? And you won't keep him forever?" Lorna asked with tears in her eyes as she wrapped the boy in a tattered shawl.

"I'll have lots of help, and you can be the judge every day."

Lorna sniffled as she handed the baby to Buck. "He doesn't have much that's clean, sir."

"Call me Buck, Lorna. I hope we'll be good friends from now on."

Lorna smiled warily, pulling her hair back into a ponytail as she watched for her father's buckboard. The crows called in the forest, and the first autumn frosts kept the leaves damp underfoot as they waited in the yard. The baby in Buck's arms acted as antidote to the bleak surroundings and Buck's usual autumnal depression.

The wheels over rocky soil made lonesome music as Jack came round the house with Buck's horse tied to the wagon. When the old veteran nodded for Buck to come aboard, Lorna kissed Noah and passed him back up to Buck.

"I promise I'll stay with Noah all night till he gets settled. I've had tons of practice at home. See you tomorrow."

Lorna ran inside, full of emotion. Jack snapped the reins against the old pony and off they went on a silent journey, each man in his own thoughts. Jack wouldn't hear of coming within the gates of the community. He unhitched the Middlemay horse and led it through the gate. The animal trotted to the barn on its own, for the Middlemayers were excellent horse trainers.

The old soldier hesitated. "Lorna will see him first thing in the morning ..."

"Of course, sir. And please do come any time. You're quite welcome here, and if there's anything else I can do ..."

Jack's jaw set. "Don't take on more than you can deliver. Why are you so set on my family?"

"I'm tired of helping myself, I guess. I don't think God just wants me studying and reading all the time."

The man almost smiled. "Well, thank you."

Buck strode up the main path as the lights were lit on the porch of the mansion. The baby was soft and round. He loved it already. The littlest ones bewitched him.

When he entered the children's wing Parmelia and India stopped reading to the toddlers and ran to him at the sight of the child.

"Who's this?" Parmelia asked.

"Lorna's little brother who's come to us to be cared for till his father gains his footing."

Parmelia raised her brow. "Has Father given permission?"

"How could he? Richard's on a boat seeing the world," India said, her hands resting on her growing middle.

"Well, he won't like it," Parmelia said, smiling at Buck's rebellion.

"Why not?" Buck asked.

"Because we're not a charity."

"Well, we should be. This little thing needs caring for, and we're God's people aren't we?"

"It's your own funeral, Buck, but Father preaches charity begins at home. Next you'll invite the whole family to come here."

"Maybe I will," Buck said with smug authority. "Maybe God has put me in charge for a reason."

Parmelia rolled her eyes and straightened the cap on Buck's head. "It's nice that you believe all the praise heaped upon you by Father."

"Why shouldn't he, Parm?" India asked. "It's wonderful that you've such a big heart."

Parmelia pretended at a disappointed frown. "Middlemay isn't the right place to take on loafers unwilling to care for their own. Haven't you read the science?"

"How can you talk of science looking at this handsome baby?" Buck asked. The child was quiet but alert.

"I'm not fond of babies," Parmelia said, tickling Noah's chin and pulling him from Buck. "Anyway, we send money to the churches in town to help with the poor—he is awful adorable though." She laughed, rubbing her nose against the baby's as she cradled him. "You weren't here when the vagabonds and shirkers were let stay. Even the children were changed by their language and riotous behavior."

"A baby wintering here when his father is still mourning the loss of his wife will be a good example for our community," Buck said.

"Is that the story the man told you to offload the child upon us?" Parmelia asked. "Buck Crenshaw, you are the handsomest form of innocence I've ever seen."

"I'm surprised at your cynicism, Parm," India said. "You haven't gotten off the farm much, but you pretend to know everyone's motives. It's sad how you turn a good deed into something shabby. I'm very impressed by Buck, but then he's always impressing me. You've never seen what it's like for poor children."

"And you have?" Parmelia asked.

"Yes, indeed. I lived in New York City, remember? There are whole city blocks teeming with unwanted street urchins. It's so sad."

"Father doesn't want his heavenly acreage turned into a tenement," Parmelia said. "Throwing trash on a beautiful cake doesn't make the garbage taste better, it only spoils the cake."

"That's not very Christian," Buck said. "I'm disappointed in you."

"Why? Are you stretching your ruling wings? I like you, but don't get ahead of yourself. I have to listen to Father, but not you. You fell from grace in my books when you threw yourself away on Miss Pious Van Westervelt."

"Yes, you remind me of that dreadful mistake every day. Aren't you tired of it by now?" Buck asked, noting a hurt look on India's face at his reply. It pleased him.

Parmelia giggled and kissed the baby.

The baby waved his arms, reaching for Buck's scarf.

"Help me find clean things for Noah," Buck said, "and let's give him a bath."

Parmelia pinched Buck's cheek. "What a sweet thing you are."

India said nothing, but Buck detected in her expression a look of admiration.

# Chapter Thirty-One

Thankful and Henry married before the judge in Martha's rose garden on a pleasant day with only a wisp of cloud cover and the slightest chance of shower. Betty made a simple meal of lamb and root vegetables from the garden with a spice cake for dessert. Martha, Betty, and Henry's parents attended. Thankful wore her grandmother's grey silk gown, taken in here and there. It wasn't quite festive on its own for a wedding, but once roses from the garden were pinned in her dark curls and around her wrist she looked the height of elegance. Mrs. Demarest pulled Thankful aside as the day turned to soft evening.

"Oh, dear, it's all happened so fast, but just like our Henry. He's such a love," she said, taking Thankful by the arm for a stroll through the small orchard. "Henry's room was just as he left it all these years, but I suppose you'd like something a little more feminine."

"No, it's all right, Mrs. Demarest. We won't be there for too long. I don't want to trouble you."

"But, dear, where will you go?"

"Hasn't your son told you of our plans for travel?" Thankful asked.

The round, old lady batted her lashes in amusement. "He's such a dreamer, our Henry. We paid for his trips to Vienna to study music with a master."

"Oh, how wonderful that must have been!" Thankful said, squeezing the woman's arm.

"Yes, he had a wonderful time," Mrs. Demarest said, adding in a whisper, "It's where he met Hilde."

"Henry's wife ..." Thankful guessed.

"Hilde was a talented violinist, but too controlling. Everything must be just so and proper. I told her first thing that Henry might dote on her for a while, but she should expect that he'd want his Friday nights to be social—he's a social creature. Hilde was too hard on Henry, but he never listened to us. He should have sent her back. We offered to pay to have them *all* shipped off."

"Are the children *horrible* then?" Thankful asked, chilled and tense.

"Oh, no. They're sweet and kind, but young in their ways. It's Hilde's parents. Henry begged us to bring the parents over because Hilde missed them. They never liked Henry and for no good reason. Poor Henry lost all confidence in his abilities and couldn't find work. They didn't approve of him playing the piano at the tavern—we didn't like it either, but our investments went sour in '73 so we had no extra funds to give, and Henry just worked his fingers to the bone. We prayed for them and sold off the last of our farmland to bring Hilde's parents here from Vienna, but they refused to contribute a penny—not a penny! We found out later that Hilde's father was a wealthy merchant back in Vienna and should have paid his own way here! He owns a watch store in Hackensack now, even wanted Henry to work as a clerk! Can you imagine Henry wasting his talents on such trivia?"

Thankful had nothing to say so Mrs. Demarest continued. "When Hilde died, the children came to live with us for a short time, but I haven't the strength for little ones. We send them things, for certain. Coats and frocks and such. I miss them too, but it's best that they live in Hackensack."

"So they live only a short ride from here?" Thankful asked, drowning in new information.

"Henry didn't tell you?" Mrs. Demarest asked in a smug and satisfied way.

"No, he didn't, but I intend to meet these children myself," Thankful replied, trying to appear secure and unafraid of Henry's past life intruding into their present.

"Good for you. Maybe *you'll* like them."

"I'm *sure* I will," Thankful lied.

Henry came up with drinks. "Is everything all right?" he asked.

"Perfect," Thankful said, kissing him lightly on the cheek. She must whip Henry into shape, for if she didn't, she could never respect him.

That night Thankful pretended to be exhausted by the day's events. She pretended while Henry changed his clothes that she had fallen into a deep sleep. He tried to wake her with whispers of love and nudges. Thankful almost opened her eyes, but something prevented her and she held them tightly shut. Henry gave up and fell truly asleep himself while she lay in the darkness wondering how she had gotten there.

In the morning she slipped from bed and dressed for breakfast before waking Henry, but when she dropped her brush he stirred with a moan. She sensed he was annoyed that she had dressed, so she sat beside him and ran her fingers through his hair. He even looks handsome in the morning, she thought, but the thought came with sadness. She didn't know why. "I'm sorry about last night, Henry—maybe tonight?"

He sat up and after a few seconds smiled his same good-natured smile. "Yes, we have the rest of our lives now, don't we? You were stunning yesterday, and I enjoyed just seeing you sleep so soundly next to me, like you finally found home. I do hope you feel that way, Thankful. I want to be your home."

She hadn't even begun to unpack her baggage. "Henry, I want to meet your children."

He gave her an odd, not-quite-pleased look. "This is sudden. May I ask why?"

"Because they're a part of you, and I don't want to live denying reality." She hoped this sounded brave.

"The reality is that I want *you*," Henry said, rubbing his hand over her shoulder in a grating way. "The children can wait. I know I'm being selfish, but marriage has rewards that you denied me last night—rather unfairly, especially with the way you looked."

She blushed. They would go on riding bicycles and watching sunsets and dreaming.

# Chapter Thirty-Two

Thankful's days changed little, but her pay did. When she tried to thank her grandmother for the more than generous raise, Martha gruffly turned the subject to other things, making sure to add at least one small complaint about Thankful's bookkeeping. Sometimes Henry and Thankful dined with Martha in the evenings. Sometimes Henry had a picnic packed, and they sat on the banks of the river eating cold chicken and playing silly lovers' games until the darkness sent them in by the piano, where Henry filled the house with new compositions he was working on but never seemed to finish. Thankful suggested he bring his pieces into the city to show people, but Henry laughed at her naiveté and brushed her off, telling her that one day she would understand the plight of a composer.

And why should Henry strive when his parents gave him just enough to get by? Thankful thought of Buck sometimes, free to find God because of their father's money. Her resentment faded when she considered the high price Buck paid to be their parents' ward. But Henry had no excuse! Thankful squirreled her money away, failing to mention her raise.

Sunsets in the field behind grandmother's house begged Thankful to linger before going to the cramped room she shared with Henry. She'd never been allowed to stand still at this time of day before. Always she was shooed in to dress for supper or French lessons back in Englewood. And nowhere in Englewood were there such open vistas. Every inch of forest and valley had been to market and bought by city folk. In these moments, she liked to think of Henry as a gift. Henry saw in the clouds casting shadows a song and a feeling. Land was no commodity to him, and he didn't hurry and fuss over the worries the rest of the world carried with them.

On just such an evening Henry hopped from his parents' sturdy carriage with a thunderstruck look upon his ruddy, handsome face as he took Thankful into his arms. "Oh, dear Thankful. I cherish everything about you especially your forgiving nature. I'm such a flawed man, and you love me anyway."

She pulled back enough to look at him. His years began to show at the corners of his eyes. "What's happened, Henry?"

Henry brightened in a hopeful, boyish way. "Remember when you said you wanted to meet my children?"

Thankful nodded in sudden panic and dread.

"Hilde's parents are annoyed at me for not telling them I've remarried. My mother saw them in Hackensack and foolishly mentioned it."

"I didn't realize we had to keep it secret," she said, all equanimity lost.

"Of course not, sweetheart. It's only I would have liked to tell them myself in my own way—at the right time. But never mind about that. The trouble is that they want the children told before too long."

Thankful took a long, exasperated breath but said, "They're right. It hurts children to have secrets."

He cupped his soft hands around her face and kissed her with exuberance. "Oh, I knew you'd understand! Mother has them over tonight for supper. You can meet everyone then."

"Tonight? But look at me! I've been at work, and I'm hot and tired!"

"Oh, never you mind! You look ravishing as always, and it's not as if Hilde's parents will ever like you—you understand. Ignore them. I do." He pulled her along and up into the carriage.

Martha came out of the kitchen. "Thankful, I thought you'd be dining with me tonight?"

Henry answered for her, "Martha, forgive us, my children have arrived and desperately want to meet the love of my life!"

Thankful noted the disappointment on her grandmother's face as she turned back into the house. Thankful sat silent and stiff next to Henry, who kept his eyes on the road, his face marble-white and frozen.

The Demarest Federal-style house of painted white brick, which at first had seemed so elegant and charming with its enormous weeping willows and shady hosta gardens, now filled Thankful with dread. Mrs. Demarest played stupid and weak by day and drank too much in the evenings, while Mr. Demarest most nights kept his head in a book. And here were the children lingering along the fence covered in rambling roses. They were fair-looking children, she thought as they eyed her when the carriage passed them. She waved at them primly. They dutifully waved back, following the carriage toward the barn. Henry jumped onto the spongy grass soaked by the swell of the river and helped her out of the conveyance.

"Thankful, this is Jacob, Avi, Helmut, Audric, Klera, and little Zala," Henry said.

"You're all so lovely," she said, wondering how she could have been afraid of them.

The youngest boy, Helmut, who looked to be about five and with a shock of black hair over his needy eyes, spoke first, "Papa, I tucked my shirt in my trousers!"

Henry glanced at Thankful. "Superb, Helmut."

They walked to the house together with the youngest girl, Zala, and Helmut hanging from their father. Henry allowed it but did not reciprocate their affection. Thankful eyed them jealously.

The older girl, Klera, who looked to be ten or eleven took Thankful's hand. "Shall I call you mother?"

"No, of course not!" Thankful said too quickly. "I wouldn't want you to think you must ..."

"I hate it here, but I'm glad to meet you since you're so pretty and the nicest person I've ever met," Klera said. The girl's mousy hair hung in her face, and the remnants of a cookie clung to the side of her sour little mouth.

"You've just met me, Klera," Thankful said, smiling uncomfortably, "but would you like me to fix your hair?"

"I like my hair *this way*," Klera said with just the smallest hint of stubbornness in her voice.

"That's fine."

Henry leaned in to kiss Thankful, but Avi and Helmut prevented it with a youthful burst of playful energy, nearly tripping their father and each other. This annoyed Thankful, and when Henry tried again to kiss her she turned from him, pretending to be interested in the foolish talk of the girls.

"Papa is going to marry her. Didn't you see the way he tried to kiss her?" Klera whispered to Zala.

"Papa kisses all the women at church that way," the little girl replied.

Mrs. Demarest, or Mother Demarest as she liked to be called by Thankful and the children, waited inside the door twisting her handkerchief as the children filed in. Thankful came next, and the old lady grabbed her by the arm. "Dear, Thankful, forgive me! I'd never have guessed that my *little* words would cause such as this to happen! I told Hilde's mother that they might come *someday* to meet you— if it was all right with you. It must be a hard thing to suddenly have so many children to care for, being so young as you are and with no experience whatever, but we'll make do won't we?"

"Mother Demarest, I have plenty of experience with children, but for how long will they stay?" Thankful asked in a whisper.

"Why, hasn't Henry told you? He's *such* a rascal, my son is! But who can blame him? It's all so upsetting." She looked past Thankful out to Henry sidetracked by his father and eldest son in the yard. "When I mentioned that Henry had finally found love again, Hilde's mother took it poorly. She's an unforgiving woman and still holds it against Henry that he dropped the children with them when he left for San Francisco with the traveling theatre troupe. How could she not understand how devastated he was after Hilde's death? He had no money to support them, and you know I'm always very fragile with my liver complaints. Henry knew, because he is such a caring soul, that minding the children would be the *death of me* ... and I always say that a stupid marriage produces *stupid* children." She paused, then whispered with a hint of mean-ness, "Bless their souls there's not a smart one among them—didn't take after Henry a bit! It's sad, but now what can we do?"

Thankful stood a moment taking it in. "So how long *will* they stay?"

"I don't mean to insult you, Thankful, but are you not listening to me? They are to stay with you and Henry *for good* now." Mrs. Demarest sighed, relieved of all respon-sibility. She smiled sweetly and made eyes as if she understood just how overwhelmed Thankful was feeling. But was there a touch of glee behind her soft features? Mrs. De-marest patted Thankful's shoulder before rushing inside to busy herself with seating the children around the table for supper.

Henry ran up now. "Mother's told you, hasn't she? Oh, I wanted to be the one to break it to you. I'm stunned by the news!"

Jacob, the eldest walked up now, tentatively, but with a certain elegance and cor-diality that endeared him to Thankful.

"Henry, now's not the time to talk," she whispered to her husband and turned to Jacob. "So I finally get to meet you. Your father speaks quite highly of you. I feel I know you already," Thankful said, to cut Henry, but she saw how much it meant to Jacob and felt a pang of regret.

"You're very pretty, Miss Thankful," he said. "I hope my father makes you happy."

She smiled and took the boy by the arm. He would sit next to her. They entered the dining room to find an old and sharp-looking couple seated at table, unhappily surrounded by the smaller children who talked and moved ceaselessly, knocking over everything in their reach. Thankful's blood boiled. The Crenshaw family never allowed the youngest children to sit with the adults, and they certainly were never allowed to topple things with impunity.

Mother Demarest feverishly spoke to her cook as the children cried out for milk and food as if starved for days. Henry stood at the door with his mouth open, unable to take charge of his offspring. Thankful sat near Hilde's mother who had not been properly introduced and gently convinced Zala and Helmut to sit at each side of her. When their hands reached for something fragile, she tapped them and whispered clever things in their ears to settle them. Jacob took her lead and made Avi and Klera be still as well. The adults seated themselves around the silenced table.

Henry's father shook his head but as usual said nothing. Mother Demarest intro-duced Hilde's parents, the Beitaks, and made an attempt at conversation which was met with stony silence.

Thankful said, "Hilde's children are lovely."

The deceased woman's parents assented silently.

The meal was a torture for all but the smallest, who seemed oblivious to tension. Coffee and brandy were brought in.

"My daughter vas a fool to marry such a man," Hilde's father, said after gulping down his drink.

Mrs. Beitak shushed him. "It matters little now, Franz. We must do vat's best for children. Miss Thankful, you are young and ve are old. Too old to care for these little ones. Franz vants to see cousin in Minnesota. You understand ve, *we* are sad to leave them, but ..."

Thankful glanced around the table. Only Jacob and Avi seemed to understand what was happening. Jacob took the news bravely and Avi with anger. He bolted from the table. Henry slowly got up as if to follow, but his father held him back. "Let the poor boy go." He shook his head again in obvious disgust.

Henry cleared his throat. "I admit that I'm a failure as a father, but to make my new wife take on something so unexpected ..."

Klera spoke now. "You're *already* married?"

Everyone ignored the girl and kept their eyes on Thankful who saw the hurt pride in Jacob's large blue eyes and the bewilderment in the eyes of the others. "Of course Henry and I will take them in. Family should not desert family. I'd be offended if anyone thought I could be so cruel to these children. They deserve better!" She raced from the room up to her own before another word could be said.

She cried for herself more than the children. Martha was just starting to respect her! And her family—if ever she told them (and she had to tell them soon)—would think her mad! If she had come up with the idea herself—to take in children—it may have felt different, but it was mortifying to be so duped by her husband. Though gentle, kind, and good-hearted, he was so tossed by the wind and befuddled! Where were the strong men? She sobbed at the thought of this, but then another thought arose. When might *she* be strong?

Henry knocked before letting himself into the room so full of clutter. "Thankful, may I speak with you?" he asked, sitting on the bed next to her crumpled form.

"Do as you like," she said but sat up now and wiped her nose with a delicate hankie Mother Demarest had made for her.

"Honestly, Thankful, I never foresaw this happening," Henry said.

"How could you not? Those poor children lost their mother and father in one go. How could you leave them?"

"Thankful, forgive me! I had no money. I'd invested it, what little I had, in a theater production that went sour. Some of the musicians had nothing, so I gave them what I had left."

"But, Henry, you had children! Why wouldn't you leave them something? Musicians have to find their own way—but children!"

"Hilde's parents had been more than generous to all of us, but living with them was suffocating! They never understood me. But I didn't want the children to be uprooted from their grandparents. I was confused. You understand my wife was dead. I loved her, though we fought dreadfully. I made decisions—my grief prevented me from good ones." He hung his head in anguish. "I wouldn't expect you to understand."

Thankful sighed. "I'm afraid I do understand. I've made mistakes too. You're such a generous soul. I believe you might forgive me anything, so I forgive you, Henry, but please, from now on we must be honest with each other."

He embraced her. "Thankful, I adore you. Such a tremendous weight has been lifted from me now that everything has seen the light of day." He looked her in the eyes. "I intend to make it up to you somehow, but for now—what will we do with my children?"

"*Our* children, Henry. We must do our very best by them," she said, resigned to her fate. She stood and fixed her hair in the mirror. She would make the children love her. "Come, let's go and start fresh."

*Dear Buck,*

*I trust you are well. I write you only because I know you will tell no one if I ask you not to. I miss you. I'm sorry over the way we left things.*

*Your words when I confided in you at your bedside helped me to see the good sense in marrying Mr. Demarest. Henry is a kind man, but in one thing he surprised me. You with your love of children might think it a blessing. Henry has six children from a previous marriage. His wife is dead.*

*I'm having so much trouble liking the children. Maybe it is God's way of chastening me for what I did to my own child. This is what I believe—which makes it worse to feel such resentment. The children are fairly well-behaved though they have been taught no manners. They have been spoiled and are quite gluttonous in my opinion. Henry is very well-read, but his children seem incredibly stupid. Of course I am painting with a broad brush.*

*The eldest boy is much like Henry, naturally intelligent and mild with a gift for music that surpasses his father's. The youngest little girl, with the frightfully foreign sounding name—Zala—is a little peach and the easiest child ever to manage and even enjoy. But the middle four!*

*How is it that a little boy who tries so hard to be good can infuriate me the way Helmut does? He is forever seeking to impress his father. It's sad really, but it seems he was raised too much at his mother's side. Helmut caresses Henry's arms and hands in a way that sickens me and upsets Henry who tries to brush it off which only makes the boy more insistently beg attention in other annoying ways. He asks insipid questions whenever there is a moment's peace. Yesterday while I was gathering flowers for the table he sidled up to me and asked if I was gathering flowers for the table when he knew that I was! I was never so violently taken with the idea of smashing a vase over a person's head. Luckily Zala came up then and turned the subject to the idea of purchasing sheep and learning to knit. We haven't a penny, I'm afraid. Henry has found work with the local surveyor, but it wears on him. His artistic soul hates to be under another's yoke, and he misses his music.*

*Klera is the oldest girl and very cunning. I believe she's stolen the few keepsakes I brought with me to Grandmother's. You may not remember or care very much for the one thing I have in common with Mama—porcelain tiny animals. Klera broke one the very first week after I showed them to her—a tiny dog I've had since I was seven. She walks and talks in her sleep. I believe she does it for show. On more than a few occasions she's knocked over her bedpan—she says by mistake. Mother Demarest thinks it unfair to make her house help do all the extra work since we've arrived so I must clean up after the children. Klera cries when I force her to help and makes more a mess anyway so in the middle of the night I scrub carpets of human waste! Henry is such a sound sleeper! Can you imagine what Mama would say to such a thing? I hardly reprimand the children because they have such sensitive faces and show no signs of any confidence in themselves. It feels wrong to berate such weaklings, though I so want to in my heart.*

*Avi is the only one with any spine, though I find him intolerable. I do respect him ever so slightly for having a personality. He hates me. I think he is the voice for the children. He stirs them against me, though they act very sweet. Avi points out every mistake I make and sneeringly takes note of every slip of my tongue. When he is reprimanded (and no one wants to do it for fear that his temper will spoil any semblance of good feeling in the house) he does not yell but scowls and generally causes a nervous discomfort in everyone. Avi should be put in his place, but then I feel sorry that he is such an angry child. I think of what Pastor Vandersar from home used to say about anger hiding pain, and I believe this poor little boy is hurt by the world.*

*Sometimes I imagine that things will be like this for only a short while, but then I remember that this is my life forever. Somehow these people are my new family, and there is no escaping them. From where you are I must look an idiotic girl with no rights to find fault with children, so I will turn my attention to the adults.*

*Grandmother will hardly speak to me when I see her and has made it clear that the children are not to come visiting. I do not blame her. On our first trip over, Helmut and Klera broke three of her flower pots and hardly apologized. It was as if they had no sense of the value of other people's things. Avi was in a temper over having to go at all and told*

*Martha that she was not his real grandmother, and he would never think of her as such. Jacob was humiliated by his siblings' behavior and reprimanded them too harshly especially taking out his frustration on little Zala whom they all believe I favor. Grandmother is angry that I quit working for her, but what could I do? Who would take care of the children? Not Henry. The dear is far too busy, and when he comes home he is no longer his old self. There is no humor in him, and he finds the children more a burden than a pleasure. On this we agree.*

*Henry's mother insists that the children call me Mother Thankful. Can you imagine? I feel an old haggard crone every time she calls me by that name. I have forbidden the children from using those words so of course they use them all the more to prick me. They pretend at forgetting that I hate it. They smile endearingly when they do not really mean it, and since Mother Demarest is in charge of her house we are forced to take meals with them. Whenever the least bit of interesting conversation has begun a child will be allowed to speak the most insufferable pile of gibberish one could ever imagine. The adults, but for me, commend the children for their great insights (of which there are none), and I am left to stew on my own. On occasion I have complained to Henry, but I see in his eyes that it hurts him to hear me say such things about his flesh and blood. I understand that, but it is hard to have no one to complain to!*

*I haven't sent a letter to Mama and Father about my marriage yet. I only tell you the truth about the problems I am having being a good wife in hopes that you will at least send me a Scripture verse to ease my suffering. I am a sinner through and through, dear brother. I intend to make this work, but I am frightened.*

*I hope you are well, Buck.*

*Sincerely, your loving sister,*

*Thankful*

Buck had taken to carrying pen and paper on Richard's advisement that God's inspiration could strike him anywhere.

*Dear Thankful,*

*I wish I were there to counsel you. God is doing a great work in me, and I see that so much of what I used to believe was just a way for the Devil to confine me and prevent me from experiencing the joy of life that God wants for us. Things are so different here, and I would not want to shock you in a letter but many girls ask after me. I am embarking on a great journey, and I have found my true home—the one God has set for me. I hope you can visit me one day soon, and I can tell you all about it.*

Buck hesitated but then surged forward.

*Thankful, I wish you were here. Here you would be treated and cared for as you deserve. You never would have had to give up your child, and it would have never been an orphan. Women should be treated with full equality. Now that I see it in action I believe it. After much study and introspection I have renounced the idea of marriage. I am committed to this little society and will spend the rest of my life serving it as God pleases. I consider myself married to all the women here as they have cared for me and I for them. Thankful, you are probably surprised by my words, but if you were to experience the beauty of truly unselfish love you would come to the same conclusion I have finally arrived at. Father and Mama are the perfect example of the sort of marriage you have to look forward to. I no longer desire that when I know there's something better and more pleasing to God. I now wish you had waited.*

*There are socials open to the public every Sunday so maybe one day you will visit. I am too needed here to get away right now, but I miss you.*

*Joyfully Serving Christ,*

*Buck Crenshaw*

A flush of excitement washed over him now as if committing his feelings to paper crystallized what up until now had been a murky mix. The sealing of this letter and the sending it to Thankful meant he would not turn back.

# Chapter Thirty-Three

The days shortened, and the chill air of Upstate New York slipped beneath doors and in through the thin windows, but Buck sat cozily now in Richard's office. He'd moved the big armchair next to the fire and brought in a few small chairs for Veronica, Lorna, and some of the boys who had become Buck's fast friends. Lily, the teacher, brought them in each day at three, and they read from an edition of *Uncle Remus* that Buck had purchased in town.

Sonja occasionally joined them for tea and cakes. Buck convinced the community that Sonja's great talent in the kitchen should be celebrated. Aside from a few insufferable vegetarians, Middlemayers heartily agreed. Boys were sent to help disabled and older town folk get ready for winter, and the general store proprietor had been so impressed with Sonja's baked goods that she offered to sell them to the hunting and ice-fishing city crowd that came through each fall and winter. Sonja was at first timid, but when Buck suggested that the profits go to her pet cause—the orphanage in New London—she gave in. Her confidence and new-found happiness attracted an admirer —an older man who had been too shy to approach her before but worked up his courage to compliment her good works. They shared regularly now. A few elders grumbled, but Richard had left orders to allow Buck to spread his wings a bit. With Richard away most sharers stopped asking the elders' permission. Buck told them they were old enough to make their own decisions, for he was decidedly uncomfortable discussing sexual unions.

Buck and Lily kept their encounters private and pleasant. He didn't like to admit to himself that most times afterward he lay in bed aching for something more. He hoped Richard would be proud of him but worried the old man might not understand a strange twist of events involving his headstrong niece, Parmelia.

For a long while Lorna made excuses for her father's failure to visit Middlemay. Buck decided to visit Jack one Friday before Christmas with treats from Sonja.

Parmelia asked to come along, and the two set off for an enjoyable yuletide errand. Buck usually tried to avoid her, jealous of Parmelia's vow of purity and ashamed that he hadn't been able to meet her on the same level. They talked and flirted a little on this day, but nothing more. The house came into view, looking more forlorn after the first dusting of snow had fallen on the weeping pines and skeletal oaks. Parmelia sighed. Lorna was with them, and Parmelia gave her a squeeze when she saw Lorna gazing up at her. They had become friends despite their age difference.

One lone candle in the window flickered as they tied the buggy to a post near the front porch. Voices inside—small ones—whispered at the sound of visitors. Lorna led them in and gasped at the sight of a Christmas tree full of old decorations. Buck and Parmelia smiled at each other and set the food on the table. The sound of a heavy boot and a light one came from the hallway, and in walked Jack with a smile. "Buck, you've brought a friend." His trimmed beard and a new light in his eyes changed the whole look of him.

"Yes, sir. This is Parmelia."

"Is she your girl?"

"No, we don't do that at Middlemay. There's no ownership," Buck said, but Jack wasn't listening. He pulled a chair out for Parmelia, who took it with a giggle.

"Thank you, sir," she said, untying her bonnet. "I think your home is so cozy. I love it!"

Jack and Buck looked amused.

"No, really," Parmelia said. "I've always dreamed of a cozy cabin in the woods with a fire to gather round—and look at the tree with those tiny carved animals! A chipmunk even!" She ran to it and cradled a small figurine. "Where did you get these? This rabbit is adorable!" Parmelia turned to the old soldier.

"I made them for the children," Jack said.

"Will you make one for me?" Parmelia asked.

Jack was taken aback but recovered with a grin. "Yes, of course. I'll send Lorna up with one next week. It's the least I can do for the lady who has been so good to Lorna. She talks about you all the time and says how pretty you are."

Parmelia blushed.

They stayed only a short while, but Buck worried all the way home as Parmelia grilled him with questions about the family.

"Oh, Buck, it really was like Christmas there. Sure it was rustic, but it felt like a real home, don't you think? And you are the one who helped them. I'm sorry I ever doubted what you were doing."

Buck looked at her sideways and laughed.

"When do you think Mr. Jack Fellows will come visit?" Parmelia asked, enjoying the sound of his name.

"I don't think he will," Buck said. "He hasn't yet. Maybe he feels bad about Noah still."

"That's silly. Anyone would understand how hard it must have been on him to lose a wife." Parmelia sighed.

The following weekend Jack Fellows arrived unannounced to see his baby and to ask after Parmelia. And every weekend since then the same had happened. Buck couldn't say a word because he saw as everyone did that Jack and Parmelia were falling in special love, and Parmelia was not one to be tamed by anyone at Middlemay. Circles of Improvement and shunning and forced readings of Richard's writings about the evils of selfish love would not stop her from writing to Jack and pining happily all week for him and dressing against the rules on the Saturdays when he arrived.

Everyone noted how much they liked her better now. She was softer and possibly prettier than ever, and Jack was quiet and unassuming. The men couldn't help admire a veteran of the war, and the women admired the way he looked at Parmelia. No one was jealous. They seemed right and sacred and beyond reproach. For now everyone just enjoyed the fairytale.

And then there was the big news of India's early delivery of her child. Of course, according to Buck's calculations the baby boy was right on time, and as expected Fred's son bore a resemblance to his father. No one seemed to notice, and luckily there was far more of India in the child's face than Fred's. India took it badly when Richard first said his return must be delayed until after he finished an unexpected tour of Rome (paid for by Middlemay), but she brightened once the baby arrived healthy. Buck discreetly sent a letter to his brother through the Middlemay post.

*Dear Fred,*

*India has just given birth to a boy. You need not worry as she is well taken care of as is Samuel Richard. I will see to it that Sam gets the best of care throughout his life.*

*Buck*

# Chapter Thirty-Four

Early March, with the sun just strong enough to send the maple sap running into silver buckets in the big woods, brought Richard home a week sooner than expected. Buck sat daydreaming with feet upon Richard's desk when Richard walked through the door. The old man gasped at the sight of his protégé so comfortably ensconced in the big leather chair moved from its place by the fire. The desk was littered with teacups and samples of Sonja's pastries, half eaten. Nothing was how Richard had left it.

Buck in stocking feet jumped from his thoughts and raced with extended hand to Richard. Just then Sonja barged in the side door which led to the common rooms with a breezy air of happy excitement over something until she saw her husband standing before her.

"Oh, dear Richard," she began in a less than enthusiastic tone. "You're too early. We were expecting you next week and had all sorts of festivities planned, and now you've spoiled it."

The three stood but said nothing as Richard's eyes landed upon first the toys strewn on the carpet and then the bookshelf with books waiting to find their homes piled on a side table. The hired girls who usually kept the books and dishes in order had been sent home, except for Lorna whose workload dropped when Buck and Parmelia decided to tutor her.

"I see you've made yourself comfortable in my absence," Richard said.

Buck stacked the dishes and gathered cups as he spoke. "Father, I'm sorry about the mess. It's my fault. I was so busy with studies and things I let it get away from me. I thought you wouldn't be here so soon."

"Maybe I should have come sooner," Richard said, reaching for a rare volume and toppling the books stacked precariously beneath it.

"I'll have the place cleaned up in no time," Buck said, gathering the books at Richard's feet. "You should go have breakfast or something."

"Now you order me out of my study?" Richard asked, his chest out with hands on hips.

"No, certainly not!" Buck said, sweating in his bulky wool sweater, feeling like a child and resenting it. "I only want to make you happy. It's all I've tried to do these last months."

Richard put his hand on top of Buck's as Buck stacked the books. "Son, let's start again." He sighed deeply, closing his eyes for a moment to gather himself. "I'm tired after the journey. I'm sure you've done your best to keep things in order. After all you are still just a student. I do forget that sometimes. God has given me many great gifts, and it's unfair to hold you to the same standards as God holds me."

Buck bristled. "Yes, sir."

"I'll take my leave while you get the girl up here to clean." Richard looked around again, nostrils flaring.

Sonja rolled her eyes. "So good to have you back, husband."

"Sonja, you look well," Richard said, icily as if he hadn't already noticed her.

"I feel better than ever, thank you," she replied in a pert and confident tone that clearly annoyed Richard.

"I will go see dear India and her child now." Richard turned to go but not before nearly tripping over an ottoman that had been moved by one of the children. He glanced back at them wearily one last time before closing the door behind him.

Buck set to moving furniture, but Sonja grabbed him. "Stop it, Buck. Let things be for a while. Richard's too set in his ways. It's time for a rude awakening."

"What do you mean?" He continued to tidy things.

"You know," Sonja said. "All of the changes you've made."

"But the elders have backed them, I think ..."

"Richard told them to support you. Rebecca is the only one with half a brain besides me, and she was gone. Of course *I* support you."

"Yes, and I appreciate it. You're a good friend."

"And then there's the baby ..."

"What about him?"

"He looks more and more like someone I know," Sonja said. "When did you share with India? My calculations make that baby a bit older than India says."

Buck held a rag doll in his hand. "I ... *did* share with her *once*. It was a mistake, and I told Richard about it."

"Oh, well then that's good."

"I'm sure this sort of thing has happened a few times before, right?"

"Yes, but not to Richard. He handpicks his girls and expects complete loyalty."

"Well, he didn't seem too troubled over me and India ... but then he thought India was already with child—*his* child ..." Buck said, collapsing into a chair. He pulled a wooden train from behind the cushion with a sigh.

"Here, have an apple turnover," Sonja said.

He waved it away. "Thank you, but I couldn't just now."

She laughed. "Don't worry so much. Everything will be all right."

\*\*\*

And at first it seemed so. The community threw together a welcome-home celebration—Sonja even made the cakes. The children sang a new song. A perplexed look passed over Richard's face at the sight of two orphan children Buck had taken in and little Noah tottering around happily with Parmelia, but the old man's blue eyes remained cheerful as he tapped offbeat to the tune.

The trouble started once the older girls stood with their tribute in song. They held each other around the shoulders swaying as if drunk and sang:

*We love you, Rich-ard, so much,*
　*We adore you, Rich-ard, more than such and such,*
　*When you're not with us ...we miss your kind touch,*
　*Oh, Richard we love you this much!*

The girls sang it leeringly, sarcastically, and they giggled, giving each other knowing looks before sitting. At that moment India strode up holding her baby and moved to sit next to Richard, but he placed his hand on her seat forcing her to sit beside the other young ladies.

Everyone came to the table set with store-bought paper decorations in festive colors. Richard looked them over sneeringly. Sonja cut the cake and Richard sampled it.

"Thank you all for this warm welcome home. Well, this cake is ... good. Of course, the confections made in Belgium by the simplest housewives reign supreme in my mind, but it's good to be back with the mediocrity here that keeps us all humbly serving our Maker."

Sonja left the room. Buck's stomach churned as India fawned over an unreceptive Richard, who picked sourly at his cake.

"I see we have visiting children at Middlemay," Richard said, pushing the cake half-eaten away. "I'm curious to know all about it."

Everyone turned to Buck.

"I ... we've ... decided to keep them. It was a cold winter, and their families couldn't care for them. We believe it's our Christian duty to help them."

"I *believe* your heart was in the right place, Buck, but you have naively put the community in jeopardy. People will talk and say we're stealing children."

"Father," Edmund said, "if we're doing good work, it's worth the risk. The children are very happy here."

"That's nice for the children," Richard said, with a troubled glance at India's child. "But children conceived without proper supervision and with no regard for God's mission here will only serve to harm the community's values and breeding stock."

Edmund glanced at Buck but said nothing more. He stirred his coffee.

Richard stood up, blessing the crowd with one of his generous smiles. "Thank you all so much for this. It's so good to be home, and while I'm a little unsettled by *certain* things, I have every confidence that the community will be brought back to the health it was in before I had to leave in service to it. I've given Verlinda a few samples of the aged cheeses I tasted in Europe to share with you all. Tonight there will be a Circle of Improvement open to all, but for now your father needs a small rest after traveling. A weary vagabond for Christ has needs too."

Buck and Edmund stood as did the other men and watched Richard exit.

"Did you tell him yet about Parmelia's plans?" Edmund asked with a sly smile.

"Don't look like you're enjoying this too much, friend." Buck half-laughed, his eyes apprehensively following Richard's exit.

# Chapter Thirty-Five

During the colder months the Circle of Improvement gathered in the auditorium decorated by the children's art league. If Richard appreciated mediocre arts and crafts, this was the best display of it. Buck had grown bored with the Circle's petty complaints. Most times he struggled to keep awake. Tonight promised to be livelier with Richard back.

The elders who had been friendly with Buck these last months kept a cool distance, whispering among themselves. Girls hung paper lanterns over the table where light refreshment beckoned. Buck wondered what they'd be like in sharing. He was a little bored in that area of his life too. He wondered how married people out in the world did it together for so long. But then there was more of a life built between them.

Parmelia came in and kissed his cheek. "I won't miss these awful things," she said to him, wrapping her arm around his.

Buck sensed Richard's eyes upon them and pulled from her grasp. Edmund walked in and motioned Buck to come sit with him. All winter Buck had endured the embarrassment of sitting on Richard's rustic throne.

Finally, it all began—the songs and familiar old speech about God and manners from Richard. Buck stared at his hands, willing himself to stay awake.

"Who shall begin? Tonight is for everyone," Richard said.

Someone spoke out.

Richard stopped them affronted. "Where are your bells?"

The bells had fallen by the wayside in his absence.

"Never mind for tonight," Richard said, waving his hand with furrowed brows.

"I'd just like to give praise to the Lord for sending us Buck," an elder member of the community who had helped Buck at the newspaper said. "He has given us a new sense of purpose and energy which now I see was lacking in recent years. God obviously does speak through you, Father Richard. I was skeptical about your choice for successor, but now I see you were right."

Richard glared at the man. "And what is your criticism? How can you help Buck to improve?"

"Well, Buckie may work a little too hard now. We wouldn't want him to tire himself."

Richard motioned the man to sit. "Yes, well now that I'm back, Buck will have plenty of rest," he said. "Anyone else?"

A young lady from the vegetarian camp stood. "Buck has a good heart, but the children we've adopted use foul language. I fear for our breeding program. Will these children spoil the results?"

"My fears exactly," Richard said with an appreciative smile.

Edmund stood now. "Our offspring—if they are indeed morally superior —should be above descending into immorality. A good experiment could be done comparing the two groups."

"I don't appreciate your readiness to throw all of our careful breeding away on a few lost souls," Richard replied.

"Jesus went after the lost souls," Edmund said.

"Since when do you care about your children?" Richard asked.

Edmund sat again, red with shame.

Parmelia stood, glancing around with a sweet smile. "Father, we appreciate your worries, but as one bred for higher spirituality I'm compelled to say that the orphans, who may not speak as properly as we'd hope, have shown me how a little love and personalized attention in a child's life can make all the difference. And Father, I've met a man whose children were poor in material possessions but rich in the spirit of God. I intend to marry this man a week from Saturday. His children have given me a real home. What I've yearned for my whole life. Buck was right to give these orphans a home too."

Richard stared at her for a long time. Parmelia met his stare with her usual insouciance. No one in the room dared shift in their seat for fear of missing something.

Richard cleared his throat. "I'm *sure* I didn't *hear* you correctly. Is this a humorous joke?" he asked with a sickened smile, his skin pale under the gaslights.

Buck stood now. "Father, I didn't have time to tell you of the events or what the feelings of the community are."

"The *feelings* of the *community*?" Richard shouted, unable to control his indignation. "Some things are *not* for the community to decide! I am God's spokesperson here, and He has told me that marriage is a destroyer of pure love! *I will not have it!*"

Sonja shouted from her seat. "You are a destroyer of real love, Richard! Marriage was good enough to get my funds but not good enough when you wanted to experience other women. I've tried all these years! I've wanted to believe that this experiment called sharing was for the betterment of humanity, but I don't believe it anymore. I want a real marriage. One with mutual love and attraction."

"I'm sorry Sonja, but I cannot give you that," Richard said, cuttingly.

Sonja stood. "I didn't mean you, Dick. I have someone else." She took her bag of knitting and left the meeting.

A few others left in support, but most stayed on.

"The marriage spirit has invaded our community!" Richard shouted as if they should all take up arms.

People yelled and squabbled.

"And the vegetarians are being tempted by good food! It's ungodly!" the sour skinny man complained, watching a friend lick his fingers after tasting one of Sonja's sausage-filled pastries.

Some defended the new and others the old. Old ladies cried and old men grumbled. Buck raised his hands, and the community quieted, anxious to see how this young upstart might reply.

Buck spoke softly as always. "Father, you're wise and inspired. While you were away I read everything you've written. I've read Scripture, and I've followed your advice to act with my heart and not my head. I've never done that before, and you were right. I've felt free and even happy. I love the people here with all my heart. I've discovered the love that isn't special—what you've talked about—but I don't believe it's for everyone."

Richard smiled at the followers and turned to Buck. "I was a fool to leave you so long to be ensnared by the Evil One. I never once said there was a love that wasn't special. I loved you in a *very special way*. I poured myself and my gifts into you—an unclean vessel. You were not the pure son you pretended to be. You are a fake, and I must apologize to this family of faith. I have been duped by the Devil!" He shouted again, pointing and cringing back at the same time. Richard turned to the rest of his followers. "I see how you all look at me with pity now. You see as I do that the child who was to be my final gift to Middlemay looks like Buck. And as you know I am quite scientific and have studied breeding for years and can count backwards on my fingers to find that Miss Van Westervelt's baby was conceived before she arrived at Middlemay. I have yet to discover the true reason for this deceit, but deceit it is! I am an old man whose time is nearly up, and I have been led astray by a pretty young girl—just like the great heroes of the Bible. All I can do is fall to my knees before God and repent!"

"But, Father!" Buck rushed to his side.

"Oh, oh, Buck," Richard said, keeping Buck at arm's length. "I am *NOT* your father! You have disgraced us."

"If only you'd let me explain!"

Edmund stood next to Buck. "Father, Buck did deceive you, but not for the reasons you think. He did it to protect you and the unborn child. Buck took pity on India."

"Did you not share with India, Buck?" Richard asked.

"Yes, I did, and I told you ..."

"You little bastard! How you manipulate!" Richard shouted. "Does the child not have your blood?"

"Not exactly ... I ..." Buck stammered.

He looked to India who remained silent, sitting in the back row.

Richard turned to her as well. "You, India Van Westervelt, are a seductress and a whore! I trusted you! I believed you when you said that you enjoyed sharing with me even as the other young girls told lies about me and reviled my body! The very body God has anointed to serve them!"

"I do love you," India said, wiping a tear away. "I came here for protection from the cruel words of others who'd judge me as harshly as you just have! I hoped you were different! I thought you of all people would understand how special love can bring special pain! Buck understands! He says he doesn't love in a special way, but he fools himself. Buck takes in children, he carries the burden of other men's sins and sets the heartbroken free."

"Even the Evil One has words of silk!" Richard replied. "I will not have Middlemay turned into a breeding ground for sons of Satan! You will be escorted back into the hell you came from tomorrow morning along with Buck's child!"

"Father!" Edmund cried. "You're a hypocrite! You believe you are more educated, more spiritual, and more human than the rest of us! It sickens me—your pride! You'd throw a child to the wolves if it wasn't a child you felt like making a show of! Next you'll go to Africa on a 'spiritual tour' and come back with an unsaved Negro to call your own as you did briefly with the Navajo baby some time ago. You've become a dictator!"

"Edmund, my son, you've always been a silly boy. Please stay out of this," Richard said with a dismissive wave of the hand.

Buck spoke now, "Edmund is a man I greatly admire, sir."

"You admire power and believe you've gotten mine," Richard said, with every last bit of sentiment gone from his eyes.

"No, I only tried to do best. I'm sorry I disappointed you," Buck said, shaken but not so very much. Hadn't he been rejected so many times before? A wave of revulsion and shame flooded his senses. He had never really believed he'd escape that thing about him—that mysterious thing that turned people's hearts against him.

"Buck, don't allow Father to bully you," Parmelia said now. "No one here can deny that Buck hasn't brought more Christian affection and activity to this place. I ask any of you to come forward who disagrees."

The vegetarian said, "Buck is good with the children, but bringing back Sonja's cakes was a mistake."

India sat by herself looking beautiful in her misery. Her eyes glistened. "Richard, Buck is not the father of my child. I had nowhere to turn but you, and I hoped I could one day tell you the details of my earlier life, but I was frightened. I just wanted my baby to be safe."

"I see the child's features in Buck," Richard said. "I'm not senile."

"I had a fiancé once—Winslow," India began. "He was so handsome and everyone loved him but my mother. She thought him reckless because he liked boats and raced them. He loved life and me, and I loved him so much I didn't care that my mother said the water would be the death of him. And it was. He had wealth and confidence, but he didn't know his new boat as well as he should have when the squall came up off the Long Island coast and he died. He was Fred's best friend."

"Who's Fred?" Richard asked.

"My brother," Buck said.

"Fred and I loved Winslow," India continued, "and when he died we spent time together. Fred is married unhappily, and I just wanted to forget about Winnie. I let things happen. I don't know why I believed Fred would leave his wife. And then I met Buck, and he was everything Fred was not and, yes, I fell in love with him too, but Richard, I believed what you said about special love—how it was selfish and hurtful. I determined to steel myself against it and love you in the way you needed."

"So you never held me in especial esteem?" Richard asked, the last bit of wind knocked from his sails.

"I did—in the way you taught us—to love as an act of service—like the way you've loved Sonja," India explained.

Richard began to speak but stopped. He looked to the ceiling and stormed out.

People milled about for a few charged minutes and then left averting their eyes and hiding any feelings they had one way or the other. Parmelia, Buck, and Edmund stood silently until Parmelia sighed and went to India, sitting beside her. They were never friends, but Parmelia smoothed India's hair at her temple and pulled her close. India wept.

Edmund kept his hands in his pockets. "Well, Buck. That went well."

Buck shook his head, playing that it didn't matter much though his heart raced.

"I think he'll get over it," Edmund continued, popping a cookie in his mouth. "These are so good." He finished chewing. "Father's human, though he'd like to imagine otherwise. None of this is your fault."

"It doesn't matter. I need to get back on his good side and send the children back," Buck said, biting his fingernail. "It's almost spring. Maybe they'll be a help to their parents now that the worst weather is over."

"Buck, we're in Upstate New York. Spring doesn't come until July, and you can't send them back just to please Father! Hold your ground. It's what people expect."

"But what if Father kicks me out with Fred's baby? I've believed God sent me here for a purpose." Buck felt a chill now. Where would he go? How would he support himself out there?

"Maybe this is your purpose—to ruffle feathers that need ruffling."

"I'm a feather ruffler? That's it? I expect more from myself than that!"

"And that's pride."

"Edmund, I don't want a lecture. This is important. I've worked so hard and deserve what Richard promised. God said so."

Edmund laughed. "Sometimes we hear what we want to hear."

"What does that mean? Are you against me?"

"Do you think I'm against you?"

Edmund offered him a treat. He pushed it away.

"My father may have some inspired moments, but the trouble is they're mixed with lots of other moments. God may have told him you were sent or that you had special worth, but he lies to himself. He's not ready to turn over this place to anyone. You've positioned yourself as his usurper."

"I didn't ask for any of this," Buck said. "I thought it was from God."

"Maybe it is, but that doesn't mean you have all the answers or can predict the future. You're a good man, Buck. It will all play out the way God wants for those who love Him."

"So what do I do now?"

"Pray."

Parmelia and India came up now.

"India, I'm sorry," Buck said.

"For what? You've been too good to me. I'm sorry that I ruined your purity."

"Father will forgive you," Buck said.

"Maybe, but I can't do this anymore," India said. "I've been unfair to everyone, and I miss my parents."

"But we consider you like family here," Buck said.

"Don't try so hard to be a leader right now. I need you as a friend. You understand that it's not the same to be *like* a family as it is to *be* family. Don't you miss home?"

"I want to go where God leads me."

"I want to read the *New York Times*," India said and laughed and cried.

"I want to see what *Godey's Magazine* is like," Parmelia said in such an innocent way that Buck had to smile.

"You're both like sisters to me," he said. "I can talk to Father in the morning and ..."

"No. I don't want halfway solutions," Parmelia said. "I'm going and I'll miss it here, but I know in my heart that God wants me to take care of Jack and his children. I'm blissfully happy about it. Nothing else will do."

"I wish I had such strong direction," Buck said.

"I'll always be just down the road." She gave him a quick embrace.

"Buck, about the baby," India began, "I think it's best to send it away. Sonja knows a nice place in Connecticut. The baby will be placed with a good family. I don't want my parents to find out. I want a fresh start with them, and you know how people talk in the city. I'd jeopardize Fred's marriage and all he wants to do with his life—you understand."

"No, I ..."

Edmund took Buck by the arm. "Enough for tonight. Let everyone sleep before making hasty decisions."

# Chapter Thirty-Six

Buck flipped through his Bible hoping a phrase, any passage, would divulge supernatural direction. His throat hurt, his head ached, and he shivered beneath his rough-hewn clothes. The candle wavered at the drafty window, and the wind howled over the barren fields and up into the quaking trees. What could Buck do to convince Richard to keep him? He listened for God in the wind all night, but heard not a word. He sifted through Richard's writings on the heaven Middlemay was ushering in, and his doubts magnified—the doubts he'd buried at the first taste of power and popularity.

Who spoke for God? Richard? Edmund? The prophets? The religious giants of Buck's studies welcomed the descents into darkness as much as the great mountaintop ecstasies for the lessons to be had. He learned nothing but the same old lesson: He was alone and God did not care for him. But no, he thought. I fall into my old self-pity. I fall when I should stand.

Buck repented the wish for Richard's quick death. When had he become so corrupted by the promise of power? Buck had convinced himself that he was being Christlike, but he should have waited for Richard's permission to change things. He begged God to intervene and turn back time.

But the morning came on icy and bright with the last twinkling star shivering before it faded. A late snow blanketed the grounds. Buck looked as grey as the heavy sky outside his window. *Did God hibernate in winter?* Muffled sleigh bells had in earlier times sounded so festive as they jostled over the backs of one of the fine teams of Middlemay horses. Buck watched as a red sleigh passed with Sonja and a hired hand bundled to their noses. Had Richard forced her to leave?

Dressing in fresh clothes, he wrapped a wool scarf around his neck. His scar never really faded, only changed with the seasons. As he ran down the hallway past the family portraits and mediocre artwork, he heard Richard yelling from down a narrow hallway. The door to Sonja's new hiding place in a broom closet was ajar. Every delectable pastry and meat pie lay splattered in a box. Richard supervised a young girl as she emptied the shelves with little enthusiasm.

"Father?" Buck probed timidly as he strode up.

"Oh, it's you," Richard replied, not turning to face him. "Sonja has left with your son—to the orphanage in New London. It's the first time she's left here for an extended stay in years. It will give her a chance to be away from her personal demons."

"But ... the cakes. Father, she so loved making people happy with them. Please reconsider what you're doing."

"Middlemay cannot afford the outlay of funds for this extra food."

"But Father, my money alone can cover all the expenses, and it means so much to her and to the others."

Richard turned now, wiping flour on his trousers. "*Your money*? You see, you are not one of us. You think the money gives you the right to bring in new mouths to feed and to foster ill will toward me."

"Father, I tried to please you. I don't want any of the money, but I should have a little say."

"*No you should not*! You are a selfish, spoiled, Godless child and an embarrassment to me! After all I taught you! You have caused lies and deceit to flourish while I was away!" Richard shook and spit as he shouted.

"I can explain everything!"

"I'm sure you can. The Devil gives great power to the wicked."

The young girl threw the last pies more quickly on to the pile.

Buck stepped back, the words lashing his confidence to shreds. "What are you talking about? I never wanted to hurt you. If you only tell me how to prove my loyalty ..." Buck's heart sank. He couldn't prove something he didn't feel, but he must somehow.

"I was mistaken. My sympathy goes out to you, Buck, but God does not want you to lead us. He wants Edmund. If you truly love God and love me then you will gladly and humbly take the seat at the lowest end of the table. You will humbly serve your masters without complaint, and you will submit to the elders in all things. I'm sorry you imagined your money meant anything to Middlemay. Your father expressed his concern about that in his letter."

"What letter?"

"The elders decided that allowing you to read it would be a great setback when you were just starting to get comfortable here."

"What did Father say?"

"He was afraid we were taking advantage of your generosity. But we were not. Money is never an issue here."

"But you just said we couldn't support Sonja ..."

"Never mind Sonja." Richard dumped a bag of sugar into the box.

"I need to go home."

"Where is your home?" Richard demanded, quickly meeting Buck's eyes. "God is humbling you here. Pray that God will comfort you and forgive me for putting you through discomfort over this. Repent, flee from Satan." Richard sighed. "I regret leaving you—one of my sheep—defenseless. I cleared out one demon and seven more entered you." Richard watched Buck struggle under his judgment and softened his demeanor. "You have become proud and presumptuous. But you like Edmund, don't you?"

"Edmund is too good for you."

"Maybe so," Richard replied, "but he shares my vision for Middlemay and would be satisfied with being a helpmate to me."

"I'm satisfied with that too," Buck said, hating the grasping tone in his voice. "You said you wanted me to lead!"

"I mistakenly thought you'd have learned enough about God's mission here to lead properly. Coming back and seeing my work on the brink of destruction was God's way of reproaching me for leaving my responsibilities to an outsider. God's will has been made clear again. I see now that I was wandering in the desert with you and not allowing God's work."

"But I don't understand. I did everything you wanted. I followed you faithfully. I don't understand why taking in a few needy children changes everything."

"False pretenses. You came in on false pretenses. At any time you could have confessed about India's child, but instead you let me carry on like a fool in front of the entire community. Am I supposed to trust you?"

"I didn't know anything about India when we first got here," Buck began, but he was afraid for India. He stopped.

"You knew her in the Biblical sense. If you can tell me that that child is unrelated to you then ..." Richard waited for a response.

Buck could not bring himself to say anything about it. The more he told the more it might appear that he was in on a gigantic ruse. Edmund would certainly not accept a leadership position. There was still hope ....

"I will take it based on your long silence that you admit to the child having your blood."

"Yes, he does," Buck replied. "But, Father, I can change. I know I've made mistakes. I was too soft with Parmelia, but I wanted her to be happy."

"After Parmelia's heroic ideas about saving that family wear off she'll come crawling back."

"They're in love. Everyone was inspired by them."

"Yes, inspired by something that will destroy Bible communism. You are a babe in the woods! Can you tell me that you don't feel something special for India's child?"

Buck said nothing.

"Exactly. Sonja has never forgiven me for putting the community before our son. But that is what God asks of us. We are to put Christ before all worldly things."

"But the Bible says to love one another," Buck said.

Richard shook his head with eyes ablaze. "Be ready to leave your parents and children and wives if God calls—hate your mother and father, hate your wife—that's what Jesus demands of us."

"I hope God isn't that cruel," Buck said, but he feared God was very cruel indeed.

"When—if ever you get to my level," Richard said, "you will see that the cruelty comes from jealousy and greed. Men go to war to have more things for their family, and I mean immediate family. If they had a broader sense of family, they wouldn't fight against their fellow man. They would see God's family as it is—one. Especial love would be obsolete. Everyone would be equally loved."

"Then why doesn't Sonja feel loved by you? And why do you care so much for India and Rebecca? People notice that your trip with Rebecca came from shared funds and that you're always with *her*."

"Only a corrupted cynic sees things in such a way!" Richard shoved the girl out of his way to bring himself even closer to Buck. "Rebecca is a trusted member of Middlemay, and I was helping India."

"Lots of people here say you favor India. People snicker over what goes on at the printing press and in Europe."

"How dare you talk to me this way!"

"But don't you want someone here to tell you what goes on behind your back?"

"I don't need a snitch! You will never convince me that communism isn't part of God's plan."

"I never said anything about communism, and I've lost a sense of where this conversation is going." Buck recoiled at the anger in Richard's eyes.

"It's because you have a weak and pliable mind, I'm afraid. In my frustration I said you weren't my son, but you are—just the weaker one—there's no shame in that," Richard said in a tempered tone that troubled Buck just as much. "You will have a home here for as long as you like, but if you can't stand up to Parmelia and the other gossips then how can you lead? Rebecca says you have writing and editing skills, and you're good with children so you can busy yourself producing the children's little newspaper from now on." Richard looked on his crestfallen servant and took pity on him, giving Buck a stiff hug which went unreturned. "God always puts us in our places when we get too big. This is a lesson learned."

Buck pushed away. He tripped over the mess of baked goods before him. "If God is anything like you he is cruel beyond reason! I'm jerked this way and that, and each time I come out with less!"

"Now don't get all upset. You still have a home and people to guide you," Richard replied, his voice syrupy sweet now.

"I believed God was guiding me, but I can't take it anymore! You used my weakness against me. And that little boy! How could you let Sonja take him to an orphanage when he has family right here?" Buck shook now. He was more lost than ever.

"Buck, settle down. Everything will be all right. You are still loved by so many here, but they need their father to guide them with more maturity."

Just then Edmund entered the hallway. Upon seeing the two he turned to leave, but Buck called to him. "Edmund, tell me you think this is all a mistake!"

"What?" Edmund blushed.

"Are you taking my spot?"

"There's no spot, Buck. I do as I'm told," Edmund replied, unable to look Buck in the eye. "You're the better man, I know, but I have to think of the community, and Father knows best about it."

"But you see all the hypocrisy, don't you? I know you must!"

"Buck, where would I go in the world? My family, my children, what little skills I have—everything is in here. You will always have my friendship, but I must help Father to keep this place going as it is for my children."

"But you saw Parmelia ... and Sonja ... they're much happier!"

"Remember when you counseled me against that sort of love? Look how much turmoil it brings. You were right. Parmelia is an exception, and we're better off with her being gone."

"Edmund! I can't believe you're saying this."

"I'm sorry. But maybe it's better for you to gain more experience. I mean, I don't want you to leave or anything."

Buck skidded through the floury mess and ran off into the day. He stood for a moment on the front porch but burst back inside to find India packing her things when he barged in breathlessly. "How could you give up the baby without asking me?"

India looked confused and angry. "Why is he any of your concern?"

"Because! Because!" Buck raced back out of doors and to the post. "Where are the letters? Where are *my* letters? Have you been hiding letters to me?"

The girl behind the counter shook her head. "I'm sorry, Buck, but there's been none for you."

He sank onto the bench outside the post office as the snow fell in earnest.

# Chapter Thirty-Seven

Lucy McCullough nursed a small crush on Uncle John and harbored the tiniest resentment toward Aunt Kate who frowned upon her eccentric insistence on old-fashioned high-waist dresses when every young girl begged for corsets and bustles. Aunt Kate had become an excellent seamstress and felt keenly the eyes of judgment at church and in town and wished Lucy might not make a show of herself—yet Aunt Kate sewed every unusual dress Lucy asked for.

The milkmaid style of Lucy's strawberry blond hair echoed that of her mother's in the photograph Lucy kept at her bedside. Aunt Kate's suggestions to wear bangs and curls in the latest style fell upon deaf ears. Lucy sensed in Aunt Kate an annoyance at her fascination with her dead mother Emily. When Lucy wore big hats in the sun to preserve the pale skin passed down to her by her mother, Aunt Kate teased Lucy about her vanity.

Uncle John, on the other hand, complimented Lucy's generous smile and easy laughter so like Simon's. Lucy suspected she could have anything she wanted from Uncle John, who adored her, but was satisfied listening to his deep voice as he read her stories—some of his own. Lucy's darkened spectacles hid the scarred corneas that kept her a poor reader, but the young lady still preferred having someone read to her anyway—something Uncle John loved to do.

Uncle John's tales of the West and the war were thrilling, but she loved best the story about a broken soldier and his girl. Lucy's chest puffed with pride every time Uncle John read the passages about her father Simon in John's unpublished but most autobiographical manuscript. Captain Simon McCullough loved his family and was loyal to his friends. Lucy vowed to be the same and longed for more such stories, but Uncle John had trouble writing and talking about Simon, and Aunt Kate always claimed to be too busy for questions.

When the Weldons smiled at a mannerism Lucy shared with *their* Simon—*her* father, the person with a strong chin and confident expression staring out from the only tintype Aunt Kate and Uncle John could bear to part with—Lucy felt as if she'd found a sliver of something that moments later would slip through her fingers. Their smiles and reminiscences made Lucy the outsider. Simon McCullough had been a best friend and brother for far longer than he'd been a father, and except for one or two letters about it, Simon's life with Emily and Lucy on the Pacific coast was a dark mystery—even the Indians who killed Simon knew more about him than Lucy did.

For hours on quiet Sundays Lucy sat alone in grandfather's study, tracing her fingers over Simon's singed West Point memory book imagining from the blurry likenesses and careless handwriting her handsome father alive. She believed Buck hadn't thrown the family heirloom into the fire that Christmas years ago, for Buck, unlike the other Crenshaw children, had always been kind. People whispered about Simon's disease and Uncle John's habit and William's drinking—none of which were Lucy's fault, but that didn't matter to the girls from the big houses up on the cliffs and even the rough girls from Undercliff and the Irish neighborhood on Waldo Place.

Lucy's favorite real book now was *Adventures of Huckleberry Finn*. She so wanted to be Huck, but what would the Weldons do without her? And truly Lucy had already found her best spot in the world right here in Englewood sitting beneath Simon's willow tree in the garden. There was something terribly sad about never having been able to call Simon Father. He was always just Simon to everyone.

Sometimes, but less often, she wondered about her mother Emily and the people who shared her blood living in Illinois. She imagined them severe and grim in the little stories she told herself because Aunt Kate said they had disowned her mother for marrying her father.

Sentimental in all things, Uncle John kept many souvenirs stowed away in a wooden box beside the desk in his writing sanctuary where Simon had slept as a boy. Uncle John gave Lucy a box to keep beside her desk too, and in it were a few of Simon's medals, a letter bragging about Lucy weeks before Simon's death, and a necklace of Emily's which Lucy wore every day.

Today on William's birthday, Aunt Kate sent Lucy out to gather flowers from the garden. The delicious fragrance of Sarah's English roses trailing the fence and the gentle buzzing of the honeybees from Uncle John's hives lulled Lucy into a quiet reverie, although the light hurt her eyes a little. A cat purred and rubbed against her skirt. She bent down to pet its velvet fur. Aunt Kate called, and Lucy, scooping up the full basket of blooms, took one last breath in the open air before entering the hot kitchen, which smelled of slightly burnt cake and a sweet ham warming on the stove top.

Though it was only noon on a Saturday, the celebration had to commence early to catch William before the drinking started. Lucy, like John and Kate, had given up on William ever changing but had not given up on habitually making life easy for him.

Everyone scurried but William. Uncle John wondered would William like his gift. Aunt Kate hurried to cook and set the table, trying all the while to do it without a sound so as not to wake William too soon, for he might run out and all preparation would be wasted. Sarah hummed by the hearth, knitting and re-knitting a piece that made no sense. Lucy set the flowers on the kitchen table and ran to reach for an old milk pitcher that served as a vase on the hallway table by the staircase. A stray kitten she'd brought home only days before tripped her, and the pitcher toppled and crashed onto the threadbare rug with a racket.

The family waited for the thud of William's feet hitting the floor of the parlor where he sometimes slept off a big night, too lazy to climb up to his attic room. The pocket doors opened with a groan, and the family braced itself. William stumbled out, cursing. He looked up with red eyes, matted hair, and parched lips. "What's all the noise?" he asked as Lucy picked up pieces of the pitcher on hands and knees. William's trousers were wet, and Kate let out a small horrified cry.

"For God's sake, William, what have you done? Your mother's worked so hard getting ready for your birthday," John said in disgust.

"Birthday? Who cares?" William grumbled, steadying himself against the banister.

"I care, Willy," Kate cried in a beggarly, pathetic tone. "We've made your favorite dinner and cake."

"I'm not hungry."

His father shook William by the collar and shoved him up the steps. "You will eat your dinner! Now get out of those soiled clothes and clean up."

"It's all right, John. Let him go," Kate said.

"No! It's not all right! William, do as I say," John ordered.

"Willy, please be good," Lucy begged, gathering the pile of pitcher fragments on the floor.

William stood, wobbling and laughing in the horrible way Lucy hated. "Good? That's your job, Lulu. You're the good one. The one who replaced my sister. I'm sorry you never got to meet your parents, but these ones are mine no matter how they try to love you!"

"Willy, for shame!" Katherine cried.

"G-Go to your room!" John yelled.

"Why should I listen to a stuttering morphine eater the rest of my life?" William asked with a rotten smile and made to punch his father, but Weldon got the better of him, smacking his face so hard William's nose bled on the new runner rug for the stairs. Lucy had helped Aunt Kate for hours cutting strips of old fabric to hook through the strong muslin to make the inexpensive and oddly nonconformist design. William lunged to get his father, but Lucy was in the way so he kicked her instead. It wasn't a strong kick, just a surprising one.

William ripped Lucy's spectacles from her face. "I hate you, Lucy. I hate the look of you. Those frosted eyes are the scariest thing I've ever seen, and the way you fawn over everyone to get attention sickens me. You're the reason I drink. You and them!

You're so blind to your place in the world, but wait. You'll see soon enough that everyone hates you in this town. You're as ugly as the rest of us!"

"But ..." Lucy wanted to say something to make it all go away, but it hurt too much, and she *did* see her place. Those blurry people she called uncle and aunt—the ones Lucy secretly wanted to call Mother and Papa like William did—they could never love her as their own. Lucy scurried to her feet as John jumped in to throw William out the front door. Lucy raced out the back and into the barn where the nice old horse Handsome once lived. The little kitten had escaped with her in all the commotion, and Lucy laughed despite herself, tucking the tiny ball of fur under her arm before climbing into the warm hayloft.

Before long John joined her, always aware of Lucy's hiding places. With his spectacles tilted and his hair nearly all grey, John looked like a daft old schoolteacher as he hoisted himself into the hay, wincing with his stiff leg.

"Are you okay, Little Captain?" John asked as he sat heavily beside her. Lucy nodded as he put his arm around her. "I'm so sorry, Lulu."

"But Uncle, it's my fault. I was in such a hurry, and it was one of the *good* pitchers."

John sighed and kissed her head. They sat listening to the baby barn swallows for a while. "Eliza was a good little girl, but you'll never replace her, Lulu. I wouldn't want you to. Me and Aunt Kate are very fond of you."

"Uncle, do you love me?"

John smiled. "I love Willy, and I love you. Your father was my b-best friend, and I wish every day he was still with us, but I'm so grateful that we get to have you. I do wish you'd known him—and your mother, but I'm a little s-selfish. Maybe we wouldn't have seen you much if ... oh, I shouldn't talk this way."

Lucy wrapped her arms around his middle. "Sometimes I'm so upset because I wish you and Aunt Kate were my parents, and I don't love my real mother and father," Lucy confided.

"If it makes you f-feel better, I've always considered you my daughter—I mean one that Simon, your father, shared with me and Kate," John said, wiping emotion from his eyes. "I wish things were different, but this is the way it is." He stood up on stiff old bones. "I have to find your aunt. Are you coming?" John asked. Even when smiling the Weldon men could not escape a handsome sadness. Every story Lucy's uncle wrote and sent for publishing at the tiny print shop had traces of his melancholy, and the old soldiers ate it up. Life was a battle to men of his generation. Moments were gifts. Women were salves to battle wounds. Lucy felt this more than she understood it. It kept her eager to please her uncle, to at once adore him and take care of him.

Lucy and John hesitated on the side porch before entering the warm kitchen where Katherine sat staring into the empty fireplace. John sighed and pushed past his feelings. "Kate," he began as he opened the door. "Has he come back, yet?"

Katherine looked up, anger flickering in her eyes but held in check. "You know he won't once he's out. Just give the cake to Mrs. Cummings to feed her chickens."

"It's a lovely cake, and we'll eat it," Weldon tried.

"No, it's spoiled. Everything gets so spoiled ..." Katherine's voice trailed off.

"Forgive me, Kate," he said.

Katherine let the words hang in the air as if mulling them over, though she'd heard such sentiment so many times. "I have forgiven you."

Lucy walked past with her kitten.

Katherine grabbed the animal. "No more pets, Lucy. It's the reason you tripped, and William is gone again." She took the kitten and tossed it onto the porch.

"Aunt Kate, I'm sorry you're upset."

"I'm not upset," Katherine said, taking her fraying shawl down from its peg in the mudroom.

John shook his head at Lucy and motioned for her to leave the grown-ups alone. Lucy climbed the stairs to her room and opened her window. She sat before it imagining the verdant pastures her father had described to Aunt Kate in one of his final letters from his new home all the way over the plains, prairies, and mountains of the continent. Lucy thought she understood why he stayed so far away.

The carelessly scrawled artifact spoke of horse rides and hope, a new life with a beautiful companion and a child. Lucy imagined her mother's perfume and imagined being cradled by her. She went to the box full of collected things and pulled out a woolen square of an old army overcoat that her father wore on the day he'd been ambushed by Indians. Lucy rubbed the scratchy fabric against her cheek. This is how it would feel to be held against his chest in embrace, she pretended. It pained her not to remember her father's voice. She imagined her own voice being much like her mother's as she talked herself to sleep most nights.

Wouldn't her friends laugh if they knew how she pretended the soothing words were her mother's? Her father remained silent inside the frame beside her bed. People said he had a solid, heartening laugh and that he attracted friends like bees to honey.

She listened to the sounds of her aunt and uncle avoiding each other downstairs. If only she hadn't broken the pitcher. If only they hadn't been burdened with an orphan. She stared at herself for a long time in the mirror. Was she pretty? She let her strawberry hair down and smoothed the waves with her pale white fingers.

Voices rose in the rooms below. A door slammed, and Aunt Kate's brisk footfall unsettled pebbles on the drive. Another walk. Another long evening. On nights such as this she was in the habit of keeping Uncle John company, but an idea troubled her: Maybe her uncle brooded because Lucy sat beside him when all he wanted was his wife's attention. Maybe Lucy was more a nuisance than a help.

She longed for the ham but could not bring herself into the suffocating melancholy and anger below. Was it only this morning that Aunt Kate had complimented Lucy about her manners? That happy moment seemed days ago.

She prayed not to hate this William from the West. She prayed not to hate her uncle for sending William away in the first place, worrying that one day Uncle John might do the same to her. She prayed that Aunt Kate might embrace her sometime and make her feel loved, and she prayed that as the hours of the day faded and the last birds sang, she might forgive the three of them for forgetting she existed and for forgetting she was hungry.

When true darkness came Lucy slipped into her white gown and under the covers of her old bed. She wondered about the moon and the stars and the vast earthly citizenry under the watchful eyes of God. Was her father Simon McCullough's name written in the Book of Life? Would Lucy be lonely even after death? Would heaven have a moon, stirring melancholy in the hearts of angels?

She turned away from the window, her legs restless and her stomach hollow. She whispered and whispered and, at the sound of her aunt and uncle making up on the porch below, Lucy fell asleep.

*\*\**

Before dawn at the darkest hour a warm body pulled Lucy close and wrapped around her. Lucy's long hair pulled beneath the weight of the person, William, mumbling beside her. She tried to squirm free.

"Ginny, darlin' come on ..." William said, his voice rough with drink and cigarettes, his breath hot with onion sandwiches from Stagg's. He snuggled in closer and kissed Lucy behind the ear.

"Willy!" Lucy cried.

He covered her mouth with a laugh. "Shush," he whispered, as he traced his fingers along her hip. "It's been so long—let me poke you ..."

She kicked him as hard as she could with her heel and pulled free. He grabbed her arm, but she hit him hard across the face. She turned up the gaslight. At the sight of his cousin William sat bolt upright. He stumbled from the bed.

"Oh, my lord!" William cried. "What have I done? Oh, *what have I done?*"

Lucy said nothing.

"Lulu—I'd never—I don't think of you like that—you're like a sister—oh, God what did I do? Lulu—tell me ..."

Lucy walked over and slapped his face hard enough to hurt her hand. "You did nothing. You stupid idiot! But you could have!"

"You mustn't tell my parents!" William pleaded. "I'm so damned sorry! I truly am! I wasn't myself. I ... I was remembering something else, I ..."

"You're a drunkard, Willy! Do you hear me? And I won't ... I won't have you drag me down to feel like nothing," Lucy said, crying as she remembered Buck Crenshaw's words on the street corner months ago. "I'm worth something," she said, wiping her eyes.

"You don't understand," William said, grabbing for her hands.

She batted him away, her mouth curled in repulsion. This stung him. He'd destroyed the innocence of his young cousin. He'd almost made victim a young girl who had adored him despite his failings. His mind raced back over the dull moments just before true waking and the kiss he'd forced upon her. His head spun as he sank into the chair beside the bed.

"I know you can't forgive me ..." he said. "I'll leave for good—only don't tell."

"Do you see me as a deal maker?" Lucy asked. "I used to trust you—and I defended you to ... people."

"I know! I know! And I'm sorry, Lucy! You don't understand what it's like!"

"I understand everything because I've been here forever," Lucy cried. "It hurts me to watch you. You're so lucky. You think you have forever to nurse this tantrum about your parents. You think drinking will keep them guilty when you're just scared."

"No. I'm not, Lulu. I ..." he said. He looked at her with his large saucer eyes for a long while as if trying to stay focused. "I've hurt so many people—when I wake up—it's what I remember first and then I think — I think — I don't want to think about any of it, but I see Mother and Papa. I see the empty barn with Handsome gone because of me. Thankful loved me—did you know that?"

"Everyone knew it."

"Why didn't anyone tell me?" he asked. "I didn't mean those things I said to you yesterday. I promise."

"I know lots of things people don't think I know," Lucy said. "I understand why I have these ugly eyes."

"They're not ugly ..."

"Willy, stop. My father made my mother sick. Everyone in town thinks because I can't see very well that I can't hear. But what I wouldn't give to meet my mother and father! I'll have these eyes for the rest of my life and that's okay, but I want *what you have*! I want parents who can tell me they love me as I am because they made me. I wish mine had lived long enough to die of sickness—no matter how shameful—because then I would have gotten to touch them with my own hands. I'd understand the jokes you all have about my father. I'd know something more about my mother besides that she was something I'll never be—beautiful. I imagine that my father must have been so funny and kind and generous to have so many people smile when they hear his name, and I'll never get to love him the way you did!" She broke down, sobbing. "Why can't you see things? You're the one who's ruining things here. Every moment we have to worry about *you*—always you! I haven't a lock on my door. Shall I ask Uncle John for one? I'm frightened of you!"

William jumped from his seat, trying to hush her while swaying slightly. "I got confused, Lulu. It won't happen again! I promise."

"I don't believe you," she said. "Get out of my room at once."

"Please give me one more chance!" he begged. "I'm done! I'm truly done! I won't drink another drop. You can follow me to make sure and empty all my bottles ..."

"I won't go near your bottles, and I would never follow you! How mortifying for me! No. I won't let you drag me down—ever again." She pointed to the door.

"Land sakes, Lulu. How old are you?" William asked. "If you look in the mirror you'll see your father."

"Mirrors are too bright. They hurt my eyes."

"I'm afraid that if I stop drinking ..." He hesitated. "I'll have to face everyone, Lulu."

"You're already facing me. You're my only friend. I don't care what the world thinks. I don't care that you've made mistakes, just come back to us like you used to be. I'm all alone here."

William walked out and up to his attic room. Lucy lay on her bed for a while, but hunger brought her down to the empty kitchen. Yesterday's cake sat on the table and the ham on the stove. Lucy dipped her finger into the honey glaze and put her apron on. She finished setting the table in the dining room and iced the cake. The house needed airing, and the sounds of early spring peepers when she opened the windows made her heart full despite the darkness of the house.

Soon she heard her aunt and uncle stirring. She called them into the dining room where she had hung garland with William's name on it yesterday. "He's home," she told them as they shuffled in.

They turned to the sound of William's feet on the stairs. She feared he was leaving, but he walked into the dining room with his old haversack. His parents waited upon his next move with drawn faces.

"I'm sorry, Papa and Mother," William began, glancing at Lucy. "I've thought of leaving you again so many times ..."

Lucy interrupted. "What have you got in the bag, Willy?"

"Oh, it's nothing, I ..." He pulled out a pastel drawing. "Lulu, this is how I remember your father in my mind. He looked like this. Like you."

Lucy took the drawing and held it close to her eyes and then a little farther back. The strong gradation of color made it easier for Lucy to see. She laughed and cried. "This is really him, isn't it?" she asked, showing the drawing to John and Kate.

They were speechless.

"Mother, I don't want to do this anymore," Willy said, clutching the back of the dining chair with white knuckles, "but I'm afraid of facing all the things I've done, and I hate who I am when I stop."

"You're the boy we always loved. Come back to us and let us all mend," Katherine said, her eyes lighting with the same mix of hope and distrust William had experienced his whole life. This time his heart broke for her—not himself.

John sat staring out the window, chin in hand.

William reached into his bag for an old drawing Thankful made him save in the West. "Papa, this was always for you. It's not very good ... but it was what I made first on my trip out to Arizona. I missed you. I've never stopped missing you. I'm just so ashamed ..."

John shoved chairs out of the way and grabbed his son, pulling him tight and close. "Forgive me, William!"

"I don't want to feel this way anymore, Papa. I forgive you."

# Chapter Thirty-Eight

William Weldon knocked at the door with trepidation. Substantial homes on quiet lanes in the country intimidated him, and he had never freed his mind of the West, where everyone lived strapped for cash and without fine things. A shower had heightened the musty scent of his woolen suit as he wiped the beads of water from his bowler hat. A tall black woman with wary dark eyes cracked open the door, since no one was expected this late in the day. Bats cast fluttering shadows in the hedge-enclosed front garden.

"Pardon me, but I was wondering if Miss Crenshaw might be at home tonight?" William said, putting his hat back on and taking it off again.

"Why are you so jumpy, young man? Do I know you?" Betty asked.

"I'm not sure. I was at Buck's funeral—with my parents—Mr. and Mrs. Weldon," William said, his eyes resting on the flowers a moment before meeting Betty's leery ones.

"Martha, we have a visitor," Betty called, but still did not invite William into the house.

"Well, why is he standing at the door, Betty? Let him in," Martha said as she came up, rolling her eyes when she saw who it was.

Betty hesitated but swung open the door and moved to let him by. He limped in, the weather always making his leg sore. The three stood in the dimly lit, wall-papered hallway for a while until Martha spoke.

"Why are you here, boy?"

"I needed to speak with your granddaughter, ma'am," William replied, his gold eyes hopeful.

"A letter would have done." Martha glared at him behind her reading spectacles.

"I'm not much for writing, and I'd feel the coward to apologize that way."

The old lady looked very much how William expected Thankful to look one day.

"You're the cause of all Thankful's trouble, and you think an apology will fix it?" Martha asked.

"No, I can't fix anything I've done, but ..."

"But you want to make yourself feel better? A new suit and a shave don't fool me. I can tell you that," Martha said. "Fred told me all about what happened between you and Thankful in Graham's carriage house after Buck's funeral."

William's face betrayed the hard feelings he had for Fred, but he replied, "Fred was right to tell you, and he's been right about me all along. Fred was looking after Thankful."

"Yes, that's Fred—misguided but loves his family as every man should. How are your poor parents? I'm sure you've been quite a disappointment to them."

William bristled a little. "They're well. I've shamed them, but they've forgiven me. They're better people than I ever gave them credit for, and I intend to repay them by never drinking again, ma'am."

"Once a drinker, always a drinker," Betty said.

Martha nodded in agreement.

"You've got a right to your opinions," William said, "and I'm a little scared there's truth to them, but I promised my cousin—I promised them all."

"Hmm, Betty, how often have you heard a grown man admit to being scared?" Martha asked her friend, keeping her eyes on William.

"Hardly ever, Martha."

"Come in, Mr. Weldon. This was a foolish time to visit. The inn is a mile off, and where were you planning on sleeping the night?" Martha asked.

"I hadn't planned on arriving so late," William said, "but the coach ride was muddy, and bridges were washed out, so it took longer than I expected. I don't mind walking to the inn if you point me in the right direction."

"No, we'll have you stay on the night. Betty has soup and bread."

"Thank you, ma'am, but I wouldn't want to trouble you, and I doubt Thankful would want me here." William felt the warmth of the fire from the paneled parlor beckoning.

Martha took him in by the hearth and made him sit near the flames in a comfortable wing chair. He worried his damp clothes would stain it so he sat on the edge of his seat.

Martha sat across from him, studying him until he squirmed.

"Ma'am, is Thankful at home?" William asked.

"You look so young," Martha replied. "It saddens me."

"Ma'am? Has something happened to her?"

"I'm afraid so," Martha said, taking up her crochet. "She's off and married Henry Demarest."

"Who?"

"A good man from a good family—he was at the funeral. You might have noticed him—rather eccentric in dress." Martha shook her head as she spoke. "Henry's doing his best to provide for Thankful and his children."

"Thankful's taking care of his children?" William asked incredulously.

"Thankful no longer lives here, you understand. And she quit working for me just when she finally learned the bookkeeping and all." Martha searched William's befuddled face. "You're too late, young man. Thankful's found someone more suited to her."

He stared into the fire. His pride and common sense took over. "Well, of course she has. She deserves to be well-treated." He put on a brave face and turned to Martha. "I only came to apologize for the bad feelings I caused between us. If she's happy then I'm very happy for her." He exhaled. "It's for the best. I can be at peace about it all, finally."

Martha smiled. "Very nice words."

"It's because I mean them, ma'am. I've cared for Thankful since I was a child, but she always deserved better, and now she has it. It's a weight lifted from me."

"I don't believe you," Martha said, "but you're right to let her go. Henry has work and a good family backing him, and Thankful loves his children as if they were her own."

William shook his head.

"Well, Mr. Weldon, you're welcome to stay the night. Bear with us though. It's lambing season, and we're in and out checking on our babies. Our hired man up and left us as the first girls were giving birth—just like a man."

"Ma'am, I'm grateful for the offer," William replied, seizing an opening. "I wouldn't mind sleeping down in the barn and keeping an eye on your flock. You hardly know me well enough to put me up in one of your fine rooms." He was discomfited by the old woman's generosity. He dreaded small talk—which he had none of—at breakfast or even for the next hour and would gladly hide out in a barn to avoid it.

Martha's severity showed softening. "You'll spoil your nice suit."

"Oh, it doesn't matter. My mother's practicing her sewing, and I have more vests and trousers than I could ever wear."

"Your mother's a nice little thing—though too quick to please people, I'd say." Martha smiled.

"Well, she pleases me greatly," William stated. "Mother's been my biggest supporter—along with my father."

"It's nice to see gratitude for parents," Martha said, fingering a lost stitch on the blanket she was making.

"I took a while, but I'm getting there, ma'am," he replied. He stood up now, putting on his hat. "Will you show me all that needs to be done in the barn?"

"You're a foolish man, Mr. Weldon, but I won't turn down help when God sends it. Come along, and I'll find you a coat to cover your fine tweed."

He slept little. Two lambs arrived, and he watched like a rapt child. The fragrance of clean, dry hay and warm, healthy animals reminded him of the army stables of his youth. The hinges on the old doors of the barn were well made, and the lanterns were polished with care. Martha had chromos framed on the rustic walls of peasants farming in the half-light of dusk—copies of famous works by European artists he'd once known but couldn't quite remember. It no longer angered him—this fuzziness of memory. What did it matter if he knew their names? He could enjoy the art till the light flickered out, and the shadows obscured it.

He remembered the important things. His sister, his uncle and grandfather—and one day he hoped he'd remember, without pain, Thankful Crenshaw. He would remember that he had always ached, but that one day he had healed—because of Lucy—because she stood up to the drinking—something he didn't think he could do. Lucy forgave the unforgivable—this awed William.

He didn't hate himself for drinking anymore—at least not every minute. Sometimes he was proud that he had finally stopped, but mostly William was humbled. Not at first, but now after a few months he began to enjoy things again—things that had been numbed or had fallen away. His mind sometimes thrilled at the little things: the warmth of the sun on a brisk day, the aroma of coffee and bacon, and the bleating of these little lambs.

He had never been a deep person and never would be in his estimation, but his fleeting memories gave him time to savor the present moment. His sister Eliza was gone and no amount of reaching back could bring her to him. Clinging to that past had left him faithless and foolish. Lucy, his sentimental cousin through her dark and humiliating spectacles, let him see the present. How did she do that? Just simple, heart-felt words.

For years William stoked the fire of his anger at his family's many flaws and missteps. Even Uncle Simon, for all of his kindness, was a diseased man when he died, and William nursed a secret gratitude his end came at the hands of Indians far away from Englewood eyes. Lucy pried open William's calloused heart. He hoped to thank his uncle in heaven for being who he had been and leaving behind a cousin who offered real friendship and inspiration. Something drove Lucy, and William wanted to know what that was, though he never asked.

He missed his family even on this short journey and smiled at the idea he had become a homebody like his father. Taking up his sketchpad, William drew lambs for Lucy.

A robin's song and the swallows flitting in the rafters announced a happy new day. Martha opened the barn door unannounced, and William jumped from his reverie. "Ma'am, good morning."

"Mr. Weldon, please call me Martha. It's less grating." With hands on hips she admired him head to toe. "You're the picture of a handsome country gentleman."

"No, that's something I'm not, though I thoroughly enjoyed my night here. Two lambs born—look there. A thing of wonder, it is. Thank you for letting me experience it."

Martha went to the animals now with a mild look on her usually grim face. "They've been a surprise. I don't know why I waited so long to have them." She spotted William's open sketchbook. "Oh, an artist with talent."

"No, just a hobbyist. My cousin loves small animals."

Martha took up the book and flipped through the pages a little roughly. "Betty has breakfast up at the house for you."

"No, I couldn't."

"You must. We don't permit wasted food, and it's already made. You gave us our first full night's sleep in weeks. Take it as payment." Martha noticed the hunger on William's face. "You never did mention what you do for work."

William pulled his wrinkled jacket over his shoulders. "Oh, well, I've burnt a lot of bridges with my bad behavior. My father insists I illustrate the little stories he sells to the magazines—old soldiers seem to enjoy them quite a lot. There's not much money in it yet though."

Martha handed him his pad of drawings. "I need a man for just a few weeks to help with the heavier work, if you'd be interested."

William's grin had won over tougher women. Martha laughed as he tucked his sketchbook into his patched old haversack. "I wonder what Thankful would say ..." he said, exposing again his true feelings.

"Thankful never comes here, and I'd frown upon you turning her world upside down. She has enough on her plate, but we're a little desperate for workers."

William rubbed his chin, having second thoughts. "I've no experience with farming and my leg is—well you see for yourself."

"I'm not asking you to run a marathon. You're plenty stronger than two old women." Martha took him by the arm and pointed him toward the house. "Now just consider my offer. Betty's cooking might convince you better. Room and board and a good salary for a month—hard to find these days."

William sent a note off at the post informing his parents he'd be delayed in returning home, but not to worry and hurried back to the barnyard where fine equipment and quality horses awaited. The chance at real money to share with his parents and be-ing out in the open doing strenuous labor roused in him a wave of bracing excitement he hadn't felt since riding out on his own on a stolen horse in the West.

After a few days of great soreness William's body strengthened. He'd never imag-ined gardening to be enjoyable, but Betty brought out cool tea in the heat, and William listened to Martha read aloud from the paper as he weeded the garlic patch in the small kitchen plot near the yard Thankful had worked in the previous year. William was handy with a gun and gamely killed the squirrels and woodchucks Martha despised, but she had a soft spot for chipmunks. When Martha spied William taming one with walnuts from Betty's kitchen she teased him, but he was so charming and good-natured that Martha relented and let him keep his pets.

As William settled in, Martha decided that Thankful must be at fault for any dis-appointment with this fine young man. Martha even took one of William's drawings and hung it in her kitchen.

Thankful never wandered over, and William pretended to be grateful for it, but knowing she was only minutes away wore on him, and he made excuses for evening walks, hoping for chance meetings but coming home disappointed each dark night with one of Martha's lanterns swinging at his side. Martha gently warned him on such nights against dreaming unchristian dreams.

# Chapter Thirty-Nine

The crisp, final leaves blew from the great oak that, in summer, Thankful sat beneath as her only refuge. From her bedroom she often watched the squirrels gathering their nuts for colder weather. Henry stood beside her some mornings peering out as wistfully as she did before sighing and dressing for his dreary work (was all work dreary to Henry?). He hardly earned enough to cover the children's schooling. Her attempts at teaching them from home ended in revolt after she proclaimed the children too stupid to learn. She apologized, but the mood soured for them all. She gladly passed the reins to a private tutor who praised his students for their ineptitude and taught them nothing.

It served the spoiled children right. Let them be fools. What did it matter to her? Thankful was not their mother and didn't want to be. She felt the outsider, longing for the Christmas holidays when Henry might be home more, and they could build something of a marriage.

She understood why Henry avoided the awful children. One night, after suffering through a day with the slack-jawed and dirty-faced hellions, she sent the last of them to bed and wrapped the final pair of stockings she had half-heartedly knit for Avi as a Christmas gift. Mother Demarest mentioned yet again the sorrowful mood that had overtaken her son—coincidentally just after his remarriage.

"Dear girl, you're young and inexperienced," Mother Demarest slurred through her wine-stained teeth. "I've set a book in your stitchery bag by the sofa—it's rather a filthy book—but I've found that men have filthy minds, and unless you can keep up with them their eyes will stray. I've taken the time to write out in the back a few phrases you might use to entice Henry."

Thankful looked at Mother Demarest—the busy, cheap, awful way she wore her jewelry—and smiled with a mix of disgust and superiority that the old lady noted at once.

"Where is our dear Henry in the evenings do you think?" Mother Demarest asked with a resigned sigh of reproach.

Thankful marched up to her room and packed a few things in a small case, pulling the last of the money she had saved from her grandmother's pay and slipped out to wait under the oak in the yard. Henry, later than ever, rode up on his sleepy horse. Thankful called out, startling horse and rider.

"Thankful, what on earth are you trying to do, kill us?" Henry said with impatience, though he smiled.

"Sweetheart, I have an idea," she said, attempting to tug him from the horse.

Henry didn't budge.

"Can't it wait till I'm in from the cold?" he asked icily.

"No. I've made up my mind about something, and it can't wait," she said, though her resolve weakened at his frosty reception.

Henry sighed and slid from his mount. "Now, what is it?"

"Remember how it was when we first met?" she asked, throwing her arms around him.

"Barely."

"Yes, well, I was thinking ..."

Henry blew into his gloved hands and looked toward the house. "What is there for supper?"

"Mince pie."

"Haven't we had enough of that lately?"

"Henry, dear, this is important. Listen to me. I see how unhappy you are. This is no way to live. We should leave. Tonight." Thankful ran to the tree and grabbed the small case as Henry looked on incredulously.

"Thankful, what are you saying?"

"Let's escape. Forever. The children will be fine with your parents, and it's not as if they'd miss us."

"I thought you *liked* the children."

"Do you?" she replied, feeling the train wreck approaching but unwilling to pull the brakes. "You're never here, and I'm expected to care for them and pretend at liking them while you're off till all hours— and we live like poor church mice and have no fun anymore."

"Fun." Henry tugged his hat off, his sweaty hair making him more ruggedly good looking than she had ever seen him. "You want fun? Try working for the most ignorant, incompetent ass in town who somehow still finds ways to lord over me."

"Are we talking about your mother?" Thankful asked spitefully.

"My mother does nothing but help us. My salary isn't enough for the schooling we now must pay for."

"And you blame me for not teaching the children?"

"Thankful, no," he said, but she didn't believe him. "I blame myself."

"Let's run away, Henry. Please, let's."

"We can't now, can we?" Henry's shoulders slumped in defeat.

"But you left them before—and they'll get by."

"Yes, I left my children—*my children*. I couldn't bear to see them so upset at the loss of their mother. But I was wrong to think I could escape them."

Thankful pulled out a wad of bills. "Look here, we have money, and we can just go now and recover our marriage."

Henry looked at her sadly. "What marriage? It was just a whim for us both."

She gasped. "Speak for yourself!"

"Thankful, do you love me?"

"You're a handsome man. I want to love you more than anything ... but you won't let me." She looked toward the house.

The answer did not satisfy his need. "I've been late these nights, speaking with an old friend ..."

"What's her name?" Thankful cried.

"Nothing's happened, Thankful. I just needed someone to talk to."

"And why not me?" she asked, her voice quaking.

"Because you're too emotional! And you're too angry at me."

"I'm not angry!" she shouted.

Henry grabbed the money from her. "You've been hiding all this money from me while I slave under Janssen?" he shouted back. "You're afraid I'll squander your money. You don't trust me."

"And how can I? You didn't even tell me you had children or a wife you once loved!"

"I knew you wouldn't understand even though you've done worse! You're a hypocrite!"

One of the upstairs windows opened, and Helmut stuck his head out. "Daddy, I love you!"

Henry turned to him. "I love you too." Turning back, he caught something and asked, "And what was that look on your face, Thankful?"

"It sickens me, the way that little boy ass-licks."

"Thankful! What's wrong with you, speaking that way? You degrade yourself with such low talk!"

"I don't care! I love you and ..."

"We're making a scene in front of the children." Henry smiled up at Helmut and Zala and waved.

"Is that all that matters now?" Thankful asked hotly. "Those stupid children?"

"Yes, and maybe that's the problem—I need to make it up to them—to put them first."

"Will your friend be helping with that?" she asked, shoving him.

"I knew you would take it badly! It's why I can't confide in you. If we're not talking about *you* then you want no part in it!"

She hit him. "How dare you! I've done nothing but care for your mistakes! I wash and feed them! I clean up after they soil the bed sheets, and you *never* have time for me!"

"I can't talk to you when you're like this! I'm going inside to bed."

"Oh, don't leave me!" she cried. "I'm sorry about everything! We have to make this work!"

Henry took her by the arms. "I don't want to leave you. But you have to understand that for now, the children come first for me."

# Chapter Forty

Martha admired the fine fiber her diminutive herd of sheep produced as she loaded her wagon with the sheared product one balmy autumn day. An enterprising young widow had just opened a small yarn shop on the banks of the Hackensack across the river from the Demarest home. Martha would see about selling her fleeces there today. William wished Martha luck, admiring the figure she cut even in her old age.

After a few sharp orders called to William, Martha trotted off, scolding her dogs to stay put. One jumped aboard, and she let him sidle beside her with an annoyed look for William's sake. They disappeared around the bend in short order, Martha being an aggressive driver. As the Demarest estate came into view with its majestic weeping willows swaying in the hazy sunshine, Martha slowed her horse. Should she lecture Thankful for not writing to tell her parents of her marriage?

Martha never liked Mrs. Demarest and had recently heard a rumor about Henry. She clucked at her fine horse now, gently urging him along as she watched the property for Thankful, but only a small girl wandered the yard. The manicured hedges and giant marble urns were too ostentatious. Martha sniffed her nose at it all. Simple was best, she said to herself, keeping her competitiveness in check as best she could. Who would want a house so close to the bridge and commerce? Just then as Martha passed almost to the bridge Thankful called out to her and gave chase. Without regard for safety, she jumped aboard the wagon, startling the old dog napping at Martha's feet.

"Grandmother! Oh, I'm so happy to see you!' she said breathlessly. "Where are you going? Of course you'll come by the house for tea on the way back, won't you? Please do!"

"Girl, you'll be the death of me and in front of all these people! Acting as if you've been let from the asylum! You're making a scene, and there's enough talk in this stupid town. I wasn't planning on visiting with you and that old crone, but if there's time when I get done ... maybe I'll stop by. Will you ever grow up? Jumping on us like that!"

Thankful looked as though she might cry.

"Oh, don't start that, now," Martha moaned, refusing to give her a second glance. "You've made your bed, dear."

"Oh, Grandmother, I know that. I just miss you terribly. It's silly." Thankful kissed her grandmother on the cheek and jumped down as fast as she'd climbed up with the wagon still slowly in motion.

Martha waved her off stiffly as she led the horse to cross the bridge, cursing to herself that she hadn't sent Betty. Too much commotion was to be had from Graham's offspring. When she thought of it that way she smiled. Poor Graham, who would have guessed he'd have such a lively bunch? Martha missed her son—and his brothers.

Selling her wool for a pretty penny, her mood brightened momentarily, but the prospect of a visit to the Demarest house caused her consternation so she trotted past. She pulled up and sat a moment, thinking. Breathing deeply, she turned around and drove up the pebbled drive. How on earth did the Demarest family afford such fine out-of-doors furniture? And the laziness of Mrs. Demarest, who in the middle of the day lay languidly in a beautiful hammock! Martha sat proudly, waiting to be greeted for quite some time. Finally her patience failing, she jumped down, adjusting her feathered town hat as she walked up, chin held high, to the snoozing old lady. "Mrs. Demarest."

The woman started with a cry. "Martha Crenshaw, whatever brings you here?" She pulled herself up and out of the hammock in an atrociously uncivilized fashion. "Are you finally here to help your kin?"

"No. I'm not. My granddaughter is capable of making her own mistakes. I don't believe in babying adults as *some do*. Leads them to misery no matter how enjoyably childish they may seem."

"Haven't you heard? Henry has found a respectable position with the surveyor Janssen," Mrs. Demarest said with tremulous pride as she wiped her forehead and fat neck of perspiration.

"Janssen," Martha said, laughing, "is an awful man. I can't see poor Henry abiding his ways for long. And Henry's no surveyor. He's many great things but not precise."

"I believe in my son even if others don't." Mrs. Demarest snapped her shawl around herself.

"What does Thankful think?" Martha asked.

"You must ask her yourself." Mrs. Demarest waved Martha in through the back porch, which led to a bright study where a dusty piano sat littered with half-written compositions on top. "Thankful's a very snippy girl, but it shouldn't surprise me. I don't like to speak with her for fear she'll bite. Come inside for something cool to drink, and I'll have her fetched."

Martha nodded grimly. Children stomped and threw each other about in a room overhead, and Martha wondered what her husband would have done to such animals.

Thankful strolled in wearing a lavender dress that was very suited to her and of fine fabric, but her eyes betrayed a desperation. "Grandmother, forgive me for my recklessness earlier. I don't know what I was thinking. I suppose I just woke up in a mood."

"Thankful, come sit with me," Martha ordered. Thankful complied. Martha wait-ed until all the children who nosily wandered in understood they were unwelcome be-fore she spoke. "Young lady, you may have fine things here, but something's not right."

"Grandmother, I am *so very* happy here," Thankful gushed, shaking her head just enough to make her pretty curls bounce. "I've worked hard and prayed *very long,* and I'm finally seeing that Henry's children are a gift to me."

Martha folded her arms in amused disbelief. "Explain yourself, Thankful."

"I *must love* my enemies. I thank you for teaching me that."

"I don't ever remember saying a word," Martha said, unwilling to take credit or blame.

"Well, your Bibles. I couldn't escape reading them now and again. Of course I knew the words before, but I never had reason to put them to use. I've always loved everyone. But here, God is showing me my weaknesses. I must try *very* hard."

"So you hate the children?" Martha said with a satisfied smile.

"It's awful, but I really do—well—I *did* but not so much anymore. I help them a lot. They just don't know how to behave. A phrenologist came for supper just recently and said the children's heads were too small for good brains so I mustn't be too harsh. One day I believe Henry will see how I've improved them as much as I can."

"I'm not certain people like outsiders to improve their offspring," Martha replied skeptically.

"Poor Henry has no time to do it himself. He's a surveyor now, did you know?"

"Thankful, honestly. We both know Henry's no surveyor. Have you met Janssen?" Martha shook her head. "Terrible man."

Thankful looked blankly at her grandmother.

"I received quite a sum of money from my sheep, and there's more to come with the meat lambs."

"That's wonderful, Grandmother."

Martha reached into her purse. "You need some funds of your own, dear."

"No, I still have money from before."

"I never would have thought about sheep if you hadn't suggested it. You're clever, and you saw a need. This money is rightly yours."

"Grandmother, thank you, but your respect is payment enough."

Martha pushed the money into Thankful's hand. "I don't respect you, dear. You don't respect yourself. This money is for a rainy day. Leave it at that." Martha stood to leave.

"Grandmother, won't you stay a little longer?" Thankful batted her lashes and a tiny tear fell.

"No, I have a great many things to get on with," Martha said. How long would Thankful use those eyes to manipulate people! Martha snapped a fan open and let herself out before Thankful could but stopped at the door and turned to her granddaughter, who sat like a neglected porcelain doll. "I miss your help in the garden, you know."

Thankful jumped to her feet grateful for the scrap her grandmother had thrown her. "Oh, and I would have loved to see the lambs. I'd looked forward to it, but I suppose I wouldn't have been able to get away for even a night what with the children," she said, trying to sound grown-up and resigned. "I hope they didn't give you too much trouble."

"Not a bit," Martha began, but hesitated. "We've hired on a young man for the season."

"Oh. Who?" Thankful asked, sensing a funny tone. "Do I know him?"

"I promised I wouldn't tell," Martha replied.

"Buck's here?" Thankful cried. "Or is it Father?"

"Of course not! What on earth would they do for me?" Martha studied Thankful and determined she'd already said too much but never was one to lie. "I told him it didn't matter anymore anyway, but he had come to ask forgiveness." Martha grew impatient as Thankful remained confused. "It's your friend Mr. Weldon."

The color in Thankful's face vanished. "Which Mr. Weldon do you mean?"

"Well, certainly not the old soldier!" Martha said, ruffled at her granddaughter's stupidity and at the look in the girl's eyes. It had been a mistake to tell. "William won't be here much longer. Said he has work with his father. I hadn't planned on hiring him on, but he has those puppy eyes, and we were short on help with the lambs."

Thankful looked out into the sunny yard from where she stood. Martha regretted the pain she had just caused, though already she rationalized it as being truthful. "Now, don't let this upset you, dear. He'll be gone before you know it."

Thankful turned on her. "Of course he will! He's not fit for work, and he'll disappoint you, you stupid old woman! I've never known you to be taken in by eyes! He'll bring embarrassment to you, and you deserve it!" Thankful ran to the porch and collapsed onto one of the expensive chairs.

Martha followed, muttering under her breath as she sat beside her granddaughter. "There, there. You've a right to be angry with me. But I felt it was my Christian duty to let William stay the night when he came so late in the day to see you."

Thankful heroically tried to regain her composure. Martha smiled a little and took her hand. "I don't like many women, but I like you, dear."

Thankful looked at her queerly and laughed in between blowing her nose. "What good will that do me?"

Martha chuckled. "Men bring pain. It's just life. They're good for heavy lifting but not much else, I'm afraid."

"Well, that's a terrible thing to say," Thankful replied, but laughed. "Oh, it's true isn't it? I suppose poor Buck should just be put out of his misery then. He can't lift a thing." Thankful meant it as a maudlin joke, but neither of them liked it in the end. "I miss Buckie."

"I'd give anything for my dead sons back," Martha said, wiping one tear away. "Let's not think too much about our poor boys. I must be off now. I'm sorry to have spoiled this nice day for you."

"It was spoiled long before you came, Grandmother. You're just the icing," Thankful said, giving her grandmother a hug before walking her to her wagon.

Martha quietly checked her horse with Thankful in tow. She turned to Thankful then. "I told William that you were happy here." Martha waited for a response and sighed when she didn't get one. "I'll keep you in my prayers, dear."

# Chapter Forty-One

The lambs were fattening and the fall harvest had long since peaked when finally William saw fit to go home. Martha sighed in relief. Though she had enjoyed his quiet companionship and promised she'd care for the chipmunk in the yard, she had been on edge fearing Thankful might come by and make an even bigger mess of things. So with a surprising bit of sadness Martha strolled with William one last time through her garden.

"Those sprouts should be taken today or tomorrow at least," he noted with a proud grin. His section of the garden was the picture of fertile abundance.

"Young man, you've got a green thumb and a way with animals. You're welcome here any time you need work—or for a visit, of course."

"You are so different from what Buck and Thankful made you out to be."

"Of course I am. To whom much is given, of him shall much be required. The Crenshaw children have been given talent, intelligence, and money, but for the most part they squander their lives. It annoys me greatly." Martha stopped to examine the last of the greens. "But you I like. You work hard and don't complain."

William laughed, his sober eyes clear and bright. "I've made some progress then."

Martha took an envelope from her apron pocket. "Here you go. Spend it wisely, my friend."

"I've enjoyed my stay so much it feels wrong to take pay for it."

Martha shook her head with a sly smile. "You *are* the charmer."

"No, I mean it."

"I know you mean it," she said with a laugh. "Now go and have a good life. I'll pray for you." She patted his face and turned back toward her fields.

William watched her for a moment then walked toward River Road, opening the envelope to find more money than he had expected. After a brief moment of confusion he turned back to Martha to find she'd been watching him. "Spend it wisely, remember!" she called to him and waved him off once more.

He shoved the envelope in his pocket and made for the road, knowing what he must do. Following the road north instead of south, he found River Edge Road and the Georgian brick home where Thankful now lived. Running up on legs improved by farm work, he pushed through the gate and up to the front door, knocking breathlessly, not wanting to lose his nerve. "Is Thankful in?" he asked a small girl who opened the door a crack.

The girl stared up.

"Is Thankful here?" he asked again.

An older girl came next and stood gaping.

William called in, "Are you home, Thankful? Are you inside?"

Thankful came from the shadows of the dark hallway, tired but fine-looking still. His heart raced despite his best efforts to steel himself. When Thankful saw him she pushed past the girls, shoving them back and closing the door behind her.

"William! You've given up the beard! What are you doing here?"

"I'm going home. But first I wanted to give you something." William pulled out his envelope and handed it to Thankful. "Take whatever I owe you. I think there's plenty there."

She opened the envelope and gasped. "Oh, this is far more than you owe. But Willy, I don't want your money. I never cared about it."

"But I did. I've always cared," he said. "I wanted to come by and apologize so many times. It's why I first went to your grandmother's. She said it was best that I leave you be and said you were happy now. I'm so glad. So here, do it for me and take the money."

Thankful pushed it away. "What would I do with it? I can't escape! Do you think my husband would like to know that I've taken money from the man I loved?"

"But it's your money, Thankful."

"William Weldon, please go home." She folded her arms against a torrent of emotions. The sun hit William's hair and every memory she had of him rushed at her from the time he walked her home from school when she was fourteen until the time they last kissed.

William stepped down the stairs. "Of course. I didn't think. I'll go." Glancing back a few times, he latched the gate and walked the hill back up from the riverfront, but before long he heard her calling him.

She jumped the fence, catching her skirts and tearing them free. Thankful ran to him, her soft cheeks red with exertion and feeling. "William, forgive me! I've always loved you. I still do. Just don't hate me forever for sending you away!"

William touched her arm. "Please stop. How could I hate you? I'm the one who messed everything up."

She laughed. "Oh, and I've been a real peach!"

He sat on the fieldstone fence that meandered up the hill. "I'll always be your friend."

"I don't want any friends!" she snapped. "I don't want us to be friends!"

"Well, I don't know what to say."

"Say nothing! Why have you shaved *now*? Why are you so healthy *now*? Why not before? Why not last year when you deserted me after—oh, I hate to think of it! I'm not one of your whores from the West!"

"I never thought of you in that way!"

"What in heaven's name *have* you thought?"

"I've thought that ... if this was a perfect world, I would have gotten into West Point and been like one of your brothers. You'd admire me, and I'd ask you—to marry me."

She sat next to him, her loose hair brushing his shoulder. "William, why did you love me?"

He scratched his head self-consciously. "I don't know."

"Well, then what does it matter?"

He saw that she would leave if he left it at that so blundered on. "You're the prettiest girl ..."

"And that's it?"

"No, no—it's that—you've always seemed so alive—like you had a secret way of seeing the world— a way of enjoying it like I've never been able to. You have that maddening Crenshaw confidence—like Fred has—but you're nice and kind. I loved your kindness to my parents even when I hated them."

Thankful took his wrist, her heart breaking at his simple admiration. "But William, that's not who I am anymore. I lost all of that since the West. I gave it all away."

"No one can really give away who they are. It's still there. I always imagined you to be so strong—nothing like my mother. Maybe I've wanted to save you from her fate. You know, she's a fine artist, but she put it aside to care for everyone else."

"I'm no artist."

"Maybe not, but you're something you haven't been given a chance to find yet. I thought I'd go to West Point and be the success my father wasn't, and I'd convince you that I was just as good as your brothers, and you'd escape all those children you were always minding. I saw how you hated it."

"I don't hate children. It's just that ..."

"You don't have to explain. I confess, in my mind, I imagined one child—a girl maybe—just so we had something that was ours, but I'd have wanted to help you."

"Why would you want to say all of this to me now—when it's too late?"

William hesitated. "I don't know. It wasn't what I planned to say."

"What did you plan?"

"I planned to say that I was sorry."

She stood. "Your apology isn't good enough."

He got up and let his eyes fall upon her round face. "I do understand. I really do. But please keep the money." He turned up the road.

The sight of him sober for the first time in years maddened her and she lunged after him. "Take your money! I don't want it! I don't want anything to do with you!" She threw it at him, and it scattered all about. "Why did you have to quit drinking now?"

William stood dumbfounded at her pent-up emotion and unwilling to retrieve the money, but sore to see it sitting in the muddy road. "My cousin Lucy made me stop."

Thankful stood for a moment. "You stopped for Lucy, but you couldn't stop for me ..."

A figure sprinted up from across the bridge. "Land sakes! What's happening here?"

"I'm just going," William said.

"No, he's not," Thankful shouted. "William is here to pay me money I stole from my father, and I won't take it! I won't!"

"Thankful, calm down," Henry begged.

"You're a liar, Henry Demarest! You said you didn't care what others thought! I'll shout if I want to!"

Henry took her into his arms. "What have you done to my wife?"

"He's done nothing, nothing at all." She pulled free of him. "Just like you. What have you done with my heart?"

"Stop this at once. This is between you and me," Henry said. "Let your friend pay you what he owes you so we can be rid of him." Henry began picking up the money.

"You want the money, Henry?" Thankful asked and went to kick him as he bent in the road, but missed. "Is that what you want? Then take it! I have no use for it in this prison!"

"You're hysterical—look, it scares the children!" Henry pointed to the children following at a distance.

"All you care about are the children! Willy, can you imagine? He never even told me about them living so near until after we were married!" Thankful cried. "And he's found another girl! Someone better than me!"

Henry gave William an exasperated look. William grabbed her arm. "Thankful, listen to me. I think you should go home."

"I hate it in this house!" Thankful sobbed.

"No, no, I mean to Englewood. To your parents. I'll take you," William said, glancing at Henry.

"I can't," Thankful whimpered.

"You must."

"How dare you meddle," Henry said half-heartedly.

Thankful turned to him. "Henry, I'm sorry. I never loved you. I wanted to, but ..."

Henry said nothing. His pride was hurt, but nothing more. His parents would fix things. Henry pushed Thankful off when she tried to take her words back, and he headed toward the river.

# Chapter Forty-Two

The washed-out bridges of spring had been repaired, and purple asters danced along every path that led them back to Englewood. Thankful and William walked the last mile together hand in hand, tired of the coach. Martha had agreed to send Thankful's things directly to the Crenshaw home on Chestnut Street.

No one awaited their arrival. No one spotted them on the bustling roads into Englewood this late afternoon. William and Thankful hadn't spoken much on the trip, but now the silence felt pregnant with unspoken thoughts and feelings.

"What now, Thankful?" William finally asked as they passed the Demarest store.

"I don't know. One day I'll be a divorced woman. I can't believe it."

"You'll always be the same Thankful to me," he said, squeezing her hand.

"I'll be forever grateful to you for this, but I really can't be that girl anymore, can I? Being that girl who you admired led me to do so many shameful things."

"You're too hard on yourself." He leaned in to kiss her, but she backed away delicately. "I love you," he said.

"Do you realize that every time I've heard that from a man I've made a huge mistake? Willy, I'm so happy for the way you've changed. It's what I always imagined for you, what I've prayed for you—but I can't make any promises right now—maybe never. I'll never be satisfied with an ordinary life."

"What does that mean? Ordinary?" William asked, his voice betraying his heart.

"It means, plain, regular ..."

"I *know* what it means—but for us," he said impatiently, his gold eyes alight in the low sunshine.

Thankful stopped walking and took his hands in hers. "I know I said I didn't want to be friends, but it's all we can be for now. I want to see your work in the magazines and talk about art and all the people you'll meet, and I want you to pray for me, Willy." She touched his face, the face she had dreamed of waking up next to her whole life. "Pray for me."

"I don't pray, Thankful," he said gruffly, rebuffed and hurt.

Thankful began to explain, to try to convince, but changed her mind and kissed him as they came to her street.

"Thankful, I just ask, as a friend, that you do one thing," William finally said after a moment's hesitation. "Use the money to do something you love. Don't give it to charity or something stupid like that."

She laughed and lingered a moment, studying him. "See you, William Weldon." She turned away then, taking the rest of the journey alone.

THE END

Adrienne Morris is the author of The Tenafly Road Series, a family saga following the Weldon and Crenshaw families of Gilded Age Englewood, New Jersey. Her first novel, The House on Tenafly Road was selected as an Editors' Choice Book and Notable Book of the Year by The Historical Novel Society.

Authors rely on word-of-mouth! If you enjoyed The Dew That Goes Early Away please leave an online review—even a short one! It makes a big difference and is greatly appreciated.

**OWN THE SERIES!**
*The House on Tenafly Road (1)*
*Weary of Running (2)*
*The Dew That Goes Early Away (3)*
*Forget Me Not (4)*
*The One My Heart Loves (5)*
*The Grand Union (6)*
***ADRIENNE'S OFFICIAL NEWSLETTER[1]***
**CONTACT ADRIENNE:**
AdrienneMorris.com[2]
Nothing Gilded, Nothing Gained[3]
INSTAGRAM[4]

---

1. *http://eepurl.com/cnCwBP*

2. https://www.adriennemorris.com/

3. https://middlemaybooks.com/

4. https://www.instagram.com/middlemay_farm/

COVER DESIGN by SAMANTHA HENNESSY

48313840R00204

Made in the USA
Lexington, KY
15 August 2019